KING OF THE BADGERS

Also by Philip Hensher

The Northern Clemency
The Fit
The Mulberry Empire
The Bedroom of the Mister's Wife
Pleasured
Other Lulus
Kitchen Venom

KING
OF THE
BADGERS

PHILIP
HENSHER

FOURTH ESTATE • *London*

First published in Great Britain in 2011 by
Fourth Estate
An imprint of HarperCollins*Publishers*
77–85 Fulham Palace Road
London W6 8JB
www.4thestate.co.uk

Visit our authors' blog: www.fifthestate.co.uk

1

A catalogue record for this book is available from the British Library

ISBN 978-0-00-730133-1

Typeset by Palimpsest Book Production Limited, Falkirk, Stirlingshire
Printed in Great Britain by
Clays Ltd, St Ives plc

Mixed Sources
Product group from well-managed
forests and other controlled sources
www.fsc.org Cert no. SW-COC-001806
© 1996 Forest Stewardship Council
FSC

FSC is a non-profit international organisation established to promote the
responsible management of the world's forests. Products carrying the FSC
label are independently certified to assure consumers that they come
from forests that are managed to meet the social, economic and
ecological needs of present and future generations.

Find out more about HarperCollins and the environment at
www.harpercollins.co.uk/green

To
The
Gang:
Bertie
and J.B.
and Sam
and Rita
and Ralf
and Julia
and Yusef
and Jimmy
and Marino
and Renaud
and Richard
and Alan again
and Lapin again
and Professor A
and Dickie Heat-Hot
and not forgetting Nix (Hi Nicola!)
and Mrs Blaikie (with love from Rufus)
and Herbert who said it's all quite laconic once
but especially and always and once more for my husband
and really just to say to all of them and probably some others too
What
Fun
It's
All
Been.

CONTENTS

BOOK ONE
NOTHING TO HIDE

That bowler-hatted major, his face is twitching,
He's been in captivity too long.
He needs a new war and a tank in the desert.
The fat legs of the typists are getting ready
For the boys and the babies. At the back of my mind
An ant stands up and defies a steam-roller.

GAVIN EWART, 'Serious Matters'

1.

Last year, at the hot end of spring, in the small town of Hanmouth on the Hain estuary, a rowing boat floated in the middle of the muddy stream. Its stern pointed inland, where the guilty huddle in cities, its prow towards the ocean, five miles down the steady current. There, all our sins, at the end of all the days and weeks, will be washed away. The boatman dipped his oars deep. There was something thoughtful in the repeated movement. The current was running quickly, and his instructions were to keep the boat where it lay, in the centre of the slow flood, the colour of beer and milk.

'Most of my customers,' he said to his single passenger, 'want to go to the same place. They want to be rowed across the estuary to the pub.'

'What pub would that be, then?' his passenger said, with a touch of irritation. He was a man fat in rolls about the middle, the top of his bald head wet and beaded. His gingery-white hair shocked out to either side, weeks away from a respectable haircut. A life of taxis, expense-account drink, and hot greasy lunches had marked him. Bachelor; or divorced more like; let themselves go in the circumstances.

'It's the Loose Cannon,' the boatman said. 'It's over there, behind you. You can see the lights. On the spit of land where the river Loose meets the Hain estuary. It's a joke, a sort of joke, the name of it.'

The man did not turn round to look. Never been in a boat before. Thinks he can drown in two yards deep. His right hand gripped the boat; the left was on the camera about his neck. At his feet, a black case, halfway between a briefcase and a suitcase in size, was laid carefully flat.

'Easier to get there this way,' the boatman went on, between his strokes. 'At the end of the spit. Between the estuary and the Loose. Car park's near a mile off. Easier to get me to row them across from Hanmouth jetty.'

'Nice pub, is it?' his passenger said. Taking an interest at last.

'Old pub,' the boatman said. 'Very. Just that and the lock-keeper's house over there. Not called the Loose Cannon properly. Someone's joke. On the licence, it's the Cannons of Devonshire. Been called the Loose Cannon as long as anyone knows. As long as I've been here. Because of the river, there, the one joining the estuary.'

On the ramshackle jetty, ten feet long, the girl with the cropped hair stood where they had left her. Two more heavy cases were at her feet. In the mid-evening light, her features were indistinct. She was an outlined shape, a black silhouette in the deepening blue, a watching upright shadow.

'You want to go there?' the boatman asked.

'?'

'To the pub. To the Loose Cannon. Most of my customers – I go back and forth like a shuttle in a loom, most of the summer.'

'No.'

'There's nowhere else to go, if you're crossing the estuary.'

The passenger gave the boatman a brief, city, impatient look. 'Just what I asked for,' he said. 'I want you to row out into the middle of the estuary and keep the boat as steady as you can for twenty minutes while I take some photographs. That's all.'

'You'd get some nice snaps from the Loose Cannon lawn,' the boatman said.

'Wrong angle. Too high.'

'That's a lot of trouble to go to just to get a nice holiday snap or two,' the boatman said.

The passenger said nothing. The boatman paused, and let the boat float a little downstream, swinging as it went. This was the time of day he most admired. A daylight wash at one end of

4

the sky, behind the far hills, and at the other, the beginning of a warm blue night. The moon was like a fingernail paring, hung above the church, flat on its back. In the half-light, the blossom of the fruit trees in the gardens shone out; the stiff little white flowers on the horse-chestnuts in the churchyard were like bright candles; over a wall, a white-flowering clematis poured and mounted like whipped cream. The disorganized up and down of the town's gables, house-ends, extensions and rooftops started to be punctuated by the lighting of windows. Here and there curtains were being drawn. The lights of a town like Hanmouth shone out across water for miles at night.

'Busy this time of year anyway,' the boatman said. 'Always busy. People like to come out for the day. For an afternoon. For an evening. Very historic town. Third most picturesque town in Devon, it won, four years back. Don't know who decides these things. Thomas Hardy came here for a holiday as a boy. You know who Thomas Hardy was?'

'Yes,' the passenger said. 'We did him for O level. I got a B. You're not from round here.'

'No,' the boatman said. 'You never lose a Yorkshire accent. I've been here twenty years. Won't start saying "my lover" to strangers now. And before that on holiday, every year, since I was a boy, almost.'

'Like Thomas Hardy.'

'Like Thomas Hardy. I worked for a steel firm in the north, thirty years. Got laid off. Firm went under. Got a good pay-off first, though. I was a manager. Good job. They said they'd see me all right. Madam says, "Let's move somewhere we want to live. Hanmouth, that's the place we want to be." She was the one who loved it, really loved it. "You can do anything," she said, "turn your hand to anything. Lot of old people in Hanmouth, very glad to have someone change a light bulb for a couple of pound." She died five years later. Cancer. Very sudden. Never get over something like that. She wanted to be buried in the church-yard, but they don't bury anyone there any more. She's in the city cemetery, like everyone else who's dead. Still go to pay my respects, every Saturday. Is that so strange?'

'Just here,' the passenger said. He opened the camera case hanging from his neck. It was a bulky black object, with a black hole where the lens should have been; not like the pocket-sized silver digital jobs people had these days. The boatman pressed against the seaward current and, fifty feet out in the estuary, they were as steady as a rooted waterweed.

The photographer bent down cautiously, and opened the case at his feet. The boatman could smell his perspiration. In the case, there were three lenses, each resting in a carved-out hollow, and there were other devices the boatman could not have named, each in its specific and bespoke place in the charcoal-coloured foam. The photographer lifted the middle-sized lens out, shutting the case with the same care, not making any sudden moves. It was as if there were some unappeased and hungry beast in the boat with them.

'I'm seventy now,' the boatman said. 'You wouldn't think it, people tell me. This keeps me fit.' It was true: his wiry arms had lost flesh, but still pulled firmly; his heart, he considered, beat slowly in his narrow chest. He had kept his hair close-shaven in a way that chimed with the way some young people kept it, though it was white now. 'There was a boatman before me, there was always a boatman. Running them as wanted from Hanmouth pier to the Loose Cannon. The old one, he'd taken it over from his father, forty years back. Had sons, they weren't interested. One's a lawyer in Bristol. Not a full-time job any more, ferryman. Hadn't been for years. I took it on. Keeps me active.'

'You must know everyone in town,' the photographer said.

'Strange lot of people in Hanmouth this week. Don't know them, never seen a one of them before. Never seen it so crowded. That little girl. I don't know what they think they'll see, though. Won't see her. She's missing.'

'Human curiosity,' the passenger said. 'There's no decent limit to it.' He raised his camera, and quickly, with a series of heavy crunches, fired off some photographs.

'Five pounds over, eight there and back,' the boatman said. 'Could have put up the fare this week, I dare say.'

'I thought we agreed a price,' the passenger said. 'You said thirty.'

'There and back in ten minutes is eight pounds,' the boatman said. 'To the middle and stay there as long as I say is thirty. Have you got permission from Mr Calvin to be taking photographs?'

'We agreed a price,' the passenger said.

'Oh, yes,' the boatman said. 'We agreed a price. I can't do you a receipt, though.'

'That's all right,' the passenger said. 'I can write my own receipt. There's no law that says people need permission to take a photograph of a town. Whatever your Mr Calvin says.'

The boatman lifted his oars and kept them in the air; in a second the boat drifted ten feet seawards.

'Keep the boat where it was, please,' the passenger said.

'Mr Calvin, he's keeping a register of all the press photographers. A lot of them. A hell of a lot. Keeps it nice and tidy, Mr Calvin says. Shame about that little girl.'

'Did you know her?'

'No,' the boatman said. 'I don't know as I even recognized her when I saw her face in the papers. There's twenty thousand live in Hanmouth and surroundings. You don't know everyone.'

He pulled hard at the oars, keeping the boat steady and parallel to the shore. They'd been out twenty minutes, he saw. Over half an hour and he'd start charging an extra pound a minute; it wasn't this bugger's money he'd be paying with. He kept an eye on his watch, worn on the inside of his wrist in good maritime fashion.

'Of course,' he said. 'There's those who won't pay the five pounds. If they run off, I don't chase after them. I phone Mike at the Loose Cannon and he takes the fare out of their change. Not much they can say to that. One lad says to me, last summer, "Five pounds? It's only over there. I can walk that." Thinking about low tide, he was. The estuary at low tide, I can't row across, but they can't wade across, neither. "No thanks, it's not deep, we'll walk across, doesn't look like much." I said, "Fair enough." Fifteen yards out, he were up to his thighs in mud, couldn't go forward, couldn't go back. The estuary, it's got its own mind. It shrinks and it quivers. The ducks walk on it; they've got webbed feet. He was in his trainers. I was in the window of the Flask, watching him. Come out and chucked him a ladder in the end. Went out making a hell of a din. Come back quiet as church mice. They only do that once. This town needs me.'

In the rich riverine gloom, the photographer held the machine to his face, and fired off more shots, taking no account of the boatman's story. From here, there was a low and extensive view of the Hanmouth estuary front, the lights in the windows shut off against the night. At the jetty, the crop-haired girl had sat down, her knees raised. Her thin body in its tight boyish denim made a geometrical figure. A half-illuminated line of smoke rose from a concealed cigarette beneath the raised knees.

The boatman pulled against the current, and the boat held quite straight. On the jetty, another figure had joined the photographer's assistant. He was talking softly to her. The low voice travelled across the water, and from the sound of it and the narrow-shouldered shape of the man, the boatman recognized Mr Calvin. He'd have something to say to a press photographer who hadn't made himself known.

'This for a newspaper, then?' the boatman said.

'Something like that,' the passenger said, continuing to photograph.

'It's been five days,' the boatman said. 'We've been under siege, it's been like. Everyone being asked, all the time, have you seen the little girl, do you know her mum, what do you know about her dad. Just to go to the butcher's or the bank. I said to one, "If I knew anything, I'd go to the police, I wouldn't be telling you." And you can get photographs of Hanmouth anywhere, on the Internet, lovely sunny day. You won't get much in this light, I wouldn't have thought.'

On the jetty, the small figure of indeterminate sex waved largely, as if she had a full-sized flag at a jamboree. Calvin, if that was who it had been, had gone. The swans and geese, misled by the wave, checked their paths and swam towards her. They were spoilt by feeders here, and took movement for the promise of generosity.

'That's enough,' the passenger said. 'Take me back.'

'I can take you over to the Loose Cannon,' the boatman said. 'There's no more to pay.'

'We'll be fine,' the passenger said, and though they seemed to be facing in the correct direction, the boat swung round in the stream, pulled by one oar, in a full circle, facing in turn the city and the roar of the motorway over the estuary, the remote blue hills where the sun was setting, and then seawards, where everything goes in the end. And on the jetty, the small figure knelt, opening up a black-backed computer, the blue light of the screen illuminating what, after all, was the cropped hair and small face of a pretty girl, intent on her digital task.

2.

Hanmouth, that well-known town on the Hain estuary on the north coast of Devon, formed a stratified appearance whichever way you looked at it. The four streets of the place ran between and parallel to the railway line to the coast and the estuary itself. Less stately thoroughfares – alleyways, gennels, cut-throughs, set-back squares of white-painted nineteenth-century almshouses and 1930s suburban 'closes' with front gardens made out of a bare foot or two of leftover land – squiggled more liberally across the four vertical and distinguished avenues. The first of those verticals ran seamlessly from Ferry Road in the north to the Strand in the south, knotting around the quay and rising to three historic pubs, a plaque commemorating the birthplace of a centuries-dead attorney general and, at its most expensive, unfettered views of the estuary and the hills beyond, crested with a remote and ducal folly-tower. On this first street lived newsreaders, property magnates, people who had made their money in computers and telecommunications. The first house in Hanmouth to sell for a million pounds was here, and pointed out by the innocent locals; but that had been seven years ago, and the figure was losing its lustre, and had long lost its uniqueness. The pinnacle of envy for miles around, for half a county, the Strand in the south was a series of Dutch-gabled houses, pink, cream, terracotta-red-fronted, and everyone, it was said, lived there, meaning that everyone, of course, did not.

Only an odd few lived in the second avenue, the shopping street; the Brigadier and his wife in a wide, flat, shallow eighteenth-century one-house terrace of brick, facing the wrong direction as if it had turned its back on the commerce. The Fore street was holding up well; the community centre, built in municipal interbellum brick, was celebrating its eightieth birthday next year with a Hanmouth Players production of *The Royal Hunt of the Sun*, among other things. Outside the community centre was a bronze statue of a boy fishing on his haunches, with an elbow on either knee and an expression of great concentration. The statue had been commissioned for the hall's fiftieth anniversary, which had coincided with the Queen's silver jubilee in 1977. It had been unveiled at the height of a street party, trestle tables snaking down the whole length of the Fore street, and was instantly and universally known, even in the hand-printed guide to Hanmouth the second-hand bookshop sold, as the Crapping Juvenile. As for the rest of the Fore street: the new Tesco out of town had had no effect on the excellent butcher, the fair-to-middling greengrocer. Had no power, either, over the knick-knack shops, the amateur jewellers making a go of it, or the Oriental emporium run by the two retired sisters, stocked by bi-annual trips to the markets of south India; they returned from Madurai with triumphant rolls of bright silk, hand-made soap, and encrusted, elaborate, tarnished silver trinket boxes to be sold at twelve times the purchase price.

On the other side of the Fore street, as the railway line grew more apparent, the bohemians, the aspiring many who had escaped only so far from Barnstaple, lived in polite and tidy houses, designed for eighteenth-century churchwardens or pre-war shop-keepers. Here, their view was of their neighbours' windows, principally. In the town, there was one school, supposed to be very good, one fortnightly French-style market, twelve antiques shops and a junk market, a fishmonger with an almost daily van and seven churches, ranging from those that turned to the east during the Creed with hats on, to one that frankly and openly prostrated itself before spiritual emanations, this last in a converted bike shed with a corrugated-iron roof. Miranda Kenyon, who taught at the university and lived in a Dutch house on the Strand, often announced that she had promised herself she would go into that last, mad church one of these Sundays.

That was the part of Hanmouth people thought of when they aspired to live there. It was the part that pronounced their town *Hammuth*. The bright upward side of leisurely high-fronted Dutch houses, their glass-punctured façades big and shining with the sun setting over the westward hills, its inhabitants pouring a first drink of the evening behind leaded, curving windows, occu-pying themselves by counting the long-legged wading birds in the shining estuary. They thought of the square Protestant white-washed houses in the streets behind, or at worst the Edwardian villas further back, towards the railway line. The railway, bearing only the trundling little train to the coastal stretch around Heycombe, was charming in final effect, rather than a noisy inter-ruption of Hanmouth's postcard qualities. The flowerbeds at the station were well kept, with 'HANMOUTH' in topiary, and a level crossing at which widows with woven wicker shopping baskets lined in gingham always seemed to be waiting patiently. A couple of hundred yards down from the station, a white wicket gate and a footpath across the track showed that this was a rare surviving branch line of the sort that was supposed to have been eradicated decades ago. It was quite charming, and harmless.

The people of Hanmouth were conscious of their pleasant, attractive, functioning little town, and they protected it. A police station with a square blue lamp and a miniature fire station added to the miniaturized, clockwork impression. Its one nuisance was represented by the twelve pubs of the town; there was a sport among the students of the university to embark on the Hanmouth Twelve, a mammoth holiday pub-crawl, which sometimes ended with drunken manly widdling off the jetty, as gay Sam put it, late-night vomit on the station platform to greet you with your early-morning train, and once, a smashed window in the florist's shop at the quay end of the Fore street. These small-town irritations, the responsibility of outsiders, were talked over in the newsagent's and in the streets. Mr Calvin, to everyone's approval, took the sort of initiative only newcomers were likely to take, and formed a Neighbourhood Watch. There was some nervous joshing that you'd have to join in a prayer circle before the meetings got going, but in the end they'd been a great success, as everyone agreed. In the last couple of years, security cameras had been put up over the station in both directions, and at the quay where people waited for buses into Barnstaple. Then a little more lobbying secured six more, and as John Calvin said he had explained to Neighbourhood Watch, and Neighbourhood Watch would explain in turn to everyone they knew, now you could walk from one end of the Fore street to the other at any time of the day or night without fear, watched by CCTV. Even quite old ladies knew to say 'CCTV' now. 'You've got nothing to fear if you've done nothing wrong,' John Calvin said. 'Nothing to hide: nothing to fear,' he added, quoting a government slogan of the day, and in the open-faced and street-fronting houses of Hanmouth, often wanting to boast about the elegant opulence of their private lives, the rich of Hanmouth tended to agree.

The security and handsomeness of the estuary town drew outsiders. It also, less admirably, persuaded those outside its historic boundaries to appropriate its name. Some way up the A-road towards more urban settlements, there were lines of yellow-brick suburban houses, a golf club, a vast pub on a round-about offering Carvery Meals to the passing traffic on a board outside. In its car park feral children romped, and, fuelled on brought-out Cokes and glowing orangeades, ran up and over the pedestrian bridge across the A-road. They had been known to shy a half-brick at lorries passing below. There was an extensive and spreading council estate on either side of the traffic artery, surrounding the Hanmouth Rugby Club grounds; it provided a flushed and awkward audience to the field's gentlemanly battles, over a leather egg, mounted for an afternoon, a drama bounded between two dementedly outsized aspirates.

All these things, encouraged in the first instance by estate agents, had taken to calling themselves Hanmouth too. They, however, called it Han-mouth, to Hanmouth's formal scorn and comedy. It was one of Miranda Kenyon's conversational set-pieces, the speculating about where the boundaries of Hanmouth would end. On the whole, Hanmouth thought little of the despoiling and misspeaking suburbs that surrounded it and had taken on its name. Though they poured right up to the gates of Hanmouth, they were obviously the city's, Barnstaple's, suburbs, not Hanmouth's. Hanmouth could never have suburbs.

In these suburbs and estates, men washed their cars on a Sunday morning; kitchens faced the front, the better for wives doing the washing-up to watch the events in the street; children kicked footballs against the side of parked cars until bawled out; support for local or national football teams was made evident in displayed scarves, emblems stuck in windows, flags flown from the back of cars; and, at seven thirty or eight o'clock on weekdays, a ghostly unanimous chorus of the theme tune to a London soap opera floated through the open windows of the entire suburb. There was no reason to go there, and Hanmouth knew nothing much of these hundred streets. It was in the early summer of 2008 that an event in these suburbs, whatever settlement they could be said to belong to, rose up and attached itself to Hanmouth, and could not be detached.

3.

No one in Hanmouth proper had ever heard of Heidi O'Connor. Unless she cut their hair, and then they still wouldn't know her surname. She did her shopping where no one hailed each other or equably compared purchases, in the Tesco's on the ring-road. She was not one for going to the pub for social reasons or any other, even to the roadhouse on the Hanmouth roundabout. She would have said she found it 'common', a word most of Hanmouth would have been astonished to discover a Heidi O'Connor knew or attached any particular meaning to. She had four children, Hannah, China, Harvey and Archie, from nine down to eighteen months. She lived with Michael Thomas, a moon-faced reprobate seven years younger than her. The four children, two with a version of Heidi's white-blonde hair, two with a dark, thick, doglike scrub on top, were said to get on with their 'stepfather', as Micky Thomas generously termed himself when events made a definition necessary. He was the third such 'stepfather' the children had known and the eldest two could remember. Only Hannah could remember, or said she could, her proper father and China's.

With four children at twenty-seven, Heidi's existence had its circumscribed aspects. She rarely went into Barnstaple – the opening of a new shopping centre represented an unusual outing. She and Micky and the four kids, walking up and down the glass-covered streets of the mall where municipal jugglers and publicly funded elastic-rope artists played with the air for one afternoon only. Here and there, Heidi and Micky said to each other that it was nothing special, really, letting the kids run in and out of the shops. Barnstaple, in general, was Micky's territory. He went in every Friday and Saturday night; he stayed out till three or four, returning huge-eyed and off his face, as he would say the next day. Saturday afternoons he spent in Hanmouth's pubs, often drinking until it was time to pick up Heidi from the salon. He waited outside on the pavement for her; he'd had to be spoken to sharply about coming in and wandering about before half five, picking up bottles of conditioner and tongs and putting them down again. He was a familiar figure in Old Hanmouth, as he called it; he was a well-known figure at the edges of the dance floors of the little nightclubs of Barnstaple, his moon face expressionless under a CCTV-defying baseball cap. He would often sell you a little bit of this, a little bit of that.

Heidi thought herself too old for that sort of thing. She spent most of her time indoors when she wasn't working at the hair salon in Hanmouth, where most of the customers were over seventy, but all right, really. She'd always said at school she wanted to be a hairdresser, and though Hannah and China coming unexpectedly had interrupted the HND, she'd made an effort, bettered herself, finished her course when she was twenty-two, and got a job here, where she worked now. Her dream was to open up a salon of her own, she said; maybe even in Hanmouth. It could do with some competition, something a bit more up-to-date. A bit less blue-rinse, she would say, though she hadn't done a blue rinse in her life, only heard of them on comedy sketches. 'I don't know how she stands them,' Micky would say to his mates and his associates when Heidi was in the kitchen, talking about the widows and retired woman civil servants of Hanmouth. 'Them old punters. Smelling of wee and asking for your blue-rinse perm.' Heidi herself didn't mind them, or Hanmouth. She didn't think too much about it. The pay could have been better, but the tips were generous, and it got her out of the house. Micky made money in his own ways. Those own ways came and went, but were a useful backup at any rate. And every Wednesday and Saturday they played the lottery. If you asked them what their ambitions were, they would both have said that they aimed at a future where an exponentially large sum of money landed on them, unearned and undeserved, and proved inexhaustible, however long the pair of them lived. It was sweet that they didn't seem to think, for the moment, of

15

a future where undeserved and enormous money would rid them one of the other.

Her childhood sweetheart she'd never married, though he'd given her Hannah and China, and he might be in London by now. Harvey's dad was the one she'd married, and never again. At the end, in the middle of one of those staircase-shaking rows, he'd said he was going to emigrate, to Australia or Canada, and had gone on saying it, with varying degrees of calmness or rage, until one day he'd just disappeared, never to be seen again. (Heidi supposed she was still married to him, all things being considered.) His name was Marcus. She remembered what he looked like, but what had really remained with her from that marriage was Harvey, of course, and Marcus's half-sister Ruth – they'd had the same father, but Marcus's mother had been from Bristol, Ruth's from Barnstaple. The father was where they'd got the black half from. There were fifteen years between Marcus and Heidi, thirteen between Marcus and Ruth. Ruth had always been the same stern-looking girl with cropped hair touched with grey, though she was only two years older than Heidi. At the wedding, with Hannah only just old enough to be a little bridesmaid in peach, China still a baby in Heidi's mother's arms with a terrible rash across her face, Ruth's constant frown hardly cracked. Some old uncle of Heidi's with a red carnation in the buttonhole of his grey suit and the red-veined nose all Irish drinkers got in the end had leant over to Heidi's mother and said he was a handsome lad, but he, he was old-fashioned, he supposed, and thought it a shame, his lovely niece who could have had her pick marrying a half-caste like that. And Ruth had abruptly turned round – people said, 'So she turned round and said,' but Ruth really had turned round, as swift as a whip in flight – and said, 'That's my fucking brother you're talking about, you stupid old cunt. His name's Marcus.' There was no answer to that. The old uncle, who had only been invited because Heidi's mother was soft-hearted, mumbled some-thing about no offence being meant, nothing personal, because he was an old man and set in his ways and could see she was half-caste too and nothing wrong with that. Mixed race; Heidi knew you didn't say 'half-caste' any more, thanks to Ruth.

Because after the wedding, the three honeymoonless months which ended when Ruth told her that Marcus was screwing the sister of some garage workmate of his, Marcus walked out. Whether he went to Canada or Australia or, Ruth thought, probably only back to his mother's house in Bristol, Heidi was left not just with a bump, which turned out to be Harvey, but also with Ruth. Ruth always knew what to do. A year ago, she had told Heidi that she ought to ask the salon for a rise in her wages; Heidi had asked, and she'd got it. Ruth knew about child benefit and housing benefit. She knew where it was best to say Micky lived. Once, in Tesco's car park, a posh woman had left the boot of her car open with all her shopping in it while she went to return the trolley. Ruth, without saying anything at all, had just calmly removed three of her bags from her boot to Heidi's, had rearranged what was left, and passed the time of day with the silly cow before getting in and driving off. A chicken, two big tubs of ice cream, loads of other stuff. Ruth always knew what to do. Heidi hadn't been left with much after Marcus did a bunk, apart from a pregnancy she hadn't wanted or recognized and which might have precipitated his departure – 'You want to take a look at yourself,' had been one of his parting shots, pointing at her fattening belly. In retrospect, spending five thousand pounds on a wedding which hadn't been made of good solid stuff that would last wasn't the most sensible thing. But she'd been left with Ruth, who was a good thing to be left with. She was worth it.

That Monday afternoon was Heidi's day off from the salon, and she'd gone round to her sister-in-law Ruth's house. Ruth's mother Karen was there too, visiting from Barnstaple. Sometimes she asked Heidi to do something with her hair, and Heidi reverted from her professional discretion to her schoolgirl hairdressing fantasy, mucking about with Karen's hair, giving it odd colours and streaks, piling it up asymmetrically for the fun of it, and

Ruth joined in too, giving her mother's hair the odd poke. That Monday, though, it was too hot to do anything much, and they'd started off in the back garden, until Karen had said it was too hot for her – it was the sort of day you liked when you thought about it afterwards – and they'd gone inside. They had put the telly on, and watched one thing after another, *Property Deals*, *Money in the Cupboard*, *Do or Dare*, *Cash Cow*, for a good four hours. At some point, Ruth brought out a little spliff, and they had quite a nice time, just passing it round. Then, at the end of *Cash Cow*, Ruth had brought out another one, and they'd smoked that. This had happened before; it was a sort of Monday-afternoon tradition, sometimes going with the mucking-up of Karen's hair, sometimes just with the telly. Sometimes it was just between Ruth and Heidi, sometimes including Karen as well – she wasn't some old granny type. Because of Heidi having Mondays off, it seemed like the end of the weekend, which could begin on a Thursday night, too, if it seemed like a good idea. Because of the spliff, and because of the sun shining into Ruth's front room and onto the screen, they'd drawn the curtains. They'd stayed drawn against the street outside.

Micky wasn't around that afternoon. He'd gone into Barnstaple to the main library. He wanted to become a member to take out books and DVDs, and he'd made an appointment. They'd told him it wasn't necessary, but Micky liked to know people were going to be there when he was, and he told them he'd not been interested that much at school, but now he wanted to develop his reading skills. The library had fallen over themselves to make an appointment for him to show him round and talk through, they said, his needs. Later, Heidi said she supposed people weren't as ready as they used to be to join a library – she knew old folk liked their Shakespeare and that. They'd treat you like royalty if you showed any interest.

Little Archie was asleep upstairs on Ruth's spare bed. The other kids had come home from school – Hannah and China collected Harvey from his infant's school, next door to theirs, and Hannah could let herself in and make them something to eat. It was quite normal; it happened like that every day, because Heidi was either working at the salon, or at Ruth's. Micky was either there or he wasn't.

Around five thirty they looked up from *The Adam Riley Show* – he was talking to Jude Vakilzadeh off *I Want To Live For Ever*. She was showing her new collection of pillowcases, duvet covers and sheets, Heidi later recalled with some exactness. One of the kids was there. At first she'd thought, muzzily, that it was China, but it wasn't. It was Hannah. She had come in through the back, which was hardly ever locked, and stood in the doorway, holding her own hands, one in each.

'I won't be long,' Heidi said. 'Put something in the oven. I'll be back home at six.' The children were supposed to know they weren't to bother her on her afternoons off, but any old worry, any crisis no matter how small – a missing cowboy hat of Harvey's, there weren't any chocolate biscuits, China had hit Hannah – would bring one of them over the road, usually in tears.

Hannah wasn't in tears. 'China hasn't come back from the shops,' she said. 'I don't know where she's gone.' Glum and slow with skunk though Heidi, Ruth and Karen were, they all agreed that was what Hannah had said. Karen thought she'd said, 'And I'm scared,' as well. That was probably just her picturesque addition to what Hannah had said, a fat little figure standing in the sun-strewn fog, making clutching gestures. In the corner of Ruth's front room in the sugary smoke, standing up against the purple-paisley dado strip, Hannah made an unconventional harbinger of catastrophe.

'She'll be back home before long,' Heidi said. 'I'll be over soon.'

But Hannah had insisted. China had been away for an hour and a half. Hannah and Harvey had gone out looking for her, and had walked the two hundred yards between home and the shop in the arcade, back and forward, four times. 'I expect she's gone to visit a friend of hers,' Ruth said, irritated. Hannah had insisted. Harvey had wanted a PB and J, and had started bawling.

19

China had gone to the shops – she knew he was sitting bawling, she'd have come straight back.

'In any case,' Heidi said to the police later, quite calmly, 'I knew China hadn't gone to visit her friends for one straight and simple reason. She doesn't have any friends. She's not been a popular girl, ever. They bully her, I expect, because they say she's fat and she smells. I don't think she smells, but at that age, it's always some reason they've got to pick on her, isn't it? I knew she hadn't gone to visit a friend. To tell the truth, I thought at first, China, she's playing some trick on her brother and sister. I'll tan her hide, I thought at first.'

When Micky came back, it was seven thirty. After his appointment at the library, he'd arranged to meet an associate in a pub by the station, and they'd sunk a fair few before Micky had said it was time for him to be getting back. (A junior librarian, the associate and a bored barmaid had confirmed all of this. The barmaid said she'd never have served him the last few if she'd thought for one moment that he'd be getting in a car and driving anywhere.) By the time he got back home, a small crowd of neighbours had gathered at Heidi's front gate. Micky got out of the car, his blue and yellow hooped T-shirt outlining ample belly and breasts. The neighbours let out a moan of satisfied excitement and interest.

'What's going on?' said Micky. The door to Heidi's house was hanging open. Ruth came out and looked at him with one of her grimmest faces. By eight, the police had arrived.

4.

There is, of course, no need to worry. There is a process. It is a police process, evolved and tested by a thousand cases that never come to court. That never last more than five hours, most of them. The process searches for a child in a succession of ways, each larger, each more serviced, each more public than the one before. There might be a metaphor here: a series of sieves, each one finer than the previous one. At first the obvious, the nearby is tested, a very few people. But more and more people fall into the sieve, and after a while, everyone is being tested. It escalates, the process, and it escalates quickly. Another metaphor: an escalator, rising like a cliff, speeding – a better metaphor – like a glass lift, rocketing upwards. A case is either solved unobtrusively and swiftly, or it arrives on the front pages of the national newspapers. Almost always it is solved swiftly, and nothing more is heard of it; nobody not related by blood to the child ever hears of it. But there is a process, and it is followed.

The police arrived around eight o'clock. There were two of them at first. They took notes. A male policeman and a policewoman. They sat in Heidi's apricot lounge, each at the edge of the sofa, smiling wanly. They balanced their notebooks on their knees. 'Don't worry,' one said. 'Children disappear, and most of them turn up quickly.' And this was true. They asked about birthday parties China had gone to. They asked about her best friends, and where they lived; about everyone China had ever known on the estate. The children came in, and could add another ten names, tumbling over each other in their urge to be helpful.

'She's not with any of them,' Heidi's friend – sister-in-law, in fact – Ruth said, walking in and walking out again contemptuously. 'You're wasting time.'

The police explained to Heidi – because Ruth had not stayed for an answer – that this was always the first line of enquiry. And then, within half an hour, they left with the names of everyone China knew, as far as Heidi and the children were aware.

The police multiplied. They went to thirty addresses, most of them similar yellow-brick houses on the estate. It was quite late in the evening by now. They knocked on the doors, and a parent came, wondering who it was. A child was summoned from bed or television. But, no, China had not been seen by any of them, not since that afternoon. She'd gone, everyone knew that, she'd disappeared, some of them said; she was there in the street one

21

moment and she was gone the next, the best-informed of them said. By midnight, the last of the names had been canvassed. By midnight in these cases, the process says, most children who have been reported missing in the day will have come home of their own accord. But China had not come home.

*

Kitty liked to get up early; make a brisk start to the day. When Dennis was still alive, after they had retired, he preferred to stay in bed if he could, sometimes until ten or ten thirty. Kitty's hours between seven and Dennis's rising were her own; she could read, or do a touch of quiet gardening in the tubs in the courtyard, or get on with any quiet little task. Or she could simply close the wicket gate behind her and go out for a walk through Hanmouth in the early-morning light, enjoying the wind, or the sun, and the weather, and the shifting moods of the estuary.

Now she was on her own, but she still liked to make a brisk start. Some people did; most people didn't. There was a small conspiratorial club of early risers, out and about by seven. That was how she had met half the people she knew in Hanmouth, after greeting them as they sailed out in search of their morning paper. Now, turning the corner into the Fore street from the little snicket that led nowhere but to her own back gate, she found herself facing Harry, another of these early risers, with the *Guardian* in his hand.

'Hell of a lot of police about this morning,' Harry said, when they had exchanged the usual greetings. 'You don't know what it's about?'

'I hadn't seen,' Kitty said. 'I've only just come out.'

'A hell of a lot,' Harry said. 'Down the Wolf Walk, poking round the car park at the doctor's surgery, and there's even a chap putting on scuba gear with his legs dangling over the quay. Dozens of them.'

'Gosh,' Kitty said. 'How exciting. The Queen's not coming, is she?'

22

'Not that I've heard,' Harry said. 'I can't think what it could be.' He waved briefly with his umbrella, and let Kitty go on her way.

The next stage of the police process had begun overnight. It had not been announced. At first light, mud-brown and frail, twenty police were scattered over the wild places of the parish; wherever was overgrown and abandoned, wherever was wild, the police were. At the edges of Hanmouth, the clouded dawn showed police eyeing empty lands: the bird sanctuaries, the abandoned huts and sheds and workshops, which can be found everywhere in England. In the warm night, the police had arrived in vans, and in the fields about the city, in the woodlands, in long waders in the muddy estuary, the police walked with a strange, crane-like gait, their faces downwards, no more than a body's length between them. They went slowly and gracefully through the waste ground, the unfarmed lands, the woods and clearings, and even along the undredged river. As Harry had seen, there was a scuba diver sitting at the edge of the quay, and soon, when the shifts ordained by the police authority changed, there were four more, at the quay, at the jetty, along the Wolf Walk. They plunged into the high water, again and again, surfacing, plunging, surfacing in further and further places. On the quay, a senior policeman stood; he did not take his own notes, but had a subordinate to do that. From time to time, he was informed of progress. Last night he had not been told about the girl's disappearance. This morning he had been told, and he was inspecting the wild places, the hiding places, the places where a child could disappear and find no way out. The mood was calm and systematic. They were working through their process. By eleven, the tide was low, and the wet, brackish mud hissed as the water drained from it, like geese or rain. The scuba divers stood in it, thigh-deep. There was nowhere to go but further towards the ocean, where the estuary still ran deep and secret.

'Apparently,' Doreen Harrington said in the coffee shop at eleven, 'they're looking for a small girl. Gone missing.' She popped a gobbet of cheese scone into her mouth, swilled it with coffee, and went on talking, her manners not being all they should be.

'I saw some police divers at work in the estuary as I was coming out,' her friend Barbara said. 'Has she fallen in, do they think?'

'They don't know,' Doreen said. 'I was speaking to a nice young constable – I saw him going into the old workshop at the back of me, the abandoned one, and I didn't see his uniform at first. I thought it might be kiddies going in to make mischief, so I went over to chase him out, but he explained everything. It's a little girl from the estate; she disappeared yesterday afternoon and hasn't been seen since. They don't know what's happened to her. The divers, it's just a precautionary measure.'

Mary and Kevin, who ran the coffee shop, had heard Doreen's informed knowledge. They now came over, he from the kitchen in a striped and flour-dusted blue butcher's apron, she in a wait-ress's frilly one, a pencil in hand. 'I do hope she hasn't been – that there's no talk of anyone taking her – that—' Mary said.

'Paedophiles, you mean?' Doreen said, in a frank, open tone. 'They simply don't know.'

'But they wouldn't be fishing in the estuary, would they,' Barbara said, 'if they thought it was paedophiles?'

'They have to exclude every possibility, systematically,' Doreen said, whose nephew was a constable in the Hampshire constabu-lary. 'They're doing all the right things, I'm sure.'

*

In the possession of the police was another list of names. Unlike the list of China's friends and acquaintances, gathered by talking to her mother, to Micky, to her aunt and her siblings and her other friends, this was kept securely on a computer, and not printed out lightly, not shown to anyone outside the police service. On it were the names of those in Devon and Cornwall who had been convicted or accused of some sexual crime against children. Some of them had fucked eight-year-old nieces thirty years ago, and had recently been released from decades of drinking prison tea, pissed in by generations of kitchen-serving muggers. Others had been found with images of carefree naked toddlers on their computers, each one fairly unobjectionable, but amounting to a collection of tens of thousands. One unfortunate had, in 1987, had sex with a bricklayer who turned out to be twenty years old and thus below the age of consent; he, too, found himself on the police's list of slavering lunatics beside the others with horrible designs on toddlers. There seemed no means of removing him from the police list, and he, like all the others, received a visit from the police in the little pink-fronted terraced house in Drewsteignton with a rainbow sticker in the window where he lived with the same bricklayer, now in his forties.

'Someone's taken her, I know it,' Heidi was saying. 'They've taken her, they've definitely taken her.'

Her apricot sitting room was crowded now: five police officers, Micky, Ruth, and a man from the local press as well as Heidi. The police didn't know how he had got there and who had asked him, but he was taking notes silently, as if in competition with the woman police officer on the arm of the sofa doing the same thing. And there was someone else no one knew what he had to do with anything; a man called Calvin, well-dressed and elegant. One of the officers knew him, apparently, and had said, 'Hello, Mr Calvin,' when he had come in, so nobody had challenged him. Heidi wanted him to be there, it seemed; she turned to him from time to time instead of answering a question. He was an improbable friend for Micky or Heidi, but he nodded and smiled, or shook his head and frowned when appealed to. He had some role, possibly self-assigned. Outside on the stairs, the children sat, Ruth's mother guarding them in watchful silence.

'She hasn't fallen into the estuary,' Ruth said. 'I said she hasn't. We knew she hadn't gone playing hide and seek, or gone off to visit one of her friends without telling anyone. We told you that yesterday. I told you she'd been taken by someone.'

'We have to explore every possibility,' one of the police officers

25

said. 'We're dedicating a very large number of officers to this case. This morning, they have started paying home visits to every individual in the area known to us with some sort of record. You needn't have any concerns about that.'

'Oh, my God,' Ruth's mother said, coming into the room. 'You're telling us that there are people who have done this, living here, living round here sort of thing?'

'Those are our first port of call,' the police officer said.

'Living here, on the estate?' Micky said. 'Who are they?'

'Not necessarily here on the estate.'

'Are they supposed to be living in Hanmouth?' Ruth said. 'Or Old Hanmouth?'

'I'm very sorry,' the police officer said, 'but I can't give you that information.'

*

'I heard,' Billa said to Sam over the telephone – he was only in his shop, not thirty yards away across the street, but it seemed altogether best to telephone, or Tom would be asking where she was going, 'that there's a little girl gone missing . . . Yes, I know. Just yesterday. A policeman came round to ask if we had a shed, or something. As if she were a lost cat . . . No, not at all. I don't think she's from Hanmouth properly speaking – I think Kitty said she went missing from up the road, on that post-war estate you drive past . . . That's right. But Tom was speaking to another police officer, I think a more senior one, and he was saying that they now think the girl's actually been taken by someone. Isn't that frightful? . . . No, nobody saw anything. Apparently she was there one moment and gone the next. No car or anything. That's why they thought at first she had run away, I suppose, but now they do think that she must have been abducted. You simply don't think of that sort of thing happening in Hanmouth. How are you getting on with that Japanese novel? I can't think why we agreed to it, I can't get on with it, not one bit . . . Yes, do drop in, six-ish or whenever you close up – bang on Kitty's door on your way over, we'll make a little party of it.'

'Have you just invited some ghastly reprobates to drink us out of house and home?' the Brigadier called from his study, just next door.

'Yes, I rather think I have,' Billa said. 'Don't be such an old curmudgeon. You really are a wretch. It's only Sam, in any case.'

'Well, I warn you,' the Brigadier said. 'There's not a drop of Campari in the house. He finished it the last time he was here.'

Billa had a couple of small purchases to make as well as the Campari, so she went out to the Co-op on the Fore street. Outside her door, there were clusters of people, twos and threes, outside the bookshop, the travel agent, the jeweller's, all talking in urgent, restrained style. She might have thought they were talking about her, from the way they hushed and broke off as she approached. And there, as advertised, were two police officers, making their way from door to door. She wondered that they hadn't made it to their house yet.

In the Co-op, she picked up what she needed – a pack of Lurpak, some emergency washing powder, some savoury biscuits and some loo roll as well as the Campari. It was extraordinary how these things ran out between trips to the supermarket. When she got to the till, on the counter there was the local newspaper. It came out in the evening, and on the cover was a photograph of a fat-faced child, grinning and gummy, evidently an unflattering school photograph. Next to her was a photograph of rather an attractive, though staring, blonde, holding that same photograph on a yellowish leather sofa; around her a thick-looking youth had his arm draped. The headline read, 'WHERE IS CHINA?'

The girl on the till could have been quite pretty, with her straight red hair and her lucid freckled skin, Billa believed, if she had only had her gravestone teeth fixed. 'Terrible, this,' the girl said, gesturing at the newspaper. 'Terrible.'

'You never think it will happen in the place you live,' Billa said. 'The poor mother,' and then, hardly meaning to, she picked up a copy of the deliriously untalented local newspaper, something she never bought or read. So when Sam came through the door an hour later, saying, 'Isn't it appalling?' Billa and, more surprisingly, Tom, who joined them for once, had found out a good deal about the case and the poor family. Tom thought he recognized the mother. Nobody recognized the little girl. It was shocking that such things could happen, virtually on their doorstep. In the end, Kitty and Sam stayed for dinner, and Billa insisted that Sam phone up Harry and ask him over, as well.

*

China was officially missing. Two police officers were assigned to sit with Heidi. Ruth was sitting in the kitchen, incessantly smoking Marlboro Lights, waiting to be called in by her friend. Karen was despatched to a hotel and told that she would be needed in the morning. The children, wide-eyed, excited and frightened, were put to bed while the adults were interviewed. Out in the streets, search parties were setting off, door-to-door, like weary electioneers. On the third day, long before nine, the house towered over a makeshift refugee camp of silver reflective canopies, car batteries, tents, aluminium stools and ladders, men and women all facing in the same direction away from the house and talking, all of them ignoring each other in their steady monologues. Behind them, a curtain moved, a small face could be seen. By the afternoon, the crowds had doubled, and the first strangers arrived on the main street of Hanmouth.

5.

At some point in the next few days, somebody in Hanmouth, behind closed doors – some cynical millionaire on the Strand, talking to some other cynical millionaire – after an hour or two of pious public conversation, paused, and judged their interlocutor, and let their interlocutor judge them. Who was it who said it first? It hardly matters, because soon everyone would be saying it. They said, 'Do you think – I mean, do you think it's remotely possible – I know it sounds simply extraordinary, but I can't help wondering—'

And by the end of the week, that was what Hanmouth was saying, and, quietly, the press and, even more quietly, the police when they were alone with each other. 'You don't think, do you, that Heidi could possibly . . .'

But they both looked at each other, whoever they were, and clapped a hand to their mouths, their eyes wide, then lowered their hands and, rather quietly, began to talk.

6.

In an upper room in a house in the Strand, looking out onto the estuary through leaded windows, a girl sat with her twenty-nine companions. This morning there had been twenty-eight; as before, she had gone out, obeying her mother's frequent instruction, 'Why don't you go out instead of staying in all day long? Go out and make some friends.' She'd gone out, mooched around the post office, where she'd bought a biro. She'd stood outside the town hall and the Crapping Juvenile. One of the grockles might photograph her and ask her if she knew about that girl that got kidnapped. Or even better, the kidnapper might turn up and try and kidnap her, and she'd scream and get the hatpin out of her pocket and stab him in the back of the hand until he bled and he was screaming for mercy down Hettie's white shirt. That would be good in front of all of the grockles. Hettie sat on the wall outside the community centre until one of her mother's friends, passing with a stupid shopping trolley with big pink flowers on it had recognized her and said hello. It was that old woman Billa who lived in the flat sideways house that always gave you the creeps because it looked so witchy. 'Tell your mother I'm looking forward to tonight,' the old woman said.

'I will!' Hettie said, smiling as stupidly as she could, and the old woman, Billa, she didn't even realize Hettie was being sarcastic, so Hettie waved, though Billa was only two feet away, and even then she didn't realize: she made a laughing noise and waved back, as though it was Hettie being stupid.

So then there was no point in sitting there because Hettie had been there for a million hours and no one had come to take her photograph and kidnap her. She might as well go. Hettie, like a prize-winning gymnast taking her bow in front of thousands as she came to the end of her routine, sprang off the wall and made a perfect finish with her feet together in the nine o'clock position. But no one saw, which was typical. On the way back home, she went first into the second-hand bookshop and said hello to Maggie who worked there. She didn't buy any books. Maggie would tell her mother she had come in, which was the same thing. Then she had got to the place she'd been going to go to all the time. She'd been delaying it, looking forward to it. She had gone inside the antiques centre on the quay, ignoring the old man, in a brown cardigan the weather was too hot for, at the front desk where you paid. She had made a pretence of looking at the stalls downstairs, with mismatching teacups and the sets of glasses and cutlery no one would want because they'd come directly from dead people. (Glasses raised to mouths that were rotting, the skull beneath the face showing as the old flesh fell away; cutlery fixed in fists in rigor mortis – she'd died over her individual cottage pie on the Friday and nobody had found her until the Monday; she'd had to be buried with a fork and a knife in each hand, and the rest of the cutlery canteen sent to the Hanmouth antiques centre.) Then she had gone upstairs. She was too impatient by now, and went to the stall she had had in mind without any delay. It was the stall that had sold her the hatpin, last year; the one Hettie had in her pocket and took everywhere for good luck. They had what she was looking for.

'Hello, there, young lady,' the one who took the money had said. 'Are you sure? Lots of other lovely dollies in the far corner.'

'Yes, I'm sure,' Hettie had said, holding out her two-pound coin.

'It's just that this one . . .' the old one said. 'It doesn't have a right arm, you see. Don't you want a dolly with all her parts?'

'I didn't know they made dollies,' Hettie said, emphasizing the word sarcastically, 'with all their parts. I don't know that I'd want one. That sounds awful.'

The old one had taken the money; she hadn't missed Hettie being sarcastic; and Hettie had taken the one-armed doll-child home to meet its fate.

There were twenty-eight participants in the upper room, and Hettie to arrange everything. Twenty-seven of them had been there for ever, and had their names in everyday life: there was Sad Child, Harriet, Lucinda, Weeping Real Tears, My Little Pony One and Two, Wedding Dress My Little Pony, Kafka, Horse-radish, Little Hattie, the Lady Mayoress of Reckham, Cappuccino, Bloodstained Victim, Dead In Childbirth, Mother, Big Hattie, Death, Widow, Child Pornography, Slightly Jewish, Shitface, Pretty Girl, One Eye Doesn't Work, Dressed As A Man, Rebecca Holden, Lipstick and Hole. Rebecca Holden in real life was a girl in her class with lovely hair, straight down, and thin, who had never spoken to Hettie, though Hettie always got better marks than her. Today they were lined up, twelve of them, including the ponies, in two rows; they were the jury. Two barristers and two juniors and a Clerk of the Court. Then there were members of the public and the victim's family and the press, and Child Pornography was the judge because of her white curly hair a bit like a wig. The new doll with only one arm didn't have a name. Hettie wasn't going to waste one on her. She was just The Accused.

'Do you have anything further to say,' Child Pornography said, in a gruff, legal voice, 'before sentence is passed upon you?'

'I have something to say,' called Slightly Jewish from the relatives' box. She lisped for some reason. 'She was my little girl and you took her away from me.'

31

'Murderer! Beast! Paedophile!' Two members of the public had called out, Little Hattie and the Lady Mayoress of Reckham, jumping up and down excitedly in either hand. Then one of the ponies, the one with the wedding dress, forgot that she was in the jury and started shouting, 'You fucking bastard.'

'Silence in court,' Child Pornography said, in the special low voice she had when she was the judge. 'I have heard the jury's verdict and all the evidence and it is clear that you are guilty of all the charges and that you kidnapped and paedophiled this innocent victim, who was as beautiful as the day is long. I sentence you to twenty years of being done with the hatpin.'

The Accused hadn't spoken so far, but now he leapt into Hettie's left hand and started pleading for anything at all but the hatpin, waving his one arm about. Too late! The hatpin and Hole the executioner were already in Hettie's left hand, and now began to stab the Accused, once, twice, three times. There were little screams and grunts as the punishment proceeded. In a moment or two it got too hard to hold Hole and the hatpin in one hand and to stab the new doll at the same time. Hettie dropped Hole, and went on stabbing with the hatpin into the doll's head, body, legs, now silently. In fifteen minutes, the doll was torn, small scraps of rubber bearing the imprint of half a mouth on the carpet; the pathetic little eye, scraps of hair torn from the fascinatingly meshed scalp; and all around, the twenty-eight dolls lined up and looked with satisfaction on what happened to people who did bad things, and on the hatpin. 'There,' Child Pornography said, but it was in Hettie's voice now, and she only moved her up and down for the sake of it. 'Let that be a lesson to you not to kidnap and torture in future.'

'You know it's my book group this evening,' her mother called from downstairs.

'Yes, I know,' Hettie said. She could hear how her voice sounded excited and stifled.

'What are you doing up there?' the voice called, with a definite inquisitorial edge.

'Nothing. Just mucking about.'

'Well, you know you're welcome to come and sit in on the book group,' the voice said.

'I'll sit up here and watch telly,' Hettie said. There was a sigh, meant to be heard up a staircase and through a solid bedroom door.

'Really,' Kafka said, in an unusually sophisticated and mature voice, 'Miranda should, to be perfectly honest, have overcome her disappointments by now. It's not as if she doesn't know perfectly well that—'

'That's right,' Hettie said, cutting Kafka off. You never knew what Kafka might or might not say when she was in a certain mood.

7.

Kenyon was running for his train across the broad and half-aimless crowd at Paddington station. The gormless, slow and humourless west began with the prevailing manners of Paddington station, and across it, Kenyon ran like a Londoner with somewhere to go. Knees up, his jacket and bricfcase-cum-weekend-bag in the other, he had only two minutes, perhaps not that, to catch his train. (The ticket, bought parsimoniously six weeks before, had cost thirty pounds, but was for this exact train. If he missed this one, and caught the next, his ticket would be invalid and he would have to pay sixty-three pounds for a new one; so he ran.) Kenyon led an orderly life, organized weeks in advance, planned in accordance with the convenience of the First Great Western train company. But there had been a last-minute query from the Department about the reported Ugandan infection rates in a paper he'd written for them; the Underground had groaned inexplicably to a halt shortly after Euston Square; pushing aside massively laden Spaniards who did not know which side to stand on, he had run up the black and greasy steps and iron escalators of the Underground, diagonal, hung and groaningly floating over great unspecified voids, like public transport envisaged in a nightmare by Piranesi. Now he ran across the 'piazza', as it was now festively renamed. The holidaymakers heading for the west, with their surfboards, rucksacks the size of a sheep, square brown suitcases dug out of wardrobes, sat in his path like deliberate obstacles, like a miniature village. He jinked and swerved among the slow-witted and the heavy-laden like a man divided between his consciousness of an almost certainly lost *something*, and his fierce intention towards that train, there, that particular one, behind the barrier.

He had read somewhere that the identity of the 16.05 train to Anytown resided in its distinction, its differences, and that presumably a train that ran only the once could have no identity at all. It remained the same from day to day, still the same 16.05, despite being constituted out of different engines, different carriages, staffed by different individuals and carrying entirely different complements of passengers. Philosophically true that might be, but the identity of this one, beyond the barrier, did not seem remotely mutable, at all capable of replacement with different units as he fumbled with his ticket and limbs and thrust-out bags in the general direction of the ticket-checking machine at the barrier and ran towards the first carriage. A guard already stood by the door of the first-class carriage, arm raised. This train, he felt, was unique, and he hardly noticed the youth on this side of the ticket barrier who seemed in no hurry to get on the train, kneeling by an open black case on the platform between waiting trains. It was as if he had nowhere very much to go. But at the time Kenyon barely gave him a thought.

'Only just made it,' said the guard, in tones of quite pointless admonition. Kenyon clambered on, and into the first-class carriage, where the other passengers gave him half a glance before raising their newspapers against him, lowered their faces to their books, or just turned their heads away. Kenyon, dripping, purple-faced, crumpled, stumbled up the aisle panting with his detritus-like luggage. He fell into his reserved seat. It faced the wrong way, with, as a man of Kenyon's age and class still put it, its back to the engine. This was either due to Kenyon's vagueness when booking or the railway company's incompetence. Around him, everyone was tactfully engaged in things that meant they didn't have to look at Kenyon just for the moment.

Out of the window, the guard blew a whistle and raised an arm. Some sort of electronic signal within signified the locking of the doors. Almost at the same moment on the platform, the young man in the nondescript camel-coloured duffel coat, completely wrong for the temperature and the time of year, raised himself in a leisurely way from his crouching position over the black case. Somewhere further away there was a cry, then a number of shouts. The noise was muffled in the compartment. The train began to move away. The man raised his right arm, his left hand gripping his right wrist. There was a popping sound, as if of a balloon, then another. The train continued to move. Kenyon's last impression was of a vague and retreating mass of people, running and throwing themselves to the marble floor, or perhaps being shot and falling to the floor. The small resolute figure stayed where it was, its arms outstretched with a firing weapon at the end of them. The train slid out from the station canopy around the concealing curve, into the sunlit railway path, lined with sunlit towers, of west London.

'Did you see that?' Kenyon said. He asked nobody in particular, and nobody answered. Perhaps nobody had seen it. The pages of the newspapers between his fellow passengers and Kenyon stayed where they were. Something in the angle of the sheets made it clear that they were not being read. They were thinking of Kenyon's sweating dishevelment, and would lower them when he might have cooled down and stopped panting like a dog. So it was left to Kenyon to read the story on the front page of all of them. It was concerned with the small town he lived in and where he was travelling to. Tomorrow, those same front pages would be filled with what he had just half seen, a teenager

35

shooting at random at strangers at Paddington station on a sunny afternoon. None of them would mention what seemed most noteworthy to Kenyon, that a train had managed its departure at the exact same moment, as if the shooting were no more than a trivial and irrelevant part of the station's normal work. He concluded, as the train went on with a smooth lack of feeling or shocked response, that he was being swept away from one catastrophe towards another. The world was experiencing an ugly abundance of news, and its experience in the face of that abundance was neglected and unshared. Nobody knew what it was like to travel from the site of a mass shooting towards the site of a child's kidnapping, and sit in a first-class compartment, the only announcements to listen to those coming from the buffet, about hot and cold drinks, snacks and light refreshments.

It could have been a delirious dream. But at the first stop, Reading, the platforms were milling with disgorged passengers beyond the extinguished trains. They had the patient and forest-like appearance of English people asked to stand and await news about an inconvenient but remote crisis. The crisis, remote as it was, had not been enough to erase the difference between travelling strangers, and for the moment they stood separately without coming together to share observations. 'Due to an incident,' an announcement from the platform began. The doors shut, the train moved on. Like a forlorn responding bird call, the Tannoy said, 'For the benefit of customers joining us at Reading, the buffet is now open for the sale of light refreshments, snacks, tea and coffee, soft drinks and alcoholic drinks. Please have the correct change if at all possible.' There was nothing in the westward direction to detain them, after all.

8.

On an early summer evening in a medium-sized city in the west of England, a more than customary crowd stood on a railway platform and noisily waited. Between the tracks, someone had once placed heavy concrete troughs and had planted them. Nobody, however, had tended them for years. A tattered linear meadow had spread. Scraggy meadowsweet and Michaelmas daisies had seeded themselves in the gravel between the lines and even along the tracks. They grew leggily, their flowers patchy and periodic as a disease of the skin.

The holiday atmosphere had spread up the line from Hanmouth. Caroline inspected the other passengers coldly, fingering the Moroccan beads at her neck. On this line, you got the squaddies from the camp at Reckham. They were bony, pimpled youths with identically applied and variously successful haircuts. With them was the miscellaneous and motley humanity, and its sourly unpromising children, that had washed up finally at the grim and dole-funded settlements where the train ground to a halt. They all came into Barnstaple to shop, to have an afternoon's spree, to be subjected to a modicum of education. Today, too, there were others: prim middle-aged couples in neat gear, as if for Sunday-morning drinks, and professionals, too, with a notebook or a complex camera about their necks. One such professional had insinuated himself into a seaside group of teenagers: a fat, womanly Goth in an unseasonable floor-length black leather coat and purple eyeshadow, his dead-black hair plastered to his scalp with sweat, and with him, three blonde girls, non-matching and clean, in floral sprigs or mini-skirts, pastel in overall effect. The professional – the journalist – was polo-shirted and knowledgeable rather than knowing in appearance. He was committing their comments to a list-sized notebook, flicking the short pages over as he scribbled. The children talked one over the other, craning over his shoulder to wonder at his shorthand.

Caroline looked away as if at a lapse in taste or judgement. She knew what they were talking about. She believed, on the whole, that if one had something to say about such stuff, one said it to the police, and if not, not.

One infrequently saw one's neighbours from Hanmouth on

this platform, though the train was at least as convenient as driving into Barnstaple, and without the terrific bore of having to find a parking space. It was particularly unusual to see Kenyon here on an early Thursday night. He was standing on the platform, this hot and celebratory night, as if no one had told him a girl had been abducted from the town he lived in. The ensemble of his professional London wear had somewhat disintegrated in the three-hour sequence that had led him from his Islington AIDS-aid office to the platform at Barnstaple. (Caroline had heard the explanation of the structures of his commuting more than once. Sometimes, at his wife's parties, people took pity on Kenyon and engaged him in conversation. If they did, he tended to fall back on explanation of how he got from Hanmouth to Islington and back again every week, perhaps rightly assuming that people didn't cross the room at Miranda's party to hear about anything interesting like AIDS outreach in Africa, which was how he spent his days.) The jacket of his suit lay in the crook of his arm. His scuffed briefcase stood at his feet, the seams unravelling at each corner. He looked mostly as if he had been recently dipped head downwards in the vat of some sugary solution, his hair anyhow in all directions, though smoothed down by the ineffective motion of his palms. His white shirt and red tie might never have been ironed at all. Kenyon was so evidently at the end of some long and exhausting journey that, for his sake, Caroline hesitated to greet him. But he saw her. With the last smile of a long, smiling, official day, he came over to her.

'The most extraordinary thing,' he said. 'Have you seen a newspaper – an evening newspaper?'

'To be honest, we've rather given up,' Caroline said. 'I honestly don't care to read about it any more. That poor little girl, and that awful family. And everyone—' She shuddered, as if shaking off everyone around her.

'No, the most – the most extraordinary thing,' Kenyon said. 'Just happened at Paddington. Just as the train was—' He gave up, unable to explain. 'It seems very crowded, doesn't it?'

'Hanmouth's' – *Hammuth*'s – 'become a popular destination these days,' Caroline said. Then, as Kenyon didn't seem to understand, or was still deep in contemplation of whatever coincidence or casual meeting had occupied his thought for the last three hours, she murmured, 'You know – the ghouls . . .' and left it at that.

'The—' Kenyon said. 'Oh. That poor little girl. And the awful family, as you say. I can't understand it either. Are they hoping to discover them, or are they just curious? Rubberneckers, Miranda calls them. She's had a new story about a group of them every night this week, every time we've spoken on the phone. One lot tried to take a photograph through our front window, as if the little girl might be bound and gagged in our sitting room. What do you think they're coming for?'

A stout family of four on a bench, raising and lowering food to their mouths in a steady, complex, four-part rhythm, caught Caroline's eye and answered the question so firmly that she said nothing.

'Have you had the police round?' Kenyon said. This had become an ordinary opening to conversation in Hanmouth in the last week or two.

'A couple of days ago. It was lucky, really. Of course we could all say where we'd been the night the little girl went missing, a dozen of us. It was Miranda's book club that evening, so everyone was round at each other's houses, boning up, I'm sorry to say – you know how Miranda leaps on one if one hasn't done the reading, so we do rather meet up in advance to see how the land lies. *Nazi Writers in the Americas*.'

'I'm sorry?'

'*Nazi Writers in the Americas*. That's what we were doing.' Kenyon still looked bemused. 'It's a book. We were all in the same two or three places, all secretly boning up on Roberto Bolaño, sharing our notes. The police must have thought we were quite a little conspiracy when they kept getting the same story back, but different locations – of course, we don't all meet at

39

once, just in pairs and threes, I suppose. Not that there's anything conspiratorial or planned about it.'

'So everyone had an alibi except Miranda,' Kenyon said.

'At the university, I believe. And you, of course, I suppose.'

'I was in London, oddly enough. I must get to my wife's reading group, one of these days. It sounds very interesting.'

'Well, we could do with another man, and if only you'd read the book I would say there's no time like the present.'

'What?'

'That's what I'm dashing back for. Miranda's book group. It's tonight, didn't you know?'

'Oh, Lord, is it really? I never get a chance to get Miranda on her own. That really is too bad.'

Caroline looked at Kenyon and wondered why he'd said Miranda only, not mentioned any failure to get his daughter Hettie on her own. Then the thought of Hettie came to mind – mouth-breathing, with an incipient dewy moustache on her upper lip, in argument hurling plates, books, knives, even, once, a small table with the unvarying refrain that nobody ever considered her needs and desires – and she admired Kenyon for being able to put Hettie out of mind, if that was what he had done.

'Well, I'm not going to complain about the book club, now that it's provided us with such a good alibi. Not that I suppose any of us were very likely suspects in the first place. It's always been a terror of mine – you know, the windowless cell, the two policeman, the "And where were you between the hours of six thirty and – and whenever"' – imagination failing Caroline here – '"on the night of September the twenty-third?" You know. On the police-brutality shows.'

'The police-brutality shows?'

'I mean the police shows on the telly. I always watch them. But if they asked you in real life, one would probably have to say—'

'"I haven't a single solitary clue." Of course one would.'

'Or just "I expect I was cooking dinner, or we might have been watching some nonsense on the telly, though I can't remember what it was one had been watching."'

'There's Sky Plus nowadays. Record and watch later. One couldn't rely on that as an alibi. A murder detective would see through it immediately.'

Caroline looked at Kenyon's red eyes in his jowly and humourless damp face. He was an odd fellow to have thought all that through.

'But luckily,' Caroline said, 'Miranda's a marvel about all of that. A date and a place booked weeks in advance. And then she writes it all up afterwards in her diary, I'm sure someone told me. Marvellous, the energy to write an entry in your diary every day. I wouldn't have the energy even to do half of what she does, let alone write about it all afterwards.'

'I expect she enjoys doing it,' Kenyon said drily. 'Here's the train. Do you want a hand with your bags?'

9.

Miranda, Kenyon's wife, was marvellous, everyone agreed. Her house, at exactly the right point in the Strand where the picturesque, in the form of old fishermen's cottages lived in by gay couples, began to give way to the imposing line of mercantile mansions, was a marvel, renewed every year. There might be more valuable houses in Hanmouth, but when she and Kenyon had bought it, five years before, it was the highest price ever paid for a Hanmouth house. Her drawing room had no taint of the rural, still less of the estuarine, but was rather defined by a Wiener Werkstätte desk in steel, an icy Meredith Frampton of a chemist holding a white lily and resting his hand on a bright array of test tubes, and two Mies van der Rohe black leather *chaises-longues* with liquorice-allsorts headrests, in the crook of which first-time visitors tended to perch like elves on the inside of an elbow.

(Returning visitors had learnt their lesson, and made for one of the three less distinguished but more comfortable armchairs.) At the door there was always a collecting box for an African cause; a small shelf in the hallway held some classics of Miranda's professional interest (Regency women poets), Miranda's two books on the subject, this year's and last year's Booker shortlist. There were also usually a couple of Harry Potters or similar pre-pubescent epics – not to suggest Hettie's reading, since she clearly didn't do any, but to indicate that Miranda was not an intimidating intellectual but a girl at heart with, just below the surface, a well-developed sense of fun. Often some of these were signed copies, since Miranda spent a whole week every summer at the Dartington literary festival. Later, the deserving few would be decanted upstairs to the study, the others donated to the lifeboat charity or the air-rescue service, to sell for a pound or two in one of their many shops.

Miranda had a grey-white Louise Brooks bob, and severe black glasses, oblong like a letterbox; her necklines squarely suggested the unspecifically medieval. With what she could alter, she tried to impose corners, lines and geometry on a general appearance otherwise curved and bulging to a fault. She was aware of the dangers to a woman of her size and age of flowing red and purple velvet, of ethnic beads and the worst that Hampstead Bazaar could do. She would not, like most of Hanmouth's women, be inspired by Dame Judi Dench on an Oscar night, and she dressed, as far as possible, in the black and white lines and corners of the fat wife of a Weimar architect. Kenyon was used to being told what a marvel his wife was; he did quite well, all things considered.

Reading groups, local groups, charities, and a party three times a year. It was obvious what Miranda thought of herself in her lovely and expensive home. Most people agreed she was marvellous, though wondering how she and Kenyon stretched to such a house on the salary of a civil servant and a university lecturer. Kenyon himself had lived for so long in proximity to the marvel that, like a waiter working in a restaurant with a view of the

Parthenon, he seemed years ago to have stopped decently appreciating it.

'What did they see in each other?' Hanmouth asked, when Miranda wasn't in the room – running late, usually. Over a long, green-baize-covered table, all of them in possession of a too-elaborate agenda produced by the committee's word-processing expert, or standing about at a party in a garden in the summer, or craning their necks backwards in the direction of a neighbour and fellow book-grouper in the row behind as they waited for the curtain to go up on the Miranda-produced Hanmouth Players production of *The Bacchae* or *Woyzeck*, they would put the same questions. How did they meet in the first place? How did they afford that house – was there money in the family? What were they like when they were young? And what – this above all – did they do or talk about when no one else was there? Hettie didn't seem enough to sustain their interest or their occupation. Bold speculations about their all-enveloping sex lives, unspoken, filled the air; and then the lights went down, the curtain went up, and Hanmouth concentrated on a production of *Marat/Sade* in the community hall.

Kenyon was not there during the week; it was just Hettie and, people imagined, Miranda being understanding but firm with her over the dinner table from Monday to Thursday. It was a surprise to Caroline to see Kenyon on Barnstaple station on a Thursday night. He worked in London. 'For an NGO,' Miranda would say, not always to the perfect comprehension of those who had asked. 'He's been donated for ten years, a solid commitment by the Treasury.' People envisaged Kenyon, reduced to two dimensions, being pushed through the slot of rather a large collection tin. Kenyon would smile, and explain that 'seconded' was really the term for the way the Treasury had concluded it could rub along perfectly well without him for the next decade.

Hardly anyone knew or understood or bothered to enquire what it was Kenyon did for a living. It was something to do with AIDS in Africa. That was an improvement, Miranda would confide, on the Treasury. Of course, she would say, when Kenyon worked at the Treasury, one knew in an abstract and uncomprehending way that he did something very important. It was something to do with the balance of payments or with incomes policy or whether interest rates were going to go up or come down – why, she went on, did interest rates *go* up but *come* down? The choice of verb was interesting: it was as if we human beings existed at a sort of base rate – at zero – that we were the nothing that interest rates pretended to improve upon, and what would happen if interest rates ever came down to zero and looked us in the face? Yes, our mortgage repayments might be less murderous, she supposed – but why those comings and goings, one really couldn't say – and why *interest* rates when of all the utterly dread and drear and tedious and unforgivably . . .

That was Miranda's style of conversation, and very good of its own sort it was, too. Kenyon would smile graciously and in a generally abstracted way, never pointing out that 'balance of payments' and 'incomes policy' dated Miranda very badly to her era of courting and seduction, when she had last paid serious attention to Kenyon's explanations of what he did for a living during the day. The Treasury hadn't touched interest rates for eight years when Kenyon was donated to the NGO. On the other hand, everyone knew what Miranda did: she was always ready to explain about post-colonial theory.

Kenyon, Miranda said, had gone on to something where at least you could see where the good was being done. Who knew whether anything was being improved, what end was being served by the vagaries of monetary policy? ('You don't mean monetary,' Kenyon said, though it was impossible to tell whether Miranda meant monetary or not, surely.) At the AIDS non-governmental organization, there were clear villains and clear heroes. There were Roman Catholic cardinals in Africa who told lies to their flocks about rubber prophylactics. And on the other side, there were orphans. The Treasury had been like that once: there had been Thatcher, the witch, and monetarism on the one side, destroying people's lives and cackling over it, and on the other, the miners. Those moral contrasts seemed to have gone on holiday for the moment. In more recent times, there had been no cardinals or orphans at the Treasury; it all seemed so vast and trackless nowadays.

At the time Miranda had been voluble about Kenyon's change of career. She had gone on talking about it ever since. Through a useful mechanism, the Treasury had gone on matching Kenyon's salary and had agreed to regard him as being seconded to Living With Aids (Africa) for five years in the first instance. In a moment of exuberance, Miranda had led him to a bank, told an unverified white lie or two, and walked out with a mortgage six times their combined salaries, with which they had moved from a fisherman's cottage to the wide bright house on the Strand. Four years had gone by, and it was as if they had always lived there. Kenyon, in private, would occasionally bemoan their lack of savings, the way things seemed to run out towards the end of the month. It was lucky they had principles about not educating their daughter outside the state system. But the house was an unarguable good. And more to the point, nothing had been said by the Treasury about Kenyon's imminent return. For some reason – some guilty reason, since Kenyon was so able and likeable – it often occurred to those she spoke to to wonder whether the Treasury might not have been keen to get rid of Kenyon for some reason. But surely not. Miranda said she hoped Kenyon would stay for the ten years they were now anticipating. It did her so much good to think of what Kenyon did for a living.

10.

The train was crowded and talkative. Kenyon and Caroline squashed into the same seat with their various bags piled up on their laps, facing forward. In a line, spread out along the aisle, seven teenagers called out. They were going to the Bear first – no, the Pincers; but one had told Carrie they would be in the Jolly Porters and they knew she'd lost her mobile, so what about that then, what were they going to do about that?

'These people,' Caroline said, shifting her bag of shopping further onto her knees. She meant to be heard. 'I don't know what they expect to see when they get to Hanmouth.'

'The most extraordinary thing,' Kenyon said. 'As we were pulling out of Paddington, a young man got out a gun and started firing into the crowd.'

'Oh, no,' Caroline said. 'On the train?'

'No,' Kenyon said. 'On the concourse. I just glimpsed it as the train was pulling out of the station. I haven't seen a newspaper and there weren't any announcements, so I don't know how serious it was.'

'How dreadful,' Caroline said. 'That sort of thing seems to happen so much more often nowadays. What a lucky escape you had. I can't imagine what these people are doing going down to Hanmouth. People just seem to go wherever they think there'll be a crowd. Trafalgar Square on New Year's Eve. People go there but they don't know why. Safety in numbers, I suppose – numbers of idiots, anyway.'

Two girls in front of Kenyon and Caroline, one talking on her mobile phone with a hand pressed against her other ear, turned simultaneously, stared from a three-foot distance, and shrugged with as much direct offence as they could muster before turning back.

'What are you reading tonight?' Kenyon asked. 'I remember now – Miranda told me to make myself scarce and not expect much in the way of supper.'

'Don't you get something at Paddington?' Caroline said. Kenyon agreed that sometimes he did, holding back the recurrence of a scene as his mind reconstructed it. 'They're terribly good, those outlets nowadays – sushi on a conveyor-belt at Paddington, isn't there?'

'Waa-raa-argh,' went the four teenagers in a scrum at the end of the carriage as the train leant into the St Martin's bend. They fell against each other, then righted themselves hilariously.

'No, I'll wander down to the pub on the quay for a bite to eat,' Kenyon said. 'Once I've done my duty and greeted my wife.'

'You'll be lucky,' Caroline said. 'Everywhere's been packed to the gills all week. Haven't you heard? Trippers, journalists, film crews, all eating their heads off. And drinking, of course. It's been precisely like a siege. Hasn't Miranda said?'

'She did,' Kenyon said. 'I thought she was exaggerating.'

'Not in this case.'

11.

There was a new noise in the air, of disagreement and disapproval and pleasure. It was like the load of a substantial lorry shifting and rumbling; it was like the bass voice that announced coming attractions at the cinema clearing its throat; it was like a Welsh male voice choir saying 'RUM' in unison. It was the sound of a community centre in the west of England, every chair filled and every spare standing space occupied with onlookers, journalists, locals, cameramen, people who had no reason or every good reason to be there. The hall was full, and spilling out into the street outside. Dozens of curious people were standing in the warm late-spring evening. From time to time one jumped up to glimpse, through the open double doors and over the heads of the crowd, the six mismatched individuals on the stage of the community centre.

One of them, the chief constable, gave a wounded, reproachful look around the hall. His face had something weak and sheeplike about it, a long, loose-lipped face topped off with hair white, crinkled, sheeplike, and his voice bleated as it attempted to assert some authority. 'I repeat: we are doing everything possible in this case, with the greatest possible sense of urgency. We are following several, a number of strong leads at this present time. The efficacy of the police operation should not be doubted by anybody here present.'

It was the use of the word 'efficacy' that roused the moan of satisfied disagreement in the first place. The policeman's first use of such a word stirred the gathering to a communal expression of disapproval and unformed hostile emotion. Now he repeated it, satisfied with the official and distant tone of the word. Perhaps he felt it conveyed calm practicality. The hall's rage and distaste rose in volume, mounted and prepared to come to a point. One of the women who had arrived early with Ruth, the mother's best friend, a woman not known to the crowd at large, now stood up. When she did so, it could be seen that she and Ruth and three other women had arrived early and placed themselves with some care: they occupied a prime position between the television cameras and the party on stage. The woman's hand was already raised, as if in a tragic gesture, as if to take a courtroom oath.

'I'd like the chief constable to know that it isn't "this case" we're talking about. It may be just "this case" to him in his big office and his forms he's filling in all day long. It's not "this case" to me and Heidi and Mick up there on the stage, and a hundred other people who know China and are missing her. Heidi and Mick are crying their eyes out and not getting a wink of sleep for worry. It's my little girl Natasha's best friend China we're talking about. It's their little girl who's been missing for ten days now. Ten days and ten nights and nothing done. Anything could have happened to her. What have they found out? Nothing. They'd done nothing.'

'I can assure everyone—' the chief constable said, holding onto the microphone, but he got no further. The woman who had spoken was, it seemed, no more than a warm-up act for a familiar and by now keenly anticipated routine. As she sat down, Ruth stood up, and the television cameras had not troubled to turn to the chief constable, but stayed where they were, fixed on Ruth, the little girl's aunt. Was that who she was? By now, all the journalists knew her well. Calvin, the media manager, had introduced all of them to her, a hard-faced black woman. They had had to admit she was nobody's fool, and had been saying the same thing to them with great energy for ten days now. The police, too, knew her and her enthusiastic but unhelpful denunciations. She had never had so large an audience for her comments as she had now, and she was going to make the most of the arguments she had been polishing.

'There's not been a policeman on the beat here for years. Where are they all? Filling in their little forms in their little offices. And they're here now, but what are they doing? Not house-to-house, they're not doing that. They know, we know, there's sex offenders living here in our midst, in Hanmouth. One of the chief constable's officers told me as much. But they won't tell us who they are or where they live. Anyone who's got a little girl in this town wants to be worried. You think, it could be your daughter or your granddaughter next. It might be as easy them that get taken as China, next time. We want to know. It's our right. What's he got to say about that?'

On the stage in front of the blue west of England police screens, next to the chief constable with his bewildered expression, the girl's mother sat, entirely relaxed. She might have believed the mission statement in fake loopy handwriting behind them, so calm did she seem: Helping People Safely. Her eyes were cast down towards her folded hands. Her long blonde hair fell like a curtain over her features. Heidi: she had been Helen in the papers, her birth name, or Tragic Helen, names nobody who knew her had ever called her. Snatched or posed, photographs of her frozen madonna-mask, refusing to weep, made a perfect front page; an old school photograph of China the usual inset. One enterprising paper had gone to Heidi's long-estranged mother in Yeovil, and printed some old photographs of Heidi, ten or fifteen years old; the mother, afterwards, had been warned off coming anywhere near Heidi or Hanmouth, and some journalists were under the impression that Ruth's mother Karen was her real mother.

Next to her was Micky, China's stepfather, with the half-wit expression and shaved head, his mouth fallen half open. The visitors had taken his expression for shock or grief. Those who lived in Hanmouth had seen his empty face hundreds of times outside the worst of the small town's pubs. They had never considered before that he came from Hanmouth, exactly. Some of them were surprised to hear that the sister-in-law, or whoever she was, was talking about 'here' as if she lived in Hanmouth, rather than in one of the grim suburbs that lay between Hanmouth and Barnstaple. Micky was known to everyone as far as Heycombe, however. He had a long-standing habit of showing his penis to newcomers and to girl students from Barnstaple, doing the Hanmouth pub crawl. His bun-like face was not made bewildered by grief or fear. That was what he looked like.

The chief constable allowed himself to think that the mother had prepared and rehearsed her sister, or sister-in-law, in these accusations. He also allowed himself to think that those involved in the rehearsal were much more extensive than that. The mother and the stepfather were, he saw, wearing new clothes from top to bottom, quite different from the new clothes they had been wearing when he had met them that morning. The price tag had still been on the sole of the woman's shoes, as he had seen when she knelt to wipe some jam off one of her younger children's chops. Newspaper money had paid for the new shoes, no doubt including a fat fee the interview in the *Daily Whatever* had brought them two days ago. The press had been full of the news that they'd asked to be paid in cash for that, though they'd all made a silent agreement not to mention any of that in their own coverage. This pair had been exploiting their opportunities and, in the eyes both of the police and the press, they knew what they were doing. It was as if they had been planning it before the child went missing, and the machinery had swung into action within hours. The way that the woman's face had fallen to her hands a second or two before Ruth stood up had had a practised appearance. She didn't want her satisfaction at the interruption and the discomfiture of the police to be too evident.

'Let me assure you,' the policeman said. 'Let me assure everyone here that we are, indeed, carrying out house-to-house enquiries. These inquiries have led to a number of fruitful leads. We are now pursuing those. It would not be helpful, in the interests of our investigations, to explain here exactly what those leads are. I should also say that, in the hours immediately following China's disappearance, we went as a matter of urgency to everybody in the vicinity who was on the sex offenders' register. Of course, that was the first thing we did. We know who they all are, and they were our first priority.'

There was another rumpus, from the back of the hall. It was a man this time, looking not at all like one of Micky and Heidi's relations, both deplorable and beyond genealogical analysis. This one looked very much like the sort of person who was supposed to live in Hanmouth, and soon people recognized him as the man who sat at the cash desk in the antiques emporium on the quay. He was the sort of person who in normal circumstances would complain about Heidi and Micky. He was wearing a tweed jacket and a tie, even on this hot spring night. His wife, by his side, nodded agreement as he shouted.

'Who are they?' he shouted. 'Who are these sex offenders living in our communities? We need to know their names. I have grand-children and – and—'

Heidi looked up, interested. She hadn't anticipated or prepared this one.

'Let me assure you—' the chief constable said.

'And that wasn't the first thing you did. The first thing you did was to go wandering round my back garden without permission and walk up and down the long field out back, questioning innocent people while time got wasted. My wife and our grand-children, our grandchildren, I tell you, they need to know—'

'Let me assure you that investigations into such persons were immediate and very thorough. We will not, however, in the light, in the light of the strength, ah, of feeling around this case –'

'This case?'

'– around this case be revealing the names of those individuals who, though on the sex offenders' register, are innocent of any involvement in China's disappearance. I'm sure you can understand the thinking behind that.'

'It's not "this case", it's—'

'We need to know—'

On the far end of the trestle table, Mr Calvin sat in his blue suit, taking notes. The chief constable had got to know him well in the last few days. He lived in Hanmouth, on the best street, the Strand. Calvin was the sort of respectable figure who would not normally have had anything to do with anyone like the O'Connors. He had announced himself to the police, once challenged, as 'a friend of the family's', who would be liaising with them and advising them. Already, the chief constable happened to know, he had told the press and television that he was the O'Connors' 'representative'. An officer with a good memory recalled that, in fact, he was nothing more than the chairman of the Hanmouth Strand Neighbourhood Watch and, last year, had lobbied successfully for CCTV to be placed not only from one end of the Fore street in Hanmouth to the other, but the whole length of the Strand and some tranquil streets behind it where no crime had ever been committed. Whether any criminal had been caught by this inch-by-inch surveillance in the two years since, no police officer could say, but the cameras, and the signs announcing their presence, had been conjured into existence by the wish of Calvin and his committee. Now, his pseudo-legal authority had allowed him to take control of the O'Connors' wishes and campaign. The police and press had, already, found common, unvoiced ground in detesting him. He gave a tight little smile to his clients, or friends, or customers, and finished what he was writing in his orange notebook. He tore out the page and passed it to Heidi, before closing the notebook.

'I'd like to invite Heidi and Micky to say a few words,' the chief constable said, with resignation. 'I'm sure we all understand how difficult this is for them, and appreciate how brave they've been in coming here tonight.'

Heidi looked up from underneath her curtain of blonde hair, and turned to her left. She did not look at Micky, but at Mr Calvin in his blue three-buttoned suit and grey-white slicked-down hair. 'Look at her,' one of the women at the very back of the hall, Billa Townsend, the Brigadier's wife, said to her friend from the reading group, and they both looked at Heidi. Despite the four children, the years of men's demands and children's commands in a small house buried a long way within the Ruskin estate on the Torcombe road, despite the lack of sleep this last week and the worst her newly acquired chainstore wardrobe could do for her, she was a beauty. Billa Townsend was indicating that in low tones, and her friend Kitty understood what she was being asked to look at. Heidi looked what she was, or had been: the sumptuous heroine of the Hanmouth Academy, and the eleven years since she had left school had done little to touch her perfect high-boned face, her green eyes, the pale stripe of hair falling like a shadow across her perpetually bronzed cheek, and that awkward but perfect element, the nose of an eagle or a duchess. They had shaken their heads when she had gone off, at sixteen, with sad, ratty Nigel. There must have been a reason for her to do that, and for the two hopeless men, one a hopeless and brief husband, since then. Must have been a reason, even, for Micky Thomas, seven years her junior. Hanmouth had hardly heard her speak since she left school, unless she had been suggesting a colour rinse in flat tones. Hanmouth had only, in the last year or two, seen her man in the worst of its pubs, heard his daft opinions, seen him manhandling different girls into the pub toilets at closing time. In her hand was the little page of the notebook Mr Calvin had passed her. She hardly glanced at it.

'I'd just like to say thank you,' Heidi said, in a flat quiet voice – the chief constable chivalrously adjusted the microphone in front of her. 'I'd like to say thank you to everyone who is helping by making a contribution to the Save China fund. It means a lot to us that people who never met China care so much that they'll send in thirty, forty, fifty pounds to help with the family expenses and the investigation that is going to help find China. China's a lovely girl. She's not an angel, she's full of mischieviousness like any other eight-year-old. I just want to say to whoever's got her that they want to think about us, think about her family, who love her so much and miss her. Her little brothers and her sister don't understand she's been taken, but they cry themselves to sleep every night. So, please, just bring her back home safe and sound soon.'

The cameras stayed for a moment at their sustained angle, waiting perhaps for the mother to start weeping. She had done so once before. 'Hard as nails,' one cameraman muttered to his sound man, and lowered the camera in disappointment. The chief constable was winding up now, giving the same appeal for information that he had given the day before, but none of that needed filming. The party on the stage stood up – the chief constable and the woman police officer in charge of the O'Connors' welfare, Calvin, the lawyer, Micky and Heidi. As at the end of a wedding, they sorted themselves out into disparate couples, the chief constable taking charge of Heidi, Mr Calvin walking with Micky's elbow firmly in his grip, the lawyer and the woman police officer bringing up the rear. The community centre rose like a congregation, solemnly and silently. At the back of the hall, the crowd, which hadn't found seats and was filling the lobby and half the street outside, pressed against each other and divided. The police officers at the back pushed and shoved, finding space for Micky and Heidi and their official attendants. 'Those sex offenders – we need to know, Chief Constable,' the man who had shouted out said again, now in quite a reasonable voice as the officers passed. Heidi smiled brilliantly for a moment; the chief constable did not appear to have heard.

The hall had been solemn, concerned and angry, but the mood petered out the further you got from the stage. Outside, in the warm spring evening, the crowd was inquisitive, unfamiliar to each other, and even festive. One man staring at Heidi and Micky's departure was finishing off a Cornetto. They hadn't bothered to change their clothes into anything respectful of the occasion. Some of the men were in swimsuits with a T-shirt or vest on top, a pair of vivid splashy Vilebrequin shorts and flip-flops, straight from the pool, their girlfriends in spaghetti-stringed tops and sarongs over wet bikinis. They stared as if at celebrity, and spilled halfway down the street as far as the Co-op and the Case Is Altered, one of the better Hanmouth pubs, and evidently doing very well out of the influx of curious outsiders. One woman had come from as far away as London, it was said, though an excited report of travellers from Germany turned out to refer to some holiday-makers who happened to have stumbled, bemused, on the happy scene.

In the middle of the crowd, blocking the street, there was a police car. Somehow a path was got through to it. Heidi and Micky, guarded by police, got into the back. Micky was openly staring at the strangers staring at him. Each of them held up a camera phone to their faces over the policemen's shoulders. The woman police officer in charge of the investigation got into the front, and the crowd, disappointed, parted. The car was permitted to set off. The chief constable, accompanied by a couple of officers, made his way as best he could through the crowd to his driver and car in the car park behind the community centre and the fire station. The stars of the show had departed. The audience, leaving the community centre, lost its focus of interest but not its excitement. Hanmouth acquaintances started greeting each other, quite happily. The outsiders, knowing no one, drifted away disappointedly.

12.

'Well, that *was* sad,' Billa Townsend, the Brigadier's wife, said to her friend Kitty. She spoke briskly.

'I *know*,' Kitty said, as if with wonderment that, of all the emotions in the world, Billa had happened by sheer chance to express the very one that she, too, happened to be feeling. 'Awfully sad, really. Rather wish I hadn't gone. Just to look at the poor mother – what she must be feeling, I can't imagine. Terribly sad.'

'We're going to be late for Miranda's book club,' Billa said. 'We'd better make a move.'

The pair of them, each with a string bag containing a book – the same book – and strong, cross, hairy old faces over their quilted blue or green sleeveless gilets, turned away from the community centre and down the Fore street towards the quay. Beyond that was the long line of Dutch houses where Miranda lived. The air of reckless festivity was strong in the street now that the police had gone. Outside the Case Is Altered, a dozen men stood and drank, smoking. None of them was known to Billa or to Kitty. A noisy record from the jukebox enquired, through the open window of the inn, whether someone wished his girlfriend was hot like the singer. Billa didn't know why it was so necessary to make such a frightful din about everything nowadays, and Kitty, throwing everything into her answer, said that she knew. Three unfamiliar children, perhaps the children of some of the drinkers, did handstands without surveillance or restraint against the white-painted carriage arch, against the land-lady's trellis. It didn't appear like a community in which a dangerous child-abductor was on the prowl.

'It all seems so normal,' Kitty said. 'And us carrying on as normal, going to the book group just as we arranged before all of this happened, as if nothing had happened at all. Talking about the same book we were going to talk about.'

'Well, I don't know what we were supposed to do,' Billa said. 'Everyone always complains that they hardly have time to finish a book even with a month's notice. We could hardly have changed the book to something more suitable, even if' – the noise of the crowd was muted as they turned down the kink in the Fore street's progress '— people really wanted to talk about a book with more relevance. A kidnapping story, I suppose you mean.'

That wasn't what Kitty really meant; she couldn't have said what she meant. Billa's flat-fronted Georgian house, like a house front on a stage flat, came into view. They inspected it from top to bottom. The Brigadier stood in the window of the kitchen, conducting with one hand the orchestra on Classic FM, which was murmuring on the sill next to the scarlet pelargoniums. With the other, he was evidently ironing; he liked to do the week's ironing on a Tuesday evening, and nothing much got between him, the ironing and *Dvořák Evening* on the radio.

He was deeply involved in his double task, and did not observe Kitty or Billa as they passed; neither did they try to attract his attention. He had had a lifetime of putting rifles together, of instructing others how to put rifles together, of walking down lines of men ensuring that rifles had been put together properly, and finally of confidence that the men had been properly trained and inspected before he walked a step or two behind Her Majesty, brimming with pride. In old age and retirement, he ensured that he maintained the orderly requirements of a lifetime, dressed with the neatness of an old soldier, and presumably had managed in the army to carry out small domestic chores when required. But little improvements in domestic items over the years had achieved the difficult task of reducing him to helplessness, and he struggled with steam irons and the programmes of modern washing-machines.

They passed on, and a new crowd outside the yellow-painted pub on the quay soon made itself apparent.

'Have you read it?' Kitty said.

'*The Makioka Sisters*?' Billa said. 'Yes, indeed. We ought to have gone through it when we were supposed to rather than tramping off to *Crimewatch UK*. Now we're just going to have to discuss it when we get to Miranda's. I suppose it's called keeping your powder dry, but I don't care for it.'

From the upper reaches of the first house on the Strand emerged the sound of the Bach G major cello suite, soupily expressive on every attained top note. It was John Gordon, straining and sobbing

57

over every unfulfilled promise of tune in the piece. At seven, every evening, before dinner, he always did this. Billa and Kitty knew what the piece was because it was John Gordon's only piece, brought out at parties and dinners, at every invitation and carefully announced. Some people said it was not only his only piece but his only accomplishment in life. He had learnt it at school, many years ago, and at seven in the evening, every day, he opened the upper window and embarked on it, playing it through twice. But everyone knew the same errors would be in it the next day, unimproved by practice and the imitation of self-analysis.

The curtains at the next house, the drawing-room windows of which were sunk somewhat below the level of the pavement, were drawn tightly. Everyone knew why. The Lovells' children had departed to the City, PR in Dubai, and that final difficult one to Oxford to read Japanese. Now, while the sun was still above the horizon and their children far away, the Lovells had taken to early-evening sex in the sitting room, kitchen or even hallway. Mr Lovell returned from his GP's practice in Barnstaple and dropped his clothes in the hall; Mrs Lovell, abundantly fleshy, would come from the garden to meet him, wriggling out of skirt and blouse as she came. Tonight, the little squeaks of joy came with treble clusters of tintinnabulating piano chords, as if in improvised modernist accompaniment to John Gordon's Bach next door. They were doing it in the dining room, on the keyboard of their untuned Yamaha upright. It happened to some people, that obsession with throwing their clothes off at an age when it would be best to keep them on. The Lovells' invitations to view their holiday photographs were only accepted once, by the unwary.

Over the road, in the detached gardens belonging to each house, a dog sat before a white-painted hen house. He was entranced. Stanley's long marmalade ears flapped to the ground, his doleful eyes on one chicken or another. They emerged, retreated, strutted like showgirls around Stanley. Stanley the basset hound belonged to gay Sam who ran the specialist cheese shop and his solicitor boyfriend, the Terrible Waste, Harry Milford – Lord Harry, properly – with the office in Bidecombe. The dog had a mania for forms of life smaller than itself, and could sit happily in front of the Kenyons' chicken coop for long hours. The Kenyons had no objection; they did not believe what the older and more vulgar inhabitants of Hanmouth told them, that that there dog was scaring they hens into fits. Miranda Kenyon didn't believe that sort of hen was much of a layer in any case.

At the very end of the Strand, where the road ran out and turned into a narrow stone pathway along a beach of mole-coloured mud for another two hundred yards, the last house, Mrs Grosjean, kept a white-slatted beehive. It looked like a miniature tongue-and-groove New England lunatic asylum. Stanley loved that even better. It must have been something to do with the rasping hum the slatted box made, or so it was supposed. Mrs Grosjean suspected him, however, of wanting to thieve the honey within, and would chase him off with a flapping tea-towel and shrieks of alarm if she saw him sitting before it. As far as anyone knew, neither Mrs Grosjean's bees nor Miranda Kenyon's chickens had the slightest objection to Stanley sitting there, manoeuvring about him with their habitual chicken or bee noises, and he certainly seemed satisfied to sit and meditate in their presence. If it were rainy, however, he might settle for the more cryptic simulacrum of colony life presented by the washing-machine in Sam and Lord What-a-Waste's kitchen once it arrived at the spin cycle. The only command he ever mastered, because everyone in Hanmouth said it to him, all the time, was 'Go home, Stanley.'

13.

'I wish they'd go home,' Miranda said, peering out of the window, although the rubbernecking crowds had only come this far in dribs and drabs, and there was no one to be seen. 'How's Lord What-a-Waste?'

'Oh, he's fine,' Sam said. He joined Miranda at the window. Once, Miranda had gone into the greengrocer just as Sam was leaving it. The two awful old crones who ran it had been rearranging some rather wrinkly Coxes and discussing Sam. Yes, he was that lord's – the one who worked as a lawyer in town – he was his boyfriend. They lived up behind the Strand in one of those old fishermen's cottages – two, rather, knocked into one. Big house, now, all wood and glass inside. What a waste, one harridan assured the other. It was as if she had believed that a nice rich lord with a solicitor's practice and a big house – two knocked into one – would otherwise have done very well for her, or her ghastly friend, or for one of their slack-jawed daughters. They hadn't said the same about Sam, who only ran a cheese shop, and who, therefore, wasn't so much of a catch. Or perhaps it was that, though Lord What-a-Waste was somewhat inclining to plumpness these days, Sam could only be described as fat. With his shaved head and full jowls, he had a certain charm but, as he said himself, no one would call him love's young dream any more. In the greengrocer's, Miranda had listened to this unbelievable conversation before buying a random bag of woolly Spanish tomatoes and going round to Sam's shop. She had told him the whole story without any delay. It couldn't have been funnier, and since then Harry had been Lord What-a-Waste, though naturally not to his face. 'He couldn't be more cheerful, actually. He's got some lovely new bit of hypochondria on the go. Full of the joys of something that might turn out to be a goitre, he believes.'

'What is a goitre?' Miranda said.

'Heaven alone knows,' Sam said. 'I only said it for the comic potential.'

'Sciatica.'

'Boils. Piles.'

'Giant wen,' Miranda said fondly, as if bringing out a pet name.

'Gout,' Sam said. The nice thing about Miranda was that you never had to explain a joke: she was quicker than any woman

Sam had ever known to catch on to an elaborating absurdity. She could catch a principle. 'And shingles.'

'Shingles really isn't amusing if you have it,' Miranda said. 'An old aunt of mine had it, and it was awful. Most of these things, it's the old names that are so amusing, like the Shaking Palsy, which is Parkinson's, isn't it? I don't know why they don't think up a non-funny, anti-funny name for shingles that would mean you took it more seriously. As if psychiatrists had to say that their patients were loony, bonkers, round the twist and nut-jobs. Shingles sounds about as serious as freckles, and it's no fun at all.'

'Miranda, freckles can be *terrifying*,' Sam said. 'Much worse than Harry's goitre, if it does turn out to be a goitre, which I seriously doubt. I don't suppose any of them are actually enjoyable to get. Some of them sound funny, and some of them don't. Goitre. Funny. Leukaemia. Not funny. Children used to get mumps, didn't they? That's a funny-sounding disease. Did Hettie get mumps ever?'

Miranda busied herself with some flowers on the walnut card table, and Sam saw that he had trodden on one of those occasional and unpredictable patches in Miranda's life where she was not prepared to be clever or amusing. 'I don't know why you should know any better than I do. Is that Stanley out there again?'

'Staring at the chickens,' Miranda said. 'They seem quite inured to him. If I were a chicken and there were an immobile great hound staring at my every doing from a foot away, I'd peck him on the nose. I haven't noticed that he even stops them laying, though they won't do it in front of him, which is what I guess he's waiting to see.'

'Like not being able to go to the loo with someone watching, I expect. I admire your hens' composure immensely.'

'Does Stanley sit and watch you on the lav in the morning, then?' Miranda said. 'Go on, you're blushing, he does. I knew he did. Doesn't it put you off laying?'

'Please.'

Sam leant forward and tapped on the window. He meant to attract the attention of Stanley, in the fenced-off garden on the other side of the road. Stanley inclined to deafness, as basset hounds do. He made no response, his attention fully on the chicken coop. Or perhaps he did hear: the sound of knuckles rapping on windows followed him around, every day of his life. Just then, a woman was passing. 'Woman. Came into the shop this afternoon. I've seen her around and about before,' Sam said. 'Bought half a pound of Wiltshire Gjetost and an olivewood cheeseboard for her new kitchen.'

'Not a ghoulish tripper, then,' Miranda said. Just then Billa and Kitty came to the door with their copies of *The Makioka Sisters*, each recognizable in a string bag, for the evening's discussion. She went into the hallway and opened the door. For an odd moment Sam could hear her welcoming cries in two dimensions, from the outside and from the inside, like a two-woman chorus. Inexplicably, the woman who had waved at Sam came up behind Billa and Kitty. Sam went into the hallway, almost knocking over a Japanese lacquer table in his haste.

'You don't know me,' the woman was saying to Miranda over Billa's imperturbable green-quilted shoulder. 'But I know you're Miranda Kenyon. It's nice to meet you. I live in the flats over there, on the top floor. With my husband. My name's Catherine Butterworth.'

They were awkwardly placed. Sam relished these moments of embarrassing social disposition, and this one was almost unprecedented. Billa and Kitty were at the door, and could not be invited in without actively dismissing the woman. They stood there, half turned between Miranda and Miranda's new friend, their smiles fixed and formal, not quite greeting anyone. Miranda's smile in turn was general and remote. Probably, Sam reflected, never in her life had Billa been greeted with the words 'You don't know me, but . . .'

'Hello there, Sam,' Catherine Butterworth said, giving him a flap of a wave. He'd evidently told her his name, though he couldn't remember doing so.

'Hello, Catherine,' he said. 'Did you enjoy the Gjetost? Unusual cheese, that.'

'Toffeeish,' Catherine said. 'Very unusual. We're saving it for an after-dinner treat. I'll let you get on. We're having a little drink next week – next Saturday at six or so. Our son's coming down to see our new place – he's bringing his new partner, so we thought he'd like to meet some neighbours, too. Any of you. That would be delightful. Over there, in the block of flats – Woodlands. Silly name. On the top floor, number six – it's the only flat on the top floor. Do come.'

'On the top floor of the flats that spoil our view,' Miranda said, once she had waved Catherine on her way and ushered Billa and Kitty towards the drinks table. A schooner of fino for Kitty, like wee in a test tube, and a gut-destroying but no doubt Colonel's Mess-ish Campari and soda for Billa. Sam knew the clearing-out effects Campari had on Billa's insides. He looked forward to the later stages of their *Makioka* discussions being accompanied by Billa's thunderous tummy-rumbles. 'I've never met anyone who lives there before. Couldn't even identify them by sight. I can't imagine what anyone was thinking of, throwing up a monstrosity like that between the Strand and the estuary. I think people must have been quite mad in the 1960s. It's so out of keeping.'

'We've been to the meeting,' Kitty burst out.

'Oh, God, how I envy you,' Sam said. 'What's the latest?'

'Yes, we must get through it before Kenyon gets home,' Miranda said.

'Is he coming home tonight, Miranda?' Billa said. 'I thought—'

'Totally placed a *tabu* on any further mention of it,' Miranda said precisely. 'I don't imagine we talked about anything else for seventy-two hours last weekend – people popping round to chew over it. Then phoning up. Then Hettie' – voice lowered at this point – 'actually coming out of her room and not telling us she hates us for once but wanting to know all the details. So' – back to normal volume – 'after three days of Heidi and Micky and Tragic China and the others –'

'Hannah and Archie and, and, and,' Sam said, counting them out on his fingers.

' – Kenyon couldn't stand it any longer and said he didn't want to hear another word, not even if Tragic China were found camping underneath the blackcurrant bush in the back garden.'

'Harvey,' Sam said with satisfaction. 'That's the fourth one. Very ugly child. Unbelievable, really. You can understand why they didn't have him abducted. Never knew a child could be both porcine and bovine at the same time. Wouldn't have thought its face would tug at the heartstrings of readers of the *Sun* when they saw it. I thought the little girl was plain but, really, when you see the others, they were making the best of rather a bad job. It is fascinating, though, do admit.'

'Simply gripping,' Billa said. 'I can't imagine why Kenyon doesn't want to talk about it all the time from the moment he wakes up. It's quite put a pep in Tom's stride in the morning, knowing that he's going to bump into someone on the Fore street with some delicious new titbit or ingenious theory. Yesterday it was that the children were in charge of concealing China. No one would suspect them of conspiracy.'

'And they were the last to see her,' Kitty said. 'Very good. She's probably in the old Anderson shelter in the back garden, or something, getting smuggled chips through the garden fence. What I don't understand is why the husband, or the lover, or the live-in, or whatever he's supposed to be, chose the library of all places for his alibi. I mean, anywhere would have done. It simply looks so very peculiar for someone like that suddenly to develop an interest in books.'

'Kitty, libraries aren't for reading *books* any more,' Sam said. 'They've given all that away. It's nothing but DVDs and computer terminals nowadays.'

'And of course it's the one place where, if he took something out, the computer records would show that it was him and that he'd been there at a specific time.'

'Oh, Billa,' Miranda said. 'If he'd walked down Barnstaple high street the CCTV would show where he'd been. I wonder what he took out. Not *The Makioka Sisters*, I suppose.'

They speculated luridly about his reading or viewing material for a while.

'I would have thought the unemployment office would have been a better bet,' Sam said.

'In what way?' Kitty said. She was not always the quickest to catch on.

'If I were someone like that,' Sam said. 'I would do roughly what he's done. I would go somewhere recognizably official to prove my alibi. Not the library, that's absurd. I would get it somewhere I could be expected to go to. The unemployment office, enquiring about my benefits, or something.'

'And the mother, how's she?' Miranda said.

'Simply terrifying,' Billa said. 'Chills the heart simply to look at her. Sits there playing with her hair, staring into space, unutterably blank. Like looking at a cloud drift across the sky. She has lovely hair, doesn't she? Bored and boring, I should say.'

'And new clothes from top to toe,' Kitty said. 'Out of the Save China fund, I should guess.'

'Do you want another drink, Kitty?' Miranda said.

'Well, I don't mind if I do,' Kitty said. 'It was awfully crowded – the world and his wife were there and then some extra, just for fun. Billa and I had to stand at the back and we counted ourselves lucky. People getting so overheated, too, calling for everyone's heads to roll. Terribly silly and embarrassing, and John Calvin running everything so.'

'There was a fight in the Case Is Altered last night, I heard,' Billa said. 'Tom bumped into the landlord on his morning constitutional *this* morning. He said they'd never seen or heard of such a thing in twenty-five years' running the pub. Townees, he said.'

65

'Grockles, they were calling them in the queue at the post office this afternoon.'

'Sam,' Miranda said. 'What an awful, frightful, yokel-like word. Never let me hear you say anything so prejudiced again.'

Sam understood that by 'prejudiced' Miranda meant, as she usually did, 'common', and carried on. 'A nice policeman came into the shop,' he said, undeterred, 'and he was saying that they were hoping, very much hoping, to make an arrest before much longer. He was pretending to question me about my whereabouts and had I recalled anything I might have forgotten earlier, but I know he just wanted a good old gossip really. And I said, "Have you got a suspect then?" and he said, "Even two," and he didn't wink exactly, but he made a sort of very winking kind of face without actually winking, if you know what I mean.'

'I'm sure the little girl's off safely in Butlin's or somewhere,' Billa said. 'Dyed her hair and sent her off for a couple of weeks to enjoy herself.'

'The thing I truly object to,' Kitty said, 'and I know this sounds trivial and I don't care if it sounds a bit snobbish, but I don't care about these awful people and I do care about this. It's that the whole world now thinks of Hanmouth as being this sort of awful council estate and nothing else, and Hanmouth people like this awful Heidi and Micky people. Absolutely everything you read in the papers is about how they live in Hanmouth and, frankly, they don't. They live on the Ruskin estate where I've never been and I hope never to go anywhere near.'

'I saw a newspaper photographer in a boat in the middle of the estuary, taking photographs,' Sam said eagerly. 'Out there in Brian Miller's ferryboat. Taking a photograph of the church and the Strand and the quay. That'll turn up in the *Sun* as a photograph of Heidi's home town, I promise you.'

'As if that family could live somewhere like this.'

'Or, really, more to the point, as if they would ever contrive a story like this if they did live on the Strand,' Miranda said. 'One

66

may be cynical, but one does think that moral attitudes and truthfulness and not having your children kidnapped for the sake of the exposure don't go with deprivation. It's material deprivation that starts all this off.'

'They've got dishwashers, Miranda,' Billa said. 'They're not examples of material deprivation. But you're right. You don't hear about children disappearing from Hanmouth proper, do you? It's just bad education, ignorance, idleness and avarice.'

'And drugs,' Sam put in. 'Don't forget the drugs. The policeman shouldn't have been saying this, but he hinted very heavily that not only had the women been smoking drugs when they were supposed to be looking after the children, but the woman's partner's got some kind of criminal record for selling the stuff.'

'What an awful story,' Miranda said. 'I can't wait for all those drunks and mischief-makers and rubberneckers and fisticuff-merchants and journalists to call it a day and go somewhere else.'

'I could wring that bally woman's neck,' Billa said.

Because belief in and sympathy for Heidi, Micky and their four children, one missing, believed abducted, ran very low among the membership of the reading groups of Hanmouth.

14.

Catherine had had such a nice half-hour in the shops of Hanmouth that afternoon. She had started with the Oriental emporium. There was hardly anything that could be described as a window display. It looked more like the random circulation of stock in the half-lit front. The door was hung with a bright purple and red throw, tied back. Out of the dark interior a jangle of temple bells and a whiff of what Catherine thought of as joss-sticks came – David had had quite a craze for the things at one stage, had been unable to embark upon his physics homework in the back bedroom in St Albans without them.

And then, saving it up rather, she'd gone into Sam's cheese shop. She'd seen Sam around, walking his dog down the Wolf Walk, reading the papers on a Sunday lunchtime outside the pub on the quay with what must be his partner. She had identified him after a month or two as the owner of the attractive little shop, white-tiled inside with built-in display cabinets. He was often to be seen swapping lengthy stories with other Hanmouthites in the street, the newsagent and the butcher. He seemed to know everyone, and Catherine didn't consider she would be a proper Hanmouthite until she'd made his acquaintance. He'd been delightful this afternoon: he had foisted the Wiltshire Gjetost on her and a Gorgonzola from a farm just up the road outside Iddesleigh, and something very unusual, a chocolate-flavoured log of goats' cheese. 'Made by lesbians in Wales,' Sam had explained superfluously. And then, not being very busy, he'd asked about the bag she was holding, from the Oriental emporium, and then, very cosily, what she was doing in Hanmouth, did she live here? He'd even clapped his hands when she said she was refurbishing the spare bedroom. It was really quite without any character at the moment, just the previous-owner-who-had-died's magnolia on the walls. It might even have been the builder's magnolia, Catherine speculated; there would be no reason to alter that in the first owner's mind. 'Well,' Sam had said reasonably enough, 'I don't want to pour cold water, but paint does yellow. It might even have been the builder's white, forty years ago.'

'I suppose it might have been,' Catherine said, enjoying this banter. She wanted to liven it up, furnish the room, give it something resembling character before her son came to visit for the first time. He was bringing his new partner, too, about whom Catherine knew nothing.

'And did they persuade you into buying their Buddha?' Sam asked, referring to the sisters with the Oriental antiques. 'A four-foot gold Buddha. Did you see it? They've had it for ten years. I don't suppose anyone will ever buy it now – it's almost a joke. Promise me you *didn't* buy it.' Catherine reassured him. 'We shopkeepers, we do have these disasters, and then we're stuck with them. So easy to get carried away, and now, I dare say, it's quite an old friend. I don't know what Lesley and Julia would do without their Buddha.'

Of course they had laughed together. She had been tempted to bring up David's new boyfriend, but she thought that might be presumptuously making connections between them. She didn't know the name of David's boyfriend, and there was no reason to suppose Sam knew that she knew *he* had a boyfriend, so the conversation would run quickly into embarrassment. (Catherine was good, she considered, at anticipating conversational awkwardnesses like that one.) After an hour, she came home with some experimental cheese, an olivewood board, a ceramic butter dish ornamented with octopuses, squid, fish and smiling underwater anemones, as well as a charming glass from next door in a padded red cloth frame, decorated with gold embroidery and pieces of mirror. 'Filling up the house with tat,' Alec said, looking round from beyond the blinkers of his green leather wing-chair as she came in, but not unkindly. That was his customary response whenever she brought anything home.

So when she heard a rapping at a window and turned to see Sam, gesturing in her direction, she naturally waved back. It was only when he rapped again, and a dog – Sam's dog – bounded past her that Catherine realized he hadn't been trying to attract her attention at all. Of course Catherine knew Sam's dog. She'd known Stanley's name since before she'd known Sam's. She had heard him calling impatiently after Stanley almost every morning as the basset hound lumbered off down the Strand. Finding out Sam's name had been more of a challenge. She still hadn't discovered his fairly handsome partner's name. Eavesdropping on a Sunday lunchtime had produced nothing but an exchange of 'darling', rather edgy in tone.

She knew Miranda Kenyon's name, however. When Miranda opened her door to the two ladies, Catherine found herself propelled into the doorway of the house. She could explain her mistake, be friendly, and at the same time offer an invitation to the little drinks she and Alec were having when David and his partner were there next weekend. They were planning to invite all the people they had made friends with since they arrived in Hanmouth. It didn't seem to go quite as well as she had hoped. It was extraordinary that four sentences could congeal in the air and fall to the floor between strangers. But the gesture had been made. The awkwardness, in the future, might lessen. Catherine stumped up the little rise at the quay end of the Fore street, past estate agent, white-tablecloth French bistro and charity shop. She forced herself to think that Sam had been very kind to her, and friendly, too, that afternoon. They were not at all the same thing, kindness and friendliness, but he had shown both. There was no reason to suppose that she and Alec wouldn't make good friends in this place.

Still, there had been rebuffs, which couldn't be shared with Alec, him being a man and not very interested in the smaller details of social life. After a month or six weeks, she'd grown confident when faces presented themselves as familiar. She had started to say hello to them, and been greeted back. She'd even got to know a few names. Every face met before nine and perhaps ten must be a resident, she believed, rather than a tripper, and worth a greeting. The return of greeting had sometimes been enthusiastic, as with a lady with a small West Highland White Terrier on her morning rounds, out and about rather earlier than anyone else. Sometimes the return was more doubtful, provisional, and sometimes rudely withheld. There was an elderly man she saw almost every morning, tall and long-faced and sinewy, with a knowing, watery, foolish expression. He had a regular route: he picked up the paper and got some fresh air, as she did. Their rounds crossed at some point almost every morning. After a month or so of meeting practically every day, she ventured a greeting, a neutral sort of comment about the weather. It was her favourite sort of day. Blue-skied and blustery, the clouds galloping at a racehorse's pace inland, the spring whiff of salt carried in the buoyant breeze from the ten-miles-remote Bristol Channel. The seagulls widely embraced the wind, wedged diagonally on the air, falling backwards and inland on the salt-swept air, and, walking over the salt-encrusted lawn of the little churchyard that was her shortcut, Catherine smiled and said, 'Lovely day,' to a familiar long-faced man. He looked at her directly, as if she were a tree or an animal of some sort, and said nothing. She had read in nineteenth-century novels about people being cut directly. Before she and Alec had moved to Hanmouth, she had been ignored or overlooked, but never cut in so blunt a way.

He was a horrible old man, as it turned out. Afterwards, she heard him laying down the law in the street, his false teeth loose, his loud, humourless Devon accent spitting over whoever he thought worth talking to. She knew people like that were proved unpleasant and not worth knowing by their parade of superiority and withholding of so simple a thing as friendliness. All the same, it hurt. You couldn't explain any of that to Alec. He would always ask why on earth you cared. He had a point.

15.

'That was a lovely town,' Catherine had said, as they drove away from Hanmouth five years before. They had come from St Albans to visit Alec's old secretary from the paper suppliers. She had retired down here with her husband. Alec and Barbara had always got on well in the office, but he and Catherine had been surprised by the invitation to come and spend a long weekend down in Devon with them. They'd had a lovely time. Barbara and Ted, her husband, lived in a whitewashed settlement around a harbour. You couldn't call it a village. The harbour was a picturesque muddy lagoon, filled with leaning skiffs and old fishing boats. In their front garden, a rowing boat was planted with lobelias and geraniums. When they returned to St Albans, agreeing that they had had a lovely time, it did occur to Catherine that Barbara and Ted might be somewhat lonely in their prettily brackish nook. They hadn't been greeted in anything but a professionally cheerful way when they went into the pub in the harbour. You might have expected more. It was the only pub in the village, and the village only had twenty or so houses in it.

Still, they had had a lovely time. Barbara had suggested they might like to drive over to the other side of the estuary to a small town called Hanmouth, directly opposite Cockering. 'Very historical,' Barbara said remotely. It gave off an air, even at a water-divided distance, of picturesque activity. It had a front of white-painted houses, a square-towered mock-Norman church flying a flag on a promontory facing Cockering over some steak-red cliffs, thirty feet high. It appeared martial and festive. On Thursday nights, if the conditions were clear, the clamour of bellringers going through their changes drifted over the estuary. They had arrived on a Thursday afternoon; at seven, Barbara had hushed them over a pre-dinner drink, and they had heard the distant hum and clanging, the mathematical variations blurring into a halo of sky and sea and seabirds. At night from Cockering, the town looked like Monte Carlo, its lights clustering like bright grapes, reflecting in the high water.

They went, and were surprised how quickly a Saturday morning passed. They had dawdled from coffee to market to bookshop. In the village hall, or community centre, there was a Saturday-morning market. The Women's Institute sold cakes and pickles on one stall, the biggest and most prominent. Other stalls sold hopeful bric-à-brac, forced pot plants, low-skill craft product such as home-made psychedelic candles, macramé hanging holders or batik throws. When you got down to the jetty and the mooring places, there were boats both large and small, neat, shiny as refrigerators, elegant Edwardian craft with shining brass fittings holding them together like corsets, and squat, businesslike, bumptious tugs. Between them swans, geese, ducks, spoon-billed wading birds and alert-headed coots swam and dived, swimming

72

out to possess the middle stream of the estuary. The boats tranquilly waited for their owners to return. From here, Cockering was impossible to identify or pick out.

There was a square brick warehouse from the turn of the century on the quayside where a bus into Barnstaple waited, the driver sitting on the step with the door open, reading a thriller with some absorption. Three geese, like old womanly friends with no urgent occupation, stood in the middle of the concrete apron, sizing him up as a likely source of bread. The building must once have been a storehouse for the fish industry but now it turned out to be filled with antiques of every description. There were pretty old pubs whose names had to have some story behind them – the Case Is Altered! On the high street, blue, white and red bunting hung from side to side in high airy zigzags. It must have been for the Hanmouth Festival with a procession led by the Hanmouth Festival Queen 2008. Catherine and Alec read about it in a series of shop windows. Alec remarked that the procession would be a short one. The high street – the Fore street, as many Devon main streets were called – was a bare five hundred yards long.

There were two Italian restaurants. One had pretensions, the other gingham tablecloths and a pizza menu. There was a French bistro where everything, white tablecloths, white walls, glassware, cutlery, seemed to polish and reflect Catherine's smile back at her through the windows. There was no Chinese takeaway or kebab shop, as far as she could see. There was a cheese shop, with a plump man in a blue and white striped apron, proffering wafery samples with good cheer to his customers. Best of all, there was a butcher. It was unexpected how butchers had become a means to register the life and independence of any English town. Until recently they had been an ordinary and unnoticed presence in a community of any size. Now they had become a thermometer measuring a body's health, and the last butcher in St Albans had given up the unequal struggle with Tesco's meat counter three years before. For no very good reason, they joined the queue in the Hanmouth butcher's and bought two pounds of their home-made sausages. 'We're almost down to the last of the free-rangers till Tuesday,' the butcher told the shopper before her. Catherine inwardly shivered for shame that the town in which she had made her home had not, it seemed, needed a butcher. The town was busy and jolly. On their way back to Barbara's for a lunch of soup, bread-and-Wensleydale and a salad, Catherine and Alec agreed that if they ever moved from St Albans, this was the sort of place that they would like to live in.

Neither of them could pin down exactly when it was that they had firmly decided to move. Their growing seriousness about the idea had been marked by their growing engagement with the Hanmouth estate agents. At first they only looked in the windows of estate agents. Frustratingly, they did not display the prices of the houses at the upper and most intriguing end. Often, the grandest houses had their own glossy brochures. They soon graduated, in a series of interviews, to pretending to be interested in buying a house. Nosily, they went round half a dozen they could never have afforded, tutting and shaking their heads sorrowfully over the lack of a utility room, a library, a music room.

It was embarrassing to have to go back to the same estate agents, a month later, after a serious conversation or two, with different aims. They had to concoct a story that they had decided, after consideration, not to move down there permanently. ('A permanent residence,' Alec had said, overdoing it.) They now wanted a holiday home. Their invented objections gave way to real ones: plausible fishermen's cottages, almshouses, inter-war semis dropped away. Too small, too expensive, facing east, facing west, too large, the worst house in a good area (embarrassment), the best house in a bad area (ostentation). A garden to keep up; a garage, which would only fill with junk. There seemed no objection that a property in Hanmouth would not meet in the most specific terms.

16.

Added to these objections were the comments of David, their son. They had told him about their intentions only at that point. He had been dubious. He had gone on living in St Albans, though he worked in London and commuted every day. Perhaps he was not the right person to consult about any adventurous enterprise. They knew people in St Albans, apart from him. They were familiar with things and services thereabouts. What if something went wrong, what if someone fell ill? At home in St Albans, they would be surrounded by willing volunteers from their circle. In this town in Devon they'd taken a liking to, no one would even know either of them was ill. No one would think of helping out. They were getting on. These things had to be thought about.

These gloomy objections were evidently weighing in Alec's mind when, for the seventh time that year, they found themselves in a Hanmouth estate agent's. One of three. It was an unpromising day for viewing anything: rain at St Albans had turned steadily colder as they headed westwards, and by now the sleet was so thick outside that you could barely see the other side of the Fore street. Maria, the untidy woman in charge, hair flying and papers everywhere on the desk, like the White Queen in steady employment, had said over the telephone that there was a nice house which had just come on the market. Should she send them the particulars? Maria had giggled as she said this, and as she said most things, though none of them were at all amusing. They had driven down the same morning. Maria had been taken aback to see them, though Alec had definitely said, 'We'll pop over this afternoon,' on the telephone. She hadn't been able to find the keys at first: she knew she hadn't popped them on the key rack, she'd just dropped them for a moment – scream of laughter – as she'd come in to take her coat off and run herself up a little cup of coffee, because she'd picked them up on her way in; Apthorpe Avenue was really the way she took from home into work – a small giggle. A Mozart piano concerto on Classic FM formed a backdrop to Maria's comments; as she turned half her desk upside down searching for the keys, she was starting in on a description of the house, very nice, pre-war, a striking sculpture in the front garden, had been lived in by the same owner for nearly forty years, but he'd taken good care of it.

Catherine started to suspect and, as Maria continued, grew sure of it, that the house she was talking about was, in fact, a house she had shown them eight months earlier; it had come off the market without finding a buyer (faced west, seller immovable on price). It had, evidently, now come back on. Maria had forgotten or never knew that she had shown Catherine and Alec the house. As inspiration started to fail her, Alec began to interject with unhelpfully general observations: perhaps David had a point. Did they want to be moving to a town where they'd be making new friends from scratch? What if one of them had a turn of some sort? And then there was the question of security, wasn't there? They'd hardly considered that. This was a rich town, but not everywhere near here was rich. What did they know about the burglary situation? Was it even safe to walk the streets at night? There were a lot of pubs, weren't there? You heard about such things in country towns – it was as bad on a Saturday night as in St Albans, or so Alec had heard.

Maria seemed to be paying little attention to Alec, dourly backsliding from his househunting obligations. She was only putting in encouraging titters, an occasional 'Oh, surely . . .' and an 'I think you'll find . . .' and an 'It's really ever such a, er, er, supportive little community we've got here,' this last bringing out a gale of laughter. Her attention moved from the attempt to find the keys to Apthorpe Avenue, which, she had started to confide, might very well be in her house, she having picked them up not on her way in but on her way home last night. She looked at the window where, between the tessellated placards of the houses for sale, a dark figure had coagulated out of the dark afternoon sleet.

'There,' she said, with finality. 'That's convenient. Here's our Mr Calvin – I wonder if he's in a great hurry to get anywhere. He can tell you so much more about that side of things in Hanmouth than I can.'

She jumped up. A desk-tidy with three pencils in it was sent flying. She poked her head outside the door, letting in a fierce blast of ozone-frozen air. After a brief exchange, she ushered the man in. His black coat and black astrakhan hat were mantled with sleet and snow. Like a magician performing a trick, he removed them in a single upwards gesture, placing them on the coat-rack, unpeeled his brown ostrich-skin gloves and placed them neatly aligned on Maria's catastrophic desk. With a quick rub of his heavily polished shoes up the back of his pinstriped trousers, right and then left, he seemed never to have been outside at all. He was thin and upright, had clean mouse-like, beady-eyed, polished features, and a smoothed-down cap of white hair. His hands went up, unnecessarily, to smooth his hair down to right and left; they were strikingly large and flat hands, like flippers.

'This is our Mr Calvin,' Maria said. The man's sleek smile went from Alec to Catherine, from Catherine to Alec, without registering any change at all. The sort of smile that dolphins have, built into their bones and into their faces, meaning nothing much, Catherine believed. She wondered what he was seeing: a woman with the anxious, motherly expression she had so often caught unawares in shop windows, and her bald, pugnacious husband, in the dim sort of beige anorak, padded, toggled and with multiple purposeful pockets that you could not believe you had ever bought with any intent to charm, beguile or seduce. If that was what you wanted an anorak to do for you.

'Mr and Mrs Butterworth,' Maria said. 'They're looking for a house to buy in Hanmouth. We've been at it quite some little time. The first houses we looked at' – gesturing at the bleak midwinter outside – 'we had to stop halfway and have a sit-down and an ice-cream, it was so hot. Can you—' her shrill, sentence-punctuating laugh went up the scale, and cut abruptly off.

'Top of the morning to you,' Calvin said. 'And a beautiful morning it be.' Then he switched disconcertingly out of his stage comic Irishness into ordinary English. 'You'll love it here. I moved down from Liverpool ten years ago, never regretted it. The weather could be better for you today, I admit.'

Alec was perking up: it was the attention of an extrovert person with a ready smile. 'We do like it,' he said.

Maria dived in. 'Mr Butterworth was wondering about how safe it was in Hanmouth,' she said. 'And then – there you were. As if sent along to answer all those questions. You couldn't possibly spare us two minutes? Mr Calvin, he's the person you really want to get on your side in Hanmouth. Came along, shook everybody up, took charge of Neighbourhood Watch, which was really a very sleepy sort of body before—' Hee, hee, hee, she went; no wonder she had no, and seemed never to have had any, colleagues.

'I don't think they did anything but stick orange stickers on lamp-posts,' Calvin said. 'Which was about as much use as a chocolate teapot, as we say in Liverpool.'

'We have Neighbourhood Watch round us,' Catherine said. 'But you would only know about it from those stickers. I don't know who runs it, or where they meet, or when.'

'Well, you'd know about it in Hanmouth,' Calvin said. 'To be sure, to be sure, to be sure. We identified some active members of the community to form a new committee. We carried out a survey on day one of the new committee, asking everyone in the town what they were most concerned about. One of the pubs that caused most trouble, the one at the near end of the Strand, we objected to the renewal of their licence – "Gaarn! Leave it ahht! You lookin' at my bird! 'E ain't wurf it, Keif!" – and had it closed down. Turned into a tea-room. Great success. The pub crawl the students go on, it's really the Hanmouth Eleven now, though the students still talk about Doing the Twelve. Can't count after eight pubs, 'tis said, so it is. All that was just in our first year, year one. Then we lobbied the police and demanded security cameras. CCTV. There's not much of the centre of Hanmouth not covered by CCTV nowadays. And that has to be a good thing. The crime rate in Hanmouth is as low as it could be. So,' Calvin slipping into mid-Atlantic telly interviewers' fake-serious accent, 'how can we justify the expense of these surveillance cameras, if there is no crime? The answer, my friend, is this. There is no crime because a criminal knows he cannot commit one. The crime is headed off at the pass, long before it is committed. *Voilà.*' Calvin considered for a moment, then added, '*Monsieur.* We aren't happy that there are still parts of Hanmouth which aren't covered by CCTV. The Fore street cameras have been there five years, and the technology has moved on. We're working on implementing some new cameras that are being trialled in Middlesbrough, with a loudspeaker and sound system attached. A police officer sees a youth up to no good in the street. Can flick a switch, say, "'Ello, 'ello, 'ello, what's all this then? Move along, move along, commit not that there nuisance in this 'ere street." And Johnny Mugger or Leeeee-roy the Burglar and his dusky friends with a jemmy and an ice-pick, they lift up their knees very sharply indeed, say, "Vat is well rank, man," and off they head to burgle somewhere a little bit less well guarded and watched, a nice safe distance away, a place which you and I do not care a great deal about. That's the general idea. We don't see why we shouldn't get the model with loudspeaker by this time next year. This –' deep breath, sincere gaze '— is one of the very safest places in this country. Ask anyone.'

Maria the estate agent had been smiling from the beginning, and as Calvin went through one accent after another, she started to titter, then giggle, then chortle, then chuckle, then snigger, then hoot, then roar, then guffaw. By the end, and Calvin imitating a black youth cowering under a loudspeaker ordering him to go away and burgle some less forward-looking community, she gave every impression of coming out into the open about her desire to howl till she pissed herself.

But by the end of the afternoon, they had viewed and made an offer on a big modern flat, occupying the whole top floor of a small, neat, well-made block right on the estuary, with walnut panelling in the lobby, rosewood fittings and banisters, black marble flooring from top to bottom. It was really very stylish. The previous owner had lived and died there, and his or her belongings had been carried away long ago. The empty rooms were clean, well-sized and open. They hadn't thought of a flat at all. The attractions of those fishermen's cottages or almshouses were fading. In practice, they always came with so individual and overwhelming a set of objections. The weather had brightened up, and the view was of silver-shining mud and a slash of light-embodying water, a thunderous zinc-black sky livid with flashes of brightness. Opposite, at the peak of the hills beyond the estuary, the castle's folly was washed in a well of sunlight as the clouds above passed on and separated. The flat's empty spaces were filled with watery light. Above in the sky, just as they were standing there, four swans flew overhead. Their wings made the regular beat of a solemn and remote drum. It was a noise that might mark the progress of an exotic and half-understood ceremony. For the first time in several months, Catherine remembered and thought freshly that she wanted to live in this place, and not in a road in St Albans where the view from the window was of a house with the precise dimensions of the one you yourself were in. She didn't really care what the people were like.

'Amusing man, that Mr Colvin,' Alec said, on the drive home.

'Calvin, I think it was,' Catherine said, surprised but not wanting to dissent.

'I think he would be a bit of a life-and-soul type,' Alec said. 'Probably worth getting to know once we're down there. Centre of the social life of the place, I shouldn't wonder.'

'I shouldn't be at all surprised.'

'I hope we're not going to hit the worst of the traffic on the M25,' Alec said.

'Just our luck if we did,' Catherine said.

17.

'Come on,' Catherine said over the telephone to David, that same evening. 'It's not as if we have one foot in the grave, exactly. It'll be perfectly all right. You'll see.'

18.

'I wasn't doing anything wrong,' the man said. On the table, a range of photographic equipment, a case lying open. A policeman was poking at the back of the camera, trying to get the digital screen to switch on. 'It's my job.'

'That's right,' the boyish-looking girl said – she was his assistant, she'd stated. 'We were just trying to get some good photographs. There was nothing harmful in it.'

'We've got to take every precaution,' the policeman said. 'It's not normal behaviour, now, is it?'

The recreation ground divided into two: the wide open grassy space, where the older kids ran and chased and played adult games, like softball and football, and the playground for the younger ones. With bright-coloured climbing apparatus and ingeniously varied swings and roundabouts, this was a popular place among the under-nines. Barnstaple Council had recently renovated the old playground, replacing the knee-crunching asphalt with some soft substance, putting in new and exotic attractions, and fencing it round. At the moment, there were few places where the young of Hanmouth could enjoy themselves. This was one of them.

That afternoon, a mother deposited her seven-year-old there after school while she went to buy a chicken from the butcher's for dinner. She had done it before, and thought nothing of it; there were plenty of other children there. She didn't believe in the existence of the child-snatcher in any case. When she came back, she was surprised to see two adults she'd never seen before: one, a fat bald man, was actually kneeling inside the playground, a large professional camera at his face. He was taking photographs of the children.

'What the hell are you doing?' she said.

The other adult, an androgynous figure, made a throat-cutting gesture. The photographer got up briskly and started walking out of the playground, straight past the mother.

'No, no, no,' the mother said. 'You don't just walk away like that.'

The pair kept on walking. The mother called to her son to stay where he was, and followed them, getting her mobile out and dialling a three-figure number as she walked.

'You see,' the policeman said, in the police station, 'that doesn't seem a very sensible thing to do in the present circumstances. Does it?'

'It's my job,' the photographer said.

'You don't have to photograph strange children playing, do you?' the policeman said. 'That's asking for trouble, I would have thought. In the present circumstances.'

'I get told what they want photographed, and I do it,' the photographer said.

'I'm not charging you with anything,' the policeman said.

'That's good, because he's done nothing wrong,' the girl said.

'Jess,' the photographer said.

'But I'm not going to let you walk out of here, for your own safety,' the policeman said. 'Feeling's running very high round here. The lady who made the complaint, who saw you photographing her little boy without permission from her or from Mr Calvin or from anyone else, sees you, a complete stranger, could be anyone, with this case going on, unsolved, the kidnapper at large – do you see what I'm saying? She feels very strongly about it.'

'Well, I'm very sorry,' the photographer said.

'That's the ticket,' the policeman said, referring not to the apology but to the camera, which, with a four-note tune, had switched on, showing the last of the photographs. 'Now. I'm not going to confiscate your camera. I can see it's the tool of your trade and I think you've learnt a valuable lesson here. But I am going to take the memory card out of the camera and keep that while we look at it and what's on it.'

'Can't you look at it now and give it back to me?'

'I can't do that,' the policeman said. 'We need to look at it very carefully.'

19.

The police car pulled away from the Hanmouth community centre. The photographers in the street pressed their lenses up against the window. Some were professional, working for the press. Others were using their little pocket digital cameras or even the cameras built into their mobile phones. Heidi and Micky sat as still as they could. In the front, Mr Calvin sat next to the driver, his brown pimpled attaché case on his lap. The police liaison officer was in the back with Heidi and Micky. She was supposed to be helping and comforting them. The police driver drove. He listened.

'Thank God that's over and done with,' Heidi said. Her little voice was accented half by London, half by America, and by Devon not at all. It could hardly sound anything but bored. 'I hate it when they stare at us. They've made their minds up and they won't help us at all.'

'Who's they, Heidi?' Mr Calvin said.

'Those snobs,' Heidi said. 'Those snobs who live in Old Hanmouth. I cut their hair, half of them, and the other half I reckon they're too much snobs to get their hair cut in Hanmouth or even in Barnstaple. I reckon they go to Bristol or to London. They know me but they don't say hello. They stare like I'm in a zoo and they've paid their entrance ticket.'

'Everyone's very concerned and worried for China, Heidi,' the police liaison officer said. 'I'm sure they wouldn't have come to find out what's being done if they didn't care very deeply about China's disappearance.'

''Ass right,' Micky said. 'You want to think of that, girl.'

'Don't you believe it,' Heidi said, as the police car slowed for the level crossing. An upright woman in a headscarf with a bounding Jack Russell on a lead peered into the back of the car and quickly looked away. Someone had breached good taste here. 'They don't care. They just want their face on the TV.'

'Oi! Oi! Oi! Look at me, Mum! I'm on the TV! I'm famous! The more people,' Mr Calvin said, 'that get involved, the quicker we find China. I know some of them aren't very nice, and they don't really take the right attitude, but they are involved. The ones who don't want to know – I expect the police will be asking themselves why these people are keeping themselves to themselves so much.'

Unnoticed, the driver felt his face harden into an expression of unbelief.

'It would never have happened,' Mr Calvin said, 'if there'd been CCTV on Heidi's street. But, of course, you put that to the police before something like this happens, and they give you a brush-off. "Not necessary, we do not consider that the above application if granted would represent a good use of current resources." And then a little girl gets kidnapped and they've no idea at all.'

The train crossed; the barriers lifted and the car drove on. Silence fell.

'You know the BBC are coming to interview you at home,' Mr Calvin said. 'They'll be round about seven, they said.'

'I know,' Heidi said.

'Am I all right like this?' Micky said. 'Should I put on my new shirt?'

'You're all right,' Heidi said. 'It doesn't look good if you're changing your clothes every five minutes. They'll be showing this in conjunction with the footage from the press conference, I reckon.'

'I don't honestly think it matters all that much,' the police-woman said.

'Mr Calvin,' Heidi said.

'Yes, Heidi?'

'I like your bag.'

'Thank you.'

'It's unusual, what it's made of, isn't it?'

'It's ostrich skin, I think.'

'I've never seen one like that before. I thought it was a design at first.'

'No, that's how ostrich skin looks. You mean the sort of puckers, the marks. That's where the feathers were.'

'Yeah. Where did you get it?'

'Milan, I think. I got some gloves from the same place in ostrich skin. They're to die for, fabulous, honey.'

'Heidi,' the policewoman said – she was not quite used to Mr Calvin's outbreaks into voices just yet.

'There on holiday,' Micky asked.

'No, on business,' Mr Calvin said. 'I shouldn't have got it – it was far too expensive. I do love it, though.'

'I didn't know you were in business,' Micky said. 'I thought you did—'

'What did you think he did, Micky?' Heidi said grumpily.

'I thought he did' – Micky gestured around him at the inside of the car, its cramped quarters of need and disaster – 'I thought he did *this*.'

'Heidi,' the policewoman started again. 'I just want to explain to you and Micky what we've been doing today to find China. And what we're going to do tomorrow.'

Heidi slumped against Micky resentfully. 'I heard you've been asking after Hannah's dad.'

'Marcus,' the policewoman said. 'Yes, that's right. We had to make an enquiry there.'

85

'And Micky's brothers, too, they said you'd been asking them where they'd been.'

'Dominic and –' she consulted her notes '– Vlad, is that right?'

'Vlad's not his brother,' Heidi said.

'That's right,' Micky said.

'Vlad's his sister's boyfriend. Avril. He's from Poland.'

'Ukraine, he told us,' the policewoman said. 'You understand we have to ask everyone with some connection to China where they were, even if it's just to eliminate them. I'm sure you can explain that to people if they feel we shouldn't investigate them. I understand that if people are concerned and working hard on behalf of China, they may feel upset if we seem to be regarding them as suspects.'

'I don't give a shit about them,' Heidi said. 'But I don't want you going near Marcus. He's scum. I don't want him turning up and saying he's worried about China. He's not been in touch for years. Ruth hasn't heard from him for years, either. I don't know what happened to him. I don't want him any part of this.'

'Heidi, you understand we have to pursue every possibility?' the policewoman said. Heidi looked for a moment as if she were about to challenge this, but then just turned her sulky face to the window and watched the fields go by. 'And then,' the police-woman continued, 'we've been making good progress on the door-to-door.'

'Does that mean you've found some indication of who might be involved?' Mr Calvin said.

'No,' the policewoman said. 'It means that we've managed to cover a large part of the community and speak to a large propor-tion of those in the immediate—'

'Well, that's frankly not very—'

'We've been concentrating,' the policewoman went on in her stolid, uninterruptable way, 'on known sex offenders in the county.'

'Sex offenders,' Calvin said.

'People on the sex-offenders register, yes,' the policewoman said.

'In our area, these are,' Heidi said. 'Who are they, then?'

'You know we can't share that information,' the policewoman said. 'Not even with you. I don't know that we've got any very strong leads through that inquiry, but we are still investigating three or four people of that cohort who couldn't give a good account of themselves for that afternoon. They might have perfectly good reasons, or just have been on their own in peace. We're still conducting door-to-door inquiries, as I said. That will go on for the next two or three days. There's a search of land in the immediate area which we're going to expand as the search goes on and' – hurrying on rather – 'we will be wanting to interview both of you and Ruth and the children again in the next few days. Nothing at all sinister, just that often when you talk over events for a second or third time, little details pop up that can be quite helpful to an investigation.'

'I've told you everything I can think of,' Heidi muttered, her hands clutching her arms. 'More than once.'

'Wasting time interviewing her and me,' Micky said. 'Should be out there locking up the sex offenders. I want to know who they are. I'll go round there and beat it out of them. No one's told us there were sex offenders on the estate. One of them's taken China.'

'Yes, well, Micky—' the driver began, without turning round.

'Don't think about it too much,' Calvin said. 'The police know everything about everyone these days. They ought to be able to find China, with all the information they've got. Everything's on computer files nowadays – who's got a conviction for looking at dirty pictures of children, who's changed their name, who's not paid for their television licence, who buys what from the supermarket. What do you think loyalty cards are for? To keep an eye on you, and the police can use that information. If they've committed a crime, the police have got their DNA. If they've been taken in on suspicion, the police will have their DNA. If I had my way, everyone in the country would have their DNA on file. Then we'd know straight away who had committed a crime if they'd left just one hair at the scene. You can really leave the police in charge these days, Heidi.'

'Police,' Heidi said. 'What have they done for us?'

'I'm as impatient as you are,' Calvin said. 'But sometimes you've got to leave it to the professionals. And here we are.'

The car slowed as it turned into Heidi's street. A bundle of photographers, television crews, idle observers and small boys, curious on bicycles, were waiting as if for visiting royalty. They all turned expectantly, made way for the car. Mr Calvin, with his lovely blond attaché case, and the policewoman got out. They shielded Heidi and Micky all the way to the front door. Through the front window, a BBC camera crew could be seen setting up. A short brilliant burst of floodlight illuminated the street from within. The two policewomen – the one at the door, the other from the car – nodded at each other. The door shut on the observers. Heidi went through to face her close-up.

'That's me done for the day,' the policewoman said, sitting back in the front seat of the car. 'Are we going back to the station now, then? I was hoping to get to Marks and Sparks before they close.'

'There's posh.'

'I thought I could stretch to their fish bake, once in a while.'

'I'll take you back,' the driver said placidly. 'I've got better things to do than hang around here. "I like your bag,"' he quoted.

'You never know what people are going to say,' the policewoman said reproachfully. 'In these situations.'

'You know what people aren't going to say,' the driver said. 'Or shouldn't. Lovely bag. What a thing to say. I think she thought he might give it to her if she said she liked it.'

'Tragic Heidi,' the policewoman said. 'It was a nice bag, though.'

'Glad I've got something else to do now,' the driver said. 'I don't think I could have stood much more of those two. And what's his name – why are we driving him about?'

'John Calvin,' the policewoman said. 'You don't have to like any of them.'

'Just as well,' the driver said, slowing down for the Ruskin roundabout. 'If I were Micky—'

'I know what you're going to say.'

'If I were Micky,' the driver continued regardless, 'I wouldn't go on about how the police ought to open up the sex-offenders register quite so much.'

'Do you think she knows?'

'About Micky? I wouldn't have thought so. Micky doesn't seem very clear about it himself.'

'What was it again?'

'Indecent exposure. Two twelve-year-old girls. Not very nice at all. Not for the first time, either. Four years ago.'

'Well, we don't have to like them,' the policewoman said.

'Just as well,' the driver said, turning into the station car park.

20.

Kenyon came in and excused himself quickly, saying that he would come and say hello properly once he was more presentable; Billa and Kitty helped out by saying how exhausting and overcrowded that London train always was. 'The most extraordinary thing . . .' Kenyon began, then seemed to change his mind, and went upstairs rapidly. He might come down or he might not, they knew. On the rare occasions when a book club meeting took place and Kenyon was there, he generally said hello, then went upstairs for the rest of the evening, exactly like that. In his wake followed Caroline, who had walked down from the station, she said, with Kenyon, only popping in at her house to drop off some shopping from Barnstaple; she'd had quite a day of it, and what about all those awful people in the Fore street?

The next to arrive at Miranda's was Sukie, Miranda's American colleague. The university operated an exchange programme every year. A small liberal-arts college in Kansas had once funded a literature professor to examine the letters of Bryher, now in the basement of the Old Library at Barnstaple University. No one had ever looked at the leavings of the lesbian poet before. The Kansas professor proposed to do so, not because of any great interest in Bryher but because it seemed to be an untouched archive a hell of a long way from Kansas, with someone aching to fund it.

In practice, the archive proved too inextensive to justify a programme on the scale envisaged by the Kansas institute, and the professor grew bored. The small Barnstaple faculty took to inviting him out to lunch and dinner and, after a dropped suggestion or two, including him on the teaching programme. (This was in 1973, when things could be done in this informal way.) After a few months, he and the department's Chaucer expert – but it could have been almost anyone – started to have an affair. One thing led to another, and the visiting professor went back to Kansas with the sad information that the Bryher archives were more substantial and potentially much more important than anyone knew. He conveyed an image of grey stacks, receding into the middle distance of a dusty basement interior, lit by flickering fluorescents. It was a great stroke of luck for a small and unnoticed college like Quincunx, Kansas. They congratulated themselves on forging links with so ancient and distinguished a foundation as Barnstaple University. The Quincunctians, who on the whole were well-read and inquisitive people, piqued themselves on the connection. For them, having a link with a place not far from the place that the man came from who interrupted Coleridge while he was composing *Kubla Khan* was as good a connection as any. Bryher, whoever she was, was an added bonus.

Small and unnoticed Quincunx might be, but it was very well funded. In two years, a proper exchange programme was up and running. The English found it a useful way to pack off the younger and more Yank-struck members of the faculty for a year. The

Americans liked to come, to soak up, they said, the theatre and the Sights. They didn't mean the Hanmouth Players or the abject university theatre, struggling through *Hay Fever* or *Oedipus Tyrannus*. Nor did they mean, evidently, the statue of the Crapping Juvenile in Hanmouth or the Romanesque parish church with twelve neo-classical marble placards of alto-rilievo nymphs weeping among bulrushes and the like, all memorials to Regency slave-owners. They meant the Shaftesbury Avenue and a girl out of *Friends* starring in *John Gabriel Borkman* and the usual doomy Holocaust-installation stuff out of Tate Modern, which they could have found in Kansas anyway.

There had never been an American exchange professor who hadn't gone through his entire year behaving as if Devon were a suburb of London. You had to travel three solid hours from Quincunx College to the next theatrical offering or one of those scraps of Corot that so pepper the North American continent, and three hours by *plane* to glimpse a soprano singing a single note in the German language on an operatic stage. A mere two hours on the train to see Simon Russell Beale in *The Cherry Orchard* seemed like a short hop into real quality.

The thrilling founding adultery had long since run its course, though the Chaucer expert was now not a waif-like youth with a tied-back swatch of black hair falling over deliciously lickable olive skin, but a grizzled boyfriendless ancient with bags under his eyes and a badly advised combination of balding top and pepper-and-salt ponytail, given to looking at himself in the mirror and mouthing the never-to-be-forgotten words 'Deliciously lickable' to the reflection. The book on the Parliament of Fowls and the long-awaited reunion with the big-cocked Kansas aesthete would both have to wait until he retired, the year after the year after next. Since then, the visiting Quincunctians had by tradition set up shop in Hanmouth. The letting agency kept a three-bedroomed red-brick Edwardian villa for each arriving American family, and they usually liked it. Since her own arrival Miranda, too, had kept a place in her book club for an American. This one had written twenty-three articles and a book about Sylvia Plath, and was a recovering alcoholic. She had turned down the offer of a drink at her very first social outing in Hanmouth, and in the same breath asked if anyone had the number of the Barnstaple AA. It was important to keep in touch, she had said, sipping brightly at her sparkling water.

'I hope you don't mind,' Sukie, said, coming through the door. She was talking about the figure with her, her elder son.

'Of course not,' Miranda said. She did think that the boy – Michael, was it? – could probably be left on his own. He was fifteen, six foot three, ripely and malodorously pubescent. What was wrong with him? Was he a pyromaniac, not to be trusted with an empty house that contained a box of matches in a drawer and a desk full of notes on . . . Rossetti, was it? 'Does he want to sit with us – no, of course you don't, Michael. I'll get my daughter Hettie down.'

There was something in Michael's demeanour as he was led into the hallway that suggested that he knew Hettie already. His posture, as he walked forward, was curved and bent, as if actually backing away. Sukie went into the sitting room confidently, greeting the others. 'And this is Michael – Michael, come on in.'

From upstairs the noises of insistence and complaint could be heard joining in response. They all looked upwards for a moment at where the floorboards creaked. Before the sounds could turn into specific and probably embarrassing words, they all started talking at once.

'How are you finding—'

'Are you at the same school—'

'I'm sure Miranda would want you to have—'

'Goodness, isn't this nice—'

Michael himself stood in the doorway, not allowing himself to come further into the house. The doorframe grazed his temples. His mouth hung slightly open to show his perfect American teeth. 'I don't see why . . .' the voice from above cried, the last word turning into a wail. There was a brief Miranda-ish rat-a-tat. Her words were unclear but the commanding tone put an end to the argument.

'And here's Hettie!' Miranda said, from the top of the stairs. Behind her Hettie made some kind of yodelling groan. Hettie was thirteen, and a well-built girl. Her face seemed organized around a newly huge nose. Her knotted hair fell about her features. She came to the bottom of the stairs holding her right elbow in her left hand, pressing her broad bosom into one mass. With her other hand, she pulled at her hair. Some experiment had been taking place this afternoon with green eyeshadow and rouge, placed centrally on her cheeks.

'Hello, Hettie,' Sam said. Hettie spent enough time in the shop demanding free samples and slivers for him to greet her. The others followed suit raggedly or heartily. She muttered something in response.

'Have you met Michael?' Sam said.

'Well, why don't you go upstairs?' Miranda said. 'Show him your things. You can watch telly in the bedroom, if you like.'

There was a moment when it was not clear whether Michael or Hettie would go along with this suggestion. They all held their breath. It was as if a military officer had issued a command to a band of unruly and potentially violent natives out of nothing but bluster. But this time the natives seemed to obey. Hettie turned, hardly looking at Michael, who followed her. ' – know why they made – come *down*stairs,' she muttered.

'Thank God for that,' Miranda said, almost before the door upstairs was closed with a perhaps excessive firmness. 'I did think that we'd have *one* more year of peace before all that started. I do blame puberty.'

'It starts so very much earlier than in our day,' Kitty said.

'I didn't begin on all that until I was fifteen,' Billa said. 'I'm sure you were the same. One didn't think it quite the thing to be much earlier. But now . . .'

'You hear about girls of nine or ten beginning,' Kitty said.

'I can't imagine,' Billa said. 'I want to ask what their parents must be thinking of, but I don't suppose there's anything you can do about it.'

'Well, I do think it's nice to see a girl maturing into a young woman like that,' Sukie said, aghast, accepting a glass of lime and soda water. 'Those little growing pains – goodness, I'm sure we all had them and were able to laugh about them afterwards. I know my mother—'

'Well, it sounds awful, but I do wish we could send them away on their thirteenth birthday and get them back at twenty to hear all the funny stories,' Miranda said. 'I know that's not awfully motherly of me.'

'I know my mother—' Sukie continued.

'There are things called boarding schools,' Sam said.

'I could never do that,' Miranda said. 'We just couldn't send Hettie away like that.'

'Well,' Sam said, getting up and pouring himself another drink, 'we could all chip in, I suppose. Want a top-up, Billa?'

That wasn't what Miranda had meant. 'Has Michael eaten, or should I take some sandwiches up?' she said.

'He has eaten, and some sandwiches will be very welcome all the same, I'm sure. When I was his age – of course, that was when I was drinking, I remember my mother—' Sukie said.

'Good, I'll do that,' Miranda said. She got up and went into the kitchen, leaving Sukie to tell the story of her juvenile nights with the vodka bottle.

The house had been extended in most directions by the previous owner. Behind the frontage, three rooms had been knocked into one sitting room; a dining room went off to the right of the hallway, not often used. The kitchen at the back was a large addition, steel and glass in a steel-and-glass shell, and lit up like seaside illuminations at night. Miranda, Kenyon and certainly Hettie were not great ones for sitting in gardens, and the loss of half the garden to this marvellous kitchen didn't seem to concern them. Twice or three times in the summer, Miranda would don a floppy hat kept specifically for the purpose. She would go and sit on one of their four deckchairs with a gin-and-tonic and a copy of a novel by Virginia Woolf. There she would stay until the doorbell rang, and she could be discovered in that position. As far as the outside went, she preferred to walk the streets of Hanmouth and look upon the estuary and its birds. You could not meet up by chance with friends and acquaintances if you sat on your own in your garden. Upstairs there were three bedrooms and a study with a futon; above that, the previous owners had converted the loft into an indeterminate space. If you were any more than Kenyon's height, you could not stand upright in the converted uppermost room other than along its central spine, under the eaves.

When Miranda had taken the sandwiches and a large bottle of some radioactive fizzy drink upstairs – 'I know . . . I've just given up trying to give them anything healthier, and they wouldn't drink squash out of a jug, anyway' – she refilled the glasses, brought out other oval plates of Marmite pinwheels, bruschetta, vegetables, dips and bought-in miniature fishcakes and Scotch eggs. Reluctantly, they left the topic of Tragic China – they had returned to it, almost without wanting to.

'Well,' Billa said. *'The Makioka Sisters.'*

She stressed it in an unusual way, and when Miranda began the discussion, she took care to stress the *o*.

Half an hour later, Kenyon, washed, brushed and hungry, came downstairs to fetch something for his solitary supper at the kitchen table. He paused at the half-open door, wondering whether to go in, to tell them about the murder he believed he had seen at Paddington station, perhaps even to ask whether he might put the television on to see if there was anything on the news. He heard his wife say, 'Well, when Kenyon and I were in Japan two years ago . . .' She was speaking with confidence. She had got into her stride. He thought of the radio in the kitchen, and the news at nine o'clock.

21.

When Kenyon and Miranda were in Japan, two years ago, they travelled first of all to Kyoto. There were reasons for that. Miranda had proposed that they see the historic parts of Japan before they saw anything more contemporary – 'To do it in order,' she said. She had researched not in guidebooks but in historical studies of the period, in works of art history, architectural analysis and garden history, many of which she had lugged home from the university library as soon as the airline tickets had been bought. She also researched online, asking travellers who had been to Kyoto where they recommended staying, what out-of-the-way places they should visit, where they might like to eat, all the time making allowances for the national origins and evident literacy of the recommender. In the end, Miranda set one of her graduate students to compile the information she had gathered in this complicated way into two separate folders, one green for Kenyon, one red for Miranda, and handed Kenyon's to him in the departure lounge at Heathrow airport, once they had left the car in the long-term car park. Guidebooks were beneath Miranda; if she ever took one, she would be careful to consult it only in her hotel room, and decant any relevant information into the back of a small diary bound in soft leather like a ballerina's practice shoes. She would be physically incapable of walking the streets of a historic city with a guidebook in her hand.

Hettie had been left behind. In fact, it might be thought that the trip to Japan was a sort of celebration, a kind of honeymoon, to mark the moment that Hettie, at eleven, was able to take her own holidays without her parents. The school had arranged an outward-bound week on Dartmoor. Some kind colleagues of Miranda's who worked in the library had offered to take Hettie for the second week. They had a daughter the same age, and Mabel was going on the same week on the moor. Hettie did not object any more than she would have to anything else. Kenyon wondered whether they were truly friendly, and previous attempts to bring Hettie and Mabel together had not been much of a success. They had been sent upstairs together, and had come down together, without making any kind of friendship. Still, Kenyon reflected on the failed family holidays from the last ten years, characterized by sulking from one corner or another; Hettie's refusal, the previous summer, to admit that the Sicilian baroque was as dramatic and entertaining as most authorities believed. Or there was the summer before that, when Miranda had first put a brave face on, then satirically descanted over her agreed fate of spending five days at Disneyland Paris. She'd enjoyed it in the end more than Hettie had. Miranda had managed to keep up the monologue about semiotic and cultural imperialism from one end of Main Street USA to the other. There must have been some pleasure in that. Hettie had only wanted to go because her classmates had gone, and hadn't really cared for the giant exaggerated animals poking their fat plush fingers in her face. Kenyon thought about these two failed holidays, and it seemed to him that their holidays together had never worked, and that Hettie's festival independence might be something worth celebrating. He wondered afterwards where it was that he might like to go, though.

(There was one afternoon with the Sicilian baroque. The argument had sent his two women in opposite directions: Hettie back to the hotel and Miranda off with her guide-folder. He was on the steps of some big building, a palace or a cathedral or a museum, or something. Above him, the yellow crumbling cliff of fantasy, curling and uprising and flowering into stone bouquets and flying winged sandstone children; about him, the marble-paved square shining in the afternoon sun as if half an inch of still water covered it. Nobody was about. It was over ninety degrees, perhaps more. Kenyon, in his Englishman's shorts and his Englishman's sandals, sat in the sun surrounded by treasures of the Sicilian baroque. He took a long drink of the cold bottle of water he had just bought, and closed his eyes against the heat and the silence. It was some long minutes before thought returned: thoughts of home, and money, and work, and budgets. Those long minutes were probably the place he wanted to go.)

'I know you didn't enjoy yesterday all that much,' Miranda said in Kyoto, after they had left their hotel and its rush-mats and paper sliding walls and endless proffered slippers. They had got through their third morning's trying breakfast of miso, cold fried mackerel, pickles, rice and a swampy dish of green tofu disintegrating into cold salty water.

'Oh, I wouldn't say that,' Kenyon said.

'Well, there's a few things I want to see, and I can get round them much quicker if we just agree to meet back at the *ryokan* at four.'

Kenyon did not object to this prepared speech. Something like it was often produced at roughly this point in their holidays. He had enjoyed the previous day, in fact. He had liked the empty yards of gravel with a rock or two in them that passed for a garden in this part of the world. He quite enjoyed looking at a stretch of moss on a boulder, and he liked the way the floors in the temples creaked, rocking back and forth on one to make it sing. He liked the restful way that the four temples they had visited had been much the same, only varying in their size and in the number of visitors there. It all seemed very nice, and not in need of the explanations that Miranda had been offering him from time to time, about Zen contemplation, representations of the Great Tortoise swimming across the void, or any such thing.

She got into a taxi and, smiling brightly, waved him off. Kenyon rebelliously put his folder of explanations into his shoulder bag, and started walking. Fairly soon, he came across a busy shopping street, of no historical interest, full of department stores and electronics shops. They had driven across it in a series of taxis a dozen or so times by now, and the area had called for no comment. He stopped at a street corner, and waited as if for the light to change. It did change, and Kenyon still stood there, enjoying the foreignness of the beeping and the foreignness of the movement. He liked looking at well-dressed people, and this crowd was uniformly well dressed. They seemed to have put on clothes according to their age and station, and not questioned the basis of their wardrobe any further.

Kenyon watched the crowds crossing the shopping street several times. After ten minutes, he went into a department store, and walked around looking at perfectly ordinary objects: saucepans, plates, clothes hangers. When he came across something he did not think existed in his country – men's fans, kimonos, displays of sweets made of bean paste, pink jelly and chestnut – he walked on austerely.

Later, he came to a quarter of the town where trees hung over a clear roadside river, and men in tight athletic costumes sat by rickshaws and waited for tourists. Their shoes were rubber socks, cleaving between the big toe and the others, as if that were something they needed to grasp and grip with. He went on, and found himself in a street of wood-fronted houses, two miniature storeys high. This was picturesque, and yet there were no other tourists. They had been everywhere yesterday, snapping at anything.

Soon Kenyon began to feel hungry. He had tried to eat the breakfast but had largely failed. He decided that when it reached twelve o'clock he would go into a restaurant and order lunch. He did not know when lunch was eaten here, but they would surely make allowances for an English tourist, and some English people did eat their lunch at twelve. Twelve came, and he came to a restaurant. Through a bamboo gate, he could see a small garden, twelve feet by four, with a miniature bridge, a pond with carp in it, a bamboo trickling device and some arrangements of moss. There was no priced menu on the front, and suddenly he wondered whether this was a restaurant at all. He had heard fantastic stories about visitors to Hanmouth, after all, opening the gate to a private garden, sitting down at a garden table and ordering tea and scones. He went on.

There was a little run of restaurants further on, and every one had three shelves of plastic models of food in the window. They shone glossily, falsely and inedibly; no one could want to eat anything that looked like that. One of Kenyon's rules was that restaurants that displayed their food in the window, whether raw, cooked, or artificial, catered for people who could not read. He did not want to eat with people who could not read. He went on. It was only a few minutes later that Kenyon realized that, after all, he could not read here either. The plastic dishes were aimed squarely at him.

As he walked on, one restaurant after another presented itself: a jolly sushi bar full of noisy clients, who all seemed to know each other; a dour American-style fast-food place; an unexplicit simplicity behind a sliding wooden front, surely indicating fifteen courses and twenty thousand yen. Nothing would do; he could not go into any of them on his own. His hunger grew. He imagined Miranda, now, having visited the three temples and two famous gardens she wanted to tick off her list, settling down just at this moment to a good but reasonable meal in a recommended restaurant. He saw the kimonoed waitress handing her a menu and bowing out backwards; he smelt the sour, attractive perfume of the rush matting in the immaculate restaurant where Miranda sat alone, raising a bowl of miso to her mouth with both grateful hands. He sat down at the water's edge, perspiring, and extracted his green folder. There was nothing in it about restaurants, and Miranda had the guidebook.

'How was your day?' Miranda said, when they met again at the hotel.

'Very nice,' Kenyon said. In the end he had gone back into a department store and bought a dozen of those chestnut and sweet-potato cakes; he had been so hungry that, not caring what anyone thought in this country of flaunted decorum, he started stuffing down the first of them on the escalator upwards. 'Really very nice. This is an interesting town, isn't it? I went where the mood took me, and I went into *a* temple, but I don't think I could tell you which one it was. There wasn't a sign in English, or anything. There was some sort of ceremony going on inside – I think there must have been ceremonial drumming – and I just sat and let myself be swept away.'

This sort of stuff, compiled from similar experiences on previous days, satisfied Miranda. Then she told him what she had been seeing.

'I thought we might go to the Kabuki theatre tonight,' she said, in the end. He agreed: he was quite glad to have Miranda with him, on these occasions, to have ideas about what to do and where to go and what to eat. 'We could have an early dinner.'

He had looked at her sideways: he had wondered if she knew.

22.

Sometimes the discussion flowed easily over the surface of the selected book. Sometimes after a decent interval – ten or fifteen minutes – the conversation turned into the tributary of an ordinary conversation, away from what Sam called the 'set topic'. After a couple of hours on holidays, the government's iniquities, an attempt by a supermarket to set up in the Hanmouth meadows, or any other subject of the day, somebody would be bound to observe, 'And we've hardly *mentioned* the book ...' They were guaranteed to talk.

Today the conversation about Heidi and the supposed abduction ran its course quickly. They had all said their piece, and with some enjoyment. But when they had reached the end of that, a little silence fell. They were all upsettingly clear that they had shared exactly these views with exactly these people. They had shared them a number of times, and nothing had intervened to refresh the views, to jolly them up a bit, or really to make them worth repeating.

Discussion about *The Makioka Sisters* had been slow to take off. Both Kitty and Caroline were very clear that they *had* read it, were rather hot on the point. But the names did slip your mind, and the story, and the events, or so it seemed. 'I *did* read it,' Kitty insisted. Miranda produced her dreaded prop, only brought out in real emergencies: a reading-group sheet of questions and topics for discussion, harvested by Miranda off the Internet and garnished with her own well-nurtured epigrammatic observations. Finally – she'd never *known* such a dull evening and would happily say so to any of the group in a day or so – she went impatiently into the hall and called Kenyon out of the kitchen. She had resolved not to offer them any more food or drink. Kenyon was getting involved in a cold-beef sandwich and a small bowl of lurid piccalilli.

'Darling,' Miranda said. 'What – I mean *what* was the name of that temple in Kyoto?'

'There were rather a lot of temples in Kyoto, Miranda,' Kenyon said, looking over the top of his glasses.

'You *do* know the one I mean,' Miranda said. 'It had a sort of squarish gravel garden with fifteen rocks in it, but you could only see fourteen from any given angle. You know the temple I mean.'

'Yes,' Kenyon said. 'I think I remember. I mean I know I do.'

By now, they were all agog. The marital exchanges between Kenyon and Miranda were anticipated and enjoyed all round Hanmouth.

'What about it?' Kenyon asked.

'What was it called?' Miranda said.

'Kenzo-ji. No, that can't be right. Kenzo's the man who makes the perfume. Senso-ji.'

'That one's in Tokyo.'

'Well, it was something like that. Why do you want to know?'

'Kitty thought,' Billa began, and in five minutes general conversation had broken out. It was striking, the group thought, that though Kenyon was a pretty dull fellow in conversation and Miranda a sparkling one, they didn't produce dull or sparkling conversation in proportion. Silence tended to hover about Miranda's most brilliant phrases, like the dull black cloth on which a diamond is laid out. On the other hand, Kenyon, not very enchanting or entertaining in what he said, acted on company like a lump of yeast on dough.

As if to prove it, Kenyon was now telling the gag about Sir Oliver Franks, the *Washington Post* and the box of crystallized fruit. '"Well," the American said. "That is amusing. I would love to see that issue of the *Washington Post*. It must have been in Katherine Graham's time."'

The others in the room had nothing to say to this. Billa regretfully turned her glass almost upside down on her nose. A roseate trickle of what had once been Campari and soda headed downwards. Kitty, in harmony, licked her finger and ran it round the fake Palissy snake-and-fruit dish Miranda used for her canapés. She licked it clean of crumbs, ran it around underneath a toad's ceramic head, licked again. Billa dropped her glass on the carpet with a soft thud. 'Golly,' she said. 'Good job it was empty.'

'Well, I guess I ought to be going,' the American said. And, as if on command, there was her blushing son in the doorway, preceded by Miranda and Kenyon's teenage daughter. Something had happened upstairs: if his eyelashes had grown blacker through some experiment with mascara, Hettie's glow had nothing artificial about it. She had taken her hair in one hand, and was chewing it, her eyes fixed and her smile enormous, gazing at the American boy. 'Well, I hope you've been having fun,' the American woman said needlessly, and her son, cued, said, 'Thank you for having me, Mrs Kenyon.' Hettie made no comment; she just nodded, unable, it seemed, to detach her gaze. Had she ever been in love before, so instantly? No one could think, and no one wanted to go on observing this passion; they had gone upstairs concrete, grey and lumpen, and come down sheer, shining, polished glass.

'I'll walk you home,' Hettie said, removing her sucked locks from her mouth.

'Don't be silly,' the American woman said. 'He's got me to walk him home, or he's there to walk me home, one of the two.'

'Dear little Hettie,' Kenyon said unkindly. 'How sweet you can be, sometimes.'

23.

The streets of Hanmouth wound away from the four stately avenues in unpredictable ways. In the uneven, curving and incomplete pathways and half-roads running between the major arteries, anything at all could be found, and had been built. There were alms cottages round a pocket-handkerchief of green, and square Georgian houses with cats in the window; there were Stanley Spencer Edwardian villas with a gap in their bow windows where a phantom aspidistra surely stood. There was a pair of white art-deco semis, curving out superbly like a liner, flat-roofed and iron-windowed; the builder had envisaged the sun, and they were gloomy, streaked and with a tendency to leak in the rain. Builders and architects had put up any number of houses without much thinking of the appearance of their neighbours. Only in recent years had inhabitants, thinking of adding to their property with a conservatory or a roof extension, found themselves being asked whether it would fit in with the town's appearance.

Halfway down Powell's Lane, there was a house that had been built in the 1890s, then altered in the 1930s, and added to after the war. Originally a prosperous shopkeeper's house, it had been rented by a pair of artistic lesbians; washed towards St Ives in the 1950s, they had got no further than Hanmouth, and the one a novelist and travel writer, the other a potter, had settled down there. An unexpected popular success had come to the writer too late in her career to think of moving to anywhere more glamorous. Instead, the book about travelling from London to Syria by train, which had found itself under many Christmas trees in Hanmouth and well beyond at the end of 1973, ended up paying for a grand studio with top-lighting and a new electric kiln for Bettie at the bottom of the garden.

Over the glass roof, creepers of ivy and wisteria lay; the glass had not been cleaned since Sylvie had bought the house from the two ladies when they retired to Aleppo. Ten years ago, at least.

The light filtered through a layer of brown leaves from the apple tree, fallen last autumn and the autumn before that. Sylvie would clear up the leaves on the lawn and in the flowerbed; she kept that tidy enough for the sake of avoiding the neighbours' comments. But to get a ladder up and clear the glass roof of the studio was more than she could contemplate. She liked the beige light, too.

At the moment, she was sitting with a cup of tea and Radio 4 on. There was an ancient kettle, filled from the sink, and two mugs in the studio – not because of guests, who weren't invited to hang around, but because it was always easier to have one mug on the go and the other on the draining-board. One said Best Aunt In The World; the other was a pink-and-blue junkshop treasure, a pre-war present from Lydd. *Woman's Hour* was running its course with a report on cookery classes for girls in a violent inner-city neighbourhood in America. The concern of the voice spooled on, against a backdrop of kitchen clank and bong. Sylvie was hardly listening. She was clutching her mug and staring contemplatively at her huge old kitchen table, squarely in the centre of the studio. On it were five folders, bellying with small cuttings, postage-stamp-sized representations, all of the same thing, collected by Sylvie in fits and bursts, roughly torn out of magazines she had travelled a hundred miles to buy fifteen of. She had caused astonishment in every shop she had been to, and could never go back there, ever again. The cuttings were organized according to a principle of Sylvie's own devising. It was time to begin the Work: her gallerist would be on the phone some time today to ask about it.

The door to the studio was pushed from outside; it jammed, and was pushed again.

'I wondered what you fancied for lunch,' Tony said. He was forty-four; trim, white-haired and bearded, with the jeans and check shirt of his youth.

'Any old thing,' Sylvie said. 'Cheese on toast.'

'Here at the Betty Shabazz Community Center,' the radio said,

'Honore and LaWonda are putting the finishing touches to their *tarte aux framboises*. They've been in patisserie class for—'

'We can do better than that,' Tony said. 'I was going to go over to the farmers' market this morning.'

'Don't go to any trouble,' Sylvie said. Tony, who taught, like her, at the new Barnstaple Academy – German, though, not art – had been living with Sylvie since his wife had thrown him out two months before. She liked Tony well enough, and had offered one of her two spare bedrooms 'for as long as you need it'. The trial separation, as Tony had initially described it, seemed to be turning into a proper one. Sylvie didn't know Tony's wife Christa, though she had heard a good deal about her in the last couple of months, how they had met in Leipzig just after the unification of Germany – 'Practically dancing on the Wall,' Tony had said. It had seemed as if they had fallen in love immediately, and married without waiting. Now, Tony said, he wondered whether his main attraction, eighteen years ago, had been as a meal ticket out of Leipzig and its long slow future rebuilding. He couldn't now imagine – Tony said – what a girl of Christa's age would be doing with an old fart eight years older than her. There was always a little pause here for Sylvie to point out that he had only been, what?, in his twenties – late twenties, but twenties. The gap between Tony and Christa had always been, it seemed, the point on which their relationship rested; perhaps if, when you started, the girl was seventeen, it would always feel like that.

But Sylvie never did point that out. She wondered how long he was going to stay. She didn't mind him being there – he was tidy, quiet and no trouble. She believed that, soon, he would stop offering to help around the place, wondering what she would like for lunch, bringing little presents for the kitchen, which he couldn't help noticing she didn't have, depositing an egg-whisk in the second kitchen drawer for her to find. She just wanted him to stop coming into her studio.

'I went past the community centre last night,' Tony said.

'There was something going on there, I saw,' Sylvie said.

'Do you know that little girl? The one who's been kidnapped?'

'No, I can't say I do,' Sylvie said. 'Was that what it was all about? Everyone seems very concerned.'

'Ironic, really,' Tony said. 'I came down here expecting to get some peace and quiet, escape from all that, and instead it follows me down.'

'I don't think it really follows you down, Tony,' Sylvie said. 'I don't think it's got anything to do with you at all.'

She regretted saying it as soon as she saw the look on his face. He was quite nice, after all. But she could not stop herself saying these brutal things, simply because he was somebody who was living with her. It came with the territory.

He bent down, and picked up one of her scraps of paper. 'You've dropped one,' he said. 'Where shall I put it?'

'Oh, anywhere,' Sylvie said, observing him place it carefully down on the table, evidently conscious that it formed the raw material of her work of art. He couldn't help it – nobody could. He cast a glance at what was on the little torn square of paper, and looked away rapidly. It was interesting to see how people looked at an image, even as small as this, of the subject Sylvie had chosen and collected. Tony had served his purpose for the morning. He had reminded her that her subject, after all, was interesting and striking.

'I'll be off now,' Tony said, stiffening and not looking her directly in the face. 'Work well.'

'And you,' Sylvie said. She watched the door close behind him; it stuck and he had to give it a proper tug from the outside. Then she got up, placed her mug on the table, and picked up the cutting that Tony had found on the floor. She examined it; it was a photograph of an erect penis, detached from any context. After a moment, she placed it in the orange folder, together with nine hundred and forty-six others of the same subject. The time was coming when she ought to stop collecting photographs of erect penises, and start work properly. Tony couldn't look at one of them in isolation. She wondered, without much interest either way, what his erect penis looked like. She thought, when her hundreds of cuttings were mounted and glued onto the disco mirror-balls resting under the table, she might call the piece 'Erect Penis'. That would be striking.

'We start the young people off by teaching them how to make shortcrust pastry,' the radio said. 'And in a week or two, they're ready for their first *tarte Tatin*.'

24.

Tony closed the garden gate behind him, and for a moment could not decide whether to turn left or right. A right turn would take him up towards the railway line, the meadows beyond the borders of the town and then the farmers' market in a new purpose-built centre, where he had told Sylvie he would be going. Leftwards was the main street of Hanmouth. That was cheaper, and made him feel more like a local – the rich of Barnstaple and around drove to the farmers' market and drove back to their homes with their expensive vegetables and artisanal cheeses. He went left.

It had been good of Sylvie to offer her spare room. She had been teaching at the academy for a couple of years. When word had got out that a proper artist had been headhunted, Tony had been sceptical. It sounded like window-dressing on the part of the new go-ahead chief executive, Ahmed Khalil. He had passed around an article about Sylvie's work from a specialist contemporary art journal, describing it in terms that Tony couldn't make sense of. He prepared himself to be unimpressed. But when Sylvie arrived, she was small, tidy and modest in appearance, and in a few weeks had proved herself to be good with the students. You heard them mentioning her name in the corridors, the tasks she'd set. She also turned out to live in Hanmouth. Most of the staff had imagined a more metropolitan figure, brought down – Jean Stevenson, the head of media, said – 'from some squat in Hoxton'. That was in her favour.

Even without Sylvie, her department was on the rise, anyone could see that. The kids were taking to art in large and increasing numbers. The same couldn't be said for Tony. When Tony was at school, German had seemed like any other subject; Germany had seemed, to him and to everyone else, like a European country you might go to. If anything, it had seemed more fascinating than other European subjects, with the Cold War and the Wall; he had led a sixth-form trip to the enclosed Berlin in 1987, and they'd gone over to the other side; that was something that those now thirty-something-year-olds would always remember. Some change had occurred since then; the smallest of ripples from the great event, the collapse of the Wall, had ended up in a West Country class-room. The numbers taking German had fallen steadily, year after year. They didn't want to study foreign languages anyway, but German had gone into single figures. The year before, Tony had realized that all but one of the students beginning German A level had some kind of family connection. He had paused, just as he was about to start a pop quiz on adjective endings, and gone round the group asking them, honestly, what the other kids in the year, the ones that weren't taking German, thought of their choice of subject. The shamefaced answer came back: no one thought the subject was cool enough to be worth all the trouble. Adjective endings, for instance? Yes, adjective endings. And Germany – the music, the food, the people, the football – a full hour of humiliated denigration had followed. Tony couldn't understand it; and in any case the demands made on students had got easier over the years. It wasn't as if adjective endings had ever been cool.

He never asked a group of students again, but after that he felt that his days were numbered. The incredible, horrible news of university departments of German closing down for lack of demand kept arriving. One day, towards the end of the summer term, Ahmed Khalil had called him in. 'Just an informal sort of chat,' he said. 'A sort of discussion about long-term strategy.' Tony knew what it was about. It was indeed informal: Ahmed Khalil had got up from behind his desk and placed first Tony, then himself in the armchairs about the coffee-table on which cups of coffee quickly appeared, brought by the smiling secretary. Not a sacking, then. (Could you sack somebody because the language they taught had stopped being cool?)

He found himself being asked whether he had any interest in teaching other foreign languages, Spanish, for instance. He didn't: he didn't speak Spanish, though he told Ahmed Khalil that he was sure he could 'get up to speed' quickly enough, and he supposed that was true in its own way.

At the top of Sylvie's road, there was a T-junction. On the other side of the road, the white picket gate that crossed the railway line. Tony looked to left and right conscientiously before going over. The alley that led beyond the line towards the water-meadows and the farmers' market was a dark, overhung place. If it had been in Barnstaple or a bigger city, you would have thought twice about walking down it alone. Tony felt a small tug of caution as he saw three figures twenty yards away, underneath a hanging slab of ivy. But they were children; one quite small. He carried on towards them, and the middle one looked. It was a girl; she made a sort of inarticulate noise. Pulling her arms into her, hardly hesitating, she ran in the other direction, followed by the two other children. At the end of the alley, a car was idling. The driver leant over, opening the passenger door, and the girl got in. The car reversed, then drove quickly forward and away, leaving the other two children behind. When Tony got to the main road, there was no sign of any of them.

Tony had been following the story about the missing girl, like everyone else in Hanmouth and well beyond. The girl – the one who had gone off freely enough in the car – had certainly looked like the missing child. Had this happened to him? Was he the one to have seen the child? He paused where he was, gathering himself. The child had been wearing a pair of white trousers, not very clean, and pink trainers – no, not trainers, they had been those rubber perforated shoes said to be comfortable. And a hooded grey sweatshirt. He tried to remember what the other two children

110

had been wearing – it hadn't registered, though their appearance had been clear enough. The biggest had looked kind of lumpy, on the edges of adolescence and carrying herself awkwardly. He remembered that flying run of the child into the car; she was younger, she ran as if she had never considered what running looked like. The car – silver. Every car was silver, these days, that was no good, but it had been a small runaround, a Fiat maybe. He hadn't had a chance to see the number-plate. But he had, surely, seen the driver. Thirty, perhaps; mixed race, wiry, a Zapata moustache, or could that have been a trick of the light?

He went home. In twenty minutes, two police officers were sitting at Sylvie's kitchen table with a notebook taking down the details, and their colleagues for thirty miles around were roaming the roads, looking for a silver car, a Fiat maybe.

25.

'I tell you what, Heidi,' the police officer said. 'It's just making it hard for you, having the children at home all the time. I'll take Hannah and Harvey out for a ride in the squad car.'

'Hannah and Harvey are fine,' Ruth said. There was a persistent unspoken hostility between this police officer and Heidi's family. She was always making little suggestions like this, and in the last day or two, Heidi had started confronting the clear implication by saying things like 'I know you think I'm a bad mother, don't you?' But she didn't, or so she said.

The front room of Heidi's house was hot and filled with smoke. It had become a public space, and police officers, case workers, victim-support officers, spokesmen, Mr Calvin and half a dozen others came in and out at will. A succession of police officers stood at the front door, like Number 10 Downing Street, Ruth said. They kept the journalists out, mostly, and stopped the photographers getting close enough to press their cameras against

111

the glass. But they let a dozen authorized figures in, and they came in without ringing the doorbell. Upstairs was sacrosanct from the casual visitor, and that had been searched thoroughly, three times. The downstairs area was as open and febrile as a 7/11, and people came and went, bearing files, notebooks, bags of groceries, replenishments of tea, biscuits, toilet paper, takeaway food. The windows stayed firmly shut, and the atmosphere inside was sweet and putrid. Heidi's hair was lank and oily; her eyes baggy and haunted. Two weeks before, she and Micky had made an unlikely couple. Now, she had grown to look much like him, and was even wearing an old T-shirt of his, advertising an Italian designer. The campaign T-shirts, reading Save China, were laid out on the back of a black leather easy chair, to be put on when the media had to be faced.

'I know they're fine,' the policewoman said. 'They're coping very well, all things considered. It would be nice for them to have a small break, and it's a treat to ride in the back of a police car. You'd like that, wouldn't you, kids?' She gritted her teeth; she was not someone with the gift of talking to children.

Hannah and Harvey looked at each other, from either end of the sofa where they perched. Hannah was a stolid sort of girl, more like Micky than her mother, though that was impossible; Harvey the sort of pug-faced child whose appearance suggested potential for evil underneath a shock of dark-blond screw curls. They had said nothing for days to the police, and their accounts of the crucial afternoon had been brutally amnesiac when the time had come for the professional child-handler to interview them. Nothing had been got out of them. Occasionally, when they were upstairs and alone, an outbreak of immense violence, of objects being hurled and voices raised in threat or wailing distress, suggested to the many visitors that their silent downstairs tolerance, like a lion and a hippopotamus in separate but adjacent enclosures, might not be the whole story.

'I don't know,' Hannah said. 'We'd like to stay here with Mom in case?'

'Mummy will be fine,' the policewoman said, correcting Hannah's inflected style, the product of being child-minded by a thousand unsuitable DVDs. 'Let's go. We'll go out of the back door.'

Little Archie, in his carrycot, slept on, deposited behind the thirty-inch television, where the hum seemed to tranquillize him and where no one could step on him.

'The thing is, Heidi,' the policewoman's colleague said, 'we may have some developments we'd like to talk to you about. And also to Ruth, if you'd like to come through to the kitchen.'

The policewoman took Harvey by the hand, and ushered Hannah ahead of her into the kitchen. The back door was unlocked, and they went through into the garden. A pathway ran between the ends of the gardens in this estate, and there would be a squad car waiting for them where it came out on the Exeter road. They would do their best to make this little trip look like what they had promised, a small treat for Harvey and Hannah. They might even let them set the siren off, if that would help them explain who it was they had been seen talking to in a quiet corner of Old Hanmouth. Confirm who it was, rather. But the policewoman was just unhooking the rusty hinge to the gate when Ruth shouted from the kitchen. The door was open, and what she shouted might even be audible to the newsmen clustered around the other side of the house; it would certainly make the state of affairs clear to Heidi, in the front room. 'Fucking Marcus!' Ruth was shouting, enraged and unable to stop herself. The children looked at each other, a message passing from Hannah to Harvey, and the message was this: 'Shut up.'

'Here we are,' the policewoman said. By some miracle, the squad car was waiting where it was supposed to be, and none of the journalists or casual rubberneckers had attached any significance to it. 'You see? It's just like an ordinary car, really, with a few alterations.'

'Do you paint it yourself?' Hannah said. 'Or do you get the people who make it to do that?'

'The police markings, you mean?' the policewoman said. 'Well, I think we paint it. This is my friend Bob. He's a professional driver. Hello, Bob.'

PC Green gave a half-wave; he was a grumpy sod, not very likely to create the right cosy atmosphere in the car, but that couldn't be helped.

'Where are we going?' Harvey asked his sister, or half-sister.

'They want to drive us round and that,' Hannah said. 'Just get in and shut up.'

'This is exciting, isn't it?' the policewoman said, turning round and smiling at the pair. 'Do your seatbelts up, kids. Bob sometimes likes to drive fast. He's allowed to, if he's chasing after people who've done something wrong.'

'Whatever,' Hannah said.

'If you like, we might put the siren on in a little while.'

'Why?'

'Well, it would be interesting for you, wouldn't it?'

The children said nothing; their jaws were clenched. They looked directly in front of them as the car slid past the end of their road. They did not even look at the mass of humanity blocking the road, idly fiddling with their equipment, talking on mobile phones, sitting on walls and playing with their handheld gaming devices and, further off from the epicentre, the casual passers-by eating ice-cream in the heat, and with their backs to this car, waiting to see some development.

'You haven't been back to school, have you, Hannah?' the policewoman said.

'Mom don't want us to,' Hannah said. 'She said she wants us by her.'

'I know,' the policewoman said. 'So you've been staying at home, have you? That's good.'

'Yes,' little Harvey added. He had a slow, grinding voice, disconcertingly deep as his colourless eyes. 'We've been staying at home.'

'Have you been staying at home all the time?' the policewoman said. 'Doesn't it get boring?'

'We want to be by Mom's side,' Hannah said. 'It's best we're by her at a time like this.'

They were clinging to a script. The policewoman reminded herself that they had nothing to do with any of this; that they were not involved; that they were only children, and not themselves evil. The ones who stuck to a script, they were her favourites. It never did any good in the end. She remembered a man last month, taken in for affray outside a pub on this side of town; he'd seen too many cop shows, and had stuck to his two-word script of 'No comment' for a good hour.

'Look,' Harvey said. 'There's a rabbit. Four rabbits.'

He was right: on the verge of the dual carriageway, just before the bridge over the estuary, four rabbits gambolled. For a moment, they were all facing in different directions; then something startled them, a glimpse of a kestrel, and they shot unanimously into the hedgerow as the police car swept past.

'Nothing you can do about rabbits,' Bob said in his way. 'Shoot them, trap them, gas them. They'll be back in the same numbers. I've got an allotment.'

'You get a bit of a breather every now and then, though,' the policewoman said to the children.

'What's that mean?' Hannah said.

'You're allowed to go out.'

There was no reply to this.

'For instance,' the policewoman said, 'a little bird told me that you'd gone out, you two, this morning for a while.'

Hannah's lips were tensely gripped, but after a few moments she nodded. 'The other coppers told you that.'

'That's right,' she said, trying to make her voice as warm and informal as it possibly could be. She thought of bedtime stories; she thought of voiceovers for chocolaty drinks; she thought of motherly speaking animals in warm-hearted cartooons, and she spoke again. 'Your mum wouldn't want you to stay inside all the time, would she? So what did you do, this morning, say?'

'Nothing,' Hannah said.

'I always like to go down to the estuary,' the policewoman said. 'When I was your age, I'd go down and watch the birds, skim some stones. My brother used to fish. Do you know anyone who ever does that?'

'We didn't do any of that,' Hannah said.

'What do you do when you want to get away from everything, then, Hannah?'

'Don't know.'

The policewoman left a long pause. The car turned right off the main road, onto a high-hedged lane, climbing up the hill. It was in the first range of the hills you could see from Old Hanmouth, on the other side of the estuary.

'We used to come here on school trips,' the policewoman said. 'I remember we came up here to Cinderham Castle. Have you done that?'

'Yeah,' Hannah said. 'We done that.'

'Did you like it?'

'It was boring,' Hannah said.

'So where did you go this morning, you two?'

'Just out,' Hannah said.

'The thing is, Hannah, a friend of mine says he saw you in Old Hanmouth this morning. You and Harvey both. Did you go there?'

'Don't know.'

'I think you do know, Hannah. You were talking to someone, I know. Who were you talking to?'

'Wasn't talking to anyone.'

'I think you were, Hannah.'

'If I was, you know I was. You've got cameras everywhere, you'll have seen us talking, but you haven't, so we weren't.'

'We don't have CCTV cameras everywhere, Hannah. Not everywhere. And my friend says—'

'Your friend needs her eyes testing. Your friend doesn't know anything. She a lesbian too?'

'That's not polite, Hannah.'

'Yeah, well, you look like one,' Hannah said. 'Doesn't she? Hey, Harvey. Look at her, she's a lesbian. She wants to do me. That's why she's taking us out.'

'Hannah,' the policewoman said. 'There's no point in pretending. I know you and Harvey saw China this morning. I think you know I know. You're not in trouble yet. Just tell us where China went, and who she was with.'

'You're mental,' Hannah said. 'You're horrible. We haven't seen China. I don't know anything about it.'

'That's what Marcus said, he hasn't seen China.'

'Yeah, well, he's a liar,' Harvey said. 'He's a big fat fucking liar.'

'Shut up,' Hannah said, and she hit him hard in the head.

'What did China say to you, then, Harvey?'

They were silent. The policewoman felt that she could take a risk here.

'I said, what did China want to say to you that made Marcus bring her over?'

They had their arms folded. Whatever happened, they were not to respond to the name of Marcus: they had heard it screamed by Ruth from the kitchen, and the hide-and-seek game of hotter, colder, warmer, hotter, boiling hot was coming to an end.

'Stop the car, PC Green,' the policewoman said. 'We know everything that's happened. If you tell us now, you won't be in trouble, and your mum won't be in trouble. But if you carry on pretending something that's not true, your mum might go to prison, and you'll get taken into children's homes. Do you understand me? And you won't go to the same place. You'll all be split up. That'll happen if you don't tell me why you met China this morning, and where she is now.'

The police car had pulled into a passing place, a yew shading it. Outside, the sounds of the country: of birdsong and a distant bleat of sheep. In the car, there was silence. Hannah looked at her lap. Quite at once, Harvey burst into a long noise; some words, indistinct, were buried in the last vulnerable wail of his short childhood. The policewoman left it. 'You shut it,' Hannah said, outraged, but Harvey had had enough, and, through her blows, the words came out – 'goodbye – had – China's saying – she said – I said – she said – we had, we had, we had to say goodbye. China wouldn't go without saying goodbye, she wouldn't.'

The torrent slowed into sobs; Hannah sat back. She had done what she could do, it seemed. In a moment PC Green started the car, tactfully, calmly, reversed it into the green-hedged space and turned back in the direction of Barnstaple and Hanmouth. The policewoman delved in her bag, and found a new packet of paper tissues. She passed them back, wordlessly, to Hannah. Hannah, without commenting or thanking, began to clean up Harvey. 'He likes China,' she said. 'It's China he likes best of all of us.'

No one felt the need to ask for any addition to this statement.

26.

'FUCK HIM.'

' – easier if you—'

'He can fucking fuck off, it's not—'

'Ruth, why did you say Marcus?'

'I never. I don't want to hear more about him, not again, not never.'

'What's going on—'

'I never, Heidi, I never—'

'What's Marcus done, Ruth?'

'That's what I'd like to know, what's Marcus—'

'Heidi, it's no good.'

Ruth was in the kitchen, two policemen over her. Heidi, in the doorway, was being restrained by Mr Calvin, who had appeared from nowhere. In the hallway of the hot little house, Micky, awed, fat-faced, neglected. A scream from baby Archie was starting up.

118

'It's best if we sit down and talk this through,' a policeman said. 'And I think it's time we went through the events one more time. Take her out, please, sir.' This one to Mr Calvin.

'I don't think I will,' Calvin said. 'I think as the mother of the abducted girl, Heidi has a perfect right to hear what's being said.'

'I think we need to establish the truth at some point,' the policeman said. 'Take her out, please, or I will.'

Almost every house in Heidi's street had the same front garden. The original architects had envisaged neat fronts of green, a path, a line of flowerbed and a patch of lawn. But almost every house, in the last twenty years, had paved over the soil, and now only cars sat in the square at the front. Only in the house opposite had an old couple maintained their garden, with a privet hedge, four rose bushes, and some clematis in pots about their front window. The kids of the neighbourhood liked to gather there and throw eggs at the house.

Underneath the privet hedge, a cat crouched. The crowd outside Heidi's house paid it no attention. They had heard a shout from the house, and that was enough to get them to wait alertly, their eyes on the front windows. At the far end of the road, a red Mondeo turned in. Perhaps the driver felt a moment of rage at the crowd that had no place here, blocking the road pointlessly; the car's engine revved, and it drove towards the scattering crowd at some speed. At that moment, the cat emerged at a run; a woman photographer saw it, a girl with cropped hair, an assistant who could have been a boy, and at the same time saw why she had not seen it under the hedge, saw that her eyes had gone over the cat in the dark shade and not seen it at all. It was an entirely black cat, black as a panther, moving like a single black brushstroke across the road in front of the red speeding car. For a moment it looked as if the cat would slip just across the road before the car reached it. But it did not; the cat ducked and swerved, but its head, its front half went right underneath the wheel, just as it saw it was too late and tried to double backwards. The car went on.

Without knowing when or how, the gathering had all noticed

it at once. They had turned from Heidi's house in silence and, with hands to their faces, were watching the cat in the road. On its side, its legs stretched out forwards and backwards, a single twisting movement repeated over and over its torso, rolling sideways; it spasmed, once, twice, three times; then it seemed to lie and to collapse, and another huge spasm, as if it were being violently sick, as if something were tossing it down. It lay absolutely still.

'Oh, God,' somebody said, and a blanket was produced from the back of a car. 'There's a vet's hospital in town,' someone else said. 'Just by the station – that's the best thing.' A woman gathered the cat's limp body up and, with a stranger, got into a car. 'Did anyone get the driver's number-plate?' someone asked. Nobody had, it seemed, and a journalist suggested that there were enough police around, you would have thought. But another said that though it was a crime to run over a dog and not stop or report the accident, there was nothing to stop you running over a cat.

'It'll be dead,' people said. 'Did you see how it went still like that? Nothing could survive that. The car went right over it.' In a moment, once the excitement was over, someone remembered where they were, and looked at the house. The curtains had been drawn back; in the window, looking out with concern and interest, were two police officers, one a man, one a woman. By them was the boyfriend and, craning to see, Heidi. The shouting and the refusals to listen inside had been reaching a new pitch of rage. Heidi, so mute and calm, had been yelling through the kitchen door that she wanted to know what Ruth was saying, what they'd done with her kids, and where was Hannah, where was Harvey? For days now, the low murmur of conversation from outside had been steady; the gathering of observers uninterrupted.

The quality of the noise changed, quite suddenly, first rising, and then abruptly downwards. A policeman had been drawn to the window. There, they saw not the car passing, but the cat, lying in the road, suffering one huge spasm after another, and the unfamiliar sight of the mass of journalists facing the other direction, their attention taken. 'Jesus,' a policeman said.

'What is it?' Heidi said.

'It's a cat. It's been run over, I think,' he said.

'Jesus,' a woman police officer said, and came to the window to look. Micky came into the room and up to the window, gawping with ugly fascination.

'That's horrible,' the policewoman said. 'Poor thing.'

It was then that she saw Heidi had been silenced by the news of this event, drawn to it. She stood there, her arms folded, walking forward to the window, waiting for the small disaster to stop taking attention away from her, and yet welcoming this small, violent event is if it were the first interesting thing that had happened to her for days, weeks, months, for ever. It struck the policewoman then, and subsequently, as the strangest of Heidi's strange behaviour, and one that witnessed not a planned front for the situation, but a fundamental and impermeable oddity in the way she was. They had complained, all of them, about the rush of onlookers, of observers, of watchers, of the outbreak of vulgar and uncaring curiosity around the larger tragedy of the child's disappearance, whatever was at the bottom of it, but to lack that was to lack some crucial element in humanity. Not to want to look at even the staged and implausible spectacle of pain and suffering was to admit yourself reduced to an animal level. Heidi cared, too, but she cared not so much about the tragedy she found herself in but, just like those onlookers, those rubberneckers, about a spectacle that, in the event, was not her own. She cared about a cat – not her own cat, but a cat belonging to someone else, a cat that had made a bad mistake on its own feline level of calculation and speculation – meeting its horrible end underneath the wheels of a strange car. She had revealed herself as human; human as the anonymous onlookers in her thirst for drama, wherever it might be found. The policewoman looked at Heidi, in an old and much-washed T-shirt of Micky's, flapping over her thin arms, at the window to share in the animal tragedy, to see what had turned them all, shamelessly, into an audience, and saw that Heidi might just as easily have been outside the window with the gawping crowd as inside, madonna-like and grieving. From that moment she knew Heidi could have done anything at all.

27.

'The truth of it is,' the policewoman said, 'the fact is, that Hannah has talked to us, and Ruth has confirmed it. We know that China has been with Marcus. My colleagues are on my way there now. We know that Hannah saw China yesterday in Old Hanmouth.'

'She never,' Heidi said.

'She's told us. She told us that Harvey wanted to see his sister, because she wanted to say goodbye to him. Where is she going, Heidi?'

The sullen surface of the woman boiled; turned; rose. Nothing for weeks had surprised her, and now something had surprised her.

'Hannah said what?'

'So you know where China has been, Heidi.'

'Hannah said what?'

'Hannah told us that China wanted to say goodbye. Where is she going, Heidi?'

'HANNAH.'

'She's not here, Heidi.'

'HANNAH.'

'Where is China, Heidi?'

'Where has she been, Heidi?'

'RUTH.'

'We've taken Ruth down to the police station to help us out some more. My colleagues are on their way to Marcus's house. Is that where China is?'

'HANNAH.'

The policeman turned round from the window, where he had been examining the waiting crowd. He looked at Heidi, gripping herself tightly, her features white and shocked, and Micky, there in the door, wearing what must be the last of the Save China T-shirts over a long-sleeved navy top. Behind him was the omni-present John Calvin. The policeman had been trying to think, ever since he came on to this case and John Calvin had crossed his path, what exactly it was that Calvin reminded him of, with his long loose limbs, his neat and close-cropped hair, his dark eyebrows and regular features, as if outlined by artificial means. Now it came to him: a painted wooden puppet. Calvin now made an unreadable gesture; it seemed like a glimpse of a longer and more considered performance, and the way he moved his arms and shifted his eyes and mouth would only make sense if you understood the character he was bodying forth at the bottom end of some strings. The policeman resisted a sharp temptation that had been building up inside him for some days now: to tell him very briskly that his services were no longer needed, and had always been somewhat misplaced. That time would come, but it wasn't necessary to make the remark in front of Heidi and Micky.

28.

It was a beautiful day; Kenyon loved these late spring days, and he loved the town he lived in. Only when he thought not of the beauty of his house and the places it looked out on but of how much he paid – how much they owed – did the beauty reveal an unpleasant aspect, like a turd under a Christmas tree. (The last six months, he had ended the month in overdraft, something that hadn't happened for ten years, and last month he had more or less started the month in overdraft, too; he didn't even want to think about the balance on the credit cards. But he had an overdraft facility of five thousand pounds, which he hadn't even asked for, and another ten thousand available on the credit cards, and then – no, he wouldn't think about it, and he wasn't anywhere near his limit just yet.) He pushed those thoughts into parenthesis; he lived in a beautiful place. The sun had wiped the estuary surface clean with a metallic shine, and seawards, in the direction of the Bristol Channel; there was the white fluttering blaze of sun and reflecting water. The folly on the hill opposite was black and silhouetted in the spring light, the hill itself a flat shape. The aching song of waterbirds, of crakes – was it? – against the humming inland motorway was broken by a deeper whoop, whoop, whoop, and above, three swans, flying from the bird sanctuary over the top of the Strand's roofs and eastwards to the other bank of the estuary. They beat on, slowly; you could not see how they kept flying, so large and steady were their wing-beats.

On his morning constitutional, Kenyon tended to turn left these days, towards the Wolf Walk and the glimpse of the open sea. The other direction went towards the Fore street. Today was Friday, and one of his infrequent days off in Hanmouth. Somebody else would be looking after the AIDS orphans in Africa; somebody else would be fielding tricky enquiries from the technical press; somebody else could discuss the budget for 2010–11 with the man from the Treasury; somebody else would be wondering out loud how it was that when people borrowed a personal mug, they never had the good taste to wash it up and leave it where they'd found it. Kenyon didn't often have a day off. They worked out around one in seven – they were supposed to be more frequent, but things often arose at the last minute. But this week he had got away, and today was his day off.

He had put on his waxed cotton jacket and his absurd but treasured deerstalker – it had been a Christmas gift from Miranda two years ago with a set of Sherlock Holmes. Nobody had expected him to wear it, but it brought out something dashing and thoughtful in him, or so he thought, and he did wear it. The road was not perfectly straight, and the houses, painted an uncontrolled mixture of pastels, leant over the street picturesquely. It was still early enough for milk bottles to sit on the doorsteps – milk delivery would be the next thing to go, Kenyon reckoned, and everyone would soon be buying their milk from the supermarket, like everything else. In the early-morning sunshine, the windows of the little 1960s block in its own trim gardens shone and flashed. A figure, made dark by the sun behind it, was coming irresolutely towards Kenyon; it was doing that thing of looking up into the sky, inspecting gardens, examining its fingernails to put off the moment when it might reasonably be expected to recognize Kenyon as a neighbour and start the process, thirty yards off, of greeting him. It must be the Neighbourhood Watch man: it must be Calvin; his name was John.

'Hello, John,' Kenyon said. 'Lovely day.'

'Lovely,' Calvin said and, undecidedly, paused. 'I suppose you've heard about Heidi?'

Kenyon had not really been around, and had found the subject distasteful. He had not listened to people discussing it if he had found any means of cutting it short; he thought it village gossip, which had somehow got into the press. He would rather not think about it in any way. He did not know Calvin at all well; he had moved into a long, awkward house at the far end of the Strand two years before, a house that had sold and then lost its buyer three times. There was some legal provision about thoroughfare through the garden, which had only come to light late in the process, or so Kenyon believed. Finally Calvin had moved in, and had told everyone he had met in the first few weeks that they had snapped up the house for a bargain price before starting to talk about his Neighbourhood Watch group. He had a wife, Kenyon recalled; but Kenyon had only very occasionally met Calvin in circumstances like this one, and Calvin's wife, to his knowledge, only once in his life. He saw no reason why Heidi might not be the name of Calvin's wife.

'No,' Kenyon said. 'I hadn't heard. Nothing serious, I hope?'

'That depends,' Calvin said, 'that may very well depend, my

lord, on my lord's definition of serious. Yes, I would think it is a little bit serious. Deceived me. Deceived us all. Led us up the garden path. That's what I would say. She wasn't abducted at all. At least, the police don't think so. Never did, they intimated. Never believed a word any of us were saying. Listened carefully to what I was asking, and in their own minds, they always thought Heidi's little girl was somewhere safe and sound, in a hideaway well known to Heidi. A Heidi-way. Ha, ha, ha.'

Kenyon had more or less caught up at some point during this, and blushed, realizing the error he had been close to making. 'So the woman . . .' He left it hanging there, encouragingly.

'Yes,' John Calvin said. 'The police more or less told me they think Heidi and her friend cooked the whole thing up. Two of the other kids were seen meeting China here in Hanmouth a couple of days ago. The police don't think Heidi knew anything about that. They think the children somehow got in touch with China, or she got in touch with them – the elder girl's got a mobile phone, it seems. She turns up, and in the car of a man looking very much like Marcus McColl.'

Kenyon tried to look vague and interested.

'Marcus McColl – he's Ruth's brother. Ruth's Heidi's best friend. Was her sister-in-law. The police told me they think the little girl was handed over to her friend Ruth's brother right at the start. Never was an abduction. It was all to get some cash out of the public. Save China. I've got a T-shirt. Might be worth something as a collector's item. Yes, sir, this is a most interesting, ah, a fascinating unique artefact. Do you have any idea as to worth? I can see it now on the *Antiques Roadshow* in twenty years' time.'

'So where is she now?'

'The police went off first thing this morning to get China out of Marcus's house. Ruth told them the whole story, and Heidi confirmed bits of it in interview. She's going to be charged later today.'

'What an awful story.'

Calvin moved out of the sun, and Kenyon took a step sideways. With the glare out of his eyes, he could see not only the customary neat outline of Calvin's turn-out, his hair slicked back and his trim long grey overcoat an almost geometric neatness. He could see, too, now that he had moved out of the sun's glare, that Calvin's eyes were bagged and haunted, rimmed with red; how the loss of a man's self-worth could rob him of sleep. He could see that Calvin had taken a resolution to leave the house and tell everyone he met the whole story, to take charge of it before Hanmouth started putting it around in its own way. Kenyon could see the virtue of that. He wondered whether, on a normal day, Calvin would have found the time to speak to his neighbour Miranda's London-labouring husband, a man he had hardly met.

'The good thing is, I suppose,' Calvin finished, 'that while the police were still taking this seriously, or pretending to take it seriously, I got them to agree to some extra CCTV cameras in Hanmouth. After all, if there had been a few more, there might have been evidence of China meeting up with the other kids. As it is, there's nothing. So that's one good thing to have come out of the whole business.'

He looked upwards, as if to heaven. Kenyon followed his gaze. He had never noticed it before, but there, on the lamp-post just by Lord What-a-Waste's house, sat an oblong grey shoe-box with an eye on it, pointing downwards. It was a closed-circuit television camera. It was pointing directly at Kenyon and Calvin, having their morning conversation. Was that new? Kenyon tried to feel safer on its account.

'Must get on,' Calvin said.

'Sorry about that,' Kenyon said, uncertainly and unspecifically.

'The thing is,' Calvin said, 'the thing that makes me so furious – it's that . . . '

Kenyon waited.

'It doesn't matter,' Calvin said in the end. Kenyon knew what he was trying to say: that the provision of new CCTVs; the extra bobby on the beat; the ability to search your neighbours' upper rooms; the taking of fingerprints and DNA samples; the idea that if you had nothing to hide you had nothing to fear; all that could fall down if, after all, nobody had kidnapped fat little China. But it rested on something. Children were kidnapped every day by strangers. Two, three times a day. Surely they were. And the bobby on the beat, dropping in for a cosy chat and to take your blood with his blunt needle and your fingerprints with his John Bull printing set. Calvin and Neighbourhood Watch had achieved that now.

'I'd better fuck off, I suppose,' Calvin said.

30.

The unmarked van drew up in the Bristol street. The area had been long colonized by students, young professionals working in the media or small advertising agencies. The street had once been lived in mainly by new immigrants from the Caribbean, replacing old working-class couples; then they themselves had been replaced by students, then white academics from the university, then impoverished couples in the creative industries; and then finally, in two houses, children of those 1960s immigrants, working on the radio and on the local BBC Television station. Everyone said hello to those two households. They were the pride of the street.

The street had been done up in stages. Only one house remained untouched. No magazine recommendations had been implemented here. The garden did not have a path made out of the fragments of smashed plates; mirrors were not embedded in the wall of the garden. There were no monochromatic planting schemes in that front garden, and no ironic or amusing use of artificial grass, garden gnomes or other ornaments; nor did it contain unironic and unamusing abstract sculptures. The stucco front of the house was not painted a bold or pastel colour; in the window were no hanging artistic objects. No political slogan pasted in the window supported a cause or a party. Marcus McColl had lived here for thirty years, his whole life, apart from two years in inexplicable Hanmouth with Heidi. He had come back with his tail between his legs to his mother's house, and when she had died, he had gone on living here. In the window was a single macramé pot-holder, a dead spider-plant in it. The curtains were not drawn; a single table lamp within illuminated to the five a.m. street an interior of dust and unobserved waste.

The police had been here before, during the day; they had knocked, in pairs, and come in when invited; they had sat and talked to the owner of the house. Now they raised the latch on the garden gate, went up the garden path and, in a single gesture with a heavy ram, smashed the door in. There were eight of them. Over the road, a light came on in an upstairs room, and the husband of the creative director of an advertising agency looked out, winding the front bedroom curtain around his naked torso. Somewhere nearby a baby began to cry. The two police officers at the front – bulked up, visors over their faces, anonymous, insectile and glistening black – dropped the ram and shouted out. The door was hanging off its hinges, and the squad thudded in.

There was nothing downstairs; the light left burning in the front room had been there all night, it seemed. The kitchen door was shut, but unlocked. A cup and a glass stood on the draining-board, and two small plates. Everything was neat and clean, but – as the police who had been here before remembered noticing – nothing in the white Formica kitchen had been new for thirty years, perhaps forty. The oven still had an overhead gas grill; the brown tiles behind the work surfaces were brown and yellow reliefs in the style of the late 1960s. He had followed his mother's working habits, and nothing was stained or dirty, even behind the oven where grease often stayed. But he could not, or had not wanted to renovate anything.

Upstairs, the noise of police boots thundering, and nothing else – no cry of complaint or disturbance, no sound of a child. They left the kitchen and went up the stairs, more slowly. As

129

they came into the large front bedroom, one of their colleagues was kneeling and pulling at an addition to the double bed. Behind the purple floral nylon ruffled valance skirt falling to the floor, home-made planks of MDF had been fixed to each other, bounding in the under-bed area. The policeman pulled, and it came away, fixed only with a strip of velcro. He took off his helmet and visor, and, lying on the dustless carpet, peered into the dark underside. Someone handed him a torch; from thick-gloved hand to thick-gloved hand, it was an awkward business.

'She's not there,' he said, but reached in. He pulled out one, then two magazines; pink and bold, the lettering advertised free giveaways, a glitter-covered pen, a picture of a puppy-eyed band of boys.

'I wouldn't have thought that was left there by old mother McColl,' one said. Because, after all, this was Marcus's mother's bedroom; like the kitchen, it had hardly been touched from the way she had left it, the florid dadoed walls, the dressing-table with its back to the front window. The kidney-shaped dressing-table with its tripartite mirror must once have held her perfumes, her powders, her medicines towards the end of her life; now the glass top with lace pinned underneath it was terribly bare. Marcus McColl probably slept in here. What would a Marcus McColl place on a mahogany kidney-shaped dressing-table with three adjustable mirrors?

'It's this week's issue of the magazine,' another said. 'My daughter reads that. I saw it on our tea table only last night.' The policeman on his knees reached in again, and his gloved hand met a small bottle, and somewhere underneath, a resistance when it pulled away, which must be some sort of sticky texture on the carpet. 'This isn't his mother's, either,' he said, bringing out a confusion, a green facecloth mixed up with a bottle of pink nail varnish, its top lost, half the contents spilt down the side and half left on the carpet, by the feel of things.

'She must have knocked it over and tried to hide it,' someone said. 'Poor little girl. She must have been afraid of what he'd say if he found out.'

'They must have gone in a hurry,' another said. 'He hasn't made much of an effort to clear it.'

The police officer dropped first the magazine, then the facecloth, then the spilt and drying nail varnish into three large ziplock bags, held open by a visored and patient constable. 'We'll get something positive off of those, easy as pie,' he said, referring to fingerprints and DNA, bodily traces that could not but be left behind. There, in the little room, the six of them, and two standing solemnly on the landing, seemed like anonymous dignitaries, serving at some last alien rite. Only one police officer had removed his helmet and visor, and he stood at the back, his blond hair tousled, his cheeks red and glowing, not much more than a boy who had been admitted for the first time to these secret exchanges. 'I'd like to know,' he said finally, 'how it is that officers visited this house more than once, in the course of the inquiry, and failed to discover any of this.'

'There'll be a time for that,' said another, perhaps more senior, a shade gruffly.

As the first of the police officers went outside with the first of a morning-long series of bags, the radio of the driver, still sitting in the van, crackled into life. The street had been woken up, and now at a couple of doors neighbours stood barefoot or slippered, hugging their dressing-gowns around themselves. They were only generally interested in the spectacle of one of their neighbours being broken into by the police; they could not have made any connection with the Hanmouth kidnapping. In the next few hours, they would all be spoken to. Now, as the police officers came out with their offerings, silent and serious, not exchanging a word as they did their task, a spot or two of rain began to fall. Then, before anyone could remark that it had started to rain, the thin drizzle of a grey spring dawn.

31.

'I'm afraid that they seem to have gone,' Heidi was told, by an official source. In the windowless interview room, lit by fluorescent light, where she could not tell whether it was day or night or dawn or dusk, Heidi shook her head, and the noise from her mouth was that of an animal. Her solicitor sat by her, her pen and her notebook to hand, and waited for something she could write down.

32.

Sometimes Gordon Jordison saw his Friday-night outings for what they were, and felt disgusted with himself. He had never heard of it, or thought that it was possible until six or seven years before, when he had read about it in the *Guardian*. The newspaper had reported what it said was a new trend. Gordon had read the story half a dozen times from end to end, while the children were arguing over who got the plastic toy in the cereal box. Marion was talking on the cordless phone to her friend Anthea, walking backwards and forwards with a mug of coffee in her hand. It was a Saturday morning in their kitchen; everything was normal. Gordon was reading about people who went to car parks in quiet places, all over the country, and had sex on other people's car bonnets with other people's wives. It was called dogging.

They made arrangements on the Internet, it said, and Gordon had gone upstairs to his study after breakfast. He knew that the Internet was obsessed with sex, and had looked at some of it himself. It had seemed to him that the Internet was like a giant version of the *Playboys* of his own youth, and he had flicked through what pictures it had to offer in a bored, passive way. It had never occurred to him that people might make their own pornography, might exchange pictures, might use it to meet and give information. But in exactly five minutes he was staring at a website called southwestdogging.com. The Friday after, not that late in the evening, he was sitting in his car with the engine off in a lay-by off the A361, not quite believing what he was seeing.

He was a second-class citizen in the dogging world, he had no illusions about that. The four licentious wives were at the top of the tree – there were only four in the whole of Devon, Gordon believed. He had seen every one of the four fucked by dozens of men over the years. He wondered what astounding impact a fifth woman would make on the small dogging scene. Sometimes, a woman would appear in the passenger seat of a car; occasionally they would lock their doors and have sex for a wanking audience. Gordon was in the wanking audience, like them grossly over-weight, reaching underneath his gut for his willie, his trousers round his ankles. He was among the solitary men, at the bottom of the pile as far as dignity and worth went. The men who brought their wives, led them out to be fucked by one stranger after another, were in this world not ludicrous and pitiable cuckolds, but heroic and bold; they clearly looked down on the crowd wanking over the windscreen, jostling like dogs towards the spread-open woman.

There were half a dozen sites within fifty miles that Gordon knew of. They changed from time to time; southwestdogging.com was a public website, and suddenly they would discover that CCTV cameras had been put up at one lay-by or other. The website had a message board, and warnings would be posted. Or occasionally a new place would be suggested. This had happened a couple of days before. Fluffysdoggingqueen had posted to say that she'd had a fantastic time in a concealed thicket two miles up the B3227. At the time Gordon had wondered whether she really meant the B3227 – in his view, fluffysdoggingqueen was an idiot with badly dyed roots, terrible halitosis and at least three stone overweight. In the world of lay-bys and car parks she was a celebrity, a star. He wouldn't cross the road to see her buggered by an Irish builder on the bonnet of a BMW one more time.

He couldn't get away until it was virtually dark on the Friday, and by the time he got to the turn-off for the B3227, he was seriously thinking about turning round and calling it a day. Two miles up the road, a farmer's gate hung half open, and beyond it some trees loomed in the dark. Was that where fluffysdoggingqueen meant? He slowed the car. There seemed to be nobody there. It was just woodland and a field running down the hill. Just to make sure, he drove the Jaguar into the half-open gate, as if to turn round. His lights swept across the woodland and there, a couple of dozen yards in, was the outline of a car. There was nobody else on the road. Gordon parked on the roadside. Anyone coming along would recognize his car, he thought. They would take it as a signal. The numbers would grow.

The weather had been dry, and the ploughed field was rough going rather than muddy. There were a few car tracks cutting across the terrain; they seemed, however, a day or two old, and as he went towards what he had assumed was a dogger's car, he began to think it was an abandoned wreck, just dumped in the woodland. He might as well make sure of that, writing the evening off as a dead loss and cursing fluffysdoggingqueen and her lack of grasp of the names of B-roads.

He stumbled over a heavy rut, almost falling, and another. He put his hand out, and it met with an edge, sharp and rock-like. He raised himself, briskly, brushing his hands as if to demonstrate to an unseen audience that he had intended to fall. But there was nobody there to see. He was sure of that now. All the same, treading carefully, he went onwards towards the dark shape of the car. There was nobody in it, he could see that now. He turned, and stumbled; not on earth or grass, but on something soft; a piece of cloth. He bent to feel, and with a burst of disgust realized that he had set off in search of bare flesh, and had found it. His hand closed around a cold and rubbery hand. Even then, his thoughts were of the doggers, and one of them was what he thought for a moment he had come across. There was no reason for him to suppose that he had come across the body of Marcus

McColl, lying with a knife in his ribs, half hidden by the long grass at the edge of the woodland, his legs lying where they had been dragged, under the back end of his abandoned old Ford Escort. That was what Jordison had seen in the dark, and he was to spend some hours explaining to the police what, in an abandoned and unremarkable shape, had persuaded him off the B-road in the dark; and considerably longer to his unbelieving wife.

33.

'So you see,' a policewoman explained to Ruth McColl, 'we just don't know what your brother's plans were. For the sake of China's safety, you have to tell us, Ruth.'

'I've told you,' Ruth said. 'I've told you everything I know. I don't know any more than you do. And my brother's dead. Don't you think I care about that one?'

'I thought we were getting somewhere,' the policewoman said to her supervisor. 'But I honestly don't know where we go from here.'

'Mobile phone records didn't yield anything?'

'Marcus didn't have one. Hardly used the landline, either. We've no idea who he was in touch with.'

'Someone must have seen something.'

'She just seems to have disappeared.'

'Sometimes,' the supervisor said, 'you just draw a blank.'

34.

The tinies, in uniform casuals of tiny white polo shirts and tiny blue trousers, lined up on the railway platform. Each had a baseball cap on, advertising their father's or mother's company, or some recent family day out; the adults waiting for a train thought that when they were young the sun had not seemed to present so much of a threat, could not remember being required by school to wear a head-covering on a sunny May morning. 'Everyone line up behind your adult,' the head of the expedition called out, and the tinies regathered, some holding their best friend's hand. 'Has everyone got their sunscreen on?' the leader said, and a forest of hands went up. 'Now, while we're waiting for the train, let's have a survey,' she called. 'What have you got in your lunchboxes for a morning snack? Who's got an apple! Good. Who's got some other sort of fruit? Good. Who's got some dried fruit – what do I mean by dried fruit? Anyone? Yes – raisins, prunes, dried apricots, anything like that – yes, good. But I don't see everyone's hands going up. Has anyone not got a morning snack in their lunchbox? No? What has everyone else got? Let's have a survey.'

Around her, the subordinate adults, each with their group, cast a stiff surveying eye over the tinies. 'What was that, Chloë? A packet of crisps. Yes. Anyone else's parents think that a packet of crisps is a sort of fruit? Because we were supposed to bring a piece of fruit or vegetable for our mid-morning snack, weren't we? A pepperoni stick, Jacob? Well, no, a piece of fruit is really much better for us, isn't it? Stay behind your adult. Don't wander off, it's very dangerous on the railway platform.'

The other passengers, some quite close to middle age, thought of telling the headmistress what they had in their bags for lunch, or what they proposed to have for lunch: the cheese strings that were supposed to be for their kids' lunch tomorrow, the prospect of a pint and a pub burger, a spliff for the park.

And on the station platform, the train was late, the tinies showing signs of wandering off from their lines, each headed by a designated adult in charge. 'Let's have another survey,' the headmistress cried. 'What did everyone have for breakfast? Did anyone not have breakfast? Jacob? Did you have breakfast? What did you have for breakfast?' Jacob was overcome with shyness, and tried to hide behind his best friend Ben. Ben found himself conspicuous; tried to hide behind Jacob. They twisted about each other for a minute. Then, without appearing to make any decision or transition, they burst into a fight, punching each other's face and tugging at each other's little polo shirt. 'Jacob, Ben,' the headmistress said, separating them. 'It's very dangerous to mess about on a railway platform.' Around the group of children, the adults thought again of their past; what they had had for breakfast when they were as small as that. One thought of porridge; one thought of biscuits; one thought of a cold London suburb with fog outside, and a father coming down and rushing his cup of tea, running for the train. His mother at the sink, smiling in her pink housecoat and morning shock of ginger hair. That had been the advice in the late 1960s, a boiled egg, a piece of protein to start the day; and on the table there had been two soft-boiled eggs, one for him in a blue china egg-cup, one for his sister in a green egg-cup.

There was a hoot round the bend. In the morning sunshine, the train emerged from between two hedges. The passengers picked up their bags; the children took each other's hands, right in left and left in right.

FIRST IMPROMPTU

THE OMNISCIENT NARRATOR SPEAKS

Kenyon left his house at seventeen minutes past eight. The time was recorded by the observing camera on the gate to the boatyard opposite their house, the fat black wires running up to its single eye like black veins. It registered Kenyon, in – if it could see in colour – a blue suit, with a surprisingly yellowish raincoat in the crook of his elbow, leaving the house and shutting the door behind him. It saw him look about him, up into the sky, hesitate for a moment and then raise his umbrella, an old-fashioned non-folding object with a knotty wooden handle. From that, any future watcher of its record could deduce that the forecast for the west of England that morning, of light passing showers, was as accurate as the meteorological record, published the day after the meteorological events had taken place, would subsequently prove to be.

The boatyard camera was not the first mechanical record Kenyon had left that morning. While his bath had been running, he had checked his emails, gaining access at seven fourteen and logging off at seven twenty-two; he read six emails, three of which were from Australia and sent overnight, concerning a conference in Canberra Kenyon was to attend in January. These emails, and the replies Kenyon sent, were recorded remotely, in several buildings devoted to the communications industry, available should any government officer wish to read Kenyon's communications. Also registered remotely were the names of three websites Kenyon logged on to and read distractedly while his bath was running, one concerning the film appearances of Rita Hayworth, whom Kenyon had dreamt making a singular appearance in the film *The*

Sound of Music: Kenyon established to his satisfaction that Rita Hayworth, contrary to his vivid dream, had not played a nun in the film of the Rodgers and Hammerstein musical. After his bath, quickly observing that his wife was still asleep, he made a short call on his mobile telephone. He did so standing at the breakfast counter with a purple towel about his waist, and another, a blue one, draped over his shoulders. The telephone call began at seven fifty-three and ended ninety seconds later, at seven fifty-four. At seven fifty-six he phoned the same number and spoke more briefly, for only nine or ten seconds. The number, the times and the lengths of the calls were relayed to the computerized records of another communications company, to remain there until summoned by an official agency, deleted, or most plausibly Doomsday. Thereafter, no one registered the movements or actions of Kenyon until he left his house and was filmed by the boatyard camera. He had a cup of coffee.

The boatyard camera, installed in spring 2004 against the worry of vandalism, and still working without any problem, filmed Kenyon walking from left to right across its field of interest. Then he disappeared from public observation until he reached, five hundred yards towards the centre of town, the quay. In turn, he was recorded by the camera attached to the pub, which looked down on its own patrons; the camera on the bus-stop, panning across the car park; the camera fixed to the entrance of the antiques centre. He passed between their fields, a small figure in a blue suit with a yellowish raincoat in the crook of his arm. Some of the cameras only observed a black shining mushroom with ribs, the dome of the umbrella. Cross-referencing between cameras would have been necessary to establish the identity of the single figure, moving between cameras like an object passed from stranger to stranger. Other cameras, pointing outwards from jewellers' shops, filmed him passing, recorded and deposited in unknown vaults, to be watched by who knew who. Other cameras merely looked plausible, but had never filmed anyone or anything, were only empty boxes, deterrents, placebos.

Kenyon stopped at the cashpoint machine belonging to the HSBC bank at the end of the Fore street, a square metal box let into the wall of a white eighteenth-century customs house, the windows discreetly strengthened against robbery or filled in with brick and plaster. The bank's records would have shown that at eight twenty-eight a.m., Kenyon took out a hundred pounds in cash, leaving him with a debit balance of £4,524.20 A curious investigator, from the bank, from a central public authority, from the sort of agencies that investigated and propagated the credit-worthy qualities of individuals to anyone who subscribed to their database, or simply some hacker who for curiosity's sake or in hope of robbery and fraud had investigated Kenyon's finances – any of these people would have discovered that his agreed overdraft facility was £5,000, that in three days his salary would be paid into his account, reducing the overdraft but not quite erasing it, and that he also owed £7,477.98 on his one credit card. They would not have discovered, either the investigators or the cameras under whose gaze Kenyon fell that morning, the fit of panic and worry that came over him when he fed his card into the machine, knowing that his bank balance was around the £5,000 limit, not knowing exactly whether it had breached the line.

It would, however, record for the benefit of anyone who was able to breach the bank's security protocols that the next person to take any money out was the sixteen-year-old Anna McLeod, staying with her grandparents, who took out twenty pounds at nine nineteen, an unusually long gap between users at this hour in the morning. It would be only the fourth time Anna McLeod had used a cashpoint machine on her own behalf – her mother had trusted her with her own card once or twice, but not a third time. Anna McLeod would use it with a sense of excitement and exuberance, and not at all with the sense that it was her own money that she was removing from its resting place with no particular objective or need. The machines and lenses of record registered all of this, and would come to register more about Anna McLeod. Before the year was out – on the last day of the year, in fact, heading away from a party in Exmouth in the passenger seat of an erratically driven old Fiat – the then seventeen-year-old Anna McLeod would be discovered by police to be in possession of two illegal pills, and the building blocks of her body and mind, her blood and skin and hair, the particular configuration of deoxyribonucleic acid, which resulted from the confluence of Marianne McLeod and (unknown to anyone at all, buried in that configuration of deoxyribonucleic acid) Marianne McLeod's boss Stewart at the Vehicle Licensing Centre where she had worked for six months in 1993 and not Marianne's Scotch-accountant husband Mungo at all, that DNA which had made an Anna McLeod out of the conjunction of an egg and a stranger's sperm in 1993 would be stored for ever more in a file, on a computer, in a database, to be drawn up and rifled through in future by bored forensic policemen whenever any kind of crime had been committed, anywhere in the country.

Kenyon took the money, which he now considered his, and walked down the Fore street. He had never come into contact with the police; had never been suspected of any crime, whether justly or unjustly. So no one had his DNA, apart from Kenyon himself, and Hettie, of course. His appearance, on the other hand, was registered on the police cameras outside the post office, the ones outside the community centre, which were trained on the statue of the Crapping Juvenile and only caught his legs from the knee down. Private security cameras outside three pubs, in the windows of the hedge-fund trader's one-man abstract art emporium, in another jeweller's shop and a souvenir shop captured Kenyon, his tense face and drawn-in, rapid walk. Perhaps the observers who followed his stride from the record on this succession of cameras might have observed the figures counting the time at the bottom of the film, might have wondered about the irregular service of the train from Hanmouth. Such an observer would have realized that at the last of the cameras, outside the Three Ferrets, Kenyon had been caught three minutes before the Bideford train left the station, with two hundred yards to run.

As the ticket machine at the station was refusing to accept bank notes or coins, it recorded Kenyon putting his bank card into the slot and pressing his four-digit code. The camera above the machine and, more remotely, the cameras positioned at either end of both platforms would have recorded the same events, though with less detail. The machine, and the database behind it, would have recorded the same user, the same bank card, the same numbers being used to acquire a train ticket every Monday morning for several years. It was unusual, however, for the ticket to be bought on a Monday morning, and the machines would have known that Kenyon was not buying a ticket this morning for his usual destination, London. His bank account, in addition to the one hundred pounds already debited this morning, was now debited a further £2.30 only. This information was stored, too, against an eventual retrieval by the authorities or those who concerned themselves with such matters.

The train that now arrived was observed by a series of cameras, but they did not observe what Kenyon saw: the bluish morning light, the veiled quality of the hills across the estuary; the sight of a large gull lodged diagonally on the wind like a back-slash, veering into the train's direction, veering off again with a call like a harsh but happy yell; a sudden and brief shadowing of the light as a single cloud fell over the early sun; the silent moon like a fingernail in the sky; a dog racing against the train in its back garden, and barking in joy as it ran. At most, shadows on the film and the digital flow, not seen at all by the mechanical recording angels along our paths, seen only by Kenyon. The cameras watched him as he got out at the central station, not mounting the London train now waiting at platform five but leaving the station instead; watched him climb the hill to the bus station; watched him wait and mount the Harvesthaye bus, paying, however, by cash (a little detective work would be needed here to go on following Kenyon's tracks); watched the bus heave itself up the hill by the hospital and, a dozen times, past some building in need of protection or observation, and then another dozen times.

By chance, the stop that he got off at was opposite a bank, and the house that he walked to, three minutes away, just past a school with two great lenses at its gates. So his progress was remarked. He had been filmed or his actions recorded fifty times between getting up and nine thirty, when he got to the place he was getting to. The remote and patiently employed angels could have discovered that he had told his employers over the phone that he was ill, that he had phoned a man who lived seven miles away, once, and that that man owned the house he now found himself at the door of, that he had got out money and would not for another couple of days: money, it could be deduced, to keep him and the man in takeaway pizza for a day or two. But they could not have told, because the door was out of sight, with what delight and happiness the man, whose name was Ahmed Khalil, as the authorities could have discovered, opened the door to Kenyon, the way in which, the door closed behind them, they fell on each other, feeding on each other with a fury concentrated in the mouth and lips, their hands on each other, roaming and gripping as Kenyon's clothes were pulled off and fell to the floor, his lover's bathrobe falling open as Kenyon went to his knees. Could not know, either, how both of them, in middle age, felt once again, for the ninth time, a rejuvenation in their lust, the sense of the teenage. The cameras in the street could not have told the secrets of the human heart; they could not and did not see Kenyon and Ahmed, meeting for the ninth time in this way. But you did, and I did.

BOOK TWO
THE KING OF
THE BADGERS

The King of the Badgers is one of Uncle's best
friends and neighbours, but he was away
arranging a loan from a foreign banker.

J.P. MARTIN, *Uncle Cleans Up*

1.

There was a spume of hurt up his innards. The dwarves with their miniature flame-thrower had been at their small-hours labour. David woke with a runnel of liquid, burning puke at the back of his throat, now actually spurting up into his mouth. He was upright already in his bed, knowing quite well that there was no heartburn medicine in the house. If there had been, he would have taken two large dessertspoonfuls, after the evening's solitary entertainment: most of a roast chicken, mashed potatoes and peas, half a sticky toffee pudding with cream, God knew how many thyme-flavoured biscuits with the Borough Market Caerphilly on top, fetched in batches from the kitchen during the commercial breaks and eaten during the entertainment. And a bottle of white wine on top of two gin-and-tonics. You deserve it, he had said to himself last night, when setting out on the first of two gin-and-tonic, thinking of the bloody horrible day he'd had, the bloody horrible week he'd had, the bloody horrible life he had. You deserve it, he said to himself now, in the dark, sweating, a burning trickle of watery vomit subsiding slowly back down his throat and his heart banging like a broken dynamo. Was that a tightening around his chest – the iron band that foreshadowed a heart attack? He sat quite still, his attention all on the uncontrollable revolts of his body, and in a few moments his hypochondria quietened itself, too.

He reached for his watch on the bedside table. His vision, or perhaps just his eyes, wobbled a little before managing to focus on the green luminous dials. It was ten to eight. He had managed, after all, to sleep through the night before the heartburn had woken him; he had not had to get up to pee. A bonus, he supposed. 'You never go through the night after the age of thirty-five,' David's friend Richard was fond of saying – it was almost his only principle in life. David himself was thirty-six. He hadn't gone through the night, as Richard called it, in ten years. He put this unusual extended unconsciousness down to the drink.

In a moment, he forced himself out of bed, wrapped his bulk in the blue cotton *yukata*. He looked around for the sash – it could be more or less anywhere in the chaos of the flat, and in the end he gripped the dressing-gown closed at the front. He shuffled through the flat, kicking aside some bit of food packaging on the floor of the kitchen where he had dropped it the night before and done nothing about it. He had not felt drunk when he went to bed, but oddly enough he felt quite drunk now. It was just tiredness. He would be fine to drive into London this morning. He gave the tap a good twist, and the water began to pour. A cup of coffee and he would be perfectly all right for the long drive down to Devon. Mauro was expecting to be picked up at nine thirty from his flat in Clapham; David didn't suppose he would make that now, but Mauro could wait.

David turned off the mixer tap and lowered himself into the bath. Outside, overhead, there was the heavy clatter of a police helicopter. More and more often, on a Friday or a Saturday night, you were woken by the police helicopter hovering over St Albans, observing some fleeing villain and a bag of weed in a stolen car with their infra-red and their ultra-violet or whatever. The villainy and the small-hours helicopter had been two of the main reasons David's parents had moved to their remote Devon village the year before. David supposed it was the same anywhere – sirens, helicopters, stolen cars, noise and chaos. He had never before heard the police helicopter at breakfast time on a Saturday morning. At that moment, it occurred to him that it was inexplicably dark outside.

He finished washing himself with the lavender soap, plunging and huffing and nose-clearing in the tub, like an oily walrus; he washed his hair with the last of the orange-flower shampoo, wetting his head by sliding backwards and putting his hair under water, rinsing the foam off in the same way. There was no clock in the bathroom, and the kitchen clock above the stove, under a thick single eyebrow of deposited grease, had needed its battery changed for at least seven months. It was really very dark for eight o'clock at this time of year; David assembled the facts laboriously, and started to wonder. He wrapped himself in a towel, and went back through the pitch-dark kitchen to his bedroom. He turned on the bedside light, observing the chaos of his sheets and duvet, and picked up his watch. It was a quarter to two in the morning. Somehow, he had picked up and read his watch upside down, and had mistaken – what? – he worked it out: ten to eight for twenty past one.

That was a new addition to the fears of the night, to add to heartburn, insomnia, three a.m. terrors of loneliness, impoverishment, hell and damnation and the so-far-evaded attentions of the authorities for some negligence or other. And the promise of dying in your sleep from being so fucking fat; that was a good one. To all those, he could add the strong possibility that, from now onwards, he might at any time wake up, mistake the time, wash and dress and probably even leave the house under the impression that the watch went that way up. No wonder he felt mildly drunk and confused; he had gone to bed only an hour and a quarter before. Normal people like Mauro were asleep now; normal people like Mauro, with his bright smile and his dark eyes and his shaved chest, sharp with stubble under an exploring hand, were at this moment being licked all over, were enjoying the best sex of their lives, the sex that had happened with any number of successful pick-ups already that week. That was probably what normal people like Mauro were doing at this hour of the morning. The thought kept David staring into the dark, long after he had turned his bedside light off. He couldn't imagine why he had asked Mauro to come with him to visit his parents and pretend to be his new boyfriend.

2.

David had met Mauro only eight months before. Three couples that David knew, knew of, or worked with had separately announced that they were going to be taking advantage of the new legislation and getting married. 'It's only a very small affair, though,' all three of them had apologetically stated to David before not inviting him. Whenever David heard of an engagement or a marriage of this sort, he was plunged into some gloom. Previously, gay life had seemed a merry series of cabinet reshuffles and rearrangements, in which everyone was single for a time, then paired off for a time. If you stood still with a welcoming smile on your face, sooner or later somebody would come over and sit on it.

The introduction of marriages for men to men and women to women rather blew a hole in David's theory. He could not go on thinking that the paired-off couples he knew were in the middle of an interlude between inevitable periods of singleness. He had assumed that any relationship was thought of by those involved as one in an indefinite series, highly provisional. Largely believing this because he tried to think that, sooner or later, his gay acquaintances would decide to resort to him as a partner, once they had run out of most other possibles, David was astonished to discover that these people, in fact, did believe that the relationship they were in was a permanent one. The regular exchanges and alterations of his friends in their twenties gave way to an immured bliss. David never saw them any more; they had just disappeared behind the garden gate and the Heal's catalogue.

It had been two years since he had gone away on holiday with anyone else, and that had been with his mother. (She had always wanted to go to Venice, and they did, while she could still get around on foot, she said; the pair of them had, in one church after another, bumped into each other with mirrors held like tea-trays, inspecting the ceiling frescos, and murmured a polite, solicitous apology. Anyone would have taken them for wife and fat husband.) It had been a year since he had had sex with another man, and the time before that had been in 2005. Both had been rent-boys, taken from an online catalogue, considered over the course of days, telephoned from St Albans and then visited in their flats in Earls Court and King's Cross. Neither occasion had been a success. The second time, no part of David's body, however minutely scrutinized, could, it seemed, raise an erection in the professional, and the rent-boy had closed his eyes and perhaps tried to think of some more encouraging flesh, without success in raising a response in his own. David had tried to be polite, then supportive, then sympathetic, then slightly catty. 'It's not me,' the rent-boy had said. 'Though I'm not a machine, you know. It's you. I can't do anything with someone as fat as you.' David had taken the rebuke humbly, got dressed, handed over the money anyway and returned to the railway station to go home with the absolutely usual thoughts in his head.

'Well, of course you're not going to find anyone sitting up there in St Albans,' his friend Richard had said, when David told him some, at least, of this. 'Your parents don't live there any more. The only people you know there are people you were at school with.'

'And the bloke in the off-licence,' said David, who was always keen to forestall accurate commentary about the defects of his life.

'Yes, I thought that might be so,' Richard said. 'We all drink too much. Our parents never did – well, they do now, they drink like fish, but they never did when they were our age. What is it with us and our best friends who are the bloke in the off-licence?'

'I don't know,' David said impatiently, thinking that the point of the conversation was getting lost in conjecture about the state of modern existence. 'I'm not going to start a relationship with the bloke in the off-licence, in any case.'

'You need to start making an effort,' Richard said. 'There's a thing called the gay scene nowadays. It happens in large cities –

153

London, Manchester, er, wherever. Did you ever hear of the St Albans gay village? There are bars, there are nightclubs, boys so off their faces they'd even go to bed with a fat slob like you.'

'Thanks.'

'A pleasure. You never know, you might meet someone who likes you for who you are. It does seem unlikely, though.'

'You could put me in front of five hundred drunk gays, and I still wouldn't know how to start a conversation with any of them,' David said. 'I just don't know how. I don't know how I ever got to meet anyone, really.'

'Well, I know how you start up conversation in a nightclub,' Richard said. 'Take in a bottle of poppers, sniff it from time to time. You'll be amazed how popular you get to be.'

'I can't bear that stuff,' David said.

'Everyone always says that,' Richard said. 'You'd be amazed, the boys who fancy a quick sniff off a fat man with a little brown bottle when it gets to three in the morning. Take my advice, seriously.'

'I've got to get back to work,' David said, because they were talking over the telephone in the middle of the day, Richard in his office and David at his desk. David's colleague-cum-boss Dymphna had been walking up and down from time to time in the carpeted aisle, not exactly looking in his direction, but walking up and down and looking at him. As if she hadn't overheard the whole conversation in this little office with just the two of them, and as if she were trying to behave like his boss.

Richard lived in London; he was a graphic designer. David admired the way he had somehow parlayed a degree in French into a career in a white office with great white desks like icebergs, swimming through a space converted from a Methodist church. He had, like David, apparently forgotten all the French he had ever known. In his dark suit and white shirt, his pepper-and-salt hair cropped tight around a tidy face, he was very different from the public schoolboy with the military delivery who had broken through his own reserve, telling David about his impossible sexual

154

desires one night seventeen years before, in a room high up in a Reading fifteen-floor hall of residence. He was very different, apart from in one feature. Then he had, when it had come to it, refused to practise his sexual nature on David, even at four in the morning when drunk. David didn't even need to ask; he certainly would refuse now.

Richard lived in Parsons Green, in a flat repainted white every other year, its furniture reconsidered every five, a new Brazilian installed every thirty-six months. He moved from one to another breathlessly, like the unwrapping prize in a game of Brazilian pass-the-parcel. The process occurred without any apparent interval of jealousy or despair. David had no idea how he had managed to stay friends with such a prodigy, such a prize, such a catch, and Richard's friends, when occasionally, unavoidably encountered, gave the impression of thinking much the same thing. David, on the other hand, had gone back to the town he had grown up in after going to university in Reading. He had stayed there ever since, wanking mostly.

'Come and stay,' Richard said. 'You can't get back to St Albans on a Saturday night. Go out and get off your face, see what happens. You might not even need to stay with me. You'll probably get a better offer.'

'That's bad luck,' Richard said, some days later, when David suggested a date. 'Rodrigo' – the current thunderously brooding Carioca – 'he's had a date in the diary for months now. His best friend's birthday party. No getting out of it, I'm afraid. We've had to reschedule it three times now.'

'Well, what about the week after?' David said, thinking that Richard's boyfriend's friend's birthday party could hardly be both in the diary for months and three times rearranged.

'Even worse, I'm afraid. Four graphic designers and their Australian accountant boyfriends coming for dinner to inspect Rodrigo. What is it with Australian accountants? People go on about air stewards and hairdressers. In Australia it's accountants, apparently. Wouldn't inflict that one on you. No, the best thing is we cut our losses, you come that Saturday night, we'll have a jolly early-evening drink, send you on your way, we'll regroup and dissect and have the post-mortem over lunch on Sunday, just you and me, and Bob's your uncle.'

'And Fanny's your aunt,' David said aimlessly. He had known how it was to be.

He went to London anyway. The Brazilian – Rodrigo – got up wearily, lazily in the L-shaped sitting room, not putting away the remote control or switching off the Grand Prix on the television, only turning down the sound to a bluebottle whine. 'Hello, I am Rodrigo,' he said, putting out his hand – the side of his hand when gripped in a handshake was surprisingly calloused for a lawyer, if he was a lawyer, as Richard had claimed.

'Hello, I am David,' David said satirically, attempting to find something unerotic in Rodrigo's appearance, barefoot and bare-chested in a pair of jeans, his grip like a lumberjack's, and not succeeding; and, anyway, he had actually met Rodrigo twice before. With a look from Richard, Rodrigo took himself off, reappearing only ten minutes before they went out. Neither of them had dressed for a party, or was taking anything with him – a present, a bottle, a bunch of flowers. As they went out, Rodrigo and Richard in well-worn athletic hooded tops, David in his newly bought disco gear, David strongly suspected the pair of them of going out to see *I Am Legend* at the Fulham Road Odeon. In the meantime, every new topic of conversation Richard had introduced had begun with the words 'Do you remember?' It was shameful to be so impossible to introduce; David wondered what he could possibly bring to the nightclub that someone else would want to take away again, and for a moment he thought of going in all his finery to see *I Am Legend* himself. Perhaps not that: perhaps *P.S. I Love You*, the other film he quite wanted to see at the moment.

He paid his money at the cash register in the black-painted hole at the entrance to the Vauxhall club. Sitting there was a thin blonde, who drawled, 'Thanks, darling,' as she rubber-stamped the back of his wrist. He was wearing an old and comfortable pair of black boots, but everything else was new: a pair of white jeans, a black shirt, a silver chain. It was disco, it was even a little bit cheesy, but most of all it was rather slimming. He had told Richard that he was heading to Soho to do the bars, going out at the same time as them. He had, but had sat in a coffee bar reading a book. He didn't want to get drunk. Then he had gone to a sex shop and bought a bottle of poppers, as suggested by Richard. Richard knew what he was talking about.

3.

But the nightclub was more or less empty. Of course, it was early still. The crowd would be gathering for a final drink or two in Soho's bars, lying about in elegant flats like Richard's, having a snort or two of cocaine, of ketamine, of whatever it was that they snorted. They would come after midnight, probably after one. He bought a drink and took it to a dark corner with a view of the entrance to the dance floor, which shook and echoed to the music. On the empty floor one man danced and twisted, his clothes eccentric, ill-assorted and miscellaneously frayed, like a farmer's, his style erratic and uncontrolled. David watched him dance; as people came in, in twos and threes, rushing almost towards the floor, then halting like birds on a wire, inspecting the man who had taken charge of their dance floor, drawing back, holding their hands to their faces, speaking behind them discreetly though no one could have overheard them. Over the dance floor, at one end, a turret with the lit DJ in it; at the other a glass-fronted balcony, the VIP room.

The floor was not extensive, but David knew from his small experience that it would be big enough once filled. It seemed, however, unlikely ever to be filled. After half an hour, the wild-eyed and rustic dancer was still alone on the floor; around the edge, men were clustering, holding their drinks up to their mouths with both hands, giggling and pointing. To join this man on the dance floor, to be the second one there, was to admit yourself into his company, and no one, obviously, wanted to do that. The second man on the dance floor would, hours from now, be going home on his own. Little outbreaks of jive and bop were happening where they were standing, but it was nearly half past twelve when a man, an unmistakable star of this place, walked on and began to groove his hips; then another, then two more, then a whole group. The spell was broken, and the night began.

It took David another hour to join in: he wanted his presence to be diluted almost to the unnoticeable, and he wanted to slip into the company of a hundred men rather than twenty. He had once seen himself at a nightclub in a mirror, dancing; it had felt to him as if he were doing much what most of the other men were doing, but the horrifying glimpse of the bear-like wobble in the mirror permanently removed any illusion about that. He stepped from foot to foot now, smiling brightly, and actually someone smiled back, making room for him. This was not so bad.

Whether you could actually meet someone in these circumstances, however, he could not say. Once here, the limit of his ambition was to have something to tell Richard about in the morning. Thoughts of Richard reminded him of the hard little nubbins tucked into his waistband; he took the small bottle out and, with a certain amount of fumbling, unscrewed the top. He raised it to one nostril, then the other, then the first; dizziness and a sick feeling was all it produced, and he put it back into his waistband wondering only how long he needed to stay.

'I love, love, love poppers,' a voice was saying, in his ear. 'Can I have a sniff off of your poppers?'

It was a small, neat, and very handsome man, dark eyebrows over dark, amused eyes; he had no top on, and he was muscular without being absurdly big. His chest had been shaved at some point, and David had a great urge to run his hands over the rough surface, to feel the texture of rough and smooth. Instead, he handed over the small bottle, and the man undid it, his eyes still on David, snorted once, twice, three times, screwed it up, popped it back in David's waistband and, amazingly gave him a peck on the cheek.

That was Mauro.

'Seems to have worked, then,' Richard said the next day, over two plates of fish pie in the neighbourhood Sloaney pub, all brass and wood and glass. They were overlooking the little common at Parsons Green, the green that had once belonged to a parson, presumably. David was dodging his own reflection in the mirrors about the public bar; it was more frightening than usual. Richard looked offensively healthy, the appearance of someone who went to bed by one without drinking and got up to have a Sunday-morning run. David was not going to ask him how the film had been.

'It sort of worked,' David said cautiously. If it hadn't worked, why would he have rolled up at nine in the morning, grinning, before giving Richard at the breakfast table a wave and staggering off into the spare room?

'Well? Did you get his name? Was it worth it? Was it fantastic?'

David gathered himself. There was the taxi back, with Mauro and his friend – what was the friend called? There was the fumbling through bags and pockets for the key on the pavement of Clapham High Street, and finally through the door between shops – Mauro lived, it seemed, above a tanning salon. There had been the production of a wrap of paper, and David had accepted one line of drugs after another, feeling that sex might be at the end of this. The friend, worse for wear than either David or Mauro, had first stopped making sense, then stopped moving, then turned his head into the sofa, a cushion over his head, and started snoring.

David and Mauro looked at each other; God knew what nonsense they had been talking in the hours before. Mauro got up. 'Don't mind me,' he said, and went into the bedroom next door. 'I've not seen you there before,' he began. 'I go there with

159

Susie. I work with Susie – did you see her? She was the girl wearing the green dress – she's tall. She wants to be lesbian. Silly bitch.' He went on chatting inconsequentially, popping in and out of the bedroom. Each time he came out, he had taken off some item of clothing; David, lying on the sofa, watched with pleasure as the small dark man came out, shirtless, shoeless, sockless, trouserless, artlessly chatting. At the end, he stood there in his clean white underpants, smiling, kind and thoughtful as a charity worker. Mauro raised his right arm above his head and pulled it over and down with his left fist. Naked, his lovely flourish of hair at the armpit like a bouquet, he yawned, scratched, turned his head from side to side and smiled in a watery way, not exactly at David. 'It's been gorgeous,' he said. 'Phone me some time.'

It took David a moment, but finally he was up on his feet, saying thank-you-for-having-me, and confusedly embracing Mauro. 'Thank you, Mr Poppers,' Mauro said. 'You could take my number, if you wanted.'

'You know,' David said to Richard, in the pub in Parsons Green. 'Yes, it really was. It was fantastic. I honestly didn't have much in the way of hopes, and—'

'That's always the way it is,' Richard said. 'Are you going to see him again?'

David considered. In the answer, there lay so many innocent deceptions. There lay, too, the opportunity to suggest to Richard, and to how many other people, that he, David, was a real person; that there was no reason why he should not have a boyfriend, though he never had; that there was no reason why a beautiful, charming Italian called Mauro, who was a vision in his underpants, standing in a doorway at eight in the morning, could not elevate David's dignity by choosing him to take to his bed. Of course, he had not done so, and would not do so. But with Mauro by his side, even just the once, if that could be contrived, they would look at him in a different light. They certainly would. And, after all, he was a real person.

'He gave me his phone number,' David said. 'So I guess I am going to see him again.'

'What an awful bore,' Richard said admiringly.

4.

When David's parents had told him that they were planning to move from St Albans, he initially didn't take them at all seriously. He had got into the habit of going round there once a week. His father had retired three years ago, with a small party for a few friends, neighbours and colleagues. Since then, David's unadventurous failure to go beyond the town he had grown up in had taken on the dimensions of a moral decision. While his father was working, their relationship must have looked like one of dependency, an unwillingness by David to venture too far into the outside world. After his father's retirement, the dependency didn't exactly reverse overnight, as if at the flick of a switch; rather, it seemed to David as if the long inward tide of dependency had reached its neap point at some parent/infant equinox, and from this point, it would begin slowly to retreat, at first hardly marking a change in David's life.

His parents lived in a neat brick detached house. Its blue front door was shaded by a porch with Swiss-style filigree wood effects. Around the porch in summer, honeysuckle bloomed, and sent its perfume into the dark little dining room at the front of the house. For David, the bashing out of a Clementi sonatina could always bring up the scent of honeysuckle; it was the scent of sitting inside, bored, at sixteen or eighteen, waiting for exam results and knowing that your future had now been decided, thinking of men seven times a minute. When he was small, the porch of his house had seemed extraordinarily pretty, like no other house in the road, like a house otherwise seen in pictures or on a jigsaw. In the same way, his mother, when dressed up to go out in silk scarf and pie-crust collar, had always seemed the prettiest of the mothers, and the nicest, quite different from anyone else's. When she sang in a crowd of singers, at a Christmas carol service or concert, or the ringing metallic song of her shoes approaching in a school or hospital corridor, her noise seemed utterly distinguished, lovely, and quite unlike anyone else's. David thought he was incredibly lucky and set apart until quite late in his adolescence.

The party was held in the church hall in his parents' road. They were called community centres nowadays. Perhaps they – his parents – might really have held the party in their own home. But they were nervous, even of their own friends. Things got knocked over; people, even with the best intentions, took a drink or two and leant on a table that wasn't meant to be leant on. So they had it in the community centre. It was not the most atmospheric place. The three of them went round earlier in the evening turning lights off here and there, trying to get anything resembling an atmosphere, but all they could achieve was a blue fluorescent glow in opposite corners and the rest plunged in gloom. And when the guests had arrived, as many as could be expected, it was seen that neither of his parents had really known how many people would be needed to fill even a medium-sized community centre. All the concern of the previous weeks, all the thinking of how to trim the guest list down to manageable proportions, proved in the event not necessary. The nicely dressed guests moved around in small groups, unbridgeably, resembling learning swimmers nervously forming islands in the shallow end. David was the youngest guest by a long way; his mother had asked him to feel free to bring someone if he would like, they would be very happy, whoever it was. But there was no one.

'We don't know what we'd do without David,' his mother said. She was talking to the minister's wife; whether in reality or just because of the peculiar and unsuccessful attempt at atmospheric lighting, both of them appeared to be dressed in almost the exact shade of turquoise. Neither seemed to have noticed this and, in fact, David's mother's dress had a best-dress, just-bought aspect, which the minister's wife, Philippa – wasn't it? – wasn't emulating.

'David's your son, isn't he?' Philippa was saying; her plump, attractive face held the generous and interested expression that was probably a prerequisite for the job. Or perhaps she was just generous and interested by nature.

Catherine made a birdlike, darting gesture, seizing David by his sleeve as he was passing. 'You've met our son?' she said.

'I'm not sure that I have,' Philippa said.

'I don't know what we would do without him,' Catherine said. 'We're so lucky to have him near us. We really depend on him.'

Philippa smiled, and with a small shock, David realized how it was to be from now on. For some years, his mother had been saying exactly this thing, that she had no idea what they would do without him, and while his father had been working, it had been clear to everyone what the intention behind the sentiment was. The son, clinging to his mother's girdle-straps, unable to venture more than a mile from his mummy's home, might look like the heavily dependent one; these sentiments attempted to cover it up by reversing the situation. But with the retirement of his father, what his mother had said was starting to become true. Not now; not tomorrow; but in years to come, they would depend on him, and when his mother said such a thing at his father's retirement party, the wives of Methodist ministers seemed to think that it might have some truth in it.

'May I refresh your glass, Philippa?' David said.

'Well, that's very nice of you,' Philippa said, and David felt like an adult, talking to adults.

5.

It was unsatisfactory, of course it was. But David believed that his having chosen to live in his flat, one of six in a converted Victorian house just behind the cathedral close and less than a mile from the Swiss-filigreed porch and the parental villa, looked to the outside world not like a sad capitulation to inevitability of a fat and fearful would-be cocksucker, but the decision of a man who knew his duties in life. Whether with self-loathing or with a sense of having got away with it in the eyes of the general public, David could see his awful job, his undistinguished flat, his decision to live in this location rather than do what everyone else did and leave home and its influences would continue more or less until one of them dropped dead.

He had thought nothing of it when his mother and father said they wouldn't be having Saturday lunch with him as usual; they were paying a visit over the weekend to his father's old secretary. He had no memory of this secretary; he had never really listened to much his father said about his workplace. These days, in fact, when he went round for his Saturday lunch, he let his father have his *Grandstand*, or whatever it was called these days, and sat with him in companionable silence. Conversation would only break out when his mother came in, fetching tureens or ladles – she liked to make a proper lunch out of it, often taking the opportunity of his regular but occasional visits to experiment with cooking, something which, during the week, his father would never permit with a good grace.

'Don't forget,' his mother said, standing in the doorway with his father's apron on – it was an ancient laminated apron showing a stripper's body with real tassels at the nipples, supposed to be for men at barbecues, and funny, but appropriated by either of them when cooking needed doing, and on his mother not funny or supposed to be, but a mournful reminder of age. 'Don't forget we're not here next weekend.'

'Why? Where are you going?'

'I thought your dad had told you – we're off for a weekend in Devon. Didn't you tell him, Alec? I thought I heard you telling him.'

'I told him,' Alec said. 'Are you watching this?'

David didn't see for a moment that his father was talking to him. He took his eyes off the television – he hadn't realized he was watching it at all, let alone with the degree of randy absorption that he was devoting to it. It was a segment about men's gymnastics, and David blushed. 'No,' he said. 'I thought we had the sport on for you.'

'Load of rubbish,' Alec said. 'Catherine – I meant to ask – if we're going down on Thursday, have you got anyone to cover your Friday-morning shift at the cathedral?'

'It's all arranged,' his mother said, talking of her volunteering commitment at the cathedral's charity gift shop.

David's regular week was thrown out of kilter by his parents going down to stay with his father's old workmate and her husband in Devon, in a town called Cockering. He didn't quite like it. He often groaned about his Saturday lunches, giving his parents some advice about this and that, asking them politely about their small-scale retirement activities and the awful friends they had seen. But, in fact, he had sometimes had to stop himself from walking the half-mile or so to their house on nights during the week. It wasn't loneliness, or an inability to cook, or really love for his parents. It was usually not being able to stand the sight of the chaos of his flat, and thinking with real longing of his parents' clean and warm house, just enough things in it, not too many, not too bleakly empty; nothing on the floor, and the laundry basket never more than half full before being emptied and dealt with, rather than, for instance, spilling its contents up the bathroom passage, across the kitchen, even across the hallway, into the sitting room and the bedroom. It was always like that in David's flat; it had long ago reached the point where he couldn't envisage asking a cleaner to come in to deal with it, and had not asked anyone, even his parents, to visit for some years. You could always drop in at his parents' house, though he did not; and so he missed them that Saturday.

They'd had a nice time, she said. What had they done? Oh, talking about old times, and they went to the pub. Yes, they'd really had a nice time. It was so pretty down there – picture-postcard pretty. But very sleepy, and the Devon people, they

165

seemed a little slow. Something guarded, something reticent in her tone struck David over the telephone line, and he wondered about their weekend. 'She's very nice,' his father said. 'I always had a soft spot for her. We were always great pals. Ted's perfectly all right, too . . .'

'He's very nice,' his mother said reprovingly. 'He really is. Your father just wanted to sit down and gossip with Barbara about people no one else had ever heard of and, of course, Ted would keep on interrupting, as he had a perfect right to, in his own house, when his wife and a guest are being a little tedious. He's really very nice. On the Sunday morning, before lunch, he saw that the whole thing was really hopeless, we might as well leave your father and Barbara alone to get it out of their system, so he said, "Come on, Cathy" – he called me that, but you can't take offence, you really can't – "let's go for a drive and leave these two to get on with lunch." And we drove to the seaside and threw bread to the gulls, and when we got back, they'd finished with every single person either of them had ever worked with, and had made really quite a delicious cottage pie for lunch. He really is nice, don't listen to your father.'

Two weeks later, David went to London to buy some new shoes. It was one of his small pieces of self-respect that he would not buy shoes in St Albans; in the St Albans Marks & Sparks he would go as far as routine white cotton shirts and socks and plain V-necks, but no more than that. He took the Friday afternoon off, and met Richard at six in a bar in Rupert Street. The stools were lined up along the glass perimeter of the bar, and on each a man on his own sat and read the free gay magazine handed out in bars, or played with the texting facility on his mobile phone. One poor sap actually had his laptop open and was searching the Internet. Even David could see that they would be better off extinguishing their battery-charged devices, turning to each other and starting to speak. But Richard was not there yet, so David, after buying a drink he did not much care for, Campari-soda, to make himself look interesting, sat down on an empty bar stool

166

facing outwards into the street, got out his mobile phone and started writing a long text, almost a diary entry, to Richard, to pass the time.

'Sorry, sorry, sorry,' Richard said, bustling in, flushed and quiffed. 'Can't believe it. Friday fucking afternoon and the fucking client calls, says it's no good, we need a rethink ASAP, Belinda says fine, hey, guys, Monday morning at eleven they're coming in to see the results, the new results. And I say let's go home and do fuck all and present them with exactly the same material and see if they notice. But apparently, according to Belinda, that won't do. How are you, darling? Bought some lovely shoes?'

When the drinks had been fetched, and Richard had greeted a couple of acquaintances, exes, casual shags, or whatever they were, they sat down in their small corner. Richard's gaze was unwaveringly on David's face, not wandering about the room. David knew this was a compliment consciously paid to him, that for the next hour Richard was all his, whatever the delights just out of eyeshot, whatever the opportunities within the range of a good spit. David found this ostentatious compliment slightly insulting, as if there could be no debate that there was something more interesting happening elsewhere in the bar. He began to talk about his parents.

'And,' he finished, 'I had a phone call from my mother this morning, saying that they're going down to Devon again, next weekend. They never go anywhere.'

'That's not fair,' Richard said. 'I remember when they went to Normandy a couple of years ago. And you went to Florence with your mother, didn't you?'

'Venice,' David said. 'All the same.'

'You know what I think?' Richard said. 'I think they're having a little break-out. It needn't necessarily be a wife-swapping, swingers sort of thing.'

'What?'

'I said, it needn't be a wife-swapping, swingers sort of thing. Going down to Cockering, was it? Lovely name. Catching up with old friends, your dad and his secretary's old husband doing a late-night high-five on the landing as they pass each other going from one bedroom to the next—'

'You really are too much,' David said.

'What? Isn't that what you meant? I thought that was the whole point of what you were saying. It seems a long way to go to find a suitable couple, but—'

'Richard, please.'

6.

Every week, David went over to his parents. He would always make a point of ironing his shirt and making sure his jeans and jumper were clean and hole-less – there had been an outbreak of moths recently in his wardrobe. He would make a point of going slightly out of his way to fetch a good bottle of wine from Oddbins, rather than stop at the all-hours shop, which was directly on the route. He would often pause to pick up a book that he'd read and enjoyed recently, to lend to his mum. He was a good son, and his regular habits proved it to them, and to him.

'We're only looking at properties at the moment,' his mother was saying. 'Nothing's been settled as yet.'

'Nothing's been settled?' David said. He felt like bursting into tears. When people said that nothing had been settled, it meant that they'd abandoned their present life. 'I don't know – it seems like an awful risk.'

'A risk?' David's father said. 'I don't know about that.'

'We're not moving all that far away,' his mother said. 'It's not as adventurous as all that.'

'The thing is . . .' David marshalled his thoughts. They were grim. 'The thing is that you're both not as young as you used to be. What happens if something happens to one of you? In a new town, you wouldn't have anyone. Here, you're surrounded by people you know. In an emergency, who would help out in – in—'

'Hanmouth,' his mother said. 'Well, I see what you mean, but it does seem a shame not to move while we still have our faculties.'

'David's right,' his father said. 'There is that to be thought of.'

'In ten years' time, it'll be too late,' his mother said, patiently explaining. 'The thing is that we're perfectly capable of making new friends, you know. It's a very lively little town. There are reading groups, the WI, Neighbourhood Watch. They're in and out of each other's houses all day long, you can see.'

'You hate the WI,' David said, almost in tears. For a terrible moment, he thought about the possibility of himself moving down to Devon – perhaps not in the same town as his parents, but in another one, a small town just up the coast, from where he could pop in every Saturday. He stopped himself.

'I don't know why you're being like this about it,' his mother said. 'It's not like you to be such a stick. Anyone would think we were talking about moving to Patagonia. It's only three hours in the car. We could practically pop back for lunch if we felt like it.'

In the months following, it seemed as if the whole process had stalled. Nothing further was said about it, though on three occasions, their regular routine was interrupted because the pair of them had gone down to Hanmouth. He felt that an awkwardness was rising between them; after that first conversation, they were tight as clams about their proposition. He cursed himself: if he had been a little bit clever, a little bit more encouraging, they would have kept him up to date; they might even have asked him to come down and take a look at the place.

Hanmouth filled his thoughts, like a neglected wife dwelling on a discovered mistress. After a week or two, he yielded to the temptation, and looked the town up on its own website. The website was maintained by a local amateur fisherman, whose ideas of what might be interesting to the outside world were curious and filled with personal anecdotes of sea-borne weather from decades back. 'The great Storm of 1954 was remembered Long

169

in Hanmouth, it carried the Benches at the present day standing along Wolf Walk right out to Sea in the course of a Single night.' The erratic style of the amateur fisherman covered the whole town in embarrassment; his parents could not be serious about moving to a place where the capital letters were so erratic, the standards of education so low. But the photographs were beautiful: an absurdly picturesque town, white-painted cottages, a church on a headland with a green churchyard and a yew, high above the glistening estuary. There were portraits, too, of many local figures – three white-coated butchers, a bravely smiling girl in the cheesemonger's, proffering Stilton at the end of a knife, a smiling plump lady with glasses on her bosom and a shelf of brownish books behind her, representing the second-hand book-shop, a whole classful of volunteers standing before the Devon Sea Rescue charity shop, and then half a dozen of the retired fisherman, his children and five blond grandchildren. The children looked appallingly prosperous, and the grandchildren hardly less so. 'The following photographs were Taken in July 2004 from a Jaunt in a friends' Light Aircraft and show Hanmouth from the Air.' His parents, David was sure, had no friends who owned Light Aircraft – the illiteracy somehow added to the uncomfort-able prospect – and he certainly did not. Following a thought, he made a search, and found some Hanmouth estate agents. 'Have you got those Chinese blurbs nearly ready?' his boss called, from the far end of the segmented room. 'I was hoping to have a look at them today.'

'Yes, almost done,' David said, investigating Devon house prices. After five minutes he sighed, and sat back with happiness. It was not going to happen. He did not know exactly what the house prices in St Albans were like, but he was pretty sure that they were not going to match the seven-figure sums in this small Devon town. He wondered that his parents had not yet discovered that: a glance in an estate agent's window would surely have revealed how unsuitable this place was. He did hope they weren't going to move to anywhere horrid, just for the sake of it.

'You seem cheerful today,' his mother said, as he arrived at their house on a Saturday lunchtime, new jersey on, an ironed shirt and even a tie underneath. 'I've made a cottage pie. And we saw a flat this week we really like. We've got the description out to show you.'

7.

The week after David met Mauro for the first time, he picked up the telephone and gave him a ring. It was practically impossible not to. He required reality to catch up with the general impression he had given out. Richard and, he supposed, Rodrigo believed that he had not just met a man at the club, but had gone to bed with him in a generally satisfactory way. David had given this impression not so much to save his own face as to save Richard's feelings; he had, after all, gone to so much trouble on David's behalf. David knew from bitter experience that a boyfriend invented from scratch, based on absolutely nothing, was never convincing – he recalled a sour little episode with Dymphna at work, whom he'd thought was his friend, first failing to ask the right questions, then asking too many, then doing it all over again in front of an audience, suppressing a tremor of laughter. But Mauro was a real person; it was none of their business what degree their intimacy had reached (he remembered the sight of Mauro in the kitchen doorway in his underpants, reaching up with his left arm, yawning and smiling sleepily). He found himself telling not just Richard, not just his neighbour downstairs as they were taking out the rubbish at the same time, but even his mother that he had met someone, that it seemed to be going quite well.

Afterwards he cursed himself for telling the neighbour; after all, Vanessa could know perfectly well, if she wanted to look into it, how many nights he spent at home, how many nights David's heavy tread up the stairs was accompanied by another, defter, more eager walk. But it was a very good idea to tell his mother about Mauro. If he was honest, his parents' departure for Hanmouth, three months before, was intimately connected to his venturing out into Vauxhall, the dance floor, the following of a handsome Italian stranger home. Without the sense of being abandoned by the most dully reliable element of his life, out of all the dully reliable elements of his life, David would probably not have thought of venturing out at all. His parents' removal had had the effect of making him see his life, and to go out in search of improvement. In part, his search, more seriously undertaken, for a companion who could be taken out in public was his sense that his relationship with his parents could be improved greatly if only he had a boyfriend to present to them, to talk about with them, all of that. The details of sexual fulfilment, of having a lover, the whole erotic caboodle of the face on the pillow and the body pressed against your own was important and fascinating to David; however, he saw the social possibilities of turning to an acquaintance at a party and saying, 'Have you met XXX, my boyfriend?' (A wave of white noise in the head at the mere prospect of a name.) That seemed most important, after persuading his parents that he was, after all, all right, that, yes, I have met someone, yes, it does seem to be going well, yes, indeed, we'll come and stay, whenever you like, it's time – a joshing, manly, even parental tone entering here – it's time you met my young man.

'Hello?' the voice said.

David introduced himself, not leaving a pause, but gabbling out the place, the time, the occasion, the consequences, and five circumstantial details about his appearance and what Mauro had been wearing the night they met, and finally referring to himself as 'Mr Poppers', fixedly staring at a blank space on the wall as he did so.

'Oh, yes,' Mauro said. 'How are you? Nice to hear from you.' In the background, there was a blitzing wave as Mauro evidently walked past a pneumatic drill, and David paused to get his next line right, and get it heard. 'Hello? Hello?' Mauro said, mistaking the silence.

'I wondered what you were up to this Saturday,' David said. It wasn't so hard, and in a moment they had arranged to meet for a drink in Vauxhall, and then maybe on to a club – they weren't going to that place again: Massimo got beaten up and thrown out by the security, and for what? David listened to the little story with pleasure. It wound on without ever getting to a conclusion. He had wondered what, actually, Mauro and he would talk about if they ever met sober in daylight, and here was the answer. He would do very well.

8.

The possibilities for improvement in David's life were not all that could be hoped for. He worked for a firm which, among other things, did something that had, always, to be explained three or four times, and then people were not quite sure about it. They provided copy, in English, for foreign businesses. 'Translations, you mean?' people would say. No, not quite: David's boss had discovered, or believed, that all across the world companies were dying for some English copy to add a touch of class, English being the language of aspiration, whether in Saudi Arabia, China or Paraguay. On T-shirts, in company brochures, on the backs of paperbacks, on tourist pamphlets, English was required not so much to convey meaning but to add an aroma of social mobility, of class, of get-up-and-go and pizzazz and vim and the rest of it. The paragraphs that David composed and sold on, licensing all manner of linguistic and physical product to remote and non-Anglophone corners of the world, were not supposed to make sense: they were supposed to sell. 'But doesn't everyone speak English?' people would say, but apparently everyone did not. Subtler enquirers would say, 'But why can't they write their own bad English?' to which David's answer was that his bad English and his reliable English company had, evidently, a solid badness all its own. 'Kiss My World of Dreams' a David paragraph would begin, and go on in similar vein. The company ventured into import-export, and David's day was taken up with other tasks, too. But three or four times a week, he was taken away from the world of invoices and dockets and online ordering protocols in favour of kissing the World of Dreams, and wrote rubbish for an hour or two.

The company had begun relations with companies in Japan, where Dymphna had spent three years teaching English as a foreign language before giving up the unequal struggle; she had acquired an unexpected range of Japanese boys to spin into a business. They used to write slogans for T-shirts – I Am Butterfly Connect, Let Each Man Do His Best Agile Sports Life, Invitation for the Proud Life, Crocodile Profusion. There was one David was particularly proud of; it was, in his view, a perfect fulfilment of the thing that Japanese T-shirt manufacturers wanted and would like to produce themselves. It read: 'Spanking! Size Case Nomadic: You can find It up completely. At any Time at Any purpose, In your life, Style. That's something Like'. He never heard back from any of the companies who formed their clients, then or when the business started to expand into other, bigger markets. He saw his job, in part, as amusing English tourists in Tokyo and Shanghai, and liked to think of the innocent Japanese who both bought and sold his wearable slogans as in on the joke, and rather enjoying it.

In the past two years, a new development had occurred. Dymphna returned from a trip to China, and had discovered that Chinese teenagers in Beijing liked to carry around books in English. As a fashion statement, not for reading: they could rarely read any English. Dymphna wondered whether they really cared what the contents of the books were, and, indeed, a teenager with bronze chrysanthemum-like hair, an English cricket sweater and tartan bondage trousers had got into trouble for carrying round a copy of *Darkness at Noon* by Arthur Koestler, probably left in a hotel room by some politically motivated tourist. If the youth could be assured that the books they were holding had absolutely no political content, and looked, moreover, rather more like the Chinese idea of an English book than an English book itself did, Dymphna observed there was money to be made.

Of course, it could be gibberish, but then the suspicion of the authorities would be raised, and their time wasted in cracking codes – and who knew what they might disinter from the ruin of a random text? Of course, they could be real books, but then the point of copyright would probably arise. An old book would be set in a typeface the Chinese would find too ugly to show their friends, and the cost and expense of resetting a book in a modern typeface could never be recouped. All in all, the cheapest option proved to be to ask members of a creative writing group, then their friends, children, acquaintances, parents, to write the books themselves, pay them a hundred pounds each and get them to sign away their rights in perpetuity.

David didn't write the books: his time was too valuable, and as an employee, he had to be paid at least the minimum wage. He wrote, however, the blurbs which were to go on the back cover, and the titles. That was the most important part: these Chinese would, perhaps, never open the books, but the titles and the blurb were there for any admiring person to observe, passing in the Chinese street. David envisaged sleek-haired girls in cheong-sams, passing each other glossily in a high-lit shopping centre of marble and smoked glass, a Chanel rip-off handbag under one arm, one of his books in another. Sometimes a member of the local creative writing group would protest that their manuscript already had a title, and its title was *Mother Called Me Cunt*. David would explain that the Chinese market in English books responded best to particular titles, and the particular title that they would respond to was *Nightingale Lovely World Dreaming, Yes, For Ever, Yes*. Sometimes he opened up and read a paragraph of one of these books, and a paragraph was all that was necessary: a waterfall of self-pity and self-reflection and self-consciousness.

But who am I writing for, thought Moron Pranxfucker to himself, striding the ruins of the post-apocalyptic ruins of New York. He sighed as he fired his machine gun at the crawling zombies which at the same time screamed and howled threateningly. The skyscrapers of New York stood blackened like giant dominoes in a game of dominoes which would end by destroying the whole world as they toppled on top of each other, one after the other. Am I writing for myself or for some audience which will never understand my words? Are these thoughts intended for anyone at all or is someone writing it all down somewhere? he thought to himself. Yes, Moron Pranxfucker was right, for maybe the first time in his life, apart from when he thought, three days before, before all of this started happening, that his girlfriend Marlena Friendly was probably the least attractive woman whose tits he had ever spunked off over. He was right, because someone was writing it all down somewhere, and someone, too, was reading it, and you and I know who was writing and who was reading it, even if Moron Pranxfucker did not and never would. Suddenly a bigger than usual zombie reeled out of a nearby doorway which Pranxfucker suddenly recognized as the ruined doorway of Macy's. He headed towards Pranxfucker like a giant rearing rat with his eyes blazing, reminding everyone of the zombies in Michael Jackson's *Thriller* video, and Moron Pranxfucker shot once, twice, three times in the head. The zombie kept on coming but Moron Pranxfucker shot him a fourth time in the head. Then the bastard stopped coming.

David retitled works like this *Moon Antelope, I Love You*, and *Rainbow Kiss the Lucky Bird*, and sent the authors in Northern Ireland a hundred quid to keep their literary blogs going. They were happy to be in print on paper, if only for the benefit of people who could not understand three consecutive words in English. Some of them had MAs in creative writing. If you thought about it, you could cry.

9.

'Got any plans for the weekend?' Dymphna said from her desk, her eyes fixed on a spreadsheet.

'Going up to town,' David said. 'Seeing Mauro.'

'Right,' Dymphna said. She paused for a moment or two, moved her cursor around the screen. It was not her way to enquire into David's life with interest. The job interview had been conducted, like a small girl playing at shops, with Dymphna in her bright red stockings and button-strapped Mary Jane shoes behind her big desk. David was sitting on a chair on the other side. The first time they had met subsequently Dymphna, released from legal restraints, had asked in a general sort of way whether he had children or not. He had told her that he didn't because he was gay. Subsequently, he heard that she had thought that gays were all right, but she wished they didn't thrust the fact of it down your throat all the time.

'I thought I'd stay in with Michael,' she said. 'Now that Toby's nearly three, we think he's mature enough for a little brother or sister. We're trying for another baby, you know.'

'Yes, I know.'

'And it's the right time of the month. We worked it all out. The peak time for conception is on Saturday afternoon, so my sister's going to come round and take Toby to the swings between two and four. It's all worked out. I don't suppose it's as exact as all that, but you can certainly pin down the peak time for ovulation to within an hour or two.'

'Oh, I see,' David said. 'No, we're just going out for dinner, Mauro and me. Maybe a film.'

'Well,' Dymphna said. She moved a figure from one virtual letterbox to another; amended it, then moved it back and amended it again. She hummed a little tune; in her way, she often hummed when trying to give the impression that she was deep in concentration. David had worked opposite her for seven years now, and had never managed to identify a single tune she hummed. It was his opinion that she made her tunes up as she went along, not at all being the sort of person to listen to music, or trouble to remember it afterwards. She would have said that, with a husband and a boy of three, she never seemed to have the time to listen to music, as she never had the time to read a book or see a film, or develop an interest in other human beings not related to her by blood or marriage. 'Well,' she said again. 'Are you going to be finishing those Chinese blurbs off today? If I send them off today, they'll be waiting for them when the printers come in first thing Monday morning.'

'How many are there?' David said. 'How many still to do?'

'I've no idea,' Dymphna said. 'I've promised them ten.'

David turned back to his computer screen and started to write. 'Happiness is the gift to everybody,' he wrote. 'Sometimes you sit in your home, and you wait for a special present. Love is a beautiful thing. Does it happen to you? You must tell all your friends that it matters if nobody loves you. Then perhaps love will come to you, when all hope and trust has gone. It will burst through your door, when you feel so alone, and take you in its arms in a huge warm embrace. It may be a dark thin man who loves you, or it may be a blonde beautiful woman. But love is everywhere, waiting to fill your life with happiness. It is like a special warm fire, burning in the hearth of your innermost soul. If you open the doors of your soul to love and happiness, then you will find that love and happiness enter in, laughing with joy. Always remember,' David wrote, remembering an Italian man in his brilliant white underpants, lifting one arm over his head and yawning as if in ecstasy as he said good night, 'the world is lovely, and loves you, too.'

'Why do we say "the cockles of your heart"?' David said. 'Nothing to do with whelks, I suppose.'

'No idea,' Dymphna said. Both of them were inspecting their computer screens, David what he had just written, Dymphna the same thing, sent across by David. 'Something to do with cochlears?'

'What's a cochlear?'

Dymphna turned from her screen, and inspected David, top to bottom. 'Someone's in a good mood,' she said, referring, he supposed, to his surging copy.

Mauro had suggested meeting in a bar David didn't know; after a bit of online research, it looked like the sort of place they had met in, but one designed for earlier in the evening. David walked through the door ebulliently; he had put on the sort of clothes he had last week rejected, and he felt as if he had been accepted by this world now. It all seemed to have gone absolutely fine.

And as if to confirm the idea, Mauro was sitting there already, on a stool, talking to the barman. David had wondered, in the previous few days, whether he would recognize him, so dense a layer of recollection and wishfulness had built up over his real features, and the only thing that came to mind was that single image of a yawning faun, his arm upwards and bent over his head. But of course he recognized him, and when Mauro turned round, his features somehow wobbling about, he recognized David, too.

'I've been terrible,' Mauro said. 'I took the afternoon off work – I wanted to go to the shops, I wanted to buy some T-shirt – but then I thought, no, I can't face it, so I just came down to Soho, and I went to a bar, then another bar, with a friend, you know, and then he stayed in Soho and I came down here.'

'Are you drunk?' David said.

'I'm so drunk,' Mauro said. 'And it's only six thirty. I've been here for ever and ever, drinking and drinking. I'm so sorry.'

'That's quite all right,' David said, smiling. Mauro dipped his head and, with both hands, ruffled and smoothed his hair, raised his face, shook his head and took another drink of beer. 'Do you want another one of those? Or do you feel you need to get something to eat?'

'Yeah, take him off,' the barman said. 'He'll benefit from a sandwich, I should say.'

'Yes, food,' Mauro said. So they went to a Portuguese restaurant in the vicinity, where David had some lamb chops, and Mauro a chicken stew with beans, of some sort. In a while, Mauro started to make more sense, to tell stories, to clarify his mind in the early evening light. After an hour or two, ordering one Coca-Cola after another, he was making quite a lot of sense; he started to listen to what David had to say, and not just to nod while David spoke. His niceness made itself evident, like a suppressed buoy resurfacing above the waves. So they went back to the bar – David paid for the Portuguese dinner, it seemed only fair – and drank some more, and by now it seemed to David that they had reached, more or less, the same starting point. Some friends of Mauro joined them, one after the other, and others, as they passed, called out in acclamation – one man, a startling caber of muscle draped with thin scraps of a vest, actually shouted hurrah, or hallelujah, or yippedy-doo, or some other ancient barely worded celebration at the mere sight of Mauro and a remembered tumble in the sack. They were the sort of men whom David, normally, would barely dare to look at in a bar; they were, he saw, the heroes of this particular bar, this particular evening. And they were civil to him. They asked about him, they laughed when he joked and they joked back at him; they made reference to past outings with confidential, sharing amusement and to future outings with the implication that David would be with them then. Mauro's imprimatur, however he had earned it, had embedded him in this lovely group, and standing there, so long as he took care not to glimpse himself in the mirror behind the bar, he could believe himself one confident good-looker among seven others. Mauro shone with a sort of pride; if it were rational, it might seem to David as if Mauro were pleased to have met him. What does he want? David asked involuntarily, before remembering that not everyone was like him. Some people were lazy, good-natured and pleased to have new people in their life. He could accept that.

Another bar, a third; a club, and at four thirty or five, they started to talk about going on to an 'after hours', including him, David saw, in the invitation. 'Oh, come,' Mauro said. But David was now as drunk as Mauro had ever been, and the trains to St

Albans were running. His instinct told him that he would lay the foundations for proper popularity if he went home at what the rest of the group obviously thought was quite an early time. He said goodbye, casually, to Mauro, smiled, and went; but the whole group, one after the other, blew him kisses across the crowd and the huge beats of the dance floor on his way to the door. It was one of the nicest things that had ever happened to David.

10.

'Over a lovely landscape in the countryside, where flowers bloom and small animals live in peace and harmony with each other, a rainbow of every colour stretches. After rain, the colours come out into the air, and everything seems fresh and cheerful. People are beautiful in a country like this, and full of their own happiness. Let them sleep together, and kiss, and share their beautiful love in the spring and the summer, in all the seasons of the year. Freshly peeled oranges lie on a dark blue wooden table in the sunshine, and bright green parrots and parakeets hop down, trying the delicious fruit. On a morning like this, anything could happen. Your life could be changed, and admit something beautiful which will never leave it,' David wrote, on his own, in the office.

11.

In the weeks that followed, David and Mauro fell into a regular pattern. They would meet in town, have dinner, go to a bar or a sequence of bars, and then to a nightclub. From what Mauro's friends said, these evenings of Mauro's usually ended with a 'chill-out', where Mauro and whoever else seemed to be around had sex in twos and threes and fours on a stranger's sofa, bed or floor.

Sometimes, David gathered, Mauro took a stranger back to his own flat when the night had gone a long way into morning. He could not help envisaging it: Mauro, naked, taking a figure into his arms in an ample smiling embrace, a figure who was not obscure or without detail, but who was just another Mauro, embracing his identical self as if in a mirror. By the time Mauro was in another's arms, David was always on the train back to St Albans. It was usually empty; once, he delayed it until eight, but could not sustain his energy any longer, and on the train back, he found himself sitting behind an old married couple, parcelling out their breakfast. The train began to move, and his eyes closed. Abruptly, he woke himself with the tail-end of a rasping snore.

'There's a bloody snorer behind me,' the old woman said.

'A snorer? You get all sorts. Got up too early, didn't he?' her husband replied listlessly. They said nothing for a moment or two. 'Has that got meat in it?'

'Yes, that's got yeast in it.'

'No, meat.'

'No, it's not got meat in it.'

'I only ask, because last time you had a bacon sandwich, you were ill the next day.'

'That's not a bacon sandwich, that's a sweet thing, look. I'll split it in half, you can have half of it.'

'I don't want half of it.'

'Well, suit yourself. Have you got sweetener?'

David looked out of the window, feeling already the sleepwards tug of the train's chugga-chugga. It had been heavily cloudy first thing, but over the roofs of Finsbury Park, there was already enough blue in the sky to make a sailor's suit, as his mother used to say; the slick of water on a long roof flashed gold in the direct sun.

What the relationship between David and Mauro was remained to be clarified. It was with a complicated series of motives that David spoke to his mother, now settled with his father in Hanmouth, about a new 'relationship': wanting to put himself in a better light than he had previously occupied, wanting to reassure her that his life would be all right, and, perhaps partly, the obscure motive of thinking that if he said something, it would make it so. Surely if someone in the depths of Devon believed as a fact that David had a boyfriend called Mauro, the universe would bring it about in due course. And there was a special bond between David and Mauro; this was confirmed for David when, two months after they had met, Mauro moved flat to a couple of streets away in Clapham. The old flat had been a knocked-together job with plywood doors and an old sofa smelling of dog; the new one was brassier, on the ground floor of a thirties block with broad low-ceilinged rooms and a lobby like an ocean liner. Mauro shared it with two other boys, off the gay rental website. The old landlord kept Mauro's deposit, and he found himself short for the two months' deposit the new landlord asked for. David was really happy that he was the one Mauro turned to, and he wrote a cheque with lightness in his heart.

There was geographical dispersion enough between the three points of this claim – David, Mauro, parents – to make it unlikely any clash would occur when the nature of the relationship would have to be clarified. But on one of their Friday nights, David had suggested a change from Vauxhall, and they had met in a bar in Soho. David had walked through the door, and there was Richard, sitting waiting for someone.

'Hello, stranger,' Richard said. 'I heard you were in London all the time these days. Never call, never write. The children cry whenever I mention your name.'

'Well, I wouldn't put it like that,' David said, with a terrible rush of confusion, his mind constructing the scene now rapidly approaching. But before he could put anything right, Mauro was bouncing through the door with an accordion-fold of shopping bags and an absurd, cheerful trilby on his head that David had never seen before. 'Hello, hello, hello, darling,' he said, and gave David the same kiss he gave everyone. 'I've had such a – oh, well, let me tell you—'

'This is Richard,' David said glumly.

'I've heard about you,' Richard said. 'We're so happy that David's met someone. And you look very suitable, very suitable indeed.'

David could only watch. But, in fact, Mauro just accepted the compliment. There was no confusion that David could see, and as the conversation went on, Mauro could hardly remain in ambiguity about what Richard thought. He clearly was under the impression that the deal was done, signed, delivered, and the curtain-rails being bickered over. The moment came when David could have said, 'No, no – he's not my boyfriend or anything.' Came and went. He stood there miserably as Richard went on about married bliss and his hope that Mauro could wrench David away from St Albans. But Mauro was perfectly cheerful, responding to Richard's questioning without a glance at David or a contradiction.

Finally Rodrigo arrived with three Brazilian friends – one of whom, David was glad to see, was enormously fat and spotty, five foot two and introduced, implausibly, as Edison. 'Well, you can light up my life any time,' David said, enjoying the chance to flirt patronizingly for once. It was good to see that even Rodrigo had his share of David-like obligations, too. Rodrigo and the pustular Edison took Richard off. David thought he would take the initiative.

'I didn't tell him,' he said. 'I didn't say you were my boyfriend, or anything. I don't know why he thought that. I would have put him right, but I wasn't sure what he meant at first, and then afterwards, it just seemed …'

'I don't care,' Mauro said, and he smiled. 'I don't care what he thought. It doesn't matter at all.'

For a moment, David thought something incredible, that what he had considered was going to take place; that the cosy but quickly static relationship really was a long wooing, whose degrees were too finely distinguished for him to perceive. Tonight, the reason that Richard's belief that their relationship had a sexual aspect to it didn't matter was that the sexual aspect was going to be offered tonight. Richard thought they went to bed together; tonight they would go to bed together; so Mauro didn't care. All the same, David was glad that Richard's error had only been brought out before Mauro, and not in front of any of Mauro's friends.

When, the next afternoon, David woke in his own bed in St Albans, hung-over and sweating, not having gone to bed with Mauro after all, he wondered why Mauro was so indifferent to being regarded as his boyfriend. For the first time, the thought of the £2,400 he had lent Mauro for the deposit on the flat, the subject of fervent promises every week ever since, started to display a different aspect.

12.

The view from Cockering was no more lovely than the view from Hanmouth. Catherine liked it, however, because from here you could see the long ribbon of Hanmouth. The town stretched along the estuary shore like bunting: from the inland side, the park and the newish school, then the shining roof and windows of the doctor's clinic, the church, high on its headland in its green grave-yard. Then the complicated knot of streets and houses and shops, rising and falling behind the berthed yachts about the stone jetty, and onwards to the Strand and its Dutch houses; the gables hock-eting and curving in a musical phrase, interrupted at the exact centre by the square pretty block Catherine and Alec lived in. From the Cockering circular harbour, now emptied of water, the sailing boats and tugs lying on their sides in the thick black mud, you could see what an agreeable, festive town Hanmouth was. They often came over here to visit Barbara and Ted, and in fact the pair of them had become much better friends with them since they had moved down here. Or, at any rate, had seen a good deal more of them than when they had lived in St Albans. One of their very infrequent arguments had erupted when Alec suggested that they'd seen Barbara and Ted only six days before, and they shouldn't 'drop in' on them by chance. 'I don't think they're always all that pleased to see us,' he'd said. 'We'd all enjoy it more if it was more occasional.' Catherine hadn't noticed any unwillingness; Barbara, at least, always seemed pleased to see the pair of them. And Alec was a typical man, always happy to go for days or weeks without any company but his own and Catherine's, cheerful with the telly in the evening, a book or the newspaper, and conversation that didn't have to be kept up, that could be a series of sporadic observations. Catherine thought that was a sure way to make you grow old before your time; her counter-image constructed itself, all those sprightly gossips of both sexes, darting between book clubs and drinks parties and Neighbourhood Watch from the far end of Ferry Road to the far end of the Strand, keeping themselves young with an interest in life and each other.

As it turned out, Barbara was thrilled to see them.

'Gosh, there's been some excitement over in Hanmouth,' she said, coming out into the front garden and wiping her hands on her apron. Behind her, in the door, Ted stood, holding the *Daily Telegraph*. 'It's all over the news and on the television. They interviewed the landlord of the pub and the headmaster of the school, and I think I saw the lady who works in the bookshop in the back of a shot while Justin Webb was talking. You thought it wasn't her, didn't you, Ted? But I think it was.'

'It was someone else entirely,' Ted said. 'And the camera moved on so you couldn't see who it was with any certainty.'

'What an awful thing,' Barbara said. 'We saw the police frogmen at work in the estuary. You hate to think of that, don't you? But even that would be better than . . .'

She led them into the house. Over the floor of the sitting room, the leaves of the paper lay scattered, the remains of Ted's elevenses in crumbs on the plate, the prize whole-page crossword just begun and a road atlas open on the coffee-table.

'Are you going somewhere?' Alec said, referring to the map.

'They think, don't they, that she might have been abducted?' Barbara said. 'They thought she might have wandered off and fallen into the estuary, or into a ditch, or – but now they're saying somebody might have taken her. Isn't that awful?'

'We're planning our summer holiday,' Ted said morosely. 'Barb likes to have it all clear in her mind before we set off. Three months before we set off. We've booked all the hotels, everything.'

'That's a French road atlas, is it?'

'All of Europe. It's a nice little production, look.'

'I don't see how a child could be just abducted, though,' Barbara said, 'in the middle of the day, with dozens of people around, and they look round and she's gone, and nobody's seen anything.'

'Frightening, isn't it?' Alec said. 'I'm glad we're not bringing a child up, these days.'

'I know,' Barbara said, with feeling. 'Everything's so much more frightening, these days. And in a place like Hanmouth!'

'I don't know,' Ted said. 'You can mollycoddle your kids, keep them inside, never let them out without supervision, and then the first bit of trouble they come across when they're grown up and left the nest, they can't cope, they've never had to deal with the like. If we were having kids now, I'd let them out just the same as ever, send them off into the woods for the afternoon, tell them, "See you at teatime, back at the ranch."'

The usual observations were made on the question of liberty versus restraint and supervision for the under-tens, dividing on sex lines. Barbara observed that letting your children loose in the woods was all very well when everyone did it, but if yours were the only ones with such freedom and there was only one child-abductor paedophile in the neighbourhood, then yours would be the ones they would go for. Alec told a story about how he'd got lost in a storm drain when he was nine on one of those afternoons in the woods, way back in the 1950s it must have been, and it was his brother who found him in the end just as it was turning dark.

'And were your parents worried that you were a bit late? I bet they hardly even noticed,' Ted said.

'Well, no,' Alec said. 'They were worried sick. They were on the verge of phoning the police.'

The observation, running counter to the shared conclusions of the conversation, introduced a silence; they sipped their coffee in unison.

'I didn't mention,' Catherine said. 'David's coming down to visit next week – he's not been here before. You must come over.'

'I remember David,' Barbara said. 'He was such a little boy, though. I remember him, always off in the corner with a book, always happy with his own company.'

Once, Catherine had attempted to explain what David did for a living to Barbara; she had nodded and smiled and said she saw quite a lot, but there was no doubt it was hard to convey any vital quality in his employment. Something must have got through to Barbara, however, and she had conflated it with whatever memories she had of David as a little boy, sitting quietly, a good little boy, in the corner while the grown-ups talked. He hadn't been particularly attached to books at all, though it had become his job.

'Well,' Catherine said, 'he's quite a bit more sociable these days. He's got a new friend, actually – they're coming down together. I don't think we've ever met a friend of David's before.'

'Yes, we have,' Alec said. 'You know we have. That girl Teresa in the sixth form – she was always over, they were thick as thieves at one stage.'

'Oh, you know what I mean,' Catherine said. 'Not friends, friends.'

'These days people say "partners",' Barbara said. 'I suppose he's getting a bit old to say boyfriend. It's not too bad when you're twenty, but it's a bit silly saying, "This is my boyfriend," and then someone bald and fifty-five comes through the door.'

'Has the window-cleaner been round recently?' Ted said, leaping up and looking through the glass at the back garden. 'It's absolutely filthy. Does he ever get back here?'

188

'What's David's friend called?' Barbara said. She was a good sort, really; after years of marriage to Ted, she could ignore his embarrassment on any remotely private subject. If Ted had his way, they would always be talking about window-cleaners but Barbara, after years of practice, just paid no attention and went on with a more interesting subject.

'I don't know, I'm afraid,' Catherine said. 'He just said there was someone he'd like to bring down, that he'd like us to meet. Did he happen to mention his friend's name to you, Alec?'

'Oh, no,' Alec said. 'He wouldn't say a thing like that to me.'

13.

Gay Sam's cheese shop had been at the corner of the curve of the Fore street for five years or so. It was sandwiched between an Oriental antiques shop and the Conservative Party headquarters. The Conservative Party could have done with a lick of white paint and a new set of curtains. There was no doubt that this was at a useless curve of the Fore street; no one really needed the Conservative Party, or the imported goods, or the sort of cheese that Fred & Gordon sold. (The name of the shop, in gold Roman lettering on a dark navy background, was often mistaken for the owners' names, and Sam had grown used to being hailed as Fred in the street by someone who thought they knew him. It stocked cheese from nowhere beyond a hundred miles' radius, though its name referred to the child-mangled names of two cheeses they didn't stock, Gordon Zola and Fred Leicester: that sort of tortuous joke, which had to be explained, was rather in vogue among the new shopkeepers of the new millennium.) Sam had run his business from a stall on a Saturday morning for years. When the terrible old ironmonger had insulted his last customer and closed up, Sam had looked longingly at the interior, unable to resist the romantic look of the space, its unswept floor scattered with the last unopened forlorn letters from the authorities. They had talked it over, and Lord What-a-Waste had thought they could manage it.

Sam took his place respectfully, self-deprecatingly, among the small-scale revivers of small trades, the inventors of new ones, the lady merchants undertaking miniature shopkeeping endeavours. Hanmouth was full of these, operating out of their houses, running stalls, rising to the dignity of a shop in the high street before sinking under economic constraints back to the temporary place they had risen from. In Hanmouth there were lacemakers, batik-printers, humble potters, potters who referred to themselves as ceramicists, the perpetrators of macramé, paper makers, conceptual artists, jewellers and sellers of jewellery, watercolourists, bookbinders, hand-printers; there were the outlets of nearby near-champagne manufacturers; there was a retired hedge-fund trader who had taken, at thirty-four with twenty-five million pounds in the bank, to running a shop, twelve metres deep, which displayed and sold nothing but twenty of his abstracts. (When, once a year, one was sold to the passing trade, another was produced from a back room to take its place; it was a process like the slicing off of Hydra heads.) Some trades were old and historic and uninterrupted; others were revived by force of will, and some were entirely novel and basically implausible. One lady, called Eunice Jorna, had founded a business that would take a cast of your infant's foot, and cast it in bronze as a keepsake. She did quite well, although five years ago an adult couple had come in and asked for their feet to be cast, a left and a right; oddly enough, they did not have unusually attractive feet or anything, and the man's bunioned pair, the hair on the toes and the hammer toes, were no more appealing rendered in bronze. Since then, she had determined to turn any custom but infants away; but the question had not arisen again.

Sam did not make anything: he just sold cheese and locally handmade pickles, cheeseboards made of olivewood and cherrywood, the bowls and dishes and plates of ceramicists from around, and even fondue sets, knives like little axes and other accoutrements. He had journeyed the country, and established relationships with farmers and cheesemakers, tiny backyard concerns and gleaming semi-industrial workers. He sold dozens of curious English imitations of more famous foreign cheeses: lesbian bleu d'Auvergne, Welsh vignotte, Essex boursin, Wiltshire Gjetost. The daughters of the town sometimes came to work for a few afternoons a week, the occasional Saturday, or Sam managed on his own. He didn't much care if a small queue sometimes built up on a busy afternoon. People liked the little shop, he believed. The cheeses were not available in many other places. Sometimes they were available in none at all, and in one case, the cheese should not have been sold even by Sam, but rather extinguished on health-and-safety grounds by the EU. Sam had often told his customers this; they laughed and then bought half a pound. They liked him. He was always ready with a sliver, a tongue of cheese. He felt creative, rather than a foodmonger, and the shop was just about breaking even, most years. He mixed in a sunny way with the foot-casters and lacemakers and a woman, four foot nine and named Eleanor Redwood, who was richly learned in *raku* and had a taste for black men. All of these were the ones who earned something from their craft; behind them, like a shadowy army of talentless Platonic forms, were those who did very much the same for no money at all, just for their own pleasure and for the sake of Christmas presents. And then there were the humble jam-makers and cake-makers and practitioners of fancy icing, who had their own hierarchies and snobberies, penetrable only to those who surrendered their identity and went, humbly, to live among them as an anthropologist might go among the Kikuyu. Ten years ago, the hedge-fund trader's abstract-painting shop had been a fishmonger.

14.

When Lord What-a-Waste – really Harry – had the morning off that partners were allowed from the solicitor's, which was at the moment on a Wednesday, he liked to come down to Sam's shop and sit in the back room. He was a sleeping partner, Sam told everyone, in the shop, and he liked to go over the accounts of a Wednesday. He went over them, it was true, but in all honesty Sam usually enjoyed telling Harry over dinner what he had sold that day, and how much money he'd made out of it, and there were only two or three things ever to tell, so even if Harry forgot, it wouldn't have taken him the whole morning to remind himself of the salient facts. Really, Harry enjoyed coming down and sitting in the back room, turning papers over, coming out sometimes if one of Sam's friends came in to hug them and complain about trade slowing or, in the past, about being rushed off their feet. He enjoyed playing at shops, as, indeed, did Sam.

'What's this?' Harry said, coming out of the back room with a receipt.

'No idea, hon,' Sam said. 'What's it look like?'

'It's just a receipt,' Harry said. 'It doesn't say where it's from or what it's for or when it was or anything, just this figure, twenty-two pounds. Could be anything.'

'Does it look recent?' Sam said. He held up, sniffed at, then bit cautiously into the croissant he'd got to go with their mid-morning coffee. The cake shop had been known to forget which were the plain croissants and which the ones stuffed with Nutella or almond paste – to which Sam believed himself slightly allergic. But it was OK and he carried on.

'Yes, I think so,' Harry said, going back into the little office and calling through the open door, 'Anyway, it was with other recent stuff. It looked as if you'd taken it all out of your wallet and just dumped it there.'

'Let me see,' Sam said. 'Twenty-two pounds. Not the butcher?

No. I got some stuff from the cash and carry but it was more than that, and it would say on the receipt. I know – I got some thrillers from Frank Cohen Books. I went in to see if they had that Japanese novel we're doing and they didn't, but I thought I'd stock up. Twenty-two pounds – was it really?'

'You are brilliant,' Harry called. 'Though I notice you've hidden them from me.'

'Nonsense. I put them on the bedside table in a pile. That reminds me –'

When Sam said 'that reminds me' it did not necessarily indicate a logical connection, but a train of thought that had started at that particular point.

'– the lads phoned to see if we wanted to go round there Saturday night.'

'The lads.'

'It was Peter.'

'Well, no, then.'

'Come on, it'll be fun. We haven't been to a gathering for three months. They'll think we're not interested any more, they'll stop phoning us. We are interested, aren't we?'

Harry came out of the back room. He had been wearing his glasses to look through the papers and to nose around in Sam's doings, as he liked to do. Now he took them off – a dashing, innocent, vulnerable gesture – and stood there blinking with his pale blue eyes in his plump, dark, hairy face. 'Well,' Harry said. 'I'm interested if you're interested.'

'We've had this conversation before, I feel.'

'Yes, quite a lot. I don't mind going to those gatherings but, you know, I've had sex with every single one of them, several times, every single time, and so have you, and I don't mind going on just as we are.'

'No, that's right,' Sam said.

'But on the other hand, the last three times, it's true that we've found something else to do, so maybe we're getting out of the habit.'

'Are you saying that I'm enough for you, that you only ever want to have sex with me for the rest of your life?' Sam said, raising his eyebrows.

'No, of course not,' Harry said affectionately. 'I'd never say that to you, darling. You know that.'

'Love you,' Sam said, beaming. They understood each other. When they had first met, they had been eight months together, chafing at the romantic bit; it wasn't that they didn't enjoy each other, hadn't feasted on each other's even then abundant flesh with nightly pleasure. But both of them had passed themselves around generously earlier in their lives, or as generously as the possibilities of Devon, Cornwall and a twice-yearly weekend in London allowed. (It was amazing they hadn't met before they had, when they were twenty-eight and thirty-one respectively.) At first, they had had those eight months of a shamefaced monogamy. Both had assured the other that they liked it, that they felt that, with the other, their life had taken a change in the right direction. They did not go as far as to say that they never wanted to sleep with another man, that Sam (or Harry) had permanently filled the wants of Harry (or Sam). But they did say that they couldn't imagine going back to their old ways of generosity and indiscrimination.

Considering that it was in those ways of generosity and indiscrimination that they had met each other in the first place, it was strange that this contract took eight months to collapse of old age. When they talked about the early months of their relationship, Sam and Harry laughed about it, these days. They had met, after all, in a bar in Bideford – not a gay bar, since Bideford had never had such a thing, but a bar that had been declared gay for the afternoon and evening, to accommodate the attendees of the one-time-only Devon Gay Pride. (Sixty-three men and nine women had turned up, marched from one end of Bideford high street to the other, retired to the well-intentioned Crown, which, despite the non-recurrence of Devon Pride, would be known for ever more to the awestruck youth of a county and a half as a gay bar and the object of yokel dares and forfeits.) They had laughed and laughed about Bideford Pride, the one trundling lorry festooned with borrowed tinsel, the parade that had lasted all of eleven minutes. After half a dozen beers and a dozen ten-minute snogs in between – you could tell, Sam firmly believed, you could absolutely tell about a person from whether you wanted to go on kissing them and if they wanted to go on kissing you too, and on those grounds he'd never for one moment had a doubt about Lord What-a-Waste – they'd taken it further, had gone into the pub toilet, where Harry had proved himself made of sterling stuff by producing two grams of top-class cocaine – in Bideford! – and then giving Sam the shag of a lifetime. Sam remembered every-thing, every fixture and fitting within the cubicle rattling like a shed in a tornado as Sam rested his foot on the toilet bowl, the top of the paper holder, and finally the cistern. And then the faces turning to them in awe, amusement or disapproval when they came back to the bar, twenty-five minutes later.

It was not very likely that, meeting in this way, either of them believed in the other's innate fidelity and monogamy. It was not likely that, as they said, the moment they laid eyes and hands on each other was the moment that a change, not just in their habits but in their nature, took place. So it was only eight months later that, at Adam and Blaise's for dinner, they'd admitted that an alteration into monogamy hadn't happened, that it wasn't going to happen, that it didn't make any difference to the way they were to each other.

They were mostly Sam's friends, though in years to come, Harry would introduce a couple of his old friends to the group. The son of his father's old gardener, a London couple from Harry's misspent youth who had moved down here to take to furniture-making, a Spanish waiter found in a pub in the middle of Dart-moor, inexplicably; those were Harry's finds. Sam's friends were people he had been at school with, had known over the years without being able to say how or where they'd first met, people who had always been some part of Sam's life, bringing boyfriends from time to time with them. Mick and Ali; Peter in Bideford; Phil and Steve, who ran the garage in Barnstaple. There was Andy, and Adam, who'd wanted to come into the business with Sam, being keen on all things African, and Blaise, whom he'd met in Senegal on the beach on holiday. Adam had gone back five times in one year to see Blaise, the fifth time bringing Blaise back with him, starry-eyed and dead set against the warning of all his friends. But they'd been wrong and Adam had been right, because Blaise had got a degree and British citizenship and now, twelve years on, did very well in the estate-agent business. It had been at their place that the moment of honesty, or the breakdown in Harry and Sam's temporary monogamy, had happened.

Since then, they had been going round the houses, once a month or so, sometimes more frequently, sometimes a little less often. They were all middle-aged, mostly fairly hairy, mostly bearded, and comfortably a touch overweight, or a little more than that. (Most of them went from fourteen stone upwards, to be honest.) The Bears met, dined, turned from booze to coke, speed, a pill or two, and then someone would start groping another, a snog would start someone else off, someone would enhance a snog with a snort off a bottle of poppers, a grope would turn into a blow-job, and then someone, overheated with a line of coke, would rip his shirt off, and it would go on from there. That first night, at Adam and Blaise's, the pair of them had disappeared in an expectant mood neither Harry nor Sam could account for, and reappeared five minutes later with a little tray of the narcotic goods, and both of them naked with (in Blaise's case) a remark-able lolling erection like a mast in a stiff breeze. That had been for the sake of the newcomers, and something similar had happened to welcome the gardener's son and the Spanish waiter to the group since then. Normally they just got on with it.

It was not a regular appointment, like Miranda's book club, every first Thursday of the month. At some point, two weeks or eighteen days after the previous encounter, a Bear would phone another. 'What's up?' they would begin, and after a bit of negotiation with the diary, a Bear would offer his and his Bear's house in a week or ten days' time. The word would spread: the date would be delayed a few days to fit in with some stragglers and busy Bears; the dinner menu would be set – nothing too elaborate, usually a roast and some roasted root vegetables, at the least an elegantly refined imitation of a shepherd's pie with Italian *ragù* and celeriac in the mash. A couple of fresh bottles of poppers would be ordered, and a couple of dozen condoms to have lying around – the Bears generally brought their own drugs. Bears drank white wine, vodka, Negronis (Sam), some bottled beer afterwards, and, to a surprising extent, sweet American fizzy drinks. Some of them were more fought over than others – you rather had to get to Harry's gardener's boy and Harry's Spanish waiter before they got to each other, and it was only a matter of time before they were going to withdraw from the group altogether, and permanently. There was a bit of a well-mannered shuffling not to find yourself next to Peter from Bideford, with his soft open mouth, baby-pink smooth belly, fluffy, patchy pubic hair and long, thin, dispiriting penis with its foreskin dribbling on unnecessarily for half an undecided inch. But everyone had had everyone else within the group, and it made a change, politely going round the group, from your usual husband or partner, and for Peter, a nice once-a-month opportunity to get some sex. Or at least they supposed so.

'I really don't want to go to Peter's,' Harry said. 'I'm sorry, but there it is. I'm sure he's perfectly nice, really. I just don't want him feeling that he can stick his tongue down my throat because he's cooked me a roast dinner.'

'If it were just the tongue he shoves down your throat . . . I know what you mean,' Sam said. 'He's not going to go for you, though. He's going to go for me.'

'Well, you've got yourself to blame for that,' Harry said. The last time they had been at a gathering, three months before, Sam had actually let Peter fuck him, out of the general goodness of his heart. Peter had phoned the next day; Harry had answered the phone, and said briefly and civilly that Sam was in the shower and would call him back. He had said the same the next day, and the day after that. After that, the phone calls had become more sporadic, and Sam and Harry had made excuses for the next two or three gatherings.

'I bet we're not the only ones,' Sam said.

'The only ones what?' Harry said. 'Oh, I see – you think no one else will be wanting to go round there. No, I dare say not.'

'Sit it out again, do you reckon?'

'If we carry on sitting it out –' a girl and a boy came into the shop '– they'll stop asking us altogether before much longer.'

Sam desisted. Pairs of schoolchildren were the bane of his life. They never bought any cheese: they were only ever interested in the knick-knacks and cheese-related gifts. This pair went from object to object, picking one up and setting it down, lifting the lids of one cheese dish after another as if there might be something inside just one of them, showing each other the comic cheese-worm-handled knife and giggling. This pair seemed completely lost in each other. Sam recognized Miranda's Hettie, and the boy seemed familiar too; it was the American's boy, the one who had gone upstairs with Hettie in a grump, and come down with her in a perfect erotic glow. It had taken Sam a moment to recognize Hettie, surprisingly; it must have been the perfect erotic glow, which was coating her in an implausible and unprecedented glamour.

'Hello, Hettie,' Sam said.

'Hello,' Hettie said, not obviously abashed. The conversation lapsed there.

'What can I do for you?' Sam said.

'Have you got any cheese?' Hettie said.

'Well, what would you like?' Sam said.

'I don't know,' Hettie said, and giggled. 'Have you seen my new bracelet?' She showed him an Oriental bracelet, fishing it out of a grubby paper bag; perhaps a love-gift from the American from the shop next door.

'Is your mother at home?' Harry called from the back room.

'Is that your boyfriend?' Hettie said.

'You know Harry,' Sam said. 'He came for New Year's Eve at your house, don't you remember?'

'Oh, yes,' Hettie said. 'I know his name's Harry. I just didn't know he was your boyfriend.'

The American boy stood by her, so wide-eyed it was clear this was some dare cooked up in advance.

'Well,' Harry said, coming out into the shop holding the remnants of his much-read and scribbled-over *Guardian*. 'I think I might be a little bit old for anyone to call me their boyfriend, these days. But I suppose that's the word.'

'Is this your boyfriend, Hettie?' Sam said, not letting her get away with this. 'No one would say he's too old to be a boyfriend.'

Hettie left off struggling to get the single bracelet over her wrist; it had been made for small Indian women and their tiny joints, not Hettie's robustness, or her fat hands. 'I hate you,' she said. 'Never, ever, come over to our house again. If you come, I'll slam the door in your face and say, "That was nobody," or "It was carol singers," if my mum asks. I hate you.'

''Bye, Hettie,' Sam said, not reacting to this at all. The American boy followed, plum-faced and sheepish, behind Hettie. 'I'd love to be that age again, to say, "I hate you." When was the last time you told someone you hated them?'

'God knows,' Harry said.

Harry went back into the back room. Sam put on a different CD, mildly bored with Nusrat Fateh Ali Khan, or whatever he was called; he put on the soundtrack to *Dil Se*. He went over to rearrange the ceramic dishes in the cabinet, thinking that he might replace the present small-at-the-front, big-at-the-back arrangement with a series of small at left to big at right. After five minutes he stood back to admire the initial effect: he did not admire the initial effect. Sam went over to the CD player, realizing as he always did that the soundtrack to *Dil Se* misled him, since he only really liked the first number, the one in the film with all the dancers on top of the train. He took it off, and put on the Scissor Sisters.

'About Peter, though,' Harry said, coming out of the back room again.

'About Peter.'

'I don't honestly see us going over there.'

'No.'

'And if we don't?'

'They're going to stop asking us altogether.'

'I suppose so. Why don't we phone everyone and ask them round to ours, then?'

'To ours? Saturday?'

'I don't see why not,' Harry said. 'I'm sure if we just phoned everyone and said, "Look, we don't want to go to Peter's, it's our turn, come round to ours." If we said that, everyone would come.'

'Even Peter?'

'Oh, I'm sure. It must have been ages since – Christ—'

Christ was Harry's response to a figure falling heavily outside.

15.

It was a beautiful day, and Catherine had decided to go for a walk. The numbers of unfamiliar figures walking the streets of Hanmouth had somewhat diminished but not fallen off altogether. The girl who was kidnapped had encouraged the visitors for a while, and then they had gone away. Alec said they naturally wouldn't be as interested now, but Catherine didn't see that. The woman herself had been arrested, though it didn't seem as if they knew any better than they ever had what had happened to the little girl. The newspapers were confused and confusing, and given to making peremptory demands on their front pages, of whom it was not clear: TELL US, they began. The numbers in the streets had fallen off, and the day-tripper quality had diminished, even though it was half-term this week. But there were still unfamiliar faces walking the streets of Hanmouth. They had a more professional quality now. They were in pairs and single. They stopped dead at the corners of streets, looking upwards. They took photographs of corners, of buildings, of individuals, in surprising ways that were not those of the ordinary person. They lay on their backs in the street, a camera to their faces; they pushed the lens right up into your terrified eyes. Sometimes these people acknowledged each other, gave each other a small, suspicious nod. They clearly did not care, and they clearly had some kind of job to do. Where these photographs would appear, accompanied by what commentary, Catherine did not know and would not enquire. A spirit of investigation had taken over the town, replacing the spirit of vulgar curiosity, and there was nothing festive about it.

Mr Calvin was coming out of the yellow-painted door, sunk below the level of the pavement, at the same time as Catherine was passing. He was wearing a light, sand-coloured suit with a blue shirt and a paisley silk flourish in his top pocket – a piece of bravado, perhaps. 'Good morning,' Catherine said and, with a short hesitation, John Calvin said hello back. Did he live on his own? He shut the door, and began to walk in the same direction as her. Catherine was about to make a further observation – she would not have mentioned anything about the investigation, or about the development with regards to Calvin's friend, client, whatever she was, being arrested. She would have made it less awkward, the walking next to each other by chance; no more than two hundred yards, it would have been, before she went into a shop. She might have talked about David and his friend coming up to stay for the weekend, for instance, and reminded Mr Calvin that she had invited him to their little drinks on the Saturday evening. 'It's . . .' she began to say, but probably a little bit uncertain. You could have mistaken it, she supposed, for a cough or a meaningless noise. In any case, Mr Calvin performed a small pantomime of forgetting, slapping his forehead, tutting, shrugging, before turning without saying anything further to rescue from the house whatever it was he was pretending to have forgotten for his morning outing. They had hardly greeted, and Catherine did not think herself justified in waiting for him to come out with his handkerchief, wallet, or Panama, whatever it was. In any case, the pantomime was clearly meant to give her the chance to walk on ahead and give him the chance to walk in solitude. Catherine did think that a bit rude. Perhaps he didn't want to go over his role in supporting the awful family with someone he didn't really know.

'Do you want to come out?' Tony said to Sylvie, in Sylvie's kitchen. In the past, they had, independently, taken the opportunity to go away at half-term. Now, the closure of the school for a week had let them both sit around. Sylvie had been getting on with her work; Tony had been talking to divorce lawyers. 'It's my sister's birthday next week. I never know what to buy her for a present.'

'Buy her bath salts,' Sylvie said, engrossed in a newspaper story. 'Do you know, this disease, here in the paper, it can strike you down without any warning, and you feel perfectly normal, there's no way you can tell you have it?'

'What – you feel normal before you get it?' Tony said.

'No, afterwards. After you've got it, you still feel totally normal. That's the scary thing.'

'Does it kill you?'

'No, it just lies in your system, and you have to have a test to know that you've got it – you'd never know otherwise. It can stay there for years, and you don't know you're ill at all. There's no symptoms.'

'Terrifying,' Tony said. 'But my sister.'

'Bath salts,' Sylvie said. 'I've bought my mother bath salts every year since I was fourteen. I don't think she likes them, but she sort of expects them now.'

'My sister's only twenty-nine,' Tony said. 'I can't buy her bath salts.'

'Buy her a PlayStation then,' Sylvie said. 'That's unusual. Are you full brother and sister, or did your dad remarry?'

'I'm only forty-four,' Tony protested. 'There's a difference, I know. I don't suppose she was planned. I remember my mother telling me I was going to have a little brother or sister. It was really pretty embarrassing.'

'Well, I don't suppose your mother and father thought about whether she was going to embarrass you before they decided to have another baby,' Sylvie said.

Tony paused. That was, in fact, exactly what he had always supposed, that everything in the family was planned with first regard for what he would think about it. 'I was a single child,' he said. 'Until I was fifteen. It forms your sense of self.'

'Well, there you go,' Sylvie said, poring over her sickness special.

'Are you coming out, then?' Tony said.

Sylvie looked up at him, a wedge of teeth torn toast in her left hand, a red smear of jam on the lenses of her big man's spectacles. 'Well,' she said, 'I was hoping to spend my morning pasting erect penises onto paper. I'm way behind.' She paused: there was no response from Tony. 'Oh, all right,' she said. 'Let's see what's going down.'

She left the toast and the half-finished coffee where it was, an archipelago of crumbs, a brushstroke of jam across the pages of the *Guardian*. With the back of her hand, she made a cleaning gesture at her face, then, in an unhurried way, went into the downstairs bathroom. Tony reached for the newspaper, shaking it, removing the jam-smeared health pages and going on to the environmental reports. Uninhibited noises as of battle, deep in the throat, the sounds of solids and water beating against each other, came from behind the white iron-riveted door. When Tony had lived here a little longer, he hoped to start to suggest that Sylvie use the upstairs bathroom for her morning shit, at least while other people were still finishing their breakfast, and not leave the door open afterwards. She emerged in time, went upstairs, descended with an unironed blouse on, hardly more presentable than what she had been wearing, then went to the coat-rack. 'What's the weather like?' she said.

203

'I don't know,' Tony said. 'I've not been outside this morning.'
'Who fetched the paper?' she said.

'No one did,' Tony said. 'It's yesterday's. I was going to get today's when I went out.'

'I thought it sounded familiar, all that about the undetectable disease,' Sylvie said.

Billa was putting on her coat, then changed her mind as she was halfway to the door, turned, took it off her, put it back on the hook in the hallway. The flagged hallway of her house was dark, hung with eighteenth-century watercolours, the fat trees like green powder puffs over heated cows at the river. The walls of the house were solid and thick, and the heavy front door had a fanlight that had needed painting for half a dozen years. The day fell through the thin, watery old glass, bubbled and warped, and cast a thin, vaporous shape on the dark flagstones. It was not hot within the house – the walls were half a yard thick, and the windows shuttered against the day. Neither heat nor noise penetrated her house, but from old practice Billa knew as she stood in her hallway whether it was hot outside, whether the streets were full of the chatter of unfamiliar folk. Without quite knowing what she was reading, she turned about and left her coat on the peg, feeling the heat of the day, and knowing that her town had lost the rubberneckers of the day before. She thought she might drop in on Kitty, buy a nice quarter of Sharpham rustic at Sam's, see what was up and what today's topic might be; might try to track down a P.D. James the Brigadier hadn't read in the charity shops and Frank Cohen Books. He liked his P.D. James, the Brigadier, was good at not letting on about the solution if Billa read it after him, or only to the extent of saying 'Have you got to the retired monk? Keep an eye on the retired monk. Not all he seems.'

'Do you want anything?' Billa called. 'Got everything you need?'

'Almost everything, my darling,' the Brigadier said. 'Important things to do. Vital things to discover. Endless novelties to propagate, I dare say. The gawping populace, full of scandal, dying to pass it on. Not for me. There's half an hour left of *Jeremy Kyle* to enjoy.'

'Now, now,' Billa said. 'Not just gossip, you know. Important things to buy. We're out of Cif.'

'Doesn't Mrs Carcrash look after that side of things?' the Brig said, coming out of the drawing room. 'It seems an ill-managed sort of affair. She's the one who revels in using the beastly stuff, I believe. So she knows when it's in need of replacement, and why she can't just pick the stuff up herself for a minor premium and then fleece us of the readies . . .'

'I'm sure there's a very reasonable explanation,' Billa said. 'It's a lovely day. I do hope you're not going to stuff away inside watching the problems of degenerates on the telly screen the whole day.'

'Not the whole day, my darling,' the Brigadier said, and Billa went out, shutting the Suffolk pink door behind her.

'Bloody queers, bloody poofs, bloody,' Hettie said, 'bumming bum-bandits, bloody fucking fudge-packers, they think they can talk to anyone like that,' she went on, muttering under her breath.

'Bloody faggots,' Michael said, but more decisively. Outside the post office they stood looking at the cards advertising dog-walkers, cleaners, pianos and canteens of cutlery for sale, and here and there a card from a forlorn town-dweller asking for property to rent, and property for sale. A mother with two children, one in a pushchair, one dragging its heels along the pavement, nego-tiated Hettie and Michael.

'That's American,' Hettie said. 'Bloody faggots. It doesn't make any sense, saying a person is a small bundle of minced meat that you could eat with peas. Why would you say that? It's stupid. Over here, we don't say faggot.'

'Fags,' Michael said, growling.

'That's even more stupid, saying a homosexual queer person is like a cigarette – that makes no sense, it's really stupid. Here in Britain we don't say "fag" or "faggot". A person might say, "Can

I bum a fag?" and there wouldn't be any untoward implication that he wanted to push his penis into the back-bottom of a man, it wouldn't mean that at all. Don't you understand proper English?'

'Yeah, we speak English.'

'We don't say those things. We speak English properly and we say fudge-packer, arse-bandit, cock-jockey, uphill-gardener, turd-burglar, shirt-lifter – we say shirt-lifter, too. Do you get that, they're called shirt-lifters because they lift the shirt, behind, you know, and then, boom! In they go, that Sam and his boyfriend, his old boyfriend, they put down their cheese and then they're at it like turd-burglars. Can you imagine them? Going at it? Shit-stabbers, that's another good one, because, you know.'

Michael shook his head. Hettie's precise pronunciation, her excited and strangulated sentences were directed not at him, he understood, but at the trickle of people going in and out of the post office. It was not clear to Michael what the post office did in Hanmouth: were the people in this town constantly sending things to their friends and relations? There were always people going in and out of the post office. What could they be doing all that time? Was there some other purpose to this business behind the stationery, the calendars at the front, the glass-shielded clerks at the back? He didn't know.

'It's boring here,' Hettie said. 'Don't you think it's boring here? If I lived in America I'd never want to leave it. New York, Chicago, LA, DC, SF, LV.'

'What's LV?'

'Don't you know anything, that's Las Vegas, it's what people call it. Everyone calls it that. No, they don't, I was kidding you, I was having a laugh. I just made that up. Imagine if you said, "I'm going to LV." You wouldn't know what a person was talking about – you'd think they'd gone mental and doo-lally in the head, you would!'

'It's not all excitement all the time,' Michael said. He considered that he was entitled to give Hettie the impression that he lived in an exciting country. His parents' view that America might not be considered by everyone in the world the best country imaginable seemed to Michael a curious, wilful, mistaken opinion. It was not so much patriotism as plain recognition of the facts that led him to tell Hettie about the excitement of his life. But in reality, the town he and his family lived in, with its sawmills, the central square and the courthouse clock, the diner and the Wal-Mart just out of town, was not so very different from Hanmouth, apart from the flags outside every commercial building and most private houses.

'I'm bored now,' Hettie said. 'Look at that weirdo.'

In the middle of the road, exactly between the sweetshop-cum-video-rental and the cheese shop, a man was squatting on his haunches; he was wearing a black polo-neck sweater and black jeans, a pair of sunglasses in his tousled hair. He was holding a camera to his face, taking a photo of the high street from a low angle. 'Stupid idiot,' Hettie said. 'If a car came up behind him, whoosh, it'd knock him over and run him down. If one hooted, even, to get him to move out of his way. Come on.'

Hettie ran away, skipping a little, and Michael followed; he had a nervous tight way of running, his elbows and knees held together like a wooden puppet's. 'Let's get him,' Hettie yelled. 'You go to the right –' and the man was confusedly standing, half balancing. Hettie gave him a little push, nothing more, as she ran past him, sending him flying into Michael, who gave him a good shove. It sent the man sprawling in the middle of the street, a crack as his camera hit the tarmac.

'Did you see that?' Hettie called. 'Did you see? That was brilliant.'

'Brilliant,' Michael yelled. Hettie could not know that he was enjoying the English word; it was just her ordinary word, and an acquisition of vocabulary for him. Only that morning, at breakfast, he had told his mother that the toast was smashing. 'Brilliant,' Michael called again, but he had overtaken Hettie and had to turn his head, and somehow, without knowing how, a woman, some old woman was there where there had been no old woman before, and he didn't know how, he was cannoning into her, and Hettie, who must have seen, who was just cannoning into him for the fun of it, was ramming into his back and pushing him and the old woman over, her voice the scream of a gull, making a noise only somewhat like laughter. Then the old woman was on the ground, and they were running away. No one had seen them. The old woman couldn't have been sure anyone in particular had knocked her over. In five minutes they were past Hettie's house, to the end of the Strand, and to the far end of the Wolf Walk, where the pavement curved round like an underlining of the estuary, the line of the sea, the hills and the sky, and fat-chested wading birds picked their way across the pimpled mud like mad, minatory headmasters. They plumped themselves down on a bench, puffing in and out, then making a parody of puffing in and out; Hettie pretended to choke and die, rolling off the bench and doing a good impersonation of someone suffocating. Finally, she got up and sat back down again.

'It's not funny, though,' she said. 'It's not. Someone might of got hurt. Did you think of that?'

'That was that old woman,' Michael said. 'That old woman that time.'

'It was the general's wife,' Hettie said. 'It was Billa.'

'It was biller?'

'She calls herself Billa,' Hettie said. '*I* don't know what it's short for. It doesn't seem to be a name at all. Perhaps she's a man and she's called Billiam. William. It wasn't your fault.'

Michael paused. He was wondering about where the birds wading went to the bathroom, whether they had a special place, or whether they just went wherever they happened to be, even if they were going to wade through it afterwards, and even put their spoon-ended beak in the same stuff, all mixed up with mud and anything. You couldn't tell.

'It wasn't my fault,' Michael said.

'Well, it wasn't my fault either,' Hettie said, outraged. 'It was

208

her fault for just standing there in the middle of the road. People sometimes they have places they need to be in a hurry and someone like Billa, she's the general's wife, sometimes she doesn't understand that, not one bit.'

'No one comes down here,' Michael said, when some time had passed. The day was tranquil beyond the ceremonies of town and river, rising forgetfully into the blue sky. 'I've never seen anyone down here.'

It wasn't true, not quite; but it was something that suited this moment, and so Michael said it. They both sat there; a *kraarque*, *kraarque* of a bird overhead, the miniature splashes of the estuary between tides, the distant humming grind of a petrol-driven boat heading north to the Bristol Channel and the open sea.

'I really love you, Michael,' Hettie said. 'I really, really do.'

Michael sat exactly as he was, and in a moment, Hettie's trembling hand crept from his elbow to his neck, cupping the back of his head in her palm. He waited, calmly; she did not seem to be expecting him to say anything in response.

'I love you so much,' Hettie said, in the end. 'I've never loved anyone as much, never, ever. Michael, I love you. I'd even show you my hatpin, Michael, I would.'

16.

Harry and Sam rushed to the door, and in the street, people had turned and returned to the figure lying on the kerb. 'I'm quite all right,' she was saying. 'It was just that I got knocked somewhat by, by—'

It was Billa, her stockings torn and her skirt riding indelicately upwards. Her hair was knocked sideways somehow, and she looked dazed and old. 'I'm quite all right,' she said, but to nobody in particular. Around her the four or five Samaritans looked doubtful, unsure: Hanmouth figures, all of them, more or less recognizable. 'Don't move,' the woman from the flats was saying, in an authoritative way.

'Billa, come in and have a cup of tea before you go on your way,' Sam said.

'Oh, Sam, thank you,' Billa said.

'Don't move,' the woman said – it was Catherine, Sam remembered. 'I was a nurse – you shouldn't move until the ambulance gets here. Has anyone called for an ambulance?'

'Oh, nonsense,' Billa said, but her voice was tremulous, weak and old. 'There's nothing at all the matter with me.'

'Better safe than sorry,' Catherine was saying, running her hands expertly over Billa's legs and hips, impersonally and without hesitation; testing and pressing quickly and, at the same time, tidying Billa's disarray up a little. 'Any pain at all? Here – here – here?'

'Well, it was a nasty bang,' Billa said. 'I came a cropper, I really did, head over heels. I can't think what happened. I've always had weak ankles. I'm often just folding up like a pack of, a pack of . . .'

'Let me fetch you something,' a woman said, in an unironed blouse, crumpled and, though clean, stained with unerasable stains. 'I'll get you a cushion – may I? Tony,' speaking now to her companion, an unlikely man for her, neat, with cropped white hair and a slightly defeated manner, 'Tony, don't just stand there.'

'I'm really quite all right,' Billa said. 'I'm most awfully grateful to you all. It is kind, but I promise you, I'm quite undamaged. It was just my ankles, my wretched ankles – they've always let me down at the worst possible moment.'

She gestured downwards, and it could be seen that her right ankle was already swelling. A sprain could be terribly bad, someone remarked, as painful as a break, in fact.

'It's so easy to fall over nothing, isn't it?' Billa said. 'There was nothing underfoot at all, either.'

'Actually,' Harry said. 'I think it was a pair of kids. Running hell for leather. They knocked you over.'

210

'Christ – in Hanmouth,' the woman said. 'You can't believe it.'

'Did you see who they were?' Harry said, turning to Sam.

'No,' Sam said. 'I don't believe I did.'

He looked down the road, and there was nobody but John Calvin, looking with great interest into a shop window, four doors down, pretending nothing had happened, and that if it had, he hadn't seen anything. It was a shame that the window he happened to be by was only the Sea Rescue charity shop, and he seemed to be examining a display of baby's bootees.

'Now,' Billa said, seizing Catherine's arm and hoicking herself upwards, 'just a quick cup of sweet tea, if you don't mind, Sam, and then I'll get myself home. I think I'll give my constitutional a miss, if that's any reassurance to you. Don't you worry yourself about me.'

Sam and Harry between them carried Billa, protesting her good health all the while, into the shop; there was a white-painted wicker chair for customers to sit in while they chose between curd cheeses, and Billa was placed solidly in it. 'What a palaver,' Catherine said cheerfully, following Sam into the little galley kitchen. 'I don't think there's anything broken, but it's probably best to call an ambulance.'

'I don't think Billa would let you,' Sam said. 'She knows best. I don't suppose she'd hesitate if she felt she'd really been damaged. Let's see how she feels after a cup of tea.'

'Do you think she would like to come to our little party on Saturday?' Catherine said. 'You remember, we're having a party on Saturday? I do hope you and your friend can come – you're very welcome.'

'Harry, you mean? That is a shame – Harry, I was just saying to Catherine, it's a great shame, she's having a party on Saturday, and we've just this second said we're having a couple of old friends round for dinner. I am sorry.'

'So am I,' Harry said, in the doorway to the kitchen, clearly wondering who Catherine was. 'But we do have some friends

211

coming for dinner. Nothing very smart, but I don't think we can cancel it now.'

'What a shame,' Catherine said. 'It's an early-evening drink, I don't suppose that makes a difference? Six to eight? And our son is coming, he's here for the weekend, with his new friend, an Italian, he tells us. It would be nice to introduce them to – to – to some new friends and neighbours. A very early party? You would only have to drop in, and it's just over the road. We live in Woodlands, the block on the Strand, you know, top floor, six to eight on Saturday.'

'I'm afraid not,' Harry said. 'It would have been nice, but I know what Sam is like when we're having people round for dinner. He's in a state of the utmost panic from four o'clock onwards. It's absurd, and they're very old friends who wouldn't mind if we did the vacuuming or not, but there it is. You wouldn't want him as your guest when he's expecting guests himself.'

'Oh, I'm sure that's not true,' Catherine said. 'Well, if you change your minds – we're only over the road, it would be a pleasure to see you, even if just for ten minutes when you find the table's been set and everything's in the oven, and you don't quite know what to do with yourselves . . . Shall I make the tea?'

In the shop itself, the hippieish woman, whose name had turned out to be Sylvie, was settled with her friend Tony; one of the Brigadier's cronies and his wife, a pillar of the amateur dramatics, had seen Billa placed squarely in the chair, her torn stockinged legs set firmly apart. There was quite a gathering as Billa explained again that she had fallen over nothing at all, that she couldn't understand it. The Brigadier's crony could be heard saying that he would run over the road to fetch Tom in a moment; Sylvie was telling the pillar of the am-dram that she had seen a pair of children knocking Billa over and running away, and that someone else had seen exactly the same thing. 'What's up, Billa?' said a voice from the open doorway. 'Always the centre of excitement, aren't you?' It could have been Kitty, or it could have been someone else entirely. Conversation divided, multiplied, chattered, and from the kitchen Sam observed one of them, with an 'oof', picking up a cow-shaped cheese dish and turning it over to see if there was a price on it. There was no cloud, he remarked inwardly; somebody would buy something; and Catherine, as she was passing round cups and mugs of tea to all and sundry, was inviting them all at the same time to her Saturday party.

'I suppose,' Harry said, 'I suppose we've rather committed ourselves now.'

'I don't mind,' Sam said, picking up the last remaining mug, a cracked and rather dirty World's Greatest Cousin left by someone or other, and shaking the pot to see if there was anything left in it. 'I'll make a shepherd's pie, shall I?'

17.

The doorbell went deep into Mauro's dream like a sword, withdrew, then plummeted deep again. He pulled his duvet into a ball, then rolled himself around it, cursing. He could not think what day it was, or what the noise of the bell signified; then, stretching backwards, pulling his arms above his head, he remembered. He yawned violently, shook himself, and leapt to his feet. He did some rudimentary exercises, flinging himself into an X shape, then back again, four or five times. Then he went to the window in his pants, looked through the curtains at the street below. There was Mr Poppers on the pavement, car keys in hand. Mauro looked down at him; at the same moment, Mr Poppers looked up at Mauro, and their gazes locked. Mauro gave his most brilliant smile, and a gesture that meant I'm coming down, or You're down there, or Hold on, or something similar. He threw on a dressing-gown and went to let Mr Poppers in.

Mr Poppers had come into Mauro's life at a convenient moment. Mauro had left Rome when he couldn't see very much alternative. The job as a waiter in the terrible restaurant by the Colosseum had come to an end. The restaurant existed solely to serve tourists – no one had ever come twice to the Incantevole, with its blue plastic sign, the image of a beckoning mermaid on the fascia. It had made a sort of living taking orders for, say, bruschetta and a plate of spaghetti, then delivering to the table unrequested great bowls of risotto, oysters buried in ice on steel salvers, *grigliata mista* and elaborate salads with egg quarters forming floral designs on top. If they ate them, thinking that they were on the house, so much the better; if they turned them away, you gave them untouched to the next customer. Either way you gave them a bill for 600 euros at the end.

The Incantevole's owner was Paolo Crichetti, a dry, professorial man with a shaved head and accurately assessing eyes, only thirty, but looking older. The restaurant did not have a long future ahead of it. Mauro's career with the Incantevole had been still shorter. He had observed that two out of three customers disputed the bill, some demanding the attendance of the *carabinieri*, and eventually the bill was reduced to, say, 120 euros. Four days a week Crichetti was away from the restaurant during lunch, leaving Mauro more or less in charge. When he returned, Mauro was trusted to tell Crichetti how many customers had paid the full amount, and how many had insisted on an informal rebate. It worked quite well for a few weeks. Then Crichetti turned up unexpectedly; he had discovered that Mauro was pocketing an extra 400 or 800 euros every lunchtime service, and he should get out and think himself lucky nothing worse was coming to him. Mauro never found out who had informed on him; it must have been the Ghanaian chef, working on the side, undeclared to the authorities, who had observed, recorded, passed it all along to Crichetti, and good luck to him. Mauro left the same day, and dropped a small unsigned note to the immigration authorities that evening, suggesting they pay a visit to the Ghanaian chef and his illegal employer.

Quite soon afterwards, Mauro's parents asked him to leave their flat; they didn't have money to spare, they said. It didn't cost them any money, having him there, Mauro pointed out, only the cost of a cup of coffee in the morning, or were they talking about the cost of the bathwater? No, they said patiently, they weren't talking about any of that. Mauro knew what they were talking about, they said, and it wasn't pleasant to think that they couldn't leave their wallets and purses lying about in case their own son . . . and it wasn't pleasant to worry about their own son taking drugs in the house, they said.

His friends melted away like ice in coffee – he had thought them his friends, all those people picked up, danced with, lent spliffs to, introduced to, kissed, taken to an Ostia open-air club on the back of a borrowed Vespa, given secrets to and listened to in the small hours in the back bedroom of a seventh-floor apartment in EUR. All those people had, on investigation, something against Mauro; they had heard some bad story about him; he owed them 500 euros, or fifty, or – they said, but it couldn't be true – 5,000; they wouldn't trust him; they couldn't help him; they wouldn't answer his calls if they recognized the number he was calling from. He'd forgotten that Paolo Crichetti was the brother of a boy he'd been inseparable from one summer, had hugged and kissed and driven to Ostia on the back of a borrowed sky-blue Vespa; that that was how he had met Paolo Crichetti and got the job in the first place. Paolo Crichetti had spread the word. No one would give him a job or a room at their place, no, not even if he paid them back the fifty or 500 or – this one couldn't be true – 5,000. 'This is a small town,' Marco Crichetti had said; he was now serious, twenty and studying at a business academy with his twin sister Su-Ellen. 'Everyone knows you, Mauro. You have to go somewhere else.'

'I haven't done anything,' Mauro said. 'I haven't done anything wrong.'

'Just go somewhere else,' Marco said.

Sometimes, Mauro thought, you could get on a plane, and make a decision on the plane, and two hours later get off and be a different and a better person. That was what had happened to him on the plane from London to Rome. The other people on the plane, accepting the harassed stewardesses' offers of hot and cold drinks, half watching the safety demonstrations – they did not notice what had happened to Mauro, but the decision should have shuddered the blue skies above the clouds. He would be a good person; he would be a good friend. To the friends he had not made yet. He would not judge people; he would not take drugs. He would be honest, even if temptation presented itself. He would not do anything with which anyone could reasonably rebuke him afterwards. He would not do anything with which he would be at all likely to rebuke himself afterwards – because, of all things, what pained Mauro most was when he had stolen money was not that they shouted at him and told him what an awful person he was. (Paolo Crichetti and his mother and some other people had said that.) The thing that pained him most was the inner voice, saying to them, 'Yes, you're right, yes, I am, yes, I know.'

For those first weeks in London, his resolution had held. He stayed in a cheap hotel in King's Cross, and when he left, he did not leave surreptitiously, but with his debt paid – in fact, they had insisted that he pay day by day, in advance, but that was the sort of person he now was. He had quickly found a short-term job in a restaurant run by Sicilians: the sort of English he had spoken to the American tourists who were the one-time clients of the Incantevole was, it seemed, good enough for a London restaurant too, if you asked the customers to point as well as speak their order. He found a room in a flat with four other boys, all gay, all foreigners, and they took him out to a bar in Soho, then another one, then a club. Mauro did not drink very much, and you only ever had to buy yourself a first drink, after which men would buy you drinks, as many as you wanted. At clubs, there was always someone who would let you in on the guest list. After two months, Mauro knew all the clubs, and people were starting to know him. Twice a week, sometimes three times a week, he would go back to a man's house, with one man, or

216

sometimes two. His resolution was holding; it was as if the old Mauro had been left behind, and here he had nothing but good new friends. He could be whoever he chose here.

Mr Poppers was an oddity. There were always people like that in clubs, fat men, bald men, old men, men who smelt and did not seem to realize why they were not so popular as fit men, men with hair, men who smelt good and looked good. By this time Mauro was living in a flat over a tanning salon in Clapham with Christian, a dark German-Brazilian boy with a firm, square jaw and a startling swivelling tic of the head, underlying unexpected words as he spoke, somewhere between every twenty seconds and every two minutes. They both worked as waiters at the chic Brazilian *churrascaria* in Gloucester Road, mastering the art of slicing beef off a vertical spit. They had fooled around together once, had shared an English boy once, but were mostly just flat-mates, these days. Mauro had been with Christian the night Mr Poppers – David, properly – had turned up. It had been a heavy weekend. The night before, they'd all gone to the opening of Sister, a club night in Vauxhall, but it had not been much good: the promoter had relied on his friends spreading the word, and he hadn't had enough friends. To make up for it, they'd all gone out the next night in Vauxhall. By two, nobody had found any drugs – the dealers had been cleared out the week before by the police, people were saying. Mauro had shared half a pill with Christian and a line with some boy he'd met, but that was it. They'd all spotted Mr Poppers with his little bottle. 'I don't care,' Mauro said, and he went right up to him, saying how much he loved poppers. And Mr Poppers turned out to be a lucky charm, because five minutes after that, three dealers, one after the other, arrived, and started selling. It was one of the best nights ever, and to top it off, it was the funniest thing ever, the one Mauro ended up going home with was, yes, a boy who fell asleep, him as well, that wasn't the funniest thing, but Mr Poppers had been the one to come home with Mauro. God knows how that happened.

There was a misunderstanding a couple of months later. At the end of the month, neither Mauro nor Christian had enough money to pay the rent. Christian shrugged and said, well, the agency, they'll have to take it out of the deposit, the two months' deposit we gave them when we moved in. 'Can you do that?' Mauro said.

'For this shit-hole, I think, yes, we can,' Christian said, poking with his finger at a hole in the plywood door. But the agency did not take the same attitude. When, at the end of the next month, Christian and Mauro found that they didn't have money to pay that month either, the agency said, quite brutally, that they could either pay two months' rent and leave at the end of that month, or they could leave within five days, to be pursued by the law. Mauro had heard about a room going round the corner, in a smart mansion block, a brick 1930s building with painted iron windows like an ocean liner. He knew one of the boys, and in fact had spent a night there with him. Christian pulled a face and said, well, he could move back to north London, this place looked like it had come to the end of its natural life.

The only trouble was that the new place was asking for two months' deposit as well, £1,200 – Mauro argued and promised and tried to get them to take just one month, but they refused. Mauro didn't have £1,200. 'Ask Mr Poppers,' Christian said. 'You'll only have to do it with him once or twice. How bad could it be?'

'Don't talk about David like that,' Mauro said. He didn't like to think of himself as exploiting David. David was his friend. When he thought of their outings, he grew quite sentimental, regarding himself with some warmth. He was helping David to establish himself, to come to terms with the modern world, and to lose some weight. He did not mock David when he was not in the room; he defended him; his kindliness had spread to other friends Mauro had thought could be introduced to him. But Mauro did not have £1,200, and, as it turned out, Mr Poppers did, and then another £1,200 on top that Mauro thought to include at the last moment. There was, of course, a price to pay for the money, which Mauro paid with a straight face. At some point, he felt, David would let him off the debt if he went on promising he would pay it, and letting people think he was David's boyfriend. He agreed – he was happy that the price was no more than this – he agreed to get into David's car and go to visit his parents in the English country. He had done much worse than that in the past.

18.

'Come in, come in,' Mauro said, lifting the latch. From the other side, a good kick came. The internal fittings of the block were stylish-looking, but most of the interiors and the communal spaces had not been replaced since the block was built, and the panelled doors and the white-painted iron windows all tended to stick. David had been here before, and knew what to do. He kicked again, and it opened. 'I'm not ready at all,' Mauro said, gesturing downwards at his bare chest and the white towel about his middle.

'I can see that,' David said, and they kissed, once on each cheek, leaning forward so that nothing but their cheeks would touch. 'Is everyone asleep?'

'I haven't the foggiest,' Mauro said, smiling brilliantly at his brilliant new idiom, learnt from David the week before. 'I think they must be. Come and sit in my room while I get ready.'

What was once the sitting room of the flat had been given over to one of the flat-sharers, so there was nowhere else to sit but in Mauro's room. Mauro took a pile of his clothes with him to the bathroom. Not for the first time, David wondered about the paucity of Mauro's possessions. David's house was encrusted, laden with acquisitions, few of which he liked, needed or could remember getting; his house was like a gift shop, a curiosity emporium, and on every surface there might be a toy policeman, uttering a harmless obscenity, or a dusty vase of whimsical appearance. One of these days he was going to put all that crap in a big sack and throw it out. Mauro's room, on the other hand, was like a hotel room that the same person had lived in for six days, no more than that. He must have a flat back in Rome, or a room kept for him, sacrosanct, by his parents. Nobody could live with so little.

Presently Mauro came back, his hair wet, black and smoothed down, wearing a clean yellow T-shirt and a pair of faded blue jeans; David marvelled at the luck he had, even knowing someone like this, even having someone like this as his friend. Mauro went on talking about a thief in the restaurant, someone taking tips meant for others, whenever cash was in a saucer; they thought one of the staff was lifting it quietly and keeping it. Nobody knew who it was, though Mauro had his idea. 'Yeah, I know who that fucker is,' he said. 'I hate people who steal. That's the one thing I hate, they're scum.' As he went on explaining, David suppressing the yawn of his interrupted and frustrated sleep, Mauro went on picking pants, socks, a spare shirt, a sweatshirt out of his wardrobe and drawers. 'Will I need a jacket?' Mauro said, and David thought he might. Mauro shrugged, and then, surprisingly, there was a tweedy sort of jacket, more yellow than an English tweed jacket would be.

'I've never seen you wear that,' David said.

'And a tie? Maybe a tie?' Mauro said.

'No, I wouldn't go that far,' David said. 'You ought to wear that more often. It suits you.'

'Not my choice,' Mauro said.

'Was it a present?' David said. 'The jacket, I mean.' There seemed to be an assent. 'Yes, I can imagine that. I bet I know – I bet it was your parents, giving it to you for, what, your twenty-first?' because it looked both slightly old and pristine, as if its few wearings had been spread out over the seven years since Mauro had been twenty-one. 'It's nice, though. You always find the best things tucked away in your own wardrobe.'

'Not a tie,' Mauro said. 'I thought you wore a tie when you go see someone's mum, someone's dad.'

'It's only Devon,' David said. 'There won't be anyone smart to meet. But they said they were having a drinks party, or something. You might feel better with your tweed jacket on.'

'I don't know if it still fits,' Mauro said, but it was difficult to see where Mauro would have gained weight; his sinewy torso must have been much the same a decade ago, and sure enough, when he slipped it on, over the T-shirt and jeans, he looked perfect, the yellow in the cloth making his dark face glow, just as the brighter, blanker yellow in the T-shirt did. Strikingly, his trousers made a smooth surface against his upper thigh, and there was nothing in his pocket to bulge; David was aware that his own pockets were capacious bags, filled with wallets, keys, handkerchiefs, odd bits of acquired goods. He wondered where Mauro put all that necessary stuff.

'You'll do,' David said. Mauro bundled the jacket up and folded it into his brown leather hold-all, on top of his other clothes. It was a more elegant bag for Mauro than David would have anticipated; he caught himself wondering who had given the bag, as well as the jacket, to Mauro. They went.

When they were in the car – David felt almost more of an erotic, a marital thrill at placing Mauro's suitcase next to his own in the boot of the silver Peugeot than he did at Mauro's slipping into the passenger seat with a natural sigh – Mauro began to talk. David had wondered about this: their usual meetings were lubricated with company, alcohol, the hour of the evening and, sometimes, drugs. There, silence or conversation seemed to matter less. He couldn't remember having struggled for something to say, to have filled in space. Now they had to drive, sober, in daylight, for hours into the deepest west, to a place he'd hardly been, to introduce Mauro to his parents, who would have to talk, sober, to him for two whole days.

'Have you ever been outside London?' David said, when they were out of Clapham.

'I went to Brighton once,' Mauro said. 'Where are we going?'

'Did you like Brighton?'

'Oh, I don't know. It was cold, it rained, we stayed in the bars, we came home again. I don't know why we went – Christian had a day off and I called in sick. He said we should go somewhere. He'd heard Brighton was nice.'

'You've never been anywhere else, though.'

'Is it near, where we're going?'

'Near Brighton? No – not really in the same direction, even. Did you hear about the town my parents live in? It's called Hanmouth – Han-mouth. It was in the news.'

'Can we put a CD on? I brought some CDs. They're in my bag.'

'It was a strange story,' David said, realizing at that exact moment that he had gone towards Vauxhall Bridge when he should have gone towards Chelsea Bridge, or further westwards. He silently calibrated his route again. 'This girl went missing – a girl in the village where my parents moved to. It was all over the papers. The girl's mother and father went on television, crying their hearts out. There were policemen all over the place, searching for this girl – first they thought she'd fallen into the river, or got lost, and then they started saying, "Whoever's got her, whoever's taken her, please just bring her back."'

'Yeah, I saw that. The girl – she was in Portugal, wasn't she, a little girl, two, three years old? They never found her.'

'No,' David said. 'That was a different case. This was in Hanmouth, where my parents moved to. It happened a couple of months after they moved there. They said you couldn't move for journalists and people just wanting to stand and stare. It's in Devon.'

'No, I don't think I heard about that, then,' Mauro said. 'That's terrible. And your parents, they knew the girl?'

'No, they'd never seen her,' David said. 'So the police were making all these announcements, and then they said, you know, we're not so sure about this. And the next thing you know, they've arrested the girl's mother. They reckoned that she'd faked her daughter's disappearance, hidden her somewhere, gone on television crying about it.'

'But why does she do that? That's crazy.'

'Well, she goes on television, says, "We can't sleep, we need money to campaign for her return," and people send in donations. Money. Lots of money.'

'How much money, you think, they get sent? A million, you think?'

'I don't know, I didn't hear. But they arrested the mother.'

'Well, but the mother, she gets to keep the money, she gets her million pounds, whatever she gets?'

'No,' David said, slightly shocked at the turn of Mauro's thoughts. 'I don't think she would get to keep any money. There's something called not profiting from the proceeds of crime, isn't there? If you rob a bank, you can't keep what you get.'

'Yes, but you need to hide it, hide it away where the police they can't find it. Do you think she did this, this woman?'

'The thing is, it gets worse. The police arrested the woman and she confesses to what she's done, tells them where the little girl is. She's hiding in the house of a friend of hers, something like that, and they go there, but there's no sign of the girl or the friend. They've disappeared. The mother doesn't know anything about it, where they've gone. Then the friend turns up dead in a field – he was murdered. No sign of the little girl. She's really disappeared.'

'Yes, but the mother, she knows really where her daughter is. She's just not saying.'

'I don't think she does,' David said.

'And I bet the mother, she's hidden the million pounds where her daughter is, they're safe together, she's going to be let out of prison and go off with her daughter and the money, *paff*, *paff*, *paff*,' Mauro said, making his fingers into a gun shape and firing, left to right across the windscreen; perhaps imagining the shoot-out as the mother and her daughter, in some fast sports car, shot behind them at the pursuing police. For a moment David thought of asking Mauro how old he imagined the daughter in the sad tale to be; his idea, that enthusiastic *paff*, *paff*, *paff*, from a

Hollywood fantasy of women running away together. But then he wondered why he cared in the slightest.

'Yeah, I bet that's right,' David said, after a moment. 'We'll be all right when we hit the A4.'

'Hey, I've got Armand van Helden,' Mauro said. 'Can I put it on?'

19.

The day before, David had written his last Chinese blurb:

Why fake being ill? Why should you pretend that that warm delirium has come over you, that you have to go to bed and draw the covers over you? The sheet and your blood turn the world a blank of pink, and you are pulsing away inside your cocoon. Some day soon your lie will catch up with you, and you will see that no one ever believed that you were ill for one second. They only allowed you to think they thought that, to let you off school, to stay home from work, to lie and be brought little sweets and bowls of soup to keep you warm and make you better. Mother-love will do this, even when you are no longer perfectly young. Mother-love knows you best, and understands that sometimes the world is most beautiful when it is rejected and hugged to yourself, beneath the pink or blue covers of your bed, waiting for things to get better. All the same, the golden day sometimes comes when your mother puts a gentle smile on her face, and she says to you, 'I know you are not really ill, but only wanted a rest. But today you can be better, you can go out and look at the world, which is still beautiful and full of bright sunshine, and forget your sickness, the sickness that was never really a sickness at all. Get up, stretch, yawn, smile and see the

224

beautiful world. Recover.' And love, too, is like this. It is always better to stop faking it.

20.

On Tuesday mornings at eleven a.m., Miranda held a seminar at the university. It was for her second-year undergraduates, and on the subject of post-colonial literature. She had been assigned fifteen students for this class, and for the first week fourteen had turned up, clutching their copies of *Oroonoko* and forty pages of photo-copied articles, looking nervous (Miranda, with her severe bob and her way of tapping the table with her pen when a student, asked a direct question, sat in silence, was feared by people she had never taught.) Miranda checked her list. There was a fifteenth name, Sophie Warren. It meant nothing to her. She began to conduct her class, in the grey, windowless room under the morose striplights. She was a good teacher, respecting her good students. In this class, for instance, she never appealed directly to Faisal Khalil on any matter relating directly to colonial theory, as if he might have special knowledge or interest. As far as she knew, he was born in Sutton, and his father, she believed, lived in Barnstaple, working for the sixth-form college. She needed a student like that on her side; and she treated him, at least, with respect whenever he felt like speaking. She was a good teacher.

The next week and the week after, there was no Sophie Warren present – those weeks also saw a couple of the first-week students fail to turn up as well, which was normal. Miranda carried out with contempt the faculty's instruction to sit there with a register, reading out students' names and ticking them off; though she was not a junior-school mistress, and she did not propose to work in a university with a truancy department, she registered the names, and did nothing more about it. She assumed that Sophie Warren, whose name appeared on her class lists, had found herself there

225

by mistake, and after four weeks must have found a home somewhere else.

On the fifth week, Miranda found a new face among the rows of girls and two boys in her post-colonial class. It was meek, downward-looking, with the familiar curtains of blonde hair falling to either side; a book lay open underneath the gaze. There was something protective about the two girls on either side of her – what was it? They had taken on the shape of her hair, her downward gaze, her hands folded in her lap. Reflecting each other, they looked like Rossetti's Sweet Symphonies, and one of them might have been called Gertrude. Miranda thought of telling them this in her best sardonic class manner, but settled for asking the newcomer who she was.

'I'm Sophie Warren,' the girl said, as Miranda expected she would.

'This is the fifth week of term. Where have you been before now?'

'I've been in family difficulties,' the girl said. 'I've caught up with all the work, though.'

'What family difficulties?' Miranda said. 'Or did you say learning difficulties?'

'I'd rather not say,' Sophie Warren said. 'Family difficulties.'

'Well, I'm not very happy about this,' Miranda said. 'You've missed half the classes of the term. You've got the burden of them from a friend who might have been listening, or who might not have been listening. The result of that kind of Chinese-whispers learning, in my experience, is that a student misses a crucial point. He or she drops five marks on an assessed paper. They sadly drop a class on the module. The result is that they narrowly miss a two:one and get a two:two. They leave university with what is nowadays a worthless degree. They have wasted three years of their life and have to get a job at Dolcis, where they remain for the rest of their lives. Nor do they marry, because nobody wishes to marry an assistant in Dolcis. It's a sad story. But the moral is this. Don't miss classes. It's too late for Sophie, of course. But it may not be too late for the rest of you.'

By the time Miranda had got to Dolcis, some of the class, at least, were laughing merrily – the sophisticated part. She was pleased to see that Faisal Khalil, who was quiet but reasonable, was one of the laughing ones – she would hate to think that the one non-white student in the whole of the first year wasn't on her side. The rest of them were looking mutinous, furious, or amazed at being spoken to like that. It was impossible to know what Sophie Warren or her two acolytes – the ones who claimed to have passed on the seminar information – thought. They were head down over their books.

At the coffee break, mid-seminar, Miranda held Sophie Warren back and asked her what was the matter. 'After all,' Miranda said, chortling inwardly, 'if the faculty knows that you are facing some difficult problems, we can deal with them, too.'

'I'd rather not say,' Sophie Warren said. 'They're just family problems, all right?'

'Well, in that case, we can't help you,' Miranda said. 'If people are just going to say, "I've got family problems," every time they don't feel like turning up or doing an essay, it doesn't seem fair on the others, does it?'

At this point Sophie Warren started making loud weeping noises, though clearly not actually crying. Miranda sat and waited.

'God,' Sophie Warren said, with real hatred. 'It's absolutely unbelievable. I've never – never – been spoken to in my life by anyone – anyone at all – in such a way. I'm really thinking of telling my father about this.'

'Yes, that would be a good idea,' Miranda said. 'If family problems are preventing you from studying, we would like to discuss them with your father, and your mother, too, if she is around.'

Sophie Warren now made another burst of weeping noises. When she surfaced, she said briskly, 'Look. It's not a new thing. It's been going on for years between my father and my mother.

227

They've never got on, and now that I've left home to come to this fucking place, they think they might be getting a divorce. I'm so unhappy about it. I felt I had to be with my mother this last four weeks.'

'Well, I do see that,' Miranda said, doing everything she could to put sympathy in her voice. 'In these situations, the faculty of course likes to write a letter to the parents, expressing their concern, and of course saying that they do hope your parents will do everything they can to keep the distress of a family divorce from affecting your work, which is, of course, the most important thing from our point of view.'

'What?' Sophie Warren said. 'No, I don't want you to do that, you mustn't do that, I'm telling you, all right?'

'But of course we must,' Miranda said. She had used this to great effect to entertain herself when lackadaisical students cited dead grandmothers, divorcing parents, and once, a brother being kept in jail in Thailand for drug-smuggling – alas, that last one had turned out to be true, and her family, the student had said, would be very appreciative of the faculty's concern. 'Of course, if I see that your situation is not affecting your work in future – in other words, if you start turning up to classes and doing all the work – then perhaps your family would prefer not to have to deal with expressions of sympathy from people they don't know. I don't know. What do you think?'

'I think you're an awful fucking bitch,' Sophie Warren said, timing this just to coincide with the first students coming back into the room holding cups of coffee, crisps and bananas.

21.

When Kenyon got back from London, on Thursday night or Friday afternoon, he liked to recover from the rigours of his

journey and of his week by cooking. He would usually drop
Miranda a note with a list of what he needed, and she would
absorb it into her weekly shop. Kenyon was a good cook, and
neither Miranda nor Hettie was a particularly fussy eater. So he
often managed to be adventurous. He kept two copies of the
favourite cookbook of the moment, whatever it might be, in his
office in London and in the kitchen in Hanmouth. During the
week he ate in London restaurants near the flat; Miranda and
Hettie ate whatever was consistent with Miranda's long-held
conviction not to be a slave to the kitchen, as her mother had
been, which meant the healthier sort of ready meal and a lot of
stuffed pasta with salad and a tomato sauce. Kenyon's returns
on a Thursday or a Friday night were highlights of the family
week, as he donned the blue striped apron and started to chop
onions and pulverize garlic, with the sharp side or the flat blade
of the knife.

On a sunny day like today, he thought something summery
and yet roasted; he found an idea for chicken roasted in saffron,
hazelnuts and lemon. There might be a herb salad with it –
perhaps just tarragon, parsley and dill, nothing else. He emailed
the details of the food to Miranda, buying some sumac, whatever
sumac might be, in Harvey Nichols. When he got home, it was
all there.

Miranda spent little time using the kitchen for its purpose. But
when Kenyon was cooking in there, she followed him in with a
glass of white wine, and chatted to him as he played about with
his complicated cooking. Boys' stuff, she referred to it as. When
cookery passed out of the realm of women, it had gone only
partially into the habits of men, who naturally took it up in too
complicated and fussy a way. She had said this to Kenyon in the
past. 'You can't help it,' she said. 'You're a man. You have to do
everything as a man does it. You love a little hobby, the more
complicated the better. It's all to do with taking control, and
directing the gaze back to you.' That had been after a notably
irrational *boeuf bourguignon*, when Kenyon had laboured with

a split pig's trotter, discarded before serving, and some home-made dumplings. He had accepted the criticism; Miranda had eaten the French beef stew; and they and Hettie had done the washing-up together.

Miranda was sitting at the kitchen table with a bowl of nuts and a glass of white wine. It was Thursday night; her teaching was over, and so was Kenyon's week. She was talking to Kenyon, ignoring, for the moment, Hettie, who had had plenty of attention since Sunday night.

'And Susie was here. I had lunch with her after she'd done her bit,' she said. 'We went out to that brasserie by the cathedral.'

'Who's Susie?'

'Susie Aboagye,' Miranda said. 'You know her. You met her when we hosted that conference in 2000. She was over from the University of Florida then. She's in England now, she's the professor at Manchester. She came down to give a paper and stayed overnight.'

'You should have asked her to stay here,' Kenyon said.

'Oh, we can't do that,' Miranda said. 'You should know. If we don't spend our entertainment and hospitality budget, it gets cut next year when we might need it. And there was a palaver with a student. She broke the record by not turning up until the fifth week of term. She said she'd been "catching up" with what she'd missed.'

'Gracious heavens,' Kenyon said politely, measuring out sumac with a spoon. The cookbook was not quite clear about its application. Parts of the recipe seemed to suggest the reddish, sour powder – Kenyon had licked his finger and cautiously tasted it – should go on before the roasting, others that it should wait until serving. He decided to do both. 'The trouble is, they want to get everything online nowadays. They don't believe in experiencing anything face to face.'

'Exactly.'

'So what was her excuse?'

Miranda explained about the family troubles of Sophie Warren, and about her own threat to write to the girl's family expressing

230

her regret for their divorce. Kenyon turned round from the oven in amazement.

'One day, you'll go too far,' he said eventually.

'Oh, I already have,' Miranda said. 'I did write to them. Very sorry I was to hear about their family troubles. Understood, on behalf of the university, that divorce was an upsetting thing in anyone's life. However, thought that they might not be aware how far their family situation was affecting their daughter's studying, not turning up for weeks on end, bursting into tears in seminars, could they please, et cetera, et cetera. She told me all her problems. I wrote them down in a letter and sent them to her parents, who, she said, were the cause of all of them.'

'I don't think you should have done that,' Kenyon said. 'I really don't.'

'Well, I've done it now,' Miranda said. 'Let them explain to her what she's done. I don't suppose they're really getting divorced at all.'

'Miranda, that's a terrible thing to do,' Kenyon said. 'If it's not true, they'll be so upset with her.'

'Well, whatever, as students say,' Miranda said. 'I don't suppose there'll be any repercussions. The point is, really, that it isn't fair on the rest of them. They work perfectly hard – they turn up to lectures, they take notes, they contribute to discussions. Why should they do all that if you can get exactly the same degree by just borrowing a few notes off someone else and trying to make some sense out of it? It isn't fair.'

At the end of the table, Hettie sat, mirroring her mother's stance. She was listening in her unnervingly absorbed way; her eyes were going from parent to parent, her mouth slightly open and breathing. In front of her was a heavy blown green Turkish glass, with bubbles still in it, full of a brown fizzy liquid, clinking with ice and a slice of lemon. Her hand went slowly, mechanically, between a bowl of the almost flavourless pastry bits she liked and her mouth. It was all part of Hettie's Thursday- or Friday-night

231

sophistication; she might even, on other nights, have changed into her best blouse.

'Is that your first Coke, Hets?' Kenyon said. 'You know we don't like you drinking too much of that stuff.'

'It's my *apéritif*,' Hettie said sharply. 'Course I don't go on drinking it, drink after drink.'

'Michael's parents let him drink as much Coke as he likes,' Miranda said, in a subdued-gleeful tone, smacking her lips silent in a mute stop like an exercising trumpet-player.

'It's my *apéritif*. It's a drink before dinner,' Hettie said. 'Course I only have one.'

'It's been known,' Kenyon said in a falsetto tone, going from larder to pan, 'for people to have more than one *apéritif* before dinner, even more than two.'

'So what's going to happen, now that you've got your own back on this girl?' Hettie asked.

'It isn't a case of getting my own back on anyone,' Miranda said. 'I don't care whether she turns up or not. I only wrote a letter to her parents to bring home to her the consequences of her telling lies like that.'

'What if she isn't telling a lie, though? What if they are getting divorced? Won't you look a bit stupid?' Hettie said. 'And she can say, "I told you so."'

'No,' Miranda said. 'They will probably agree that their petty disputes are deleteriously affecting their daughter's academic labours, and put a sock in it.'

'What was that word you said?'

Miranda explained, almost sure that 'deleterious' had actually come up before. 'In any case,' she went on, 'I have some really good students in that class. There's a boy who comes every week, does all the reading. He makes an effort; he takes notes; he came to see me to discuss some feedback; he's getting a proper education out of a university. They either have a work ethic or they don't, and I don't see why I should help the ones who don't want to be there.'

232

'What's he called?' Hettie said.

'He was just an example, his name doesn't matter,' Miranda said. 'Faisal Khalil.'

'Is he Asian? Because they work hard, it's well known. I heard—'

'Yes, I expect so,' Miranda said, in her most helpful manner. 'Or perhaps he feels he ought to make more of an effort, being the only non-white student in his year in this fucking university. I don't suppose it's anything innate, really.'

Kenyon had picked up a jar of cinnamon, put it down again; squared off the Pyrex dish by a couple of millimetres; opened and shut the cupboard door without taking anything out of it; turned on the tap and turned it off again; walked three times round the kitchen table and finally stood looking out of the window at where Stanley the dog was defecating mournfully in the middle of the street, apparently unaware of an approaching John Lewis lorry. Miranda and Hettie exchanged an unusual sisterly look of pity and concern.

'Are you all right there, darling?' Miranda said. 'You don't seem altogether sure of yourself.'

'I was just thinking,' Kenyon said. 'I was just thinking whether – I can't remember whether I put pepper in the marinade or not.'

'I don't think you did,' Hettie said. 'But I've not been watching all the time.'

'Is that the Asian boy whose father works at the sixth-form college?' Kenyon said, and took the largest of the knives, the oblong butcher's cleaver; he raised it with both hands above the squatting body of the neckless chicken.

'Yes, I think that's right,' Miranda said. 'Khalil. I can't remember the father's first name. Went to university in his home town, not living at home, though, I think he said once. How clever of you to remember, darling.'

22.

'And then David here – he's only fourteen, I think it's the first time he's ever been in a bar – he goes back into the bar, and he's had one big beer, and he doesn't know what they call them in France. He does his best, poor lad, he says to the barmaid, "Can I have half a kilo of beer, please?" – half a kilo – and she says, doesn't she, David?, she says – what was it she said? She said—'

It was a favourite story of David's father, but he hadn't got to the end of it. He was overtaken with hilarity, and Mauro sat and waited politely, a glass of gin-and-tonic in his hand. David's mother was mopping her eyes at the story, and for a moment David wondered whether the pair of them had been drinking before he and Mauro had even got there; but of course company had this effect on them, egging them on and geeing them up. I could tell you a story about that holiday in the south of France, a couple of decades ago, David thought. It would be a much better one than yours, which was just how I got my weights and measures mixed up; I could tell you about the day I said I had a headache and wanted to stay in the dark in the hotel, and you two went off to see a Roman amphitheatre, and the second you'd driven off, I went down the swimming-pool with the German man who was staying in the hotel, and we came back to the hotel afterwards, and he fucked me in his room. I was fourteen, and he was twenty-eight, and he must have been terrified, because he gave me a false address afterwards, somewhere in Munich where I know he didn't live. But fourteen and twenty-eight – that's a story.

David's father seemed to have come to an end. 'So you see,' he said inconsequentially; he had gone quite red in the face. 'It's nice to meet you, Mauro.'

'What is that castle over there?' Mauro said politely. The big picture windows of the flat gave over the estuary. The room was quite elegantly furnished, with a new beige carpet and a Persian rug David didn't recognize. His parents had had a good clear-out when they moved, offering him quite a lot of furniture he certainly didn't want if they didn't, and this flat held only the best and most treasured pieces from their old house. David thought it had a winnowed-down air, like the soulless end-result of a TV de-cluttering show or, worse, like a retirement home where nothing comfortably related, where all the little links and piles and untouched matter between and under stuff had been removed and thrown away. From the window, as Mauro was indicating, there was a good view; the puckered and pleated silver of the river – the estuary – succeeded by water-meadows, a lonely white-painted pub on a kind of headland, a glint of some more river, and then a narrow road and the hills rising beyond. The castle Mauro was asking about might have been a folly, or might have been the inhabitable turret of a Victorian eccentric, placed dramatically at the crest of the hill.

'Ah,' David's father said urbanely. 'The View. Yes, it's rather special, isn't it? It was the thing that persuaded us to buy this flat.'

'We knew we liked the town,' David's mother said. 'But we had some difficulty finding the right place to live. We never thought we would want to live in a flat, to be honest. But after a while . . .'

David's thoughts wandered. Mauro's stance was exactly the right thing; he was not a tall man, and yet, standing there, in his ordinary weekend clothes, he looked quite noble as the afternoon light fell on him. David inwardly apologized for having thought Mauro's choice of clothes inadequate, casually chosen or thoughtless. He saw, now, in his parents' sitting room that this T-shirted, barefoot figure with its five-second grin struck exactly the right raffish note of the short, charming urchin – Mauro had cast off his brown-and-orange Onitsuka Tiger trainers almost as soon as he entered. It was some sort of gesture towards domestic politeness. Clearly, prepared, they had taken to him. David wondered, again, what Mauro was going to do for clothes for the rest of the

235

weekend, and the question brought another piece of mental discomfort to mind: the way his mother had ushered both of them into the same bedroom, with one double bed, without asking. Mauro had casually thrown down his bag, turned round and gone straight back into the sitting room, just as David's mother – 'Catherine' to Mauro, immediately – was explaining that she expected he'd like to have a rest and a lie-down. David supposed that he would have to have some kind of conversation with Mauro about what his father referred to as 'the sleeping arrangements' at some point. He did hope Mauro wasn't going to ask him to sleep in the armchair in the bedroom.

'That castle?' Alec said to Mauro. 'It's on the ridge behind our friends' village – I mean the village where our friends live. It belongs to the old manor house – it's the earls of Bakewell, I believe. They say you can see three counties from the top of the tower. We've never been.'

'Pay no attention to Alec, Mauro,' Catherine said. 'That's his idea of a joke. You can't see three counties from up there, not unless you can see right across the Bristol Channel. I know it's old, though – they've lived there for hundreds of years. Maybe we'll go over there tomorrow, have a nice day out.'

'I'm sorry we have to go back so soon, after lunch,' Mauro said smoothly. 'It looks beautiful.'

'Well, you must be used to old things,' Alec said. Then he seemed to see an ambiguity, and said, 'Coming from Rome.'

'That's right,' Mauro said, and it stayed there, rather taking something away from the conversation than adding to it. 'Could I have another drink, please?' And David took his glass and poured himself a fat one, too.

'Seems very nice,' Alec said, when he and Catherine were washing up the glasses, and 'the boys', as they seemed to be called for the purposes of the weekend, were preparing and titivating and chatting in the spare room. 'You couldn't take offence,' he went on.

'Nothing to take offence at,' Catherine said, drying a glass, holding it up to the light and placing it on the work surface. These were not the glasses they would be using for the party tonight: those, hired from Oddbins, were in cardboard boxes underneath the breakfast bar. The best ones would go back into the cupboard, safe and sound. 'He seems very nice. I always . . .' She paused, not quite knowing what to say, how to put the sense of an intuition into words. 'I always *wonder* about David, though.'

Alec dried his hands, shook them once more, inspected his nails. 'Shall we have a little walk?' he said. 'We'll be inside all day if we don't make a bit of an effort. Might as well show them Hanmouth.'

'It won't take long,' Catherine said, wondering whether she had spoken at all; she had not quite understood what she meant about David, so it was strange that Alec accepted it without remark. Perhaps she had heavily struck one of many soft and embarrassable patches that appeared to be lying around in Alec's vicinity today.

23.

Once the Bears had been invited to Sam and Harry's instead of Peter's, a number of them found that, after all, they didn't have something else to do that evening. It turned out that, like Sam and Harry, five or six of the Bears had talked about it, and decided that they didn't really feel like going out to Peter's. Not that they had anything much against Peter, but an evening he was in charge of was an evening that some of the other Bears would avoid. So they second-guessed each other, like small children, saying, 'Well, I'm only going if everyone else is going,' but not quite getting round to canvassing opinion. The turnout had been looking rather grim; Sam and Harry were relatively popular, generous hosts. It was ruthless of them to announce without any real consultation that it would be better if they held the party, since – the brilliant excuse – Harry needed to be in Hanmouth that night, and otherwise, they wouldn't be able to make it to the 'get-together' at all. Peter put up only token resistance at first; then, a couple of days later, called in bored tones to say that it was just as well, since he'd forgotten it was his brother-in-law's retirement party and he had to go to that. So no Peter either.

All this phoning around resulted in – Peter apart – a full house. More than a full house: Steve had phoned to ask if he could bring a lad, a mechanic of his, just moved down from London with his wife and baby. 'I've had him,' Steve said. 'In the back office, twice. Can he come?' And Blaise had acquired a couple of keen admirers too in the last month, or so it seemed, and Adam thought they might as well be asked. This sort of thing had happened before. You did a small scout round, picking up anything small and valuable – a silver Georgian snuff box, a cloisonné cigarette case thought to be Cartier – or breakable. The coked-up Bears would fling their limbs and members about the floor of the drawing room, and glass and porcelain treasures were best tucked away for the night. Stanley, the basset hound, had a graceful knack of walking between the precarious treasures, but a Bear after a drink or two would have lost whatever knack he ever possessed. It had to be admitted, too, that some of these last-minute invitations were not the most trustworthy people imaginable. In fact, that was sometimes their attraction, and a year or two ago, a boy called Darren, whom Phil had somehow met, announced frankly as 'a burglar', had had a high degree of success one evening. Never returned: serving a four-year stretch.

It looked like being the most successful evening for a while. Usually people phoned afterwards, the next day, to chew it over, what had happened, who had done what, and usually to say, 'Never again,' about some overindulgence or other. This time, half the Bears had phoned up in advance, the day of the 'get-together', to say they couldn't wait, to see if they could give anyone a lift, to offer to bring something or other. The anticipation was keen. Harry observed that Peter, without anyone really admitting it or even understanding it, had been a cup of cold water on the festivities for a while now. 'How did we get to know him?' Sam said, but Harry couldn't remember. Someone had brought him, and he had stayed, his wandering hands making no kind of contribution to their communal pleasure. Tonight, a brother-in-law was having a retirement party, and they could get on with it. There was no reason why he should ever be included again. It was hard, but there it was.

In the end, there were fourteen Bears coming. Harry and Sam's drawing room was no more fussy than anyone else's, but they'd acquired a fair number of objects over the years that had to be cleared away – ceramics from Sweden and the five Hagi tea-bowls, a vase from a local ceramicist with a kiln on Dartmoor, blazing red and three feet tall, resting precariously on a base only three inches wide. The heavy Victorian silver from Harry's family he'd taken good-naturedly, and it was locked away in the cellar, never to be used; it was fair to say that the other valuable residues from Harry's family treasures were unlikely to be walked off with by any of the Bears or their guests. They were too massive: a Tabriz carpet acquired by a great-great-great-uncle in Iran; or, as well, too ugly – a five-foot greeny-orange Fuseli of (Sam had to peer) 'Bertram of Roussillon In Thrall To Helena, His Wife'. The white sofas and armchairs were covered up with shawls acquired by Sam during Indian adventures. Stanley's bed was carried upstairs for the evening – Stanley had always sighed and spluttered when he saw them lifting up his bed. He knew what it meant. Then they totted up the stores.

Harry had driven to Plymouth to meet with his long-term dealer, now running a fairly respectable mini-cab company, and had come back with a dozen grams of coke and some K. Six bottles of poppers had arrived via mail-order, and the condoms and lube were placed in (non-valuable) bowls here and there about the place; a plastic bowl full of dildos had been put under the sofa out of sight, if anyone felt like using them later in the evening.

Sam had driven to Sainsbury's, and had got three pounds of mince, potatoes, onions, tomatoes and mushrooms, enough for a big bowl of salad, and a couple of litres of ice-cream – the pudding was never much of a draw at these events. The wine merchant had delivered a case of white wine and a couple of cases of beer, placed in the fridge next to the bottles of poppers. It was all looking very cheerful.

'I thought we had some carrots,' Sam said to Harry on Saturday afternoon.

'Carrots?'

'I thought we had some.'

'What do you want them for?'

'What do you think? For the shepherd's pie. You need them for shepherd's pie.'

'Well, I don't know,' Harry said. 'I thought we had some, too. I wasn't really paying attention to the carrot stores, though. Can't you do without?'

'It's only up the road, and I only need three,' Sam said.

'Doesn't make any difference whether it's three or thirty,' Harry said. 'I've still got to walk up to the greengrocer's, apparently.'

But in the end Sam thought he'd drop in on the shop, to make sure things were 'under control', as he put it, and Harry had nothing else to do, so they went out together.

'I'm sure there are other things I'll have forgotten,' Sam said to Harry, as he closed the front door, incidentally pushing Stanley out into the street – he had been sniffing the air for rain, unwilling to commit himself to a walk if the weather was uncertain. 'I'll only know when we get to the shops. Come on, Stanley.'

'I'm sure it'll be fine,' Harry said. 'And no one's coming for the shepherd's pie.'

'You'd be surprised,' Sam said. 'The number of times I've found myself in the kitchen at a party, discussing what it is exactly they've put in the vol-au-vents. Did I ever tell you about the Transvestite Goulash Challenge in Berlin?'

(A German friend of Sam's had once told him about a bar in

240

Berlin where a transvestite had told another transvestite, one night, that her mother's recipe for goulash sounded rubbish, and an argument had broken out. The landlord had settled the argument by inviting the two of them, and any other drag queens in the district, to cook their mother's goulash and bring it in so it could be judged by the regulars. This story had tickled Sam's fancy, and he retold it quite regularly, on the smallest encouragement.)

'Yes, you did,' Harry said. 'Look – remind me, I've forgotten . . .'

They were walking down their road towards the junction with the Strand, and walking along the road, not having seen them just yet, was the neat and birdlike woman Sam seemed to know – she was newish in town, she was having a party some time, she was perfectly nice, a chatterbox, she'd bought some Gjetost, and her name, her name was— 'It's Catherine,' Sam said. 'I knew I knew it.' With her was her husband, a beige-padded anorak type, resembling a retired policeman, and behind, a fat man in his thirties, balding, a morose and withdrawn expression in, surprisingly, scarlet corduroy trousers and a blue sweater. He had a startlingly red face, full of blood and breathlessness; he looked, frankly, ill. But with him was a dark, small, beautiful, neat man, his mobile features and thoughtful, expressive dark eyes alive with pleasure and sex. He radiated availability from twenty yards, and Sam and Harry passed a look between them, not needing to say anything to indicate whom they were talking about.

'I do hope you're going to come to our party tonight,' Catherine said, when they had greeted each other, the fat son, as it turned out to be, introduced, and the sex object described as 'David's special friend' by David's mother.

'Lucky David,' Sam said drily, shaking David's hand; he blushed and said nothing.

'It's tonight, is it?' Harry said. 'Well, we do have friends coming round, but later – perhaps we could drop in at some point. What time is it?'

Sam was almost certain that the last time the question had been

241

raised, there had been no possibility of their finding time in their busy evening of stress and bother. He did not blame Catherine, however, for asking again, now that she could dangle the gorgeous prize of this Italian in front of them in person, if that was what she was doing.

'I'm sure we can get over for half an hour,' Harry said. 'It's only over the road, and we're only cooking shepherd's pie – that's not going to spoil, I suppose.'

'Who's the cook in this relationship, then?' Sam said, to make everything absolutely clear to the hot Italian, and he flirtatiously punched Harry on the shoulder. 'Honestly,' Sam said confidentially, and as camply as he could manage. 'Some people – and I include Harry in this – they have no idea, no idea at all, what cooking dinner for guests entails. He really is terrible. He thinks it's just shoving something in the oven and then shoving it on the table afterwards. He has absolutely no idea what I'm going to have to do for the next few hours.'

'So you can't come, then?' Catherine's husband – Alec – said. He seemed a bit slow.

'No, no,' Sam said. 'We'd love to come. Just for half an hour, though, I'm afraid.'

'Looking forward to it,' Harry said brilliantly, shaking the hand of the Italian one last time and looking him warmly in the eye; the Italian, it was clear, needed no encouragement whatsoever.

'Lucky old David,' Sam said, when they had gone in different directions.

'Let's get an extra carrot,' Harry said. 'You never know who might drop in after dinner, after all.'

Sam paused at the cashpoint machine – all that shopping, all that drugs-buying, the whole lot, had cleared him out – and struggled, as ever, to remember his security number. 'Let's get another *carrot*?' he asked, as the machine tongued two hundred pounds into his hands. 'Let's get another *carrot*?'

'They're really a very nice pair,' Alec was saying to Mauro confidentially, as they peered together at the collection of posthumous donations in the window of the Devon Sea Rescue charity shop – a china house saying 'A Present From Exmouth', a Cabbage Patch doll, a lace doily the size of a goatskin, and seven novels by Barbara Taylor Bradford. 'We don't know them well, but they're always very friendly. He runs a shop here, on the high street, a cheesemonger's. I don't know what he does, the other one.'

'They seem *very nice*,' Mauro said warmly, smiling at Alec, and everyone – Alec, Catherine and David – thought how very well Alec was getting on with his son's boyfriend, how easy it was all proving to be.

24.

There was little more to do before the party. David had looked, and there were four oval plates of finger-food, dominoes of dark bread with pink, green and black toppings, small potatoes roasted and Xed open for a dollop of cream cheese, pastry barques ready to be filled with finely chopped tomato, garlic and parsley mix in a bowl to the side. The plates were covered with clingfilm. David had peeled one, then the other, and quickly, while nobody was watching, eaten half a dozen from round the edges. He wasn't hungry – the late lunch in a quayside pub had finished only an hour before – but he thought he might as well since, in his experience, you never got enough to eat at parties under the gaze of the other guests, counting how much you were eating and how much they were eating. He carefully unrolled the clingfilm, and put it back in place.

In the sitting room, his father was sitting with the paper, his mother perched on the windowsill, which looked down towards the town. 'Mauro's just gone out,' his mother said, carefully and politely pronouncing his boyfriend's name. 'He said he needed to make a phone call, and he couldn't get reception here.'

'There's nothing wrong with the reception here, is there?' David said.

'No, he just wants a bit of privacy, I expect,' Catherine said. 'You can't blame him. He seems a very nice young man, David.'

The objects about the sitting room were all familiar from David's childhood. Not all the possessions from twenty years back had made it into this smaller collection – Jubilee plates, the tasteless china presents David had thought to give his mother for Christmas and birthdays, things too markedly 1970s, like the bouquet of flowers preserved under a glass dome, in a vacuum: these had all been removed and given away to charity shops. The inherited adornments of both sets of grandparents, too, had been reduced, as far as David could see, to a Bavarian wood-carved cherub on his father's side, and a geometric vase on his mother's. They could be seen as cropping up on *Antiques Roadshow* and, though hideous, might have some value, so – David reckoned – they had stayed. But not everything his parents had possessed was ugly, and not everything had needed throwing out. All through his childhood, David had loved a sideboard ornament, a small enamel bird, a pheasant, beautifully made and swarming with brilliant colour, with garnets for its eyes, and which, if you took its upper body and lifted, turned out to be a box with a warm blue coat of enamel inside, a swimming, liquid colour. David had always thought, in an unelaborated childish way, that the Chinese pheasant was not just a jewel-box, but was itself in some way made out of jewels; the colours were of that order of brilliance. Even when he understood that it was made out of enamel – had connected, with a shock, the process that had produced this lovely object with a process they had spent three weeks in Metalwork on – it had still retained its magic aura. David didn't suppose it was, in fact, particularly valuable, but the freshness of the colour, the shine and cleverness of it made it precious to him.

For some reason, it wasn't on the console table where it should have been. 'Mum,' David said.

'David,' his mother said, but then David thought better of it.

Why did he think it should have been on the new console table? It had always been on the sideboard at home in St Albans, as long as he could remember – the thing, in fact, that the console table had replaced. He realized that he had, in fact, seen it on the console table that morning, when they had arrived; he had particularly noticed it, had been pleased that his mother and father had kept something they knew he had always liked a great deal. He wondered whether his mother had removed it for the sake of the party, but that was unlikely. There were more fragile and probably more valuable objects still out on tables, and it didn't seem likely that his parents knew people who would snaffle or swipe anything, not even those two fat queens his mother had, bafflingly, greeted as friends. 'What is it, David?' his mother said.

'I just wondered when people are going to be coming,' David said.

'In an hour or two, I suppose,' his father said. 'We'll have a cup of tea in a minute.'

David got up and went into the spare room – their room, his mother had called it. His dark blue weekend suitcase was on one side of the bed, upright; Mauro's bag had been thrown down carelessly on the bedroom armchair. David went to the window, but it was facing the other direction, towards the hills on the other side of the estuary: he could not see Mauro, if he was, in fact, making a phone call on the street. Probably making a date for Monday night. Even Sunday night; Mauro's schedules were tightly tessellated, David believed, with a spare hour quickly filled with a man or two.

David hovered, undecided, then swiftly ran his hands over the crumpled leather surface of Mauro's bag. It was no more than ordinarily lumpy and, hardly believing he was doing this for anything but lecherous reasons, David unzipped the bag and plunged his hands into Mauro's underwear, socks, crumpled shirt and trousers. The dizzying sensation that followed, as he saw himself as if from outside rifling through Mauro's intimate and private possessions, sweating and panting, was a complex one of sex and passionate, transferred guilt. He did not know what he would say if Mauro came in now; he could not be expected to absorb this behaviour in his assessment and acceptance of David's public relationship with him, and he would – David thought – be justified in taking his bag, walking to the station, and going straight back to London.

But then, underneath, swaddled in a pair of impossibly tiny Y-fronts, there was something hard and unyielding: well, David reflected, that was what he had wanted, after all. He unwrapped it without bringing it out, his two arms plunged into Mauro's bag, and in a moment the cloth texture revealed something hard, sharp and smooth. It was David's mother's enamel pheasant, as he had known it would be. David quickly placed the thing in his pocket, and zipped up Mauro's bag, not really caring that Mauro would know he had been inside from the mess he had made of its contents. He would find out soon enough that someone had reclaimed his stolen object.

'What's that on the floor?' he said casually, once back in the sitting room, having performed a small and secretive pantomime.

'Pardon?' his mother said. 'How did that get there? I must have knocked it off when I was dusting. It's that little jewel-box. We've had it for years – I always liked it. There's Mauro, now. That was a long phone call.'

25.

The buzzer from the front door went at five minutes past six exactly. The four of them had been sitting in an artificial way – Catherine had pushed all the chairs back against the walls, so that people could sit if they wanted to, but most of the party would roam in the central space in the room. The television, normally the intense focus of interest, the chairs turned to its face, had been pushed back squarely against the wall as if it were an occasional, temporary distraction. When people started arriving, it would look more nearly normal; but before the guests arrived, it seemed foolish to stand up, so the four of them sat against different walls awkwardly, as if waiting for the dentist.

Catherine had been getting up and sitting down again for twenty minutes, checking and rechecking. Alec had never been to Rome, but he and Catherine had been, two years running, to Lake Como, the second time not so much of a success, and of course Catherine had been to Venice, with David, a couple of years ago. Catherine had always had a wanting to go to Venice, and they'd enjoyed it, he believed, but it had been difficult to get away from the tourist traps, in the event. Mauro had never been to Venice, although he knew people who came from there, and he knew there were good pasta dishes, including one with the black ink of a squid. 'I'll make it for you some day,' Mauro said, in a burst of enthusiasm, though it was not clear when this would happen. David and Mauro were leaving after lunch the next day, and to David and, presumably, to Mauro, too, in his different way, it must seem unlikely that they would meet again. Unlikely, too, that Mauro would take or be given the opportunity to go out and buy cuttle-fish ink, which was what David thought he meant by squid, even if such a thing could be had in Hanmouth between Saturday evening and Sunday lunchtime. The conversation went its way, absurdly; David could hardly listen to it. Any forgiveness in his heart for his boyfriend's chatter, his father's attempts to keep the conversational show on the road was gone; any allowance for the nervous half an hour between near strangers before a party they bore some kind of joint responsibility for was gone. David levered himself to a standing position before his father could dredge anything else up about Italy from his experience or knowledge. Before he could go in search of his mother, the buzzer at the front door went.

'They're prompt,' his father said, with a glance at his watch. 'I'll let your mother get that. She knows who she's invited.'

There was a bustle in the hallway, as his mother said, 'Hello?'

in an unpractised way into the speakerphone and buzzed them in. Quickly, she wiped her hands on her blue and white apron, and took it off, going into the kitchen to hang it up. She came back quite partified, her green shift dress like one a much younger woman would wear. For the first time in years the thought came to David, like a pang, that his mother was as pretty as anyone; he did think the shade of green exactly the right one for her, and exactly paired with an uncomplicated amber necklace and an amber and silver brooch.

'Hello, my dear,' the woman was saying, as she came through the door. 'It's so nice to get to know new neighbours.'

She had a distinctive appearance: square-bobbed and squarely spectacled. She sailed into the flat like a landlady on an impromptu inspection. 'How nice of you to come,' Catherine said. 'Nice and early, too – it's always a terror, that, in case someone not very . . .'

She floundered a little here, having made a suggestion that she might have invited some not-very people to her party.

'No, don't shut the door,' the woman said, as Alec came into the hallway to greet her heartily enough. 'Hello – I'm Miranda Kenyon, I don't think we've met. Have we? How awfully rude of me. Yes, of course we have. Catherine, don't shut the door – I came in with Sam, you know. I saw him passing in his party finery and I dashed out to have an escort to arrive with.'

'Is he there?' Catherine said, popping out to peer down the marble and brass stairwell. 'Yes, here he comes.'

'Toiling upwards,' Miranda said. 'I took the lift. Kenyon's coming along very shortly.'

'And my husband too,' Sam said, smiling and wiping his brow. His party finery turned out to be a pair of faded pale blue jeans and a lumberjack shirt. 'I have to climb stairs whenever I can – it's the only exercise I get. How lovely!'

His panoramic and sweeping gaze made a general compliment out of his words, but Catherine merely said, 'Yes, I do think we've got it looking nice now,' and went to pour everyone a drink. The others went into the sitting room.

248

'Charming,' Miranda said, with warmth. 'Kenyon would have come with me, but – well, I don't know why he didn't. I was going to say he had to wait in for the babysitter, but my great lump hardly needs a babysitter beyond *The X Factor*, so I don't know. I'm sure he's on his way.'

'Have you come far?' David said, in a general sort of way.

'No, just over the road,' Miranda said. 'What a beautiful view you have from up here – we don't have anything like such a nice one. Our house is, as it were, sunk down into the earth rather than raised up as you are. How beautiful!'

'I expect you had a nicer view before they built this block,' Alec said. 'It must stand completely in your way, doesn't it?'

'Well,' Miranda said. She paused. 'Of course, we haven't lived here much longer than you have, not ten years, so this was the view when we bought and we can't complain. We don't complain, I should say. Champagne! How lovely! How generous of you!'

There was a knock on the front door. 'I left the entrance ajar,' Sam said, taking a glass of wine and popping a fistful of peanuts into his mouth. 'I hope I did right. Save you from getting up and down again all night. Hello, we sort of met earlier.'

'Hello,' Mauro said meaningfully, but then the attention was taken by the new arrivals, who, in fact, were the retired sisters who lived two floors down, and their Bedlington terrier.

'I hope you don't mind,' Isobel, or possibly Marian, said – both were big-haired, big-jawed, big-voiced women with broad bottoms and hairy chins. 'We brought Poppet up. She gets bored.'

'Bedlingtons, very intelligent dogs,' Marian, or possibly Isobel, chipped in. 'Intelligent dogs, they need distraction, problems to solve, games to play.'

'Walks to go on,' the other one said.

'Drinks!' they said in unison. 'Well, just a small one,' said one. 'I'm Isobel Wallace, how do you do? And if Poppet could have perhaps a small bowl of water, that would be lovely. Very intelligent, Bedlingtons,' Isobel Wallace said, closing down the range of her remarks from the whole room to David. 'You see, the thing is . . .'

'You should have brought Stanley,' Catherine said, daringly, to Sam. 'He'd have been quite welcome.'

'Oh, you know Stanley, do you?' Sam said. 'He's a card, dashing here and there, making pals behind our backs. No, he's perfectly all right where he is, and besides – he pongs rather a lot. He and – what? Poppet, is it? – they're old friends, he never gives up a chance to bite her savagely.'

'I'm sure that's not true,' Catherine said. 'We hear Poppet sometimes in the evening. She's a little over-excitable.' Together they looked at the small, sheep-like object, like an incompetent drawing of an indeterminate four-legged creature, fresh from having her hair cut, dashing about yapping and begging for canapés. 'And here's Mr and Mrs Calvin . . .'

John Calvin's arrival was a surprise, particularly to Catherine, after he had snubbed her. He was clutching something in tissue paper, an awkward shape. By his side stood a tall, thin, nervous woman; her face and her hair were long and unkempt. She seemed to have made little or no effort in coming out. The Wallace sisters and Sam eyed her with interest. They didn't remember ever having seen her before.

'This is a small present, a housewarming present,' John Calvin said. 'It'll come in ever so 'andy abaht the 'ahse. I bet you'll say, "Ooh, I've never thought of that, I've never imagined I could have lived ever without one of them, and now it's there, I dunno how I ever managed without it."'

'John,' his wife said, perhaps restraining Calvin's shrill joke falsetto. Her voice was low and gracious, her eyes flickering backwards and forwards.

'Anywhere, there it is,' John Calvin said. 'It's just to welcome you to our little town.'

'Well, that's very nice of you,' Catherine said. 'But it's a little bit late to have a housewarming party – we've been here months. But, anyway, I suppose if we'd had it earlier, we wouldn't have known people to invite to it. You know everyone, do you? This is our son, David – he works in . . .'

It was awkward to help John and Laura Calvin to drinks, introduce them to whoever they didn't know and to open the ill-wrapped present all at once. With some enjoyment, Sam observed that the housewarming present was from his own shop, but not something he had sold for at least two years. It had been a hideous mistake, the scale of which had slowly revealed itself in the years it had sat on the shelf. In the long months it had waited for the right person to come along and buy it, Sam and Harry had started referring to it as the Home Beautifier. Eventually someone had bought it, though certainly not Calvin – who had it been? To a small-town shopkeeper like Sam, the means of production and distribution were all too clear, particularly around Christmas time. The Home Beautifier, a sort of papier-mâché bowl with hollows for different-shaped cheeses and an Indian elephant ineptly rising in the middle, had originally been made by a cheese-maker's teenage daughter, and Sam hadn't had the heart to refuse to try and sell it. It had been given as a present from the forgotten buyer to a mystery recipient, and had afterwards been passed on, perhaps the very same season, to someone the mystery recipient hadn't liked much. It might even have been John and Laura Calvin, who were very much the sort of people to turn up at Christmas time bearing presents when no exchange of presents had been envisaged. They liked imposing an obligation.

'How nice!' Catherine could be heard saying. 'Alec, look, it's . . .'

Sam found himself in conversation with a middle-aged couple.

'Did you find it hard to park?' the man said.

'Well, no, I only live over the road, so, well, I left the car where it was, and—'

'It took us for ever to find a place to park,' the woman said. She was in a camel-coloured blouse with purple jewellery round the neck; her hair was tight and cropped around her skull, her close bud of a mouth like a flower about to open.

251

'It's legendary, Hanmouth, for being difficult to park in,' the man said.

'We thought it might be easier on a Saturday night,' the woman said. 'But in the end we went round and round, and we had to park right up at the doctors' surgery, at the pay and display.'

'Did you have to pay and display at this time of night?' Sam said.

The couple looked at each other doubtfully.

'I just assumed,' the man said to his wife.

'Your trouble is, you always sodding assume,' the woman said. 'I suppose it's up to me to go back up and put some money in the machine.'

'No, I'm sure you don't have to,' Sam said. In fact, he had no idea at all. As far as he knew, the traffic wardens patrolled the quiet streets of Hanmouth twenty-four hours a day, slapping yellow clamps on the wheels of pay-and-display delinquents. 'How do you know Catherine and – and Alec?'

The pair had simmered down a little. 'Well, my wife, Barbara, the genius who's probably just landed us with a sixty-pound fine here, she used to work with Alec in St Albans, and then we retired down here, and they sort of followed us.'

'Do you live in Hanmouth?'

'No, over the estuary, over there, in Cockering. It's a hell of a journey from Cockering to here, whichever way you look at it. Tell me, Sam, how would you set about driving from Cockering to here?'

'Bedlingtons, you see, they're what I like to call a very *intelligent* breed,' Isobel Wallace, or possibly Marian, was saying to Miranda and, for the second time, to David. Without shifting his eyes from her for a second, he leaned backwards and took two canapés from the sideboard, eating first one, then the other without chewing, just a large swill of wine. 'And intelligent dogs have their downside as well as their upside, let me tell you . . .'

Kitty had arrived all in a fluster, clutching a last-minute Co-op bottle of Chardonnay-Semillon in raggedy flying paper. She was, she said, expecting to see Billa. 'I thought you were going to call for her,' she said to Miranda, pulling her away from explanations about Bedlingtons. 'Or did you think I was supposed to call for her?'

'I honestly didn't wonder how she was getting here,' Miranda said, eyeing Kitty's well-known party dress in gloomy swirling shades of pot-pourri. 'Was it my responsibility? Someone might have told me. I'm sure the Brigadier's perfectly capable of bringing her himself.'

'Oh, no,' Kitty said seriously. 'Tom wouldn't come out to something like this. When was the last time you saw him at a party? He never comes out, if he can help it, at all. Happy for people to come to him.' She dropped her voice an octave and her chin into her bosom, in supposed imitation of Billa's husband's parade-ground voice. 'Perfectly happy. Delighted. But never go to other people's parties to sit in other people's chairs and drink other people's ideas of wine. Very picky, Tom, about that sort of thing. Quite unreasonable. No, I think really the best thing is if I go back and collect her.'

'Or Kenyon could pick her up on his way,' Miranda said. 'Is she still tottery on her pins?'

'Oh, dreadfully,' Kitty said. 'I can't imagine how people could be so awful as to knock her over like that and not stop to make sure she was all right. Her legs were a mass of purple from knee to hip. It really turned the stomach to look at them. But here she is – Billa, what are you doing?'

'What on earth do you mean, what am I doing?' Billa said. 'Hello, hello, hello – how nice of you to ask me, Catherine, and Alec, too. So nice to get to know new neighbours, at our time of life, you know, so difficult, one never meets anyone new. Charming. What a wonderful view you have. Champagne! I say. No, I'm quite all right standing for the moment – I'll yell out if I need to plop myself down. Well, I just came along, came out of the house, turned right, walked down to the quay and a bit further – I don't know what Kitty means, it hardly seems so very extraordinary.'

'Well, I thought Miranda was going to call for you, and she thought I was supposed to call for you, and we'd just decided that it was probably going to be best if Kenyon called for you.'

'Well, here he is,' Billa said. 'Kenyon, I do hope you haven't been fruitlessly calling on me, or for me, or whatever everyone seems to think I need.'

'No,' Mauro was saying. 'I come from Rome. I know David, he is my friend from London, though he does not live in London.'

'Oh, David's their son, isn't he?' John Calvin said.

'John,' Mrs Calvin said, in her low, restrained voice. They all looked at her. 'Don't,' she said, quite as if they were entirely alone.

Calvin did not say whatever he had been preparing to say, and whether it was an impersonation of a London homosexual or a routine in stage-Italian, nobody could not be glad of it.

'We've known David since he was a very little boy,' the old friend from Cockering, over the estuary, was saying. 'I used to work with David's father Alec, and I remember him coming into the office. He was very shy – he used to try to hide behind things, the hatstand, the filing cabinets, under the desks – he'd never speak to you unless you put on a specially kind voice.'

'I always thought he was a bit of a mummy's boy,' her husband put in.

'Well, you can see he was,' the woman said. 'Obviously he was. You don't need to make the point, Ted. Some things go without saying, I would say.'

'We went to Italy on a driving holiday, not five years ago,' Ted began, addressing himself to Mauro. 'We thought about putting the car on the train, the Eurostar – Eurotunnel, do I mean? – but then we thought, we've got all the time in the world. So we drove to Poole, to get the ferry to Cherbourg, and I know what you're going to say, we could have gone Plymouth–Roscoff, or even Weymouth to St Malo, that would have saved us quite a drive at the other end, or we could honestly have gone from Portsmouth, and even now, with the competition from the Channel Tunnel, there's a lot more choice from Portsmouth, as far as destinations go. But we talked over all those alternatives, and we decided in the end to go to Cherbourg from Poole.'

'It was nice, the ferry,' the woman said.

'So on the other side, we had quite a choice of routes,' Ted said confidentially to Mauro. 'Remember, we had designated a good week to get down to Tuscany – we'd decided that the journey was really going to be part of our holiday. So if you were us, what route do you think you would have taken, Cherbourg to Chiantishire, as we call it in England?'

'That's what people call Tuscany in England, because there's so many English people there, apparently,' the wife put in.

'Well, I'll tell you,' Ted continued. 'Oh – he's gone. Gone to refresh his drink. Very sensible of him. It was a nice holiday that one, wasn't it?'

The room was filling up nicely, and unlikely people were starting to talk to each other; people who did not know each other well, or at all.

'Yes, she's ours,' Marian Wallace was saying to Kenyon. 'She's called Poppet. She's a Bedlington terrier – they're awfully intelligent. No, she is naughty, she knows not to bark inside, and most of them, the breed, they don't bark a great deal. Just Poppet, but I expect we've got used to it now. No, she can't have a sausage – no, you can't – no, no, no, and . . . in it goes. I do find her irresistible, when she holds out her paw like that and cocks her head.'

A short burst of music now filled the room; a crackling piece of noisy jazz. It was not obviously party music, but it could not be taken off without confessing a mistake, and now music had come to the party, it would seem strange to take it off and rely on silence and the noise of talk. Alec straightened up – the hi-fi was kept on a low table in the corner of the room, the CD collection in a wall-mounted rack – and smiled generally. He went into the kitchen. Mauro had just preceded him in there. The man they had met on the street this afternoon – it was Sam, Alec believed

– was leaning against the sink holding a glass. Neither of them paid any attention to him. He took a bottle of champagne from the fridge, and went out again to do the rounds of the party.

'So,' Sam said, watching Alec's apologetic back retreat.

'So,' Mauro said, and shrugged, and grinned, and like a pair of dancers coming together at the beginning of a routine, they moved towards each other. Out of the window, the sun flashed on some remote and unobserved castle window at the crest of the far and wooded hillside.

26.

Harry had stayed at home to do a last lot of phoning round, to encourage stragglers, to remind them that there was going to be food – there wasn't always – and to make sure of numbers. There'd been a lot of phoning round already, but he believed you could never have too much, to egg people on. He was really quite excited about tonight, and was going to pass on his excitement. He liked to call landlines for this. You never knew when a Bear was going to be in the car with his mum, doing the weekend shopping. Fewer and fewer people used their landline at all. Once, recently, when he had called a London friend, there had been a puzzled 'Hello?' and then, when he'd identified himself, a drawled 'How deliciously retro', meaning, to call a landline from a landline.

Sam had gone off to his party, Harry saying he'd join them later, and he was installed in the window of the sitting room when an unfamiliar car drew up, a woman at the wheel. Harry wasn't much interested in cars, but he could see this was a glamorous or an impressive one in some way. It was perhaps vintage, perhaps American, but there was something restored and exotic about its appearance, the powder blue, the upsweep of the fins at the back, like diamanté spectacles. There was something redolent of the hobby about it, and he could believe that it was the possession not of the plump woman at the wheel, but of the tousled blond unshaven bloke, good-looking and trim in his worn and frayed weekend clothes, who was now getting out of the passenger seat, a bottle of wine in his thick fist. The man must be bringing the bottle to a party; but as he got out, he raised the bottle to his lips, glugging the wine himself. The woman hooted and drove off, manoeuvring the car with some difficulty down the awkward, narrow and twisting lane; the man watched her go, obviously concerned for the safety of his car's sides, and so did half a dozen observers, owners of parked cars, from the curtained windows of their white-painted cottages, concerned for the safety of theirs, too, at the expense of those back fins. Unexpectedly, the man came straight to Harry's front door and rang the bell, placing the now empty bottle in their window.

'I'm Spencer,' the man said. 'Steve's mate. Steve said I could come, yeah?'

Harry remembered the mention of a mechanic, Steve's employee, just moved down from London, whom Steve had had twice in the back room of his garage, over the desk.

'Nice car,' Harry said. 'I'm Harry. You can bring that bottle in – better throw it away than leave it there.'

'Yeah, thanks,' Spencer said, coming into the hall. He handed the bottle over, shutting the door behind him. 'Restored it myself. It's a 1961 DeSoto. Pillarless hardtop. Had to respray it, but the colour's authentic. Hear the growl it makes?'

'Was that your wife?' Harry said, dropping the bottle into the recycling box by the front door. 'At the wheel?'

'Yeah,' Spencer said briefly. That wasn't unprecedented: there were Bears who couldn't drive, or who were banned from driving, who had got lifts from family members, sisters, mothers, fathers. 'She don't care. I don't ask her where she's going, she don't ask me what I've been up to. So, we're going to have a good time, yeah?'

He was a good-looking man, but the way he jammed his hand, hard, against Harry's crotch and rubbed himself up against him

257

was more aggressive than inviting. 'It's been a while,' he said, and then he made a growl himself, possibly in imitation of a 1961 DeSoto pillarless hardtop.

'It's going to be a while yet,' Harry said, smiling but disentangling himself. 'I don't think anyone else is coming for an hour or two – two hours, actually. Never mind. You're welcome. Come in.'

'Steve told me half six,' Spencer said. 'I think he did. No one else here yet? Never mind. We'll sit down and make ourselves comfortable, yeah?'

He flung himself down on the white sofa, kicking off his trainers onto the Persian carpet, and lay back with his eyes closed and his legs spread, running his thumbs across his chest. 'Yeah,' he murmured. 'Eighteen thirty he said, yeah?'

'I think he must have said eight thirty,' Harry said. 'Were you in the military?'

'Yeah, I was,' Spencer said, carrying on with what he was doing. 'Was it the eighteen thirty that made you think that? Like a squaddie, do you?'

'I'll get you a beer,' Harry said, amused.

'Yeah, that'd be great,' Spencer said, sitting up. 'Nice place. A beer'd be good, but, Harry – Harry, yeah? – you know what'd be good with a beer? You know what'd be good with a beer, I reckon. You got anything else?'

'Whisky, gin, wine . . .'

'No, I mean – Steve says – I mean, you know what I love, I love coke, me. I don't know where you get coke, down here in the country. But I heard, you know, mate . . .'

'All in good time,' Harry said. He feared he had sounded too much like an old-school nanny, a little bit discouraging, a little bit priggish; Spencer might be, from all appearances, a madman, but they'd invited him and they'd want to have some fun with him later on. 'If you want some now, that's fine.'

'Yeah,' Spencer said, adopting a new, open, available posture halfway between the sofa and the floor. 'I reckon I want some.

Is that your dog? Can you get him to go somewhere? He's putting me off my stroke, mate.'

When Harry and Sam hosted a party like this, it was agreed between them that the drink should be on display, and freely available; the other stuff should be somewhere more discreet, and probably in two or three separate places, in case a greedy guest discovered one stash and polished it off. Harry went to the fridge for the beer, and then went to the back window, lifting up the base of a lamp and took out a Ziploc sachet. 'Stanley,' he said, going back into the sitting room. 'Fuck off. Upstairs. Upstairs, now.' He had thought that Spencer might take the opportunity of his temporary absence to take all his clothes off, but in fact, he had only taken his T-shirt and jeans off, which now lay in a pile to one side. He lay on the rug in white socks and Aussie Bum tight whites. Stanley had seen more surprising things, but now he gave a shake of his head as if coming out from water, averted his eyes and bounded heavily upstairs. Perhaps his short doggy memory erased anything genuinely traumatic, until the next time.

'Good boy,' Harry said. 'Up you go. Nice tan. Have you been away?'

'No, mate,' Spencer said. 'Just been on the sunbed this week. D'you think it looks all right?'

'Very nice,' Harry said honestly. He put down the beer and the sachet on the table and, kneeling, gave an encouraging rub, up and down Spencer's hairy, solid, almost bony torso, pausing to twist once, twice, his nipples, then down again, weighing the heavy contents of Spencer's pants like a bag of fruit.

Spencer moaned. 'Oh, yeah,' he said. 'Yeah, yeah.'

'The thing is,' Harry said, seeing a way out of the apparently inevitable sequence of the next few minutes. He withdrew his hands. 'You're really a couple of hours early. I don't know why we've got things in a muddle, but we have. And I said, I promised, really, that I'd go to a party over the road, just for ten minutes, half an hour, something like that.'

259

'That's all right,' Spencer said. 'I can stay here, no trouble. Anyone else comes, I'll let them in, we'll make a start.'

'I've got a better idea,' Harry said, thinking of the Fuseli and the best – the fourth from the left – of the Hagi bowls. 'Let's have a beer and a quick line here. Then, I tell you what, you put your clothes on and come over the road. We won't stay, we'll just go in and pick up Sam, my husband, and come straight back.'

'Are they blokes, too?' Spencer said. 'Christ, you know how to live in Hanmouth, I'll say.'

Harry took a moment to see the direction of Spencer's thought. 'No,' he said. 'It's nothing like that. It's just our neighbours, having a little drinks party. Nothing exciting. We'll just go in, pick up Sam, come back. You can behave yourself for five minutes, can't you?' Then Harry somehow doubted this, and said, more honestly, 'You could wait outside if you didn't want to come in.'

'Well, I could fucking well wait here, couldn't I? I'm not going to nick anything, mate, if that's what you're thinking.'

'I'm sure you wouldn't,' Harry said. Maybe the best thing was to phone Sam with apologies, ask him to come back, abandon his project of luring that cute Italian over to the Bears' night. 'Here. Let's have a line.'

27.

The party was filling up nicely: probably nobody there had expected to come into a crowded room, perhaps nobody had come from any motivation other than mild pity, not wanting their new neighbours to announce a party to which nobody came. That would not show a good side to Hanmouth. 'So you haven't lived here that long, either,' Catherine was saying brightly to Miranda.

'Not ten years, I think,' Miranda said.

'We've been here a little longer than that,' Billa was saying. 'Fifteen, I think, in September. Of course, we had the house before

260

that, some years, just as an investment at first, then with the idea of moving into it when Tom retired from the army. But we've only lived here properly for a decade and a half now.'

'Me too,' Kitty said. 'I moved here just before you did, a year or so, I think. I well remember the excitement of your moving in, Billa.'

'Oh, nonsense,' Billa said.

'Really,' Kitty said. 'Of course, it's your house, it's so prominent, everyone walks by it, and if it's empty, everyone would wonder about it, you know. And Sam's not been here for much longer than that, have you – Sam? Sam – oh, he's gone.'

'I think he's in the kitchen,' Catherine said. 'Do you know, that's surprising. I thought everyone was born and bred in Hanmouth, or at any rate, in Devon. I thought this was one of those places where no one accepted you until you'd lived here for fifty years and then probably only your children, you know. Is nobody a proper Devon native?'

'Not me,' said the man who rowed the ferry across the estuary. Alec had had a long and informative chat with him one morning and invited him along. He seemed, Alec said, to have what might be a slightly lonely life, and there was no harm in him. 'We moved from Sheffield, eight years ago. Retired from a steel firm. My wife, she died five years back.'

'There are people born in Hanmouth,' Kenyon was saying. 'After all, there was that girl, woman I should say, the one behind that awful case last month. Her family had never lived anywhere else.'

There was a small pause: the conversation of Hanmouth had moved on from Heidi and China. Nothing more had happened since Heidi had been charged, and people of good taste had moved away from the subject. Perhaps it was that Kenyon had been so much in London during the hunt and the panic that he hadn't had his chance to discuss it at the time, and was making up for it now.

'There must be someone we know who's a native,' Miranda

261

said. 'I can't believe everyone's a newcomer, comparatively speaking.'

'But you all seem so very settled, so much a part of the place,' Catherine said. 'That is encouraging.'

'We moved here, too,' John Calvin's wife, Laura, said, but so quietly nobody took any notice of her.

'I know,' Miranda said. 'I've thought of someone. Harry. Sam's Harry, Lord What-a-Waste. Here he comes, as if on cue. Harry, hello, we were just talking about you.'

Behind Harry was a man none of them knew; he was barely dressed for a party, if the party had been held by anyone over the age of sixteen. He was unshaven, his hair scrunched up and uncombed; his gaze was a little wild, not directed at anyone in particular. His broad grin was not reassuring; it roamed about the room, not engaging with anyone, like the sweep of a light-house.

'I hope you don't mind,' Harry said smoothly to Catherine. 'A guest of ours for dinner tonight, his business in Barnstaple this afternoon finished early and he came straight over. An old friend of ours – I thought you wouldn't mind if I brought him, rather than leave him alone in the house with Stanley.'

'Oh, yeah, with Stanley,' the man said, and burst out laughing.

'Stanley, the dog,' Harry said mildly. 'You forgot the name of our dog.'

'Of course not,' Catherine said brightly. 'Have a drink, both of you.'

'What's your friend's name, Harry?' Miranda said. Harry stared at her, quite blankly. Miranda exchanged a look with the man, who looked frankly back at her, engaging with an expression for the first time since he had entered, and then, once more, he broke into open laughter, joined by Miranda.

'I'm Spencer,' he said, without hostility. 'Who the fuck are you?'

'I'm Miranda,' Miranda said. 'Fucking nice to meet you.'

David saw, with some surprise, his parents' party filling up rapidly with handsome gay men. Where had they come from? There was one Hanmouth gay in the kitchen, talking to Mauro; another Hanmouth gay had just arrived with a man whom David could not believe his parents knew. It seemed to David that, in natural justice, he ought to be the fulcrum of this particular aspect of the party, but he had hardly made any impact on it. He was stuck in a corner with one of the two sisters, who had been taking shifts at the David-face for three-quarters of an hour now. Every time one of them drew a breath, or ran out of things to tell him about their Bedlington terrier, Poppet, the other one came over and relieved her. The dog herself was still running around through a thicket of legs and making whining noises. It seemed unlikely to inspire such a sequence of amusing or poignant stories. In the meantime, Mauro was grinning as if he had never had such fun at a party, and one of the Hanmouth gays had his arm on his shoulder; the pair of them were drawing near the other pair, the other Hanmouth gay and the sexy gatecrasher, and David could see that he would be stuck in this Bedlington-virgin corner for ever, excluded from the quadrangle where he wanted, needed, to be.

He had never been good at parties, even as a child, when parties were run along strict rules with their phases and their games and their gifts and their consequences, when parties were much easier. Once, when he was coming up to eleven, he remembered what parties were like, and told his mother that he didn't want to have a birthday party that year. For some reason he had it in his mind that birthday parties were childish things that he should make himself grow out of. What did they do instead? He had no recollection; only that, bad as parties were, always ending with him crying and running out to find his mummy, to general amusement and contempt, it was worse not to hold a party at all. That year, hardly anyone in his class invited him to their parties; in retrospect, it seemed that he had only ever been invited in recompense for an earlier invitation. And he had been completely wrong: parties were things you were never allowed to grow out of, with their jeweller's clusters of brilliant amusement and, round the edges, the dreary extras making laborious and egocentric conversation with each other for the sake of it. 'Excuse me,' he said to the two sisters, one to his right, one to his left, shining with the joy of having been allowed to talk about themselves for forty-five minutes. He remembered a conventional phrase. 'I mustn't monopolize you,' he said. But they looked at him in surprise and bewilderment; and perhaps in a room containing only seventeen people, that was a strange thing to say.

'Yeah, there's never been a club like Trade,' the handsome gatecrasher was saying. He took a moment and wiped his nose with the back of his hand. 'Ten, fifteen years ago, there was nothing like it.'

'Oh, come on, Spencer,' the posher of the two gays – Harry, was it? – was saying. 'Fifteen years ago, how old were you?'

'Seventeen,' Spencer said. 'I was seventeen. I never saw anything like it. The things I saw in Trade, my days.'

'It's not the same now,' Mauro said. 'I hear it was fabulous in the old days.'

'Back in the day,' Harry said, and laughed. 'What's good now?'

Mauro, in his good-natured way, introduced David again to Sam, Harry and Spencer; they all greeted him, friendly, but quickly. Mauro ran through Soho, Vauxhall and Shoreditch. 'And there's Bitch – it's OK,' he finished up. 'That's at the Rooms in Vauxhall.'

'That's where we met,' David said, to get some kind of purchase on the conversation. 'You and me. Remember?'

'Yeah,' Mauro said. 'Is that right? I can't remember.'

'Must have been a good night,' David said, and laughed on his own.

'Hey,' Spencer said to Mauro, running his hand down his back and resting casually on his bum, 'are you going to come over later?'

'Coming over where?' David said.

The look that now filled the air between Sam and Harry was one of those looks between couples that could mean anything to an outside observer, that to the couple could hardly have any more decisive meaning: it was a consultation in an expressive look. 'We were having some friends over,' Harry said.

'A bit later,' Sam said.

'You're welcome to come, if Catherine and Alec can spare you,' Harry said, and then he, too, made the same gesture of a back-handed wipe under the nose. With astonishment, David realized that they had all snorted something before they came out; he was amazed that Mauro hadn't discovered this, and wheedled something to take off to his parents' spare bedroom.

'A party?' Mauro said.

'They're famous, these two's parties,' Spencer said. 'You're in luck, coming down on the right weekend. You don't want to miss out on this.'

David knew that if he said, 'Well, I don't know,' or made some kind of acknowledgement that they had come down to see his parents, that he could see no way of explaining to them that he and his boyfriend were going to go off and spend the evening with two people they'd only just met, if he said any of that, then the invitation would be extended to the one they actually wanted to come, and Mauro would certainly accept. He had no particular reason to be the perfect guest. As for David, he did not believe that the invitation had been extended to him, if it had, indeed, been extended to him, for any reason other than politeness. They wanted Mauro to come, and Mauro would go. To look at it another way, Mauro was David's ticket to an orgy of sex and drugs.

'Yeah, why not?' David said. 'We'll just slip off. What time?'

'What sort of party?' Mauro said.

'Just a few mates coming round,' Sam said.

'Are they like you?' Mauro said.

'What do you mean?' Harry said.

'Are they Bears?' Mauro said. 'Is that what you say? Are they Bears?'

Sam and Harry exchanged another look, but this time they

looked, expressively and with agonizing amusement, at David. It was as if they had all known each other for ever, in some sympathetic world of the overweight and lecherous, and in a moment, the three of them burst out laughing.

'Come on,' Sam said, lowering his voice. 'It'll be fun.'

With a swift, open, undisguised movement, Harry now took a small paper wrap from the inner top pocket of his jeans and handed it to Mauro. 'There you go,' he said smoothly. 'That'll start you off on the right foot.' There was no hesitation or surprise in the exchange; it was as if Mauro had been expecting exactly this small gift ever since he had arrived in Devon, and here it was, astoundingly in David's parents' sitting room, just as everything ought to be. The wrap went into Mauro's inner top pocket in return, quite naturally. In the room there were incompatible multitudes: there were two grumpy sisters – spinsters was the only word – talking about their terrier, which was pestering their ankles; there was his mother whom he loved, flushed and pleasant, feeling that her party was a success, feeling justified; there was a posh old woman, saying, 'Well, I mean to say,' to a thin man, his arms wrapped tight about himself, hand to elbow, other hand against his face; there was his father doggedly filling glasses, and Ted and Barbara discussing A-roads with each other; there was the lovely vista from the picture windows; and there was the man, the thief, impersonating his boyfriend, taking a wrap of drugs from a stranger in front of all the rest. When worlds collide, David thought in his best Chinese-blurb manner, the result can only be shame in the heart.

'It's beautiful, the view from here,' Mauro said. 'Really beautiful. Do you have so nice a view from where you live?'

'No, not really,' Sam said. 'We like it, though.'

'The nice thing about Hanmouth is that you can always walk down to the estuary,' Harry said obstinately. Spencer was pawing at him and muttering into his ear. 'Well, you can have some when he comes back, you can't go with him, it's too much, you'll get us into trouble. I can't imagine living anywhere else.'

266

'Hey,' Sam said, as Spencer's gestures grew more importunate. 'You see that guy over there. The tall thin guy. He's Neighbourhood Watch round here. If he sees you, he'll call the Bill. Wait your turn and keep it discreet.'

'I do love these long summer evenings with the sun setting behind the castle,' Harry said. 'Always have. My idea of heaven. When I die and go to heaven, it's going to look exactly like that.'

'They were saying,' David said, 'I think I heard them saying, that you're about the only person here who didn't move here. Everyone else is a bit of a newcomer, apparently.'

'I suppose that's true,' Harry said, as Mauro appeared to judge that enough innocent conversation had followed the exchange to insulate it, and sauntered off to the bathroom.

'It's been a lovely party,' John Calvin could be heard saying in farewell to Catherine, whose attention was on this unexpected, half-invited group of men. She hadn't meant her party to be filled like this, you could tell. 'Thank you ever so for asking us but – heigh ho, heigh ho, we've got to go back home –' and he had actually broken into song.

'Goodbye,' the wife said to Catherine. 'It was nice to meet you.'

'What are you lot gossiping about?' Miranda's husband said, coming over to Sam, Harry, David and Spencer, still pawing Harry. Everyone called him Kenyon; David had no idea what his first name was. 'I know a good old chinwag when I see one.'

'Oh, you wouldn't understand,' Sam said. 'Straight men, they're hopeless for gossip.'

'Who are you calling straight?' Kenyon said equably. 'We can all start calling each other names.'

'Oh, come on,' Harry said. 'What about those shoes? I can tell you – there's not a gay man in the world would even know where you could buy shoes like that.'

The shoes were palest brown, and padded somehow; their tops were stitched like eiderdowns, their sides spreading. They were comfortable shoes, catalogue shoes, shoes bought by Mummy or

267

wife. They inspected, in turn, Harry's shoes – Australian Chelsea boots, polished to a conkery shine; Sam's shoes – an elaborate set of silver buckles and fastenings, breaking out into a showy ankle-collar, left louchely undone; and then they turned away, as if in shame, from the shoes with which David was letting down his sexual tribe.

'Anyway,' Spencer said, in a quick, flickering drawl, 'what the hell do they do when they go down to Neighbourhood Watch? That guy – the one who's left – the Neighbourhood Watch guy. What the FUCK. Do they DO. FUCK knows.'

'I really don't know,' Kenyon said. 'I really don't. I think they meet on Tuesdays, but I honestly don't know who takes an interest. I know John Calvin does. But I don't know anyone else who goes. I know they're awfully powerful and influential, though. What time is it? Don't you have people coming for dinner, Harry?'

'Yeah, for dinner,' Spencer said, bursting out laughing. 'Lovely, lovely dinner. Is he coming over?' nodding at Mauro coming back from the bathroom with a sudden shine on his features.

'Look at Mauro's shoes,' Kenyon said brightly. 'They're not so different from mine, surely.'

'Well. They're brown,' Sam said, because even Kenyon ought to be able to see the difference between a pair of Onitsuka Tigers in brown with this season's orange trim and the squashed Cornish pasties Kenyon was wearing.

'Are they as bad as all that?' Kenyon said, and Spencer raised his voice a little, bored with this nattering about shoes. The seventeen people in the room, who had broken up into half a dozen or so conversations, fell subordinate to his urgent and alien noise.

'Hey, gorgeous,' Spencer called. 'You're coming over later, yeah? We'll look forward to that, I reckon.' Mauro, returning, smiled, and Spencer slid his arm round his waist, assessing his firm sides, his silky skin. Without making any concession to the place or the people around, he boldly pushed his hand down the back of

Mauro's jeans, and for a moment his hand writhed under the denim like a suffocating vole. Mauro went on smiling, not doing anything to discourage this frank and coked-up move; and David could see that he might quite like it. 'Yeah,' Spencer said. 'When you come over, I want . . .' but then his voice sank into intimacy, and he muttered into Mauro's ear the deeds he would do to him, the deeds Mauro would be commanded to do to him '. . . cos I bet you love that,' it finished, Spencer withdrawing his hand and returning to the land of the audible. He might have been talking in a strange language to Mauro, who went on smiling, and not responding, and wishing him well with his benevolent face. Sam and Harry were masks; Miranda's face was interested; Kenyon was giving him that calm, deciding judgement with his pale blue eyes, the look of a schoolmaster waiting for someone to stop fooling about and give an attempt at the right answer. Behind them, Alec, with a sad bottle in his hand, offering top-ups, confused and unhappy. It was as if he were wondering who it was that his son had brought into the house; as if he blamed David for bringing in this remote and shameful member of his tribe, this Spencer, and despoiling their party, which might have been quite nice. Then Alec caught David's eye, and there was the opposite of an exchange of complicity; there was an exchange of disavowal. It occurred to David that his father might not be objecting to Spencer, who was the sort of party accident that might happen to anyone, the sort of party disaster who could be brought once by people you hardly knew anyway. It might not be Spencer; it might be Mauro his father was registering such distaste for, who was standing with an aura of unnatural brightness, a hired glassful of champagne from the in-laws in one hand, and letting a stranger shove his finger down his bum-crack. Yes, it might be Mauro.

'Anyone for a top-up?' his father muttered.

'Yeah,' Spencer said malevolently. 'I'll have a top-up, old chap.'

'No, you won't,' Sam said. 'We've got to go. We've stayed too long. It's been lovely. David – David? You come too, if you like. We'd like to see you.'

'It's been fucking great,' Spencer said, to Alec. 'But now I reckon it's time to get on with some other stuff.'

Not ten feet away, Billa was obstinately telling Kitty that they'd got a roast leg of lamb for their supper, that she'd be welcome to join them, and Kitty thought that would be delightful, she thought it would be just perfect, as they concentrated their full attention on each other's faces.

28.

Like timber dislodged by spring floods; like unmoored boats swept into the stream; like cast-off objects driven before the force of a renewed river, taking possession of a dried-up channel at the end of a hot Devon August; like the return of beasts to their place of spawning at the close of their season of youth; like all of that, the Bears turned and followed the scent back to the house in Hanmouth, upriver, along the country routes, speeding up, shedding their concerns as they went, flying in their Toyota Civics, their Ford Primeras, their VW Golf GTis, their Peugeots, their Fiats, their Ford Kas, their Jaguars, their Bentleys, in shades of royal blue and silver, and silver and white, and red and silver, and silver, silver, blue and silver, catching the evening light like trout turning in a stream. They had come from Ashreigney and Iddesleigh, Bishops Tawton and Bratton Fleming, from brown fat houses like mushrooms in moorland, from first-floor flats with peeling paint in Barnstaple, from town terraces in Cullompton, from Chittlehampton, Huish, from almshouses in Cheriton Fitzpaine and Clyst; from towns commended for a reredos, for a pub as old as the monarchy, for a manor-house carving of Shadrach, Meshach and Abednego, and for King Charles I's belief that if there was anything certain in this world, it was that rain was falling over Tavistock. They had put themselves in leather, in green combats, in jeans, in tartan shirts, in a red and blue kilt, in clean white underwear, in none at all, and with bottles at their side or in their pockets, large and green or thumb-sized and brown, they drove, in pairs and singly. Mick and Ali, Phil and Andy, and Adam and Blaise and Steve, who ran the garage in Barnstaple; men solid and beefy, men stout, men verging on the definitely fat, ninety kilos, a hundred kilos, a hundred and ten and twenty, men whose waking breath resembled a lady's light snoring, and a couple of men who just liked that sort of thing. There was the son of Harry's old gardener, and Charles and Robert and Kevin; and they drove fast, with Lady Gaga on the stereo. They were in a hurry because they had all heard about Steve's mechanic, whom Steve had had twice over the desk in the back room of the garage. Whose name was Spencer. The CCTV watched them go along the roads, breaking the speed limit as they went.

They came along roads that ran along rivers, hardly thinking of the names of the floods and trickles; their county sent the rain water to this Channel or that, to the Bristol, to the English; the Dart with its salmon, the glimpse of the Erme, the Avon, the Lynn, the deep-hidden Tamar, the Torridge, the Tavy, the Taw. They saw them, they crossed them, they passed within two miles of them, unseeing and unthinking, not like people going to something, but like those fleeing a threat behind them. They feared, as adults do not, to be late; they thought and talked to each other, in their cars pelting in top gear, of sex, of men, of the evening to come. A mild heated confusion had already settled on most of the passengers and a couple of the drivers, who had drunk a beer, a glass of wine, had taken a pill, had snorted horse anaesthetic or the ground-up leaves of a South American plant, and now were talking nonsense about how and when in the process the leaves lost their green and turned to white. When they reached the borders of the larger town, they deliberately slowed, grew stately, in homage to the stately observing cameras; some even turned down the stereo as the houses about them thickened. They passed the ugly estates with their backs to the road where – some remarked – that little girl had lived, where her mother stole her away and lost her, perhaps for ever. And then the houses grew pretty, and Hanmouth turned into itself. Some of them noticed each other, arriving more or less simultaneously, all of them afraid of turning up late and missing whatever they had come for, and hooted and gave a manly thumbs-up. They had come from miles away, sometimes, the Bears, and they knew what they had come for.

'It's a fucking nightmare parking here,' Mick said, plucking at his crotch, tight and hot in black leather. 'Always has been. Always will be. It'll be a ten-minute walk from that car park by the station, you wait and see.'

'Oh, for fuck's sake,' Ali said from the passenger seat. 'It's not you they'll be staring at.' Because he was wearing a kilt in green camouflage material and, under his leather jacket, nothing but a harness of steel rings and leather straps. 'Stop going on about the fucking parking.'

29.

Half an hour later, it was as if no party had ever taken place in Catherine and Alec's flat. The guests had gone, and could be seen to have trodden like cats through the furniture, the drink, the food; nothing was disturbed, nothing was moved, nothing was knocked over. The scrupulous new carpet – still giving off a faint metallic odour of the showroom and the carpet fitter – bore the marks of its vacuuming. The guests had been neat in their eating, and no crumb or spillage had fallen anywhere to show that anyone had visited at all. Alec had been good with the cloth and with the bottles, removing and stacking as the party had gone on; and now, as the four of them waved the last guests off, they returned to a smokeless, unstained, well-ordered room, more ready to hold a party than anything else.

'Goodbye, Marian,' Catherine was saying. 'Goodbye, Isobel. Oh, yes – mustn't forget – goodbye, Poppet, yes, goodbye to you too . . .'

'Know more about Bedlington terriers than I ever thought I would,' Alec was saying in the sitting room, busying about. 'Could go on *Mastermind*. Specialist subject.'

'Extraordinary, bringing their dog to a party,' David said. 'I don't see why they couldn't leave it at home for half an hour.'

'Bloody thing,' Alec said. 'I must have tripped over it half a dozen times. You hear it yapping in the stairwell in the mornings.'

'It makes your eyes hurt when you're in the same room as it, yapping like that.'

'I saw you give it a good kick, David,' Alec said. 'Well done, that man.'

'I thought no one was looking,' David said, sniggering.

That was a nice moment of companionship between father and son, agreeing about Bedlingtons. Then it passed, and Alec went back into the kitchen.

'In Italy,' Mauro said, turning round from the window, 'nobody brings their dog to a party if it can't behave. Maybe not even then. I never saw a dog at a party, running round like that. That's what we say, the English, they love their dog, they have it instead of sex.'

'Yeah, maybe.'

'Hey, David,' Mauro said. 'Did you have some of that stuff? It's good stuff, that. I don't know you can get such good stuff here. I'll come again.'

'No, I didn't,' David said. 'No one offered me.'

'Well, you only have to ask,' Mauro said. 'I think you're crazy. When are we going to their party? Can we go soon?'

'Well, that was nice,' Catherine said, coming back in. 'And we did only say from six to eight, and it's nice that people don't hang around for hours afterwards. They came when they were asked and they went before we got bored with them. Did you meet some nice people, Mauro?'

273

'Yes, very nice, very nice,' Mauro said.

Alec stood in the kitchen doorway. He had put on his nipple-tassel pinny over his best shirt and his cavalry twill trousers. Behind him, the two dozen glasses, clouded, obscured, lipstick-edged, still half- or quarter-filled with champagne, stood in three neat rows above the dishwasher like an improvised and reprehensible musical instrument; Alec could have been about to play 'Edelweiss' on them. 'Have I got the lot?' he murmured, but this had not been a party inclined to smash glasses, even by accident, even considering Spencer, and he went back to his domestic task.

'Yes, those funny boys,' Catherine said, and she involuntarily looked about her at her objects, her bibelots, her table-top treasures. As well she might – but David looked, and even the little jewelled bird was there still. 'We don't really know them, I suppose, though I've often exchanged a few words with Sam. He runs the little cheese shop. I bought some of that brown cheese no one's tried from there. I do think it's important to support local businesses in ways like that. And his friend, his partner, Harry, seems awfully nice. Do you know he's a lord? Not a proper lord, not one that sits in the House of Lords, not that they do any more, but someone's son, someone important, he's called Lord Henry something. You'd never know. Perfectly nice, very ordinary, no trouble at all, not pompous, no side to him.'

Catherine was going on talking as if to fend something off, to delay the moment. Was it Spencer – was something going to be said about that impossible and, now he had departed, unimaginable appearance? Among the Bedlington-fanciers and military widows, the shy and unadvised men with clothes ambitiously posher than their weak and even somewhat silly faces, Spencer had come in with his tight-clad body canted backwards like a model and his sleepy, lecherous glare under unkempt hair and blond eyebrows. He had seemed like a mistake, a delivery for downstairs, a party changeling whose true identity had been uncovered too late. But he had been in the right place after all; he and Mauro had gone towards each other like elementary principles in a physics experiment, hand drawn to arse. They could not have helped themselves.

'They're having a little party themselves tonight,' David found himself saying. 'Harry and Sam. They asked us if we'd like to go over a little later.'

'That was nice of them,' Alec called from the kitchen. 'I don't know that I really feel up to it, though.'

'David didn't mean *us* when he said "us",' Catherine said. 'He meant that Harry and Sam had asked them, David and Mauro, to go over.'

'Not very polite,' Alec said. 'Are you sure they didn't include us as well?'

'They don't want old people like us at their party,' Catherine said.

'Anyway, you said you didn't want to go,' Mauro said. 'Do you mind if we go?'

Catherine flushed. She hated bad manners more than anything, David always believed; it was a blessing she didn't always notice it, when it happened. Small snubs, small jibes, the raised eyebrow and the moment of being ignored; she was always ready to overlook that, to find excuses for neighbours, fellow workers at the charity desk at the cathedral, acquaintances and even strangers at the bus stop. 'They've got a lot of troubles,' she would observe, or 'They're very busy.' But Mauro clearly had no troubles; he was not busy; he was their guest for the weekend and, his eyes shining like plastic with the coke he'd taken, his request to go and find something more amusing was not something David's mother could ignore.

'Of course,' she said. 'It sounds like fun. Anyway, I hadn't made much in the way of plans for dinner. No, you go. Enjoy yourselves.'

Alec was making a good deal of noise in the kitchen.

30.

'Well done,' Calvin said. 'Ever so well done. They'll think, Ooh, must have Mr and Mrs Calvin back, they're ever so entertaining, full of conversation, especially her. I. Don't. Think. Standing there like one of the elect, like a bleeding duchess. Disapproving look on your silly face like you could smell rotting fish. Or dog droppings.'

'That's not fair, John,' Laura said. They were walking down the Strand towards their house. Calvin was carrying a woven hessian bag-for-life in which there was a bottle of Spanish cava. They had brought it, just in case it was the same sort of party that Calvin gave, the sort where people brought bottles of Spanish cava and were expected to – in fact, the bottle in Calvin's planet-saving bag had been brought to them by an only marginally less mean guest, and been set on one side. But they had come through the door, and Calvin had seen that there was champagne in the kitchen. He had placed the bottle in the bag, underneath the telephone table in the hallway, to pick it up without comment on their way out, as if they always brought their shopping to parties. 'That's not fair. Not everyone finds parties as easy as you do.'

'You've had plenty of opportunities, my girl,' Calvin said. 'Oh, yes, begorrah and Goddammit, that you have. The parties I've taken you to. The festivities you've adorned. Over the years so to speak.'

'John, not in the street,' Laura said.

'And you still can't bring yourself to show an interest in other people, just standing there like a prize turnip. Do you know what you look like, standing there with your mouth open? Some great white root vegetable, that's what. Why do you think people ask us out? Do you think it's because of you, standing there with your great silly look and saying nothing? It's just selfishness, that's what it is, what you call your shyness. You see, I make an effort. You can see I do. And people want to have me, li'l ol' me,

276

at their parties, but you, they put up with you, no more'n that. And—'

Calvin's commentary froze. Out of a silver car – a sleek silver Saab with a soft top – two men were stepping, both in sunglasses despite the half-light of the evening. Both had shaved heads, one with a trim ginger beard. One, slightly shorter, wore a skirt, a kilt, in combat material, and above, nothing but an arrangement of leather and steel, a sort of harness. The harness was tight about his flesh, perhaps bought when he was less fat, or fastened a notch too far; its side straps made capital Bs of his bulging waist, and about his peg-like nipples, the flesh was forced into breasts like rhomboid chicken flesh. His friend, less startling, wore leather trousers, folded and creased like an overfilled sofa and a black T-shirt with an obscure slogan on it. 'You see?' the kilted man said. 'Right outside their house in the end.' The car was locked, and they walked across the Strand, up Little Matcham Street. They hardly glanced at Calvin and Laura.

'Gays,' Laura said superfluously. 'I heard those two say they had some friends coming round. That's why they left early.'

'Disgraceful,' Calvin said. 'Walking the streets like that. There could have been—'

'There could have been anyone,' Laura said.

'It's practically a matter for Neighbourhood Watch,' Calvin said.

31.

The table had been cleared, but most of the dishes had only got as far as the work surface just inside the kitchen; it had been cleared in a hurry. It was two hours later. The curtains were pulled tight: Harry had sometimes suggested that, on the Bears' evenings, they might be fastened tight with clothes pegs, but nothing had been done, and Harry accepted that he was being too nervous about the neighbours. On the table – a four-pinioned mahogany Victorian structure, as solid as a dining-table could possibly be, resting on voluted and square-legged pillars – a man lay on his back with his knees flexed, his head backwards over the edge, his face inverted. This was Spencer. On the floor, lying on the carpet, another man, his position echoing Spencer's, on the table, but his legs stretched straight upwards, his hands gripping the back of his knees. This was Mauro. Like everyone else in the room, they were naked, though Mauro had left on a pair of white socks. They were now twitching in the air like an upside-down pirouette with the forceful rhythm of what was happening to him at either end. Almost everything that could be occupied was occupied; a bottle of poppers was doing the rounds, passing from Ali, who was fucking Spencer with a steady, circular, *andante* rhythm, to Spencer, who took his face away from Harry's inquisitive, craning, rhubarb-pink cock to sniff the bottle; left nostril, right nostril, and then, dangerously, held underneath the open mouth and a deep breath. Harry took it from him, and ladled his balls once more into Spencer's mouth; he sniffed once, twice, and, like Spencer, a third time, before passing it over his shoulder to Steve, who with a businesslike snap stretched and dropped a condom on the solid trunk of his cock, Viagra-sustained, jabbed twice before forcing it into Harry, who let out a slightly rehearsed groan; Steve bit Harry's ear from behind, licked his neck affectionately, and then started up a rhythm of his own, sniffing from time to time as it went on. Underneath, there was a hand cupped confidently, encouragingly, under Steve's motion into Harry; it turned out to be Robert's hand, or perhaps, underneath him, Kevin's.

'It says play that funky music,' Ali said to Blaise, collapsed in a two-man pile to one side. 'Do you hear what it's saying? It's telling a funky music, no, it's telling a white boy to play that funky music.'

'I'm not a white boy,' Blaise said. 'So it ain't be talking to me, yeah?'

'I know you're not a white boy,' Ali was saying. 'You're lovely. Look at that, isn't it lovely?'

He ran his fingers over a part of Blaise, which responded alertly; they had finished what they were doing for the moment, but they would begin again in a second.

'Oh, you,' Blaise said. 'I want some more charlie. Oh, it's so good, that charlie, and I want it, some more.'

'Let's have some, then,' Ali said, and raised himself up to the level of the sideboard, where a fat scattering of the stuff lay. He took a quilled-up ten-pound note resting there and, with a single eye closed, the better to see the coke, made vague figure-of-eight movements over the rosewood surface. He was too fucked to form the stuff into a line, and in a moment fell back onto Blaise's thighs like a sack of potatoes.

About Mauro everyone was busy, mouth and arse and hands and cock, and their mouths and hands and arses and cocks; he was being a considerable social success. Perhaps it was only his neat, diminutive scale that drew such attention to the parts of him that were rather remarkably out of scale. But for at least a year the Bears had mostly been making do with each other; putting up with occasionally having to endure even Peter, who wasn't here tonight. His absence, and his two spectacular replacements, assured the success. They had heard about Spencer, whom Steve had had, twice, over the table in the back room of his garage, and had looked forward to him; they hadn't anticipated a second gift in the shape of Mauro. The Bears feasted. They would still be talking about tonight in a year or two. Adam and Phil and Mick and Andy and the others, almost crushing each other in their eagerness, were passing nipple and cock and Mauro's open lips from mouth to mouth, passing his arse from finger to cock to mouth to clenched and arrowed hand, filling, grazing, flicking, biting, and stuffing. Mauro was wriggling, crying out, 'Madonna,' opening his big eyes, grinning, flinging his neck-thick arms wide behind him, letting Adam and Phil and Mick and Andy and the others do what they wanted to him. They seemed to have a list they were working through.

279

For long months now, David had had a film playing in the inside of his skull. In the film, Mauro was taken and seized and fucked, and his naked body passed of its own free will from one hairy man to another, in London at the exact moment David was lying sleeplessly, fraught, in his solitary bed in St Albans. The rubbish grumbleflick with which David's lying brain liked to torment itself was here, in front of him, running its course. The small and tinny collection of porn David kept in St Albans, industrial fucking preserved in the shape of shiny beermats, kept by David in an envelope between two of Nabokov's novels, *that* did not run on a permanent night-time loop as his thoughts of Mauro's entertainments tended to; on the other hand, that rubbish porn had a fast-forward, had an off-switch, and there seemed no end to Mauro's pleasures, happening here, before him. Another part of his fantasizing brain had, for long months, dwelt happily on what might happen if lovely Mauro ever came to the point of showing him his bum or even his penis – in less ambitious moods, what would happen if Mauro ever came out of the shower when he was there, his grip on his white towel weak and faltering and accidental . . . His weak and apologetic imagination was being fulfilled here, in a stranger's house with twelve hairy men, none of whom Mauro had ever met before, taking turns to fuck David's love. Did they even know Mauro's name, all of them? David was not altogether sure he liked it and, naked, he squatted by the wall with his back against the wallpaper and his balls dangling between his heels, a drink in his hand and a mild smile on his face, as if he had been enjoying himself, were just taking a little rest, and would be returning to the fuck-wrestle in a moment or two.

'The thing is, it's telling the white boy to play that funky music,' Ali was saying.

'Yeah, I know,' Blaise said.

'But it doesn't make any sense,' Ali said.

'I think it makes sense,' Blaise said.

'No, it doesn't,' Ali said. 'Because when it says that funky music, what it means is this funky music.'

'No, man, I don't get what you're saying.'

'It doesn't mean there's some other funky music which is, like, better than this funky music, I mean, this record, this one, going, white boy, play that funky music.'

'Yeah, they're great, these old records.'

'So it's saying, white boy, play this record, which is extremely funky, but it's telling you this in the form of the record which is already playing, which the white boy has already started playing, because if he hadn't, it wouldn't be playing to tell him to play that funky music. You see what I'm saying?'

'Yeah, but that's no good, man,' Blaise said. 'Because it might not have been a white boy that put the music on in the first place. It might have been a black boy. Or it might have been a black girl. Or it might have been . . .' His head wavered back and forth as he focused on something. 'That Italian bloke,' he finished. 'He can't get enough, can he?'

'What an arse,' Ali said. 'I'm having another go on that in a bit, I reckon.'

'That Italian bloke,' Blaise said. 'He don't like this music, does he?'

'What – why do you – what—'

''Cause he keeps asking for Madonna,' Blaise said. He was straight-faced, tremulous, his eyes on Ali's face. In a second, Mauro called out, 'Madonna,' in pleasure or amazement or just because he had his mouth free for a moment, and the pair of them burst out laughing, chuckling and wheezing like two old men at a comedy rodeo.

32.

'Hi, David,' said Sam, dropping down on his haunches, facing him. He was solid rather than fat when his clothes were off; he gave the general impression of burliness, even of stoutness, in his

281

clothes, but naked, his chest came out like a sergeant major's. He was a curious, cuboid sort of shape, and a curious, rather appealing animal odour came from him. Clothed, in the street or in his shop, he seemed languid, indulged, lazy, with probable areas of softness at waist and big arse. Naked, he gave the impression of compressed hairy power, as if he could fell a policeman, chop down a tree, outrun a milk float. In a friendly gesture, he reached out his big hairy right hand and weighed David's balls where they hung. 'All right? Having a good time?'

'Yeah,' David said. 'Fantastic. Just taking a breather.'

'Yeah,' Sam said. 'He's having a good time, your boyfriend.'

'Yeah,' David said. 'Mauro. It looks like it.'

They paused for a moment to observe the stage Mauro's pleasures had reached.

'People say that we've got a strange relationship,' David offered. 'But it seems to work quite well for us.'

Sam burst out laughing. 'Yeah, I know all about strange relationships,' he said. 'Didn't you notice? It's my husband who's got his fist up your boyfriend's bum.'

'Oh, yeah,' David said miserably.

'You've got to give us your telephone numbers,' Sam said. 'If the two of you are going to be coming down regularly. It's usually once a month we meet up, every six weeks or so. You want to come again.'

'You mean,' David said, 'you want Mauro to come again.'

'I didn't say that,' Sam said. 'And you said you were having a good time. You want to . . .' And, boldly, he made a glib, intimate gesture with his hand; it might have been the surprise of it, or Sam's hand, cold from gripping a bottle of beer, but David really flinched.

'It's not compulsory, you know,' Sam said. But David said again that he was having a good time.

'I was watching you earlier,' Sam said. 'Making your way round. Your heart just wasn't in it, was it? First you try one, then another, but you don't go for it. You put your hand out, you touch some-

282

one's bum, but you do it – it's like it's all tentative with you, it's like you know you're going to be refused. That's no good, Dave. It looks like you're asking for their permission. Oh, please may I . . . and I tell you, if you waver and look nervous and think that they're going to say no, and look as if you think they're going to say no, they'll think about it, and they probably will say no. I mean in real life. Not in here. They're not going to say no, none of this lot. Slags.'

'Slag yourself,' Steve called over. 'It's not us who met our boyfriend in the toilet of a pub.'

'Yeah, well,' Sam said. 'But they are. They're not going to say no. Look at your boyfriend. It's never occurred to him in his life that anyone's going to say no, once he takes his shirt off. I bet they never have.'

'But—'

'I know what you're going to say. But he looks like him, and you look like you,' Sam said. 'It's true. But how do you think you get to look like you? It's not what shape you are, or the size of your nose. It's – you know what it is – it's that hunted expression. You really do. You have a hunted expression. When you were going round the room, you copped a feel of all of them, one after the other. Usually a pretty quick feel. You didn't even give them a chance to say, piss off, fat boy. They aren't going to say that, you know. It's just that hunted expression on your face. It's not doing it for anyone. And when you got near anyone you thought was out of your league – when you got anywhere near Spencer – it was like you were waiting until he was turned in another direction before you were going anywhere near him. You didn't want him to realize it might be you putting your finger up his bum. I tell you, he wouldn't care. And then you get near Mauro, and it's like you just don't dare come within a foot of him. That I don't understand.'

'I guess it's embarrassment,' David said. 'Doing it in public.'

'Yeah,' Sam said. 'Some people are like that. When people fuck – whether there's someone else there, or not, it's a whole different ballgame. Some people just don't have sex with each other, not unless there's . . . Harry and me, we're all right, we like it if there's just the two of us, and we don't care if there's another one. But Ali and Mick – you know Ali and Mick?'

'That's the guy with the kilt on, yeah?'

'Mick told me he hadn't had sex with Ali, just the two of them, without someone else, or another couple, or another fourteen like tonight, for two years. Just didn't fancy it. But it's not like that with you and Mauro.'

'I suppose we've just grown out of it,' David said. 'It's true – we don't have sex together any more, not much. I love him, but he does his own thing and I do mine.'

'Yeah,' Sam said. 'I can see him doing his own thing. I don't see you doing much of yours. I see you watching your boyfriend getting fucked, and I don't think it's doing you much good. It's like you've forgotten what it's like to fuck with him, and you're watching because it's interesting, that's all. It just doesn't seem to be reminding you of anything. You know what I mean? Maybe it's just that hunted look. You do have a hunted look, you know.'

'I'll do my best to do something about it,' David said gallantly.

'I tell you what,' Sam said. 'I'll fuck you, if you like. I don't mind. It would be a total pleasure.'

'Sam,' David said. 'That's the nicest thing anyone ever said to me. Would you really? Would you really fuck me?'

'Well, of course I would,' Sam said, who hoped that David would not take him up on the offer. 'Do you want a line first? There's plenty more where that came from.'

33.

'It's such a shame you have to go back so soon,' Catherine said. 'We were hoping to have you for lunch, at least.'

They were at the breakfast table, the next morning. The night before, David had had the impression that they were tottering in in the small hours; but of course they had gone to Sam and Harry's party around eight, and the promised dinner had run its course in half an hour. Spencer had seen to the quick succession of events, like a kid at Christmas calling out, 'Now can we? *Now* can we? Sam, now, please?' So even after Sam and Harry's party had come to an end, and Sam had graciously and smilingly done to David what he had offered and Mauro had levered himself up off the floor, wiping himself down, dizzy and limp and grinning slackly, noisy with gratitude towards Harry, who had saved himself until last and had found himself hugely appreciated – after all of that, the two of them had walked back in wavering parallels, hardly knowing how to return home, and had come quietly in to find Catherine and Alec watching the Saturday-night film. It was only eleven fifteen. They were a sight, David and Mauro, and Mauro would have happily stayed up and talked gibberish to his parents. David had no idea how he persuaded Mauro that it was time for bed. Now, in the morning, the four of them were at the table in the little dining room, with toast in the toast-rack, two boxes of cereal, and jars of jam, marmalade and honey next to the butter dish and the cafetière.

'Yes, I've got to be back,' Mauro said. 'I didn't realize – I have to work tonight.'

'Such a shame,' Alec said, and both David and Catherine looked at him with surprise. He made an amused face. Mauro had tried to steal an ornament; had been groped by a gatecrasher; had snorted coke in David's parents' house; had gone out to be gang-fucked by half a dozen strangers. But David had not expected his father to take a dislike to him. He had thought his father would like Mauro as much as he did.

All over Hanmouth people were talking about Catherine's party, and a few about Harry and Sam's. 'I don't see why we should put up with that,' John Calvin said. 'Fancy dress is one thing, but that?' His wife reminded him of past successes of Neighbourhood Watch. Billa told her husband about the party, omitting the conspicuous parts and concentrating on the Wallace sisters and their Bedlington. Over their breakfast honey and toast and the babyish cereal they both seemed to like, she made a funny story out of it, as she had made many funny stories out of things Tom had not got to. Isobel, coming back from a nice long walk with Poppet, made her dinner, the dog bounding and barking. She said to Marian, who was still in her dressing-gown, that they had met some interesting people last night, but all the same, they seemed to know some jolly peculiar people too, and that she had enjoyed going last night, but she was quite sure that she wouldn't want to go again tonight. The amateur boatman thought of telephoning one of his children; he knew they worried about his isolation, and it was good to tell them when he had gone out and made some new friends. Sylvie read a three-day-old copy of the *Guardian*, and Tony a four-day-old one.

'Christ,' Harry said, looking at the state of the downstairs; things spilled and two glasses broken and, despite the three bins, someone had dropped and left a condom on the carpet where they had missed it last night. Stanley had followed him downstairs, after sleeping the sleep of a basset hound, and looked up at his master in an inquisitive way. 'Not just yet, you fool,' Harry said. Sam was still asleep upstairs; the air rippling past his tonsils supplying the house with an adorable, warm background sound. Harry was in his old dressing-gown, and the morning constitutional Stanley was about to insist on seemed inconceivable. Harry's thundering headache must be not just down to the drink and the drugs from last night, but to an overpowering odour of feet, making the air swim. Someone had left an open bottle of poppers on the rosewood sideboard. At least they hadn't spilt it. Harry went to the french windows and opened them wide, then to the side window to create a through-draught. 'Go on, you fool,' he said to Stanley, and Stanley lumbered out for his morning shit. He preferred the street, but the garden would do at a pinch.

'Is there any coffee?' Spencer said, coming down the stairs, a white guest towel round his middle.

'Christ, I thought you'd gone home,' Harry said. 'Go home. Go home, Spencer.'

'It was awfully nice,' Kitty said to her friend Angela in Clun, over the telephone, clutching it between chin and shoulder as she went through her kitchen cupboard – she was sure she had some juniper berries, but maybe not. 'It was vintage,' Ali said to Blaise. 'It was really much more fun than I expected,' Miranda said to Hettie. 'We ought to ask them round for dinner,' Kenyon said, chomping hard at the muesli, thinking, not for the first time, that the way to make the stuff edible was to start soaking it the night before, as he knew the Swiss did. 'Or maybe just have a meal at the Case Is Altered. That might be best.' 'One of the best nights ever,' Steve said to Andy over the telephone. 'I've got to get Spencer to come back,' and then some miscellaneous comments about the sorts of things ex-soldiers in their early thirties with wives were always going to get up to.

David had put their bags in the boot of the car; there was no return of that marital frisson as he placed them together. 'Well,' he said to his father and mother, standing in the car park of their apartment block. There was a keen wind blowing from the direction of the sea. 'Well,' he said.

'It's been nice to see you,' Catherine said. 'However briefly. And lovely to meet you, Mauro.'

'It's been lovely,' Mauro said, and kissed her on one, both cheeks, before turning to Alec and shaking his hand. For the first time, it struck David that the normal thing to have done, surely, would have been to bring a gift of some sort. But Mauro had brought nothing. It went onto what was now becoming a long line of grievances; it was astonishing to David that an infatuation could develop into pure resentment without a conventional relationship coming in between. He wanted to divorce Mauro and to embark on an affair with him more or less equally.

Once they were out of Hanmouth and on the road to the motorway, Mauro said, 'I'm going to sleep. I didn't sleep well last night.'

David hadn't slept well either; the first time he had lain next to Mauro in a bed, and knowing nothing would or could happen after the evening. He had endured Mauro turning himself over like a dolphin in open seas, every five, every ten minutes. 'It must have been the coke,' he said.

'Yeah,' Mauro said. 'It was good stuff. You had some in the end?'

'Sam – you know Sam – he gave me some to take away,' David said. 'He gave me, like, half a gram.'

'Oh, you're lying,' Mauro said. 'He never gives you half a gram like that.'

'Well, he did,' David said. 'It's in my wallet.'

'Yeah, you took it,' Mauro said. 'There was enough, they'll never miss that.'

David controlled a surprisingly fierce uprise of temper. He pressed down on the indicator; the slip road for the London motorway unrolled in front of him. 'No,' he said. 'I didn't steal it. You shouldn't assume everyone's like you.'

His meaning came across Mauro slowly, but when it came, it had to pain and insult him. 'Fuck you, David,' he said. 'I don't have to come away with you for the weekend.'

'Yeah, well,' David said.

'I don't think it was such a good idea,' Mauro said.

'Probably not,' David said.

'Hey, David,' Mauro said. 'If you've got some coke, give it to me. I'll snort it off a key, while you drive. That'll be fun, yeah?'

'Forget it,' David said.

'Ah, you don't have any,' Mauro said. 'You're full of shit.'

'I've got some,' David said. Mauro took his sweater from his lap; rolled it up into a pillow; rested against the side window. Then, clearly, he thought of something to say.

'Your parents, I don't think they like me, not really,' Mauro said. 'I think they know we're not together.'

David agreed, morosely.

'I don't think anyone would think it's so likely,' Mauro said.

288

'I mean, those boys, the Bears – you know what they all said to me, about you? They all said to me—'

'I can guess what they said,' David said. 'I can guess they said that you were fabulous, an amazing guy, so what were you doing with – yeah, I can guess. I've heard your stories before, Mauro.'

'You think I make up the stories?' Mauro said. 'Hey, Mr Poppers. Look at yourself. You really think it's so likely some guy like you, he's with someone like me? What would be the sense in that, you know? You – what are you like?'

David admired the quick ear for idiom Mauro had, while recognizing that Mauro had not quite got it right: *what are you like* was, surely, an expression of admiration and wonder at excess, an affectionate comment that might have smoothed the way between the two of them this morning. But it would have been for David to say, 'What are you like?' with a shake of the head, to Mauro. In Mauro's mouth it was a real question, and what David was like could only be answered with 'I have no idea.'

'I think I would like,' David said carefully, 'when we get back to London, I think I would like you to make a start on paying me back that two thousand four hundred pounds I lent you.'

'That's fine,' Mauro said. 'I don't give a shit. I can pay you back now if you like.'

'Good,' David said. 'Pay me back, then. It's been fun, but, you know—'

'I'm happy with that,' Mauro said. 'I want to see that guy again.'
David said nothing.

'That guy, you know, that guy at the end. His name – he was the guy whose house it was. He was the lord. I liked him – he was the best. He was a fantastic shag. I want to see him again.'

'Good luck,' David said.

The motorway was clear and they did not speak. There were no lorries or coaches; there were only cars, widely separated and relaxed. On either side, green banks, planted with spindly and ineffective trees, and where the road curved round, a remote vista of moorland and high cloud revealed itself. A sign said it was hundreds of miles to London, where Mauro lived; it said nothing about David's town. For a moment he envisaged his untidy, solitary flat, with nothing in it but detritus, as he had left it, and as he must return to it. Twenty miles of silence passed; Mauro put on a CD of dance music. It played for three or four minutes before David found he did not care for dance music of any sort, and never really had. He pressed the button and ejected the CD. Mauro said nothing, but rested his head on the side window, turning his face to the view.

In another half an hour, a sign came up for a motorway service station. 'I'm stopping here,' David said. Mauro said nothing. David signalled, slowed, turned off. The motorway had been quiet, but the car park was surprisingly full. He drove about, and then, not caring at all, parked the car at an angle, in the disabled bays. David considered that when the guardians came to berate the owner of the car, it would only be Mauro, who would not be getting out.

'Do you want to get out?' David said.

'No,' Mauro said. 'I'll stay here and sleep some. Can you leave the keys?'

'Can I leave the keys?'

'Yeah, so I can, you know, listen to some music while you're gone.'

'You must be fucking joking,' David said. 'You think I'm leaving the keys to my car with you?'

'Fuck you,' Mauro said. 'I'm not stealing your car, David.'

David got out, nevertheless, his keys in his hand. In the old days – when he and his parents had taken a trip, when he was a child – these places had had their own identity. You would not confuse one for another: a bridge over the motorway that one boasted, the fish restaurant another was noted for, the blue plastic façade of a third. Now they were all subsumed in a general international corporatism; the sign on the motorway had been crested with a double identification, an American burger bar, a coffee chain. Whether they owned the site or not, their franchises were

290

conspicuous to either side of the spread-open entrance; the floor-to-roof red-framed windows had been conceived as giving cheerful face-stuffing families a fine cheerful view of the car park, and indeed, some of those exact families were filling themselves up with complex interactions of sugars and fats without any reference to the time of day. To the right the coffee shop; to the left the burger bar; straight ahead the yob-symphony of the one-armed bandits and the sad CD choices of the miniature supermarket. David turned left. It seemed a long time since breakfast. Just today, he didn't care what he ate. It hardly seemed to matter, and the burger bar's sugary, vinegary, salt-imbued contraptions glowing in the illustrations above the servers looked like just the thing for a Sunday mid-morning comforting giga-snack.

He paid for a burger, a paper hod of chips, a catastrophic pail of vivid liquid, and sat down. Inside the box, the burger and bun had a sat-on appearance as ever, a flat grey tongue in the middle, far in appearance from the plump pillow in the photograph. He didn't care: he ate it, feeling eyes on him. 'Someone's hungry,' a Birmingham voice from the next table announced. He went on, hardly breathing between a mouthful of bun, a fistful of chips, a huge swill of fizz; he could feel in his mouth how disgusting it was, but could hardly stop filling it up; it was some lack in his mouth he was comforting by filling, and he went on, breathing heavily through his nose as he ate. He stared morosely, emptily, ahead of him, not engaging with a single gaze around him, feeling that he was making himself stupid as he stared and chomped and did not think, wanting to be ugly and gross and alone in the eyes of the world. Too soon, the burger was done, the last chips in his mouth; he felt that his mother would refuse to believe that he could make such a spectacle of himself over this gross, cheap, plebeian food at no later than eleven in the morning, and he got up, still chewing on the last of it, to buy another one.

If they had stared before, the other customers and, indeed, the servers now started to nudge each other as he came back with a new tray laden with another burger, chips and another huge fizzy drink. He didn't care. Only in retrospect did it seem to him that the first burger had been delicious; he only understood that by the quick excess of this second burger, the way it formed a resistant bolus as if of cotton wool, expanding in the throat and blocking it. He made a nauseous, laborious gulp – it stuck for a moment, and he felt it would never go down, wondering for a second whether it was possible to Heimlich yourself in extremity. His face was wet with sweat after the effort of eating, his fingers greased, and gritty with salt; he felt flushed, hot fluids pumping, banging, through his limbs and joints. He hated Mauro. He never wanted to see him again. How could he have descended so low as to give such a person – such a thief, such an indiscriminate whore, such a – such a Mauro – the impression he could have been his boyfriend? He pushed more dry, heavy, fat-soaked food into his grease-and-salt-edged mouth, and thought very little of Mauro, waiting outside in the car.

In time, it was finished. Not caring, he wiped his fingers on his cherry-red corduroys, and got up. There was a pain in his side; just a stitch. It was an old-fashioned word, but a correct one. A needle and thread had been through his side and pulled tight. He could feel his heart thundering with the sugars and fats and stodge limping their way complainingly down his oesophagus. If he went back to the car, he knew, Mauro would suggest that they took some of Sam's cocaine before they started again, and would probably finish it before they got back to London. David turned decisively towards the toilets.

There was nobody much about and the cubicles were the convenient sort without a gap below or above to discourage drug-taking and sexual congress. If I ever wanted to recommend to a traveller or tourist, David thought, the best place to shag, snort and shit in privacy, this would be top. It proved to have, too, a ridiculously convenient shelf above the cistern. David ran his finger along it, and it came up white; as he suspected, he was not the first person along this morning to have had the thought of a quick pick-me-up in the service-station toilet. Sam had been generous: there was a good half-gram in the little sachet. Enough for David; not enough to share. He poured out a fingernail's breadth; hesitated, then, thinking of Mauro and his greed, poured out almost as much again, and then a little more. He fastened the sachet, returning it to his wallet – it was surprising how quickly you could get through half a gram – and then with credit card and twenty-pound note fashioned the drug into a neat, arm-long line, and snorted it in two quick motions, left nostril, right nostril.

It was good stuff, and almost at once David felt the need to shit. He unbuckled his trousers and sat down, plunging down on the seat more suddenly than he expected. It was good stuff. His heart was banging around the well-padded cage of his torso, like a volley with a wet sponge. This was good stuff. And he felt strange, cold at the extremities, though his face and head were pouring with sweat. Not for the first time, he wondered whether he really enjoyed cocaine as a drug at all. He would have to have a nice long sit-down before he got back into the car. And, actually, he wasn't sure that he really did want a shit. If only he could have a shit, he would probably be perfectly all right. But it was good stuff, a fact that had sort of escaped him the night before. Mauro would kill, he thought, Mauro would kill to get his hands on a bit more of this coke.

34.

Mauro watched Mr Poppers go off towards the service station, stomping as he went. He would have something to eat, and his temper would improve. Anyone would see in a while that Mauro had done everything he was supposed to. The party with the Bears had been an unexpected extra, and what was David complaining about? He'd got fucked, too, hadn't he? Mauro watched him go into the building. It was a shame he hadn't left the keys so that he could put on Miss Platnum. He was stupid to think Mauro was going to steal the car; stupid, and insulting and rude, and not the sign of someone of education. But Mauro, who did not really care, rolled up his sweater into a wedge, placed it between his head and the window, and in a moment fell asleep.

When he looked again, twenty minutes had passed. Mr Poppers was calming himself down with food, Mauro expected. He yawned, a quick, feline motion, and shook himself, making a brisk, alert movement with all his limbs. He remembered that it was a record jackpot in the European lottery that weekend – it was 105 million – and for a few minutes, Mauro occupied himself thinking what he would spend it on. He would buy a villa on the Costa Smeralda; he would buy a jet-ski; he would have a palace in Rome; and a Ferrari, and a Rolls-Royce, and he would give his mother and father a hundred thousand euros each, and send Paolo Crichetti a thousand, too. He would have a blond German lover, who would always be twenty-four and exchanged for another on his twenty-fifth birthday, weeping. Oh, yes: Mauro would behave like a total bastard. There would be a huge red sofa curving round half a room, the one he had seen in a furniture shop in Milan once for twenty thousand euros; no, the room would be big enough for two, a double-height, double cube . . .

After a while, his invention ran out. 'And I would buy a Tintoretto,' he said to himself defeatedly. But he only knew the name and the three paintings they had had to study in school; he couldn't really think what one you could realistically buy would look like. Mr Poppers was making too much of a point now. Mauro took out his mobile phone, and called Christian, who was on answerphone, and then he realized that for probably the first time ever he was sober and awake after eight hours in bed on a Sunday morning. There was no point in calling anyone else. He fumbled in the glove compartment. There was a bottle of water, half evaporated and warm, which he drank, and a bag of gelatinous sweets, two-thirds finished. He took the sweets out, one by one, peeling them one from another, and sorted them out in order: the red, the green, the orange, the black, the yellow, the purple. Mr

Poppers hadn't liked the black ones, of which there were seven, and he'd liked the green ones and the red ones, of which there was only one each left. Mauro tried a black one; it seemed all right. He lined them up like the material of a stained-glass artist on the dashboard. He wished David had left the coke, at least. That would have been friendly.

Mauro looked on his mobile phone, and he'd been sitting there for three-quarters of an hour. That was too much. He was going to fetch Mr Poppers. Not much caring about the car, he got out and slammed the door without having the means to lock it. He went into the burger bar, the coffee shop, the amusement arcade, the shop. David was nowhere. For a moment he considered whether David might just have left him in some way, now on his way back to London, or wherever it was he lived. But that made no sense. He wasn't in the toilet, either, because the toilet was closed. A man in the service-station blue trousers and white shirt, with a serious-looking colleague, was telling customers that the toilet was unfortunately out of order, and being told off angrily. 'No, I'm sorry, but you could use the Ladies,' he was saying.

'What is it, then?' a man said.

'Someone's been taken seriously ill,' the man was saying.

'My friend came in, nearly an hour ago,' Mauro said. 'I can't see him anywhere.'

The two service-station staff exchanged a look. 'What does your friend look like?' one said.

Mauro described Mr Poppers as honestly as he could. 'He was wearing red trousers this morning,' he said.

'And his name is . . .?' the man said.

Mauro did not understand the man's pause, and they stood there contemplating the silence. 'Oh,' he said. 'He's called David. He's my friend.'

'David . . .' This time Mauro really did not understand the intonation, and the man had to say, 'I mean, David what? What is your friend's surname?

Mauro thought. It was a question he was sure he had once

295

known the answer to. But in practice the answer had never – hardly ever arisen. What should he say? He said in the end, 'I don't know. I just call him David.'

'OK,' the man said, and it was only then that Mauro saw that though both men were wearing dark blue trousers and a white shirt; one of them was, in fact, a policeman. How could he have failed to notice that immediately?

'I don't know his name,' Mauro said. 'He's my friend. I never knew his name. I don't think he ever said. I called him—'

'You don't know his name,' the policeman said.

'Where is he?' Mauro said.

'I think I'd like you to come with me.'

Mauro gave the door to the toilet a long, penetrating stare as if some solution to his situation, to his future and to his past might lie behind it; and at that exact moment a policewoman came out of the men's toilet. Mauro caught a glimpse inside; there was a huge, lumpish shape, lying without ceremony on the floor, a blanket over what must be a face and torso, but leaving the trouser legs uncovered in their vivid and surely unique scarlet. What had Mr Poppers – what had David— But in an instant, Mauro's thoughts went to the car keys in David's pockets, and the responsibility he was going to have to take, and also the £2,400, which no one knew about and no one would now care about, and how the fuck he was going to get himself home, and all that *che cazzo*, all that how-the-hell. Then the door swung shut again behind the policewoman, and Mauro, at the top of the stairs, went into the manager's office and started answering as best he could questions about next-of-kin. He had never heard the English expression before, and he filed it away for future use.

SECOND IMPROMPTU

TWO HUNDRED DAYS

He had his breakfast, then he washed up the dishes carefully, humming a tune as he went. It was a nice day outside. You could see three miles off, easy, from the ridge. The house was tucked away. From the lane that ran along the top of the ridge, all that presented itself was a heavy thatch, in need of redoing; its surface was mossy and green, and small animals, he knew, were living in it. The house sat like a mushroom in the earth. Few people passed along the lane. It led to nowhere very much and never had. The road in and out of Hartswell, with its one pub and its bleak central square, ran on the other side of the village. There was almost no reason for anyone to come up here. He heard a strange step on the lane outside perhaps twice a week, no more than that. After the sun set, the outside was enveloped in a thick dark. When there was no moon or stars, your eyes might have been bandaged in wool.

The house was old. Nobody knew how old. He had always lived here, and his father before him. He had kept the house in good condition, mending and repainting and replastering when it was needed. Five years ago he had had a grant from the council to replace the old iron-framed windows with good, solid, double-glazed windows in white uPVC. Nothing but the old black range was needed now to keep the house warm, what with the uPVC windows and the insulating thatch. And in any case he was used to cold. The kitchen floor was heavy stone flags; they were worn and rounded with all the people who had gone over them, his father and his grandfather, and beyond that, too, he was bound. He had never married, of course.

Probably it had once been three cottages, until the families had intermarried and interbred and knocked holes in walls, and in this haphazard way, the three tiny houses had become two, and then one. The doors were of peculiar size and shape, positioned in unexpected places. Perhaps the families had had to guess where the house bore itself up, and where there was just a wall, holding nothing up. Even to him, who had lived his whole life here, it was difficult to understand how the rooms fitted together. There were spaces between rooms, and a room upstairs, which, entered in an indirect way, and without a proper window, could only be used as a boxroom, giving all the adjoining rooms awkward and inexplicable shapes. There were inferrable spaces and shapes in this house that you would puzzle over.

He went into the kitchen and listened. There was no sound. He did not expect one. The stone flags were heavy and thick. He lowered himself to the cold floor, and now pressed the side of his head to the ground, like an Indian listening for far-off horses. Through the stone came a dampened mewing, impossible to inter-pret or understand, and when he stood up again, the noise retreated to an imagined reverberation, like a ringing in the ears. Perhaps nothing at all.

The day before, he had gone to the supermarket in Bideford where no one knew him or would remark on what he was buying. He had bought some fresh fruit – grapes, tangerines, fruit for little fingers – and some cheese, bread, ham and pickles. In time, he would find out what she liked to eat. Standing in the kitchen, he made a sandwich, then put the unused food back in the fridge. He took out a raspberry Petit Filou, a sort of yoghurt, but smaller, and placed it next to the sandwich, the tangerine and a glass of water barely clouded with orange squash. Hot food would be better; he would get some soup next time – it came in cartons, these days, rather than tins.

It took a certain knack to raise the flagstone – it took a knack to identify the one that could be raised at all. He took an iron bar from its place on the wall and, with a quick levering action, raised the flagstone. The noise from the cellar clarified itself into a girl's wordless voice for a second, then stopped, all at once. He had turned the light off the night before, to let her get some sleep; now he knelt and, feeling under the rim of the concealed cellar trapdoor, he switched it on again. He stood up, fetched the tray with the food on it, and walked down the stone steps nobody knew about. He made love to the little girl. Then he came up again without the tray, shut the trapdoor behind him and went to work. It was eight o'clock on a Thursday morning.

The next day was Friday. It was raining densely when he got up. The tor was hidden from view in the clouds; there was a steady spatter of water on the surface of the lane and a drumming effect from the thatch above. He took a bath, the boiler juddering as it often did in wet weather for some reason, and thought about the tasks for the day. They revolved around twelve horses, and the soft faces of Molly and Sugar came up before him, as if they were approaching him across Mrs F's upper field. 'Little devil,' he said out loud, remembering the antics of the week before, the horse twisting and biting, but remembering it with fondness. He had allowed the bathwater to go cold, and he quickly rinsed his head with the shower attachment. 'That's better,' he said, towelling himself. 'Nice and clean.' He had not taken a bath since Tuesday, believing a flannel wash twice daily and a bath twice weekly would do him now as it had done him since he was a boy. When he was dry, he put on a clean shirt and a weekend pair of trousers. 'Going to see my darling,' he said to himself. Then he went downstairs and raised the flagstone. He went down into the cellar and made love to the little girl. Then he came up, made a sandwich for her, and took it down again with some fruit and a raspberry Petit Filou. He went to work. It was eight o'clock on a Friday morning.

The next day was Saturday. The weather had cleared up a little – my, he'd got muddy yesterday. The clouds scudded like yachts across the blue, far up over the moor, running like wild things through the sky. He watched them from his bedroom window.

He could have watched them all day. He dressed. From the laundry basket, he picked out the brown corduroys and the shirt he had worn yesterday, a yellow, brown and green checked shirt, a proper country shirt, he would have said. He had put them in the laundry basket when he went to bed. Some men, living on their own, turned into slobs, dropping their clothes anywhere, not doing the washing-up from one week's end to the next. Not him. He didn't want anyone to think he couldn't cope now his mum had died. And no one did think that. No one had even suggested coming in to do for him, and he could even cook, after a fashion. He took the dirty laundry downstairs, some pants and socks as well as a couple of other shirts. He would do another load later, and then the laundry basket would be empty. He put the laundry in the washing-machine, a new one, an energy-saving one, which took all day to wash your clothes. The old one, his mum had had it for thirty years, only took an hour and a half. He put powder in the drawer, turned the knob to D, and the water started to gush and hiss within. He could hardly ever resist the temptation of opening the little drawer at this point, to see the jets of water washing the soap powder down into the drum. That ringing sound in the ears started again. It was her, under the flagstones, responding to the first noises of the washing-machine. It was true she would not have heard it before. This was his first laundry in a week. He fetched the iron bar from its customary place. He raised the stone flagstone. Today, the noise carried on, clarifying and hurting his ears. He went down into the cellar and he made love to the little girl. Then he came up, prepared food for her for the day, and took it down again, a sandwich, a bunch of grapes for little fingers, a raspberry Petit Filou. She seemed to like them. He might try one himself. Then he came up and closed the stone trapdoor and went to work. 'No rest for the wicked,' he said to himself, as he always did on his working Saturdays. It was nine o'clock on a Saturday morning.

The next day was Sunday. He did not work on a Sunday. He had managed to get to the supermarket late yesterday. It had been

busy, and they had had no tangerines left. They had had mandarins, but he'd never liked mandarins, neither he nor his mum. 'I
don't know why,' he remembered her saying, 'I just don't like
the taste they've got.' He had got some plums instead. He had
remembered to get some soup, and also some ready meals, which
would only take putting in the oven. The soup she could drink
from a mug. The ready meals she would have to eat with her
fingers when it had cooled down a bit. She couldn't have a knife
or a fork. But all the same, she would like that, the little girl. He
would save that for the evening, no, for Sunday lunch. For a
moment he envisaged him and the little girl sitting on either side
of the kitchen table, a big roasted goose between them; she would
be in a clean white frock, her hair in plaits, a real old-fashioned
little girl, she'd be, and clapping her hands with pleasure at the
food and at being with him. She'd look pretty like that. But then
he remembered that she'd got no clothes, apart from the three
tracksuits he'd bought for her in the big Asda in Exeter last week,
guessing her size and getting it mostly right. One top was white
with a sparkly pierrot on it, one pink with a fairy on the front,
one green with a design of rainbows. The trousers were in
matching colours, white, pink, green. It was the pink one she was
wearing now, that she had been wearing for a week. He went
down into the cellar and made love to the little girl. Then he came
up and made her a bacon sandwich, which was what he ate on
Sunday mornings, too. There was no work to go to once he'd
closed the cellar door. So he sat and watched the television all
day long. He watched *The Andrew Marr Show*, and *Something
for the Weekend*, and two episodes of *Friends*, and the *EastEnders*
omnibus, and *Columbo*, and a film called *Shoot-out at Medicine
Bend*. Towards the evening it began to rain again.

The next day was Monday. He got up and went down into the
cellar and made love to the little girl. 'Going courting,' he said
to himself, as he descended the cellar steps. Then he went to work.
It was eight o'clock when he left. He wondered what they would
say.

The next day was Tuesday, and before he had a bath or anything he went straight down to the cellar, switching the light on and walking down with a heavy tread. She was sitting on the edge of her bed. He had made it nice for her down here, with a duvet and pillowcase, and, because it could be cold in the cellar, an electric bar-heater fixed to the wall, which she could turn on if she wanted to. There was even a toilet and a washbasin. He'd put them in himself. She was just watching him come downstairs, staring at him. He didn't know what the expression on her face meant. 'I hate you,' she said. 'I'm sorry,' he said. 'I hate you more than anyone I've ever known,' she said. 'Where's my mom?' 'Your mum,' he said – he hated it when she asked for her mom; he hated the word, the foul American noise it made in her mouth. 'Forget about that. You've got to learn, you can't do that again. It can't be like that again.' She gazed at him dully. He made a gesture at his face where a long double scratch ran from edge of eye to corner of mouth. He'd had to tell Mrs F and the others a story about catching himself on some barbed wire. He didn't know if they'd believed him. 'If you do that again,' he said, 'things will get bad for you. Do you understand?' She looked at him with the dumb look that you had sometimes from a dog that had hidden something, eaten something, been in a fight. 'Do you understand? You've got to understand.' Finally, she nodded. He was glad of it. He didn't want to make things worse for her. He didn't want to have to come down into the cellar with a big knife in his hand, he didn't want it to come to that. But then he went upstairs without making love to the little girl, because she didn't deserve it, and he went to work without giving her something to eat, because she didn't deserve that either. It was eight o'clock on a Tuesday morning.

On Wednesday morning, he woke up thinking it was Tuesday. He couldn't understand why he thought that so strongly. Then he realized that it was because he could smell himself. He had not had a bath on Tuesday. He didn't know why. It was not like him to forget to have a bath on his Tuesday, on his Friday. He had always had his bath then, on those two days. He got up and had his bath. She had been quite grateful last night, and quiet, when he'd come in finally with some hot food. He hadn't stayed long. This morning he was in a forgiving mood. It was a beautiful sunny day. You could see the larks over the moor, rising and plummeting, their singing descending from high in the sky as they rode the thermal currents. He ran the bath, and even put some of that bubble bath in it, his mum's really, a giant bottle she'd never used up and he hardly ever used, but still it sat there. He wanted to make himself nice for the little girl. When he had dried himself and dressed, he made a proper breakfast on a tray, with the cereal he'd bought at the Sainsbury's in Bideford. He'd have put top-of-the-milk on it, but milk came in cartons, these days. It didn't have top-of-the-milk like he'd had as a special treat as a boy, saved for him by his mum. And he made some toast and spread some butter and pink strawberry jam on it, so she wouldn't have to be troubled with a knife or anything, and even poured a paper cup of orange juice from the fridge. It was his way of saying sorry, to ask her nicely to be nice to him. Then he went down into the cellar and made love to the little girl. He came up with the empty tray, closed the cellar door and went to work. It was eight o'clock on a Wednesday morning.

'If you promise not to run away, or try to hurt me,' he said, the next morning, to her, 'if you promise that, you can come upstairs and I'll let you have a bath. Would you like that? But you've got to promise first. You've got to or I won't let you.'

'I don't care,' the little girl said. It was a Thursday morning. 'I don't care whether I have a bath or not. Where's my mom. She's going to kill you. I mean, she's really going to kill you, with a knife. She will. You don't know my mom.'

'Wouldn't you like to have a bath?' he said. 'I don't care,' she said. 'I don't want a bath in your bath.' He could be angry now. She needed a bath. He thought that she could wash properly down here in the handbasin with a flannel and soap. But still she was dirty. He had made things nice for her; there was even a

305

square of carpet down here, nice and warm under her bare feet, the old carpet from the spare bedroom with a pattern of flowers on it, before his mum had redone the spare room, thinking she might start a bed-and-breakfast. 'Fine,' he said. Then he made love to the little girl. He went upstairs and made her a sandwich – an angry sandwich, not caring that the cheese was cut thick and carelessly, not even bothering to butter both pieces of bread, and just a dollop of pickle and a glass of water. He balanced a raspberry Petit Filou on the plate by the sandwich. He'd tried one. He hadn't liked it. It tasted of chalk. He took it down to her. Then he went to work. It was eight o'clock on a Thursday morning.

The next day it was a Friday morning. Everything was out of kilter and because he had had a bath later in the week than normal, he didn't feel he wanted one now. The wind was up and howling through the trees, pouring off the moor like a river of air. With decision he threw on an old jumper and a pair of trousers. He went into the bathroom and began to run a bath. Barefoot, he went downstairs. He switched on the radio. Terry Wogan was chuntering about his imaginary friends, and he turned it up, almost as high as it would go. He went to the kitchen's front windows and drew the neat yellow curtains across. He drew up the stone trapdoor; the smell he had noticed yesterday was still stronger today. He went down and, without saying anything, picked up the little girl, his arms round her waist, lifting her. She screamed and kicked as best she could, behind her, but he was used to the kicking of animals and walked her up the stairs, his legs planted broadly apart. She was twisting her head, trying to bite him, anywhere she could reach, but he had a hold for that, and she could not reach anything. Her screaming, the violent juddering of the old boiler upstairs, Terry Wogan going on about his listeners and their pets and their gardening gloves: it all made an unfamiliar noise in the little house. But no one was near, no one could hear. 'Fuck you! Fuck you!' the girl was screaming, and it shocked him, as it shocked him the first time she had said this. He took her upstairs, where she had never been, and into the bathroom. The bath was full enough and, with a struggle, he removed her tracksuit top, her tracksuit bottoms. She wore no underwear: that would be too much. There was more screaming, more struggling, another attempt to bite and kick, but he got her into the water. It never got too hot, the water out of the old boiler, and he scrubbed her and pummelled her with the soap, washing her hair as best he could with the soap, her twisting and head-butting and wriggling as she went. The showerhead sprayed everywhere as she punched and pushed and bit. It was like washing a beast terrified of water, terrified in its nature. But finally it was done and, without speaking, he dropped a sage-green bath sheet over her, rubbing and drying and constraining her all at the same time. You needed three hands for this job. She seemed to subside, all at once, to let him continue with the drying. He paused; let his guard drop; a mistake. She came at him, and something glinted in her hand; she had somehow grabbed a pair of nail scissors. But he caught her fist, and with pressure he made her drop it. She gave a cry of pain. 'That was stupid,' he said. He carried her downstairs, wrapped in the sage-green bath sheet, writhing and howling, and down again into the cellar. There he made love to the little girl. After leaving her a sandwich and a piece of fruit, he went to work. It was eight o'clock on a Friday morning.

The next day it was Saturday morning. He felt defeated, dutiful, obligated at the thought of the little girl down there like an unre-turned library book. He had a bath himself: he thought he might change the days of his twice-weekly bath. Then he went down to the cellar. 'Why are you doing this?' the little girl said, calling out as soon as he opened up the trapdoor. 'Where's Marcus? Marcus wouldn't let you do this. I want to see Marcus. You know Marcus. He's Ruth's brother. I want my mom.' He had an answer to this, but not today. There was no work for him to do today. It was not his turn to work. He made love to the little girl, then made her some food to eat. He sat down and he watched the television, turning it up when the noise like a ringing in the ears made itself felt. He watched *Saturday Kitchen* and *The Crocodile Hunter Diaries* and two episodes of *Friends* and a film called *Fools Rush In*.

The next day it was Sunday. He went down to the cellar straight away and made love to the little girl. Then, instead of going upstairs without saying anything, he stood up and said, 'Marcus isn't coming for you. Marcus sold you to me. I knew Marcus for ten years. He sent me photographs and I sent him photographs and we sometimes met to talk. Not often. And I bought you from Marcus. Marcus gave you to me for a thousand pounds. I gave him the thousand pounds, and afterwards I took it back again. But Marcus isn't going to come for you. And your mum's in prison. Do you know why your mum's in prison? Because she tried to pretend that you'd been stolen away by the fairies when really you were just with Marcus. And your mum knew that. She'd arranged it all with Marcus, hadn't she? But your mum, she didn't know Marcus as well as she thought she did. That was really stupid of your mum. Really stupid. So she deserves it, being in prison. And it's your fault, too. Because you could have said something, or just walked out and found a policeman. But you can't now. Do you want to know what's happened to Marcus?' She was crying now, and shaking her head. She didn't want to know. He went upstairs and made her a sandwich. He wanted to go to work, but it was a Sunday morning.

He went out in the car, which was his mum's old car, a red Fiesta, and he drove around for three hours. After some time, his car found itself on a main road; then on a smaller road; then a smaller still. The road to either side was dense with green moss in dark and light colours, like soft cushions, like a growing mess of colour. You wanted no flowers when you looked at such warm wet moss. It was so good, all the greens of the moss in the woods. The road came to a halt with parking for just three or four cars, an ash gate to the moor at its northern boundary. He got out and went through the gate, closing it carefully behind him. There was nobody else about. He saw the name of the place: Scorhill. He knew it. He wondered where he had heard the name before. The moor here was close-cropped grass, trimmed by sheep, by the rabbits whose black shit like clotted marbles was everywhere, by the three beefy ponies on the other side of a stone wall, one rubbing its arse on a bleak and bony tree. At school, boys had said that here, just beyond the wall, was a place where magical mushrooms grew, without his knowing exactly what magical mushrooms actually were or what they did. The hill was there to be climbed, rising up as if into the sky, the saturated earth yielding new puddles under every step, pouring out water, and at some points he jumped from granite rock to granite rock, placed like stepping stones in the sweet and wet earth. Below the summit of the gentle slope, a torrent of gorse, florid with yellow. At it, he remembered why he knew the name of Scorhill; there was nothing below him but a great mass of moorland, dappled yellow and brown and green. Below that, there was nothing in the way of civilization to see; no house, no village, no manor, nothing but a plantation of trees and a rude bridge over a narrow stream. Around him the whole landscape spread. The horizon went all the way round, as if he were at the centre of a gigantic bowl. Why the horizon did not always do that, he had no idea. Above, in the sky, the larks sang and plummeted and leapt into the blue air with its stacked flight of clouds, and other birds – who knew what? The druids had come here. Below him, at the centre of this mass of nature and unplanned perfection, a circle of stones stood or lay, the grass between the stones trimmed and neat as a bowling green. It had been here for ever; the old druids, the old folk, they had known what they were about when they said, 'Here . . .' It captured the horizons, the sunrise and the sunset, the smell and the light of this place in its twenty-foot circle. He had been here before. He was glad to have seen it again. It was really a beautiful day.

BOOK THREE
NOTHING TO FEAR

Die Andern lachten
Und gingen vorbei.
Wir aber dachten
Wie schön es sei:
So still zu gehen
Durch's freie Land
Im Abendwehen
Und Hand in Hand.

John Henry Mackay

1.

At the first ting of the alarm clock, Hettie was upright in her bed like a meerkat, silencing it with a downward thrust. It was five in the morning. Outside, only the faintest trace of light, like a dim old film.

She was already dressed. She had gone to bed that way. All she had to do was to put on her shoes, which were neatly paired by the side of the bed. On the floor was a bag-for-life, and a round blue washing-up bowl she had removed from the kitchen just before going up to bed. From under the bed, Hettie took a bottle of white spirit, similarly stolen, from the cupboard-under-the-stairs. What was the dusty bottle meant for? She had no idea. She placed it neatly in the washing-up bowl. From the regular row of dolls, blank in the morning half-light, she took Child Pornography, the doll with the curliest hair, who played the role of the judge when the game needed it. Hettie was sorry, but she would say goodbye to her this morning. She was the perfect corpse for a Viking funeral. She, too, went into the washing-up bowl, and then a large box of kitchen matches.

Finally, from her bedside table, Hettie took her favourite possession ever, her hatpin. She would be sorry to say goodbye to that, sorrier than about Child Pornography. But she had bought it and carried it and placed it on her bedside table and taken it to school in her bag, all that for a whole year. Now she had Michael, and the hatpin had reached the end of its use. She put that, too, in the blue washing-up bowl. The objects were neatly lodged with each other. She placed it in the bag-for-life. All this

Hettie had done in the half-light of early morning. She had not wanted to wake her parents by putting her light on.

But as she was going down the stairs, she must have made a noise.

'What are you doing, Hettie?' her father's voice asked from their bedroom.

'Nothing,' Hettie said. Behind her father's sleep-vague question, there was the familiar and yet annoying noise of her mother's snoring. In-out, in-out, it went, like a punctured vacuum cleaner.

'Where are you going …?' her father said, in his horizontal voice, already drifting back to sleep, hardly needing an answer.

'Nowhere,' Hettie answered, carrying on down the stairs. She would have said 'bird-watching'; she had her excuse ready for her return, some time before breakfast. But now, as she headed out towards the Viking funeral that Child Pornography was about to be rewarded with, no answer was necessary. She had told her father *nowhere*, and walked out of the house with her bag-for-life and its tragic contents.

At this time on a Sunday morning, no one was up. Even the motorway bridge over the estuary was silent. A remote high song of a bird, a blackbird perhaps, that was all. The sky was thinning far away, like water dropped into ink. It was strange how at the other end of the day, as night was falling, it made you nervous to walk the streets. (That was why Hettie had bought the hatpin in the first place, because of all the rapists and paedophiles and abductors hanging about Hanmouth's streets.) At the other end of the day – i.e., like NOW – no one would be scared of anything, although there was probably only about the same amount of light in the sky. She walked briskly towards the quay, past the antiques shop and a dead, abandoned dark bus, waiting for a Sunday-morning driver to reclaim it for the first trip of the day. She went down Ferry Road, by the thicket-like boatyard with its thin legs in the air, not stopping to read the adverts for speedboats and tugboats in the blue-framed glass case. Soon she came to the stone jetty. On it were dozens of ducks, their heads under their wings, like mushrooms.

Miranda and Kenyon religiously bought a small yellow booklet from the newsagent, one every month, entitled *Tide Tables*. They probably felt they ought to know when the estuary was high and when low, if they lived by its banks. It lived on the hallway bookcase, replaced every month. Hettie thought she was the first member of the family ever to have picked it up and read it for a purpose. Within half an hour, she had worked out that the tide would be high at five thirty in the morning on this particular Sunday. She had waited weeks for a good time to roll round. Here it was, the perfect time for her undisturbed Viking funeral. The estuary was full. The jetty sat in the water like a tongue.

On the jetty, she unpacked the components, and placed them in a row. She squatted on her haunches. First, she folded the bag-for-life in four, fastening it with the hatpin. It went at the bottom of the washing-up bowl. Then Hettie opened the child-proof top of the white spirit. She had always been good at opening the child-proof tops of things. She had had the push-twist-click knack since she was little. Miranda was always saying to her, 'Child, come and open this child-proof bottle,' of aspirins, or Valium, or whatever it was. That was supposed to be funny.

Hettie poured the white spirit all over the woven jute bag until it was sopping and an inch of liquid was at the bottom of the bowl. She took the doll – 'Goodbye, Child Pornography,' she said, and thought of kissing her. 'You had a noble life—' She stopped, because the funeral oration came later. Child Pornography was good at sitting upright. That was why she played the judge. Now she went torso upright in the bowl, her legs stretched out, and Hettie decided to put her arms straight outwards, in supplication and despair.

She took the bowl down to the water's edge, disturbing the ducks as she went. The little mushrooms produced surprising sleepy heads and legs, walked, barking, a few paces, disturbing other mushrooms, settled again. She carried the bowl solemnly, the liquid slopping from side to side, soaking Child Pornography's

315

blue and white floral dress. She placed the bowl on the stones, half in the water, and had to go back to fetch the matches.

'Farewell, O child,' she said. 'Go in peace, and remember your great deeds as you go. Every one of them. Farewell, farewell.'

Then Hettie struck a match, and dropped it into the bowl. She had imagined a faint blue flicker like a Christmas pudding. But it went up with a satisfying *woof*. All around, a great eruption of quack and flight, as the waterbirds took to the air, ran flapping for their lives. Never had they been woken up like this, with the smell of plastic burning and feathers singeing. Hettie could see that it would have been more sensible to bring a stick to poke the burning bowl into the stream. But in a second the flames died down somewhat and, with a deft shove of the foot, the bowl went into the water, still burning. By the jetty, the water was still, and the funeral boat twirled in the flood ineffectually. 'Go on, you stupid thing,' Hettie said. Then some kind of current took it, and it began to move purposefully. Child Pornography's hair was beginning to catch. It burnt beautifully, and each strand was a little line of flame, hissing and winking up into the air, detaching and rising into the morning like a prayer. Her dress was ablaze; her face might be melting.

Into the middle of the estuary stream the Viking boat went, its cargo of flames and the stoic forward doll in its middle. It was working well, this floating blaze in the dim dawn light. Hettie, as she had planned, began to sing what she could remember of Siegfried's funeral march. 'Bash-bash! Baa – bash-bash! BAA – bash-bash – baa – bash! Da-daa – dit daa – didi DAA –' she sang, running breathlessly back to the road. She had planned a funerary oration, but now she could see that running alongside the water-borne pyre would be more fun. It floated, the flames shooting high, the doll sitting impassively, all the way down Ferry Road, across the quay and, Hettie running alongside, to the beginning of the Strand. Its smoke was high and black and evil. Hettie had hoped that it would carry on, down the estuary and out to sea. But just there, the blaze seemed to be too much for it. The floating bowl suddenly collapsed into the water, drunkenly pitching the now black-faced and bald Child Pornography into the flood. The heat must have burnt through the bottom of the washing-up bowl.

'Child,' Hettie declaimed, standing in the herbaceous bed of the garden opposite number seventeen, the naked Lovells'. 'Child, your life was brave, and your end was noble. We give you a hero's end, as a hero merits. You passed judgment on many, and now you go to meet your judgment.' Hettie wondered whether she could, after all, wade out and rescue the sacrificed hatpin when the tide was low. She dismissed the thought as not very dignified. 'Farewell! We mourn for you, and for that man who died –' she couldn't remember that man's name – 'and for the general, and for that girl who died a death of heroes! Farewell! Farewell!' Out in the stream, an object, twisted, blackened, melted, turned in the flood. It seemed to be caught on something. Hettie looked at her watch. It was six, and the sun was rising. From beginning to end of her Viking funeral, not one person had witnessed any part of it. They had slept through the whole thing.

2.

The four rooms at the corners of the university building were much fought over. They were the largest, and they had a double aspect. Some of the occupants managed to introduce a sofa and a coffee-table into their offices as marks of their superiority. The rooms to the front of the building looked out over the university's immaculate gardens, acres of woodland, miniature lakes with mock-Renaissance sculptures spouting water, and glossy ericaceous shrubbery, just now coming into pink, purple and white flowers. The gardens were looking their best. They had become significantly sprucer in the last couple of years, and prospective parents often commented on their groomed beauty with approval. The appointment of twelve more gardeners with funds made available after the closing down of the chemistry department had had its desired effect. From the window of the head of the English department's office, on the left-hand side and on the second floor of the building, the head of department looked at the university's gardens. He found it restful; a change from budgets and research grants and learning outcomes; a change from books and literature, things that over the years he had come to detest; a change from Miranda Kenyon.

Miranda Kenyon was sitting on the head of department's sofa. He had asked her to come and see him on a matter of some delicacy, and she was currently reading the matter of some delicacy. There was no doubt in the head of department's mind that she was a difficult colleague, a problem colleague, whose demeanour could never have been described as collegiate. She was older than he was, but there was no reason for her to refer to him as 'Benjamin', 'Benjie', 'Darling little Benny', or, he had been told, 'Cliff'. It was true that, as other people had remarked, his appeal was boyish – the word had recurred in verbal testimonies to his charm, as he himself thought of it. There was no reason for her to have remarked, however, in a faculty meeting in front of twenty colleagues that she would be obliged if he would leave off laughing reflexively after every sentence, as it seemed to be threatening to bring on her migraine. He regarded that as actively hostile. In any case, he prided himself on chairing professional meetings with good humour and some warmth. To talk of migraines being brought on by his good humour and warmth – that was definitely hostile. He looked at Miranda, sitting reading a letter, slightly flushed with the effort of climbing the stairs, smiling somewhat, with frank dislike.

'Miranda,' he said.

'Yes, Benjamin,' she said, looking up with affected pleasure and surprise. She might have been a researcher, dutifully hard at work, accepting with delight the diversion offered by a chance acquaintance.

'I'll let you finish,' he said.

318

'It's true that I haven't quite finished reading,' she said, and returned her attention to the sheet of paper. He could have sworn that she had finished reading; that now she was just gazing at the sheet of paper, waiting until she could declare herself finished. To keep him waiting.

'And now I have finished reading,' she said, taking off her glasses, looking with kindly warmth towards Ben – what a fuss this young man seemed to be making, her expression said. 'I can entirely see why you thought you would like to speak to me, Benjamin.'

'Well, I think I should ask you whether you recognize Mr and Mrs Warren's account of your letter to them, I suppose,' Ben said. 'Did you write a letter like that?'

'Like . . .' Miranda looked again at the letter, putting her glasses back on. 'Oh dear. I think I may well have done. But should we take this from the very start, Benjamin?'

'Perhaps we should,' Ben said, defeated.

'I was told that Sophie Warren's poor attendance at my seminars and very poor work were due to some family problems. She told me this herself. I pressed her, and she told me that her parents were undergoing some serious marital problems, and that this was affecting her work. I was naturally very concerned.'

'Naturally. So you wrote her parents a letter.'

'As you see, I wrote a letter to her parents.'

'And they have written back – well, you can see what they have written back. They wrote to me, as you see, not to you.'

'Yes, I can't understand that. I really can't tell you why they should do that. It seems almost rude.'

'They say that they don't know why you think they were divorcing. They're very happy, they love their daughter, they can't see what it has to do with, blah, blah. They seem pretty angry, in fact. Ha, ha, ha, ha, ha.'

'Well, I can understand that. I would be awfully angry if my daughter went round claiming that we were divorcing when there was no truth in it. I'd be furious with her.'

319

'No,' Ben said. 'They're angry with us.' Ben laughed lightly again; then he remembered what Miranda had said about finishing statements with laughter, and stopped short.

'I see,' Miranda said, and smiled like a pupil taking a lesson.

'I can't help feeling,' Ben said, 'I can't help feeling that your behaviour may be construed as somewhat disingenuous.'

'Well, you are entirely entitled to your own feelings,' Miranda said. 'You must own your feelings. I would never seek to deny anyone a right to hold and express their feelings.'

'Miranda,' Ben said. He took a deep breath. He looked at the horticulture. Three lacrosse players were helping a fourth, his arm evidently broken, up the hill; they looked like the helpless seasons in Poussin's *Dance to the Music of Time*. 'Miranda. When a student with poor attendance claims that a grandmother has died, or that they have had glandular fever, or that, or that their parents are undergoing a traumatic divorce – do you generally believe them?'

'Ben,' Miranda said. 'Are you saying that we ought to call our students liars when they tell us these things? I don't think I can quite square that with my conscience.'

'No,' Ben said. 'I'm not saying that. But I wonder whether it was quite necessary to write a detailed letter of condolence, on behalf of the faculty, to the parents of a delinquent student, saying how sorry we are that they are getting divorced.'

'And that we urge them not to let their family difficulties affect their daughter's work. That's where we start to get concerned, surely. Isn't that rather a worry? Benjamin?'

'Ben,' Ben said.

'I'm sorry, Benjamin?'

'I prefer to be called Ben,' Ben said. He had been trying, and failing, to think of an unwelcome abbreviation of Miranda's name. Randy? Anda? Mira? She wouldn't even have recognized that he was addressing her.

'In any case,' Miranda said, 'the students are always saying that they want more contact hours, more supervision, more interest in all of their affairs. I thought I would be helpful and aid Miss

320

Warren with some more direct contact. Isn't that what we are always being enjoined to undertake?'

'So you wrote this letter.'

'Not this letter,' Miranda said, handing back the letter to Ben. 'This letter seems to be from Miss Warren's father. I believe he still has the letter I sent. Benjamin.' She had read it, and now he read it again. They seemed to have reached a complete impasse.

Ten minutes later Sukie, standing in front of the German department's noticeboard, examining a disconsolate claim that learning German could be fun, was startled by Miranda pushing open a pair of double doors and breaking into 'Dontcha Wish Your Girlfriend Was Hot Like Me'.

'You're in a good mood,' Sukie said.

'I've just had half an hour with poor little Benny,' Miranda said.

'Poor old Benny,' Sukie said.

'Oh, he just needs speaking to, now and again,' she said. 'He's perfectly harmless, really.'

3.

At the far end of Hanmouth, if you turned left at the far end of the Wolf Walk, you found yourself in a land of mud and water, of meadows and standing pools. Birds landed and settled here; migratory birds, wading birds, a small dull bird with a ringed collar that was never seen anywhere in Britain but here, in the Hanmouth estuary on the north coast of Devon. The ring-necked pipit was so choosy, it would not even cross the Bristol Channel and breed in Wales. For some reason, this ornithological star had been officially adopted as a symbol of the estuary, and a dreary Pipit Lines boat grunted up and down between Hanmouth and the sea, and the train that stopped at Hanmouth was officially called the Pipit Express as it chugged and hooted its slow way northwards, between road and water.

The bird came to the notice of the Royal Society for the Protection of Birds, who declared that not enough was being done on behalf of the ring-necked pipit. At the millennium, seven years before, a platform had been erected above the ring-necked pipits' breeding ground, the stretch of meadow, bush, water and mud where Hanmouth gave out. On the platform was a hide of plain, unstained pine with a letter-box slit running around at roughly eye level, where the birdwatchers of Hanmouth and around could gather and watch that unremarkable bird, the ring-necked pipit, without scaring it off. It had cost £150,000 of Lottery money matched by public funds, and had been opened in 2000 with pipit-terrifying pizzazz by the newsreader who spent his weekends here.

Hettie and Michael came here to be on their own. They had never been disturbed, never seen anyone else here, and they thought of it as their private place. When they came back, the cigarette stubs on the floor were the ones Michael had smoked the last time they had been here. Hettie didn't smoke: she thought it was disgusting, it smelt, but she didn't mind Michael doing it because it was Michael, and she liked it when she saw the cigarette butts lying on the floor, exactly as he had left them the time before. No one came here; no one cleared it up; and Hettie was glad of it. Today they had come separately; they sometimes ran down the Fore street together, went for a walk before they ended up here, but Hettie had phoned Michael yesterday, saying, 'I've got to see you. At the hide. Tomorrow after school. I'll see you there.'

In a corner of the hide, Michael squatted. It was not cold. On this September day, the summer was holding on with some determination. But he was pretending to be cold: the sleeves of his shirt had been drawn down to cover his hands, and the cigarette poked out from the wrist hole like a strange beast, fire-snouted, from its lair. Sometimes it was hot in the world and sometimes it was cold. That was an ordinary thought which anyone might have. But also you could say that when it was cold it was impossible to imagine what it was like when it was hot, and when it was hot you could never think it would ever again be cold. These thoughts had never occurred to Michael before he and his family had come to Britain. Britain was good for having the sorts of strange, interesting thoughts he now had all the time. He was putting his hands inside the sleeves of his shirt and then pretending he was cold and shivering – he shivered, he held his forearms to his chest, he gripped himself – as an experiment in whether you could make yourself remember what cold was like by doing all the gestures of a response to cold. He had found out that you could make yourself sleepy by opening your mouth wide until you yawned. It didn't seem as if you could stop yourself feeling hungry by making chomping noises – Michael was often hungry, his mother always commenting on how much he was eating directly out of the fridge. Now he was seeing if you could re-create the memory of cold by making yourself shiver. Sometimes Michael surprised himself with how totally mental his thoughts went. 'Totally mental,' he said in the empty hide, being as British as he knew how to be. Perhaps it was all over Europe that you could think in this interesting way. He clutched his forearms to his chest and, in the warm, dusty atmosphere, half lit from the slits in the upper half of the hide, a winter's day momentarily rose up, the dust on the floor becoming hoar frost. He blinked; the warm day was back; there was a racket and thunder as Hettie came tearing up the pine steps of the hide.

'I had to see you,' Hettie said, plumping herself down on the floor. She looked haggard, distraught, big-eyed. 'I had to see you, Michael. I don't know that there's anyone else who would understand. No one else knows what we did, that day, what happened. It was wrong, Michael, I'm not saying it was anything but wrong, I'm not saying it was right – that would be crazy, stupid, bonkers! I'm not saying that. But I never meant this to happen, I never did, I promise, I swear. You know I never meant this to happen.'

'Hey, Hettie,' Michael said. 'I know you're not a mean person. I don't know what you're talking about. What happened?'

'That's always the way,' Hettie said. 'You're thinking what you're thinking, all to yourself, and it goes round and round and round, whee, whee, whee, inside your head until you meet someone. Then, BANG, it comes out just as it is, how you've been thinking of it, and they don't know what you've been thinking, how can they, you're bonkers for thinking they know what you're thinking, they're off on a train of thought of their own. The Brigadier.'

'I know what you mean,' Michael said.

'The Brigadier!' Hettie said.

'The—'

'The Brigadier, that's what I'm talking about. You could have knocked me down with a feather when I heard. I came down to breakfast, and my mum was sitting there, looking very solemn, you know my mum Miranda, and she said she'd heard the night before but she hadn't told me. The Brigadier. Tinkle, tinkle, the phone went, when dear little Hettie was tucked up in bed and I was looking at things on YouTube so I only heard the phone ring downstairs. I didn't hear the conversation which Miranda, my mum you know, had with Kitty, that old woman. It came out of the blue, like a rumble of thunder, no one thought that would happen, he'll be seriously missed. The Brigadier.'

'I don't know who the Brigadier is,' Michael said.

'Oh,' Hettie said. Her eyes rolled about in their sockets; her hands fluttered about in search of something to do. Her fingertips found the raw pine board, tapped, one, two, three, four, five, six, seven, along it; then became a great pianist's hands, and she played a C major scale on the floorboard. When Hettie was in this trying-out state, everything about her agitated and experimental, Michael wondered if she were, in fact, seriously insane. 'Oh, but you do. You do, Michael. Do you remember once we were running down the Fore street and we ran into an old woman and she fell over, bang? That was the day I told you I loved you, remember?

324

I must have been out of my tree, I must! What was I thinking? But we knocked her over and we ran away and no one else ever found out who we were, the hooligans who had knocked dear old Billa over.'

'But who's the Brigadier?'

'I'm coming to that. Billa, she's married, she WAS married, to the Brigadier. We knocked her over and now her husband, he's dead, he's tragically dead, it's AWFUL.'

'That's awful,' Michael said. He got up and looked through the slits in the hide. The ring-necked pipit might be the bird flapping around in gangs of a dozen; or that could be some other bird entirely. It was an odd thing to be fascinated by, a particular bird. 'That's awful. But it's not anything to do with knocking her over – how can it be?'

'You don't understand,' Hettie said. 'He died because of us knocking her over. He was trying to do something in the house, I don't know what, he was trying to do something which, normally, it'd have been her job, it was woman's work. But she wasn't doing it, Billa wasn't doing it, because she couldn't, because we'd knocked her over, she was bruised from head to toe, a solid mass of bruises, Kitty said she was. The Brigadier couldn't do it, naturally he couldn't do it. He'd never had to do it. And he got in a tangle and a muddle, he was all wrangled up and he fell over and he got himself killed. That's the story. If WE hadn't knocked her over SHE would have been able to do it and HE wouldn't have tried to do it and been a big failure because HE didn't know how to do it and HE wouldn't have died. It's ALL OUR FAULT.'

Michael looked at the case from one end and from the other end. A small paw rose up, streaked with mud, and with its back stroked his cheek.

'I do love you, Michael,' the owner of the small paw said. 'I really do. I'd go all the way with you, Michael, I would, if you only asked me.'

Michael said nothing to this, not even what he had said before, which was that he wanted to be sure, and he thought it was

325

wrong to go all the way before you were married or possibly engaged to be married. He considered the case. It did seem to him that he and Hettie had done something that had led to the death of the Brigadier.

'What are you going to do?' he said.

'We can't put things right,' Hettie said. 'We can't pick her up off the pavement, we can't go back in time and remember to swerve round her, or not to run at all, walk, maybe, like good little boys and girls. Because if we'd done that, if we could go and do that, she would be alive today, I mean he would be alive today. I wish that with all my heart, Michael. I am profoundly moved and he will, I believe, be much missed, I think that with all my heart, Michael.'

'When you've done something wrong,' Michael said. 'You can apologize. You can go and explain.' Then he told her about his mother's twelve-step programme, and about the eleventh step, the apologizing to everyone. Hettie listened, her eyes tranquil, following only the movement of his lips, and nodding from time to time, and saying, 'I see,' now and then.

4.

After the Brigadier's death, Billa felt herself, in the eyes of the village, flitting between incompatible states. She never knew when she was going to be invisible, as widows and women over a certain age were said to be, and find herself standing by while a conversation of terrible intimacy unwound between strangers; and then, without any warning, she would have the sense that she was being pointed out, observed, described. It seemed to Billa that her place in the village had been altered at one stroke by the Brigadier's dying, and the style of his death. She had always felt a little anonymous, in the shadow of his local celebrity, and the invisibility, enhanced by widowhood, was only to be expected. The celebrity and notoriety, in which she knew some strangers must find a comic aspect, was quite new. The Brigadier's local fame now fell on her, and was compromised and magnified by the absurd and horrible story. She felt herself pointed out, discreetly, but also, by others, not seen at all.

Billa had said thank you effusively at first, when Kitty had come over with the first plastic-covered dish. After that, she had retreated to the Brigadier's study, upstairs, to sit in the Brigadier's red leather thinking chair. She left the kitchen door open, and now watched Kitty bustling backwards and forwards, carrying one plate after another, each glistening in the March sunlight with its transparent polythene sheathing. 'I don't want you to do a thing,' Kitty had said, and she wasn't going to. 'It's no trouble,' she had gone on, when the response she'd expected wasn't quite forthcoming. Even an old friend like Kitty had difficulty in not ending her sentences, these days, on an unfinished cadence, a sort of dash, —, hanging in the air. Like many people in Hanmouth, she seemed to think any comment, if voiced quizzically, might well call out Billa's innermost thoughts on the whole affair.

Billa's big square house, and Kitty's smaller L-shaped white cottage; were attached, and curved round a paved semi-courtyard lined with lobelia pots. The fourth, open, side gave onto the churchyard, where the salt-encrusted grass grew leaning in the direction of the wind off the estuary. Day-trippers, who had an extraordinary mania for reading the ancient tombstones, would sometimes walk quite confidently into their courtyard, even peer into Billa's or Kitty's kitchen windows as if they expected to see an aproned Mrs Tiggywinkle taking scones out of the oven. Billa's house proprietorially fronted onto the comfortably sinuous high street, with its navy-blue front door and brass knocker. Kitty's crowded cottage, unmistakably the house of a widow who had lived in a larger, more urban house, faced directly onto the estuary, overlooking the mudflats where the avocets picked and strode in their fastidious way. That side, thanks to the salt winds, had to be painted every two years at, Kitty said, appalling expense.

Kitty's opulent caravan of funeral dishes – the sum of her party dishes, acquired and tested over a lifetime of party-giving – was at last drying up, and she was trotting over now with what must be the last offerings. She had brought them through her green kitchen door and across the courtyard in eating order, the objects skewered on cocktail sticks first, the substantial cold ham and coronation chicken next, and finally a bowl of fruit, of cheese and, surprisingly, a cake. At the sight of the cake, Billa rose and went steadily downstairs, gripping the banister. She hadn't expected a cake, and wondered if it was quite the thing. She couldn't remember having seen, or been offered, one at a funeral ever before. With a nod to the parties of her childhood, she contemplated the funeral-goers accepting a slice, taking it home wrapped in black-edged paper napkins to eat later. For Kitty, who had won prizes at the Women's Institute, any occasion was a good excuse to make a cake. This time, it was a good dark sombre fruit cake, and she'd restrained herself enough, as Billa saw coming into the kitchen, by not indulging herself with icing. It stood there on the shelf of the Welsh dresser, monumental and sadly bulging with cherries, in austere solemnity. In any case, had she iced it, what could Kitty have found to pipe on the top?

'You shouldn't have gone to all this trouble,' Billa said.

'No trouble at all,' Kitty said, and then surprisingly added, 'I was awfully fond of the Brigadier – of Tom.'

'I hope it all gets eaten up,' Billa said. 'One never knows.'

'Well, if not, it won't go to waste,' Kitty said. 'Do you have any idea about the numbers?'

'I can't remember how many we wrote to,' Billa said.

'I think it was a hundred and eighty in the end.'

'I've certainly had a lot of letters back. And there were quite a lot from people we hadn't thought to write to, who had just read about it.'

'Yes, of course,' Kitty said. One of those hanging sentences, waiting for Billa, at the end of this long and difficult week, to come out at last with what she actually felt about the Brigadier dying in such a fashion. To most people, now, he'd become Tom; Billa thought still of him as 'the Brigadier', inexplicably a more intimate address. But her eyes dropped, the moment passed. 'You probably ought to start thinking about changing,' Kitty went on practically. 'They'll be here in, what, three-quarters of an hour?'

Kitty was already in her funeral garb, or what passed for such: it was black, certainly, but the bodice was gleaming with jet. It looked like a frock for an outing, like the matinée garments of the aunts who, years ago, would take the young Billa to the theatre. Of course, people didn't have devoted funeral outfits, these days.

'I know,' Billa said. 'It just seemed awfully sad to get up and put on one's black straight away, eat one's breakfast alone in it.'

'I quite see.'

'Of course,' Billa said, 'I dare say in another week or two I'll be shamelessly eating my breakfast in my dressing-gown. But not quite yet.'

She said this because she knew quite well that Kitty did that exact thing, had often seen her watering the plants, or opening the kitchen door to the postman quite late in the morning in a purple quilted dressing-gown. She wasn't quite convinced, either, that it was a habit Kitty had fallen into since her widowhood; from what she had heard of Dennis, it might always have been her way. The Brigadier had often commented on it; daily, it might have been. But now Kitty gave an enigmatic chuckle, and reversed out of the kitchen. She paused at the door.

'It just seems . . .' she said.

Billa raised her eyes. 'Ironic?' she said, at last supplying the word for the whole situation, which not just Kitty but most of the village had evidently been waiting for.

'Not that, exactly,' Kitty said gratefully. 'But terribly sad. I'll be back in half an hour, walk over with you.'

'Thank you,' Billa said. 'Thank you so much.'

Kitty looked at her with curiosity; and perhaps she had struck the wrong tone with so old a friend and neighbour.

5.

'Ironic' was the word that the village, the county, the newspapers and even the television had used about the Brigadier's death. But in fact the word they wanted to use was 'funny'. If she had ever thought about the matter while the Brigadier was alive, she would have realized that his eventual death would have had its public aspect. But she had always presumed that the reason for that would have been his public career. He had been a brave man, and for forty years, uncomplaining, the pair of them had gone all over the world, to some terrifying places. He had stood upright as flags were hauled down in half a dozen colonies, or once – it was a favourite story of his – running for his life for the gunboat in Aden as the marauding tribes closed in on them, about to turn and plunge the country into a hell, not a very upright one, of impenetrable internecine slaughter. He had done his very best in Northern Ireland and, with Billa at home in Hanmouth watching and reading every scrap of information she could gather, had led his men into the Falklands and out again with the minimum of fuss and bother. He'd been rewarded for that in a more than routine way: the medals were in the small mahogany chest upstairs, lying on top of his dress uniform. She was proud of him – indeed, the village was proud of him, near-strangers always calling out, 'Good morning, Brigadier,' across the street as he set off on his constitutional – and had taken it for granted that, at the end, the pride would be expressed in newsprint. No scandal or impropriety had ever touched his conduct; the army esteemed him, his men always loved him, and he volubly hated any sense of the army's disgrace. He had taken, in his last days, to turning off the television news when the subject of Iraq had come up; the self-serving decisions of politicians, the incomprehensible and wilful conduct of individual soldiers towards their prisoners, all that was hateful to him. She could not imagine a more upright man; never could.

She had left him alone for a morning while she went into

Barnstaple for some shopping – the village was quite all right for the day-to-day things, but there were some things, like the Little Scarlet jam they had both always liked at breakfast, you had to go into Barnstaple for. She never minded. She had called a cheerful 'I'm back,' on opening the door, but there had been no response and, in the hallway at the foot of the stairs, the sprawled, ugly scene she would never be able to get out of her mind. She called an ambulance, though he was obviously dead, and, absurdly, she felt guilty at using the emergency services when there was no emergency any more. Who else were you supposed to call? She put the telephone down. Immediately, there was a knocking at the front door; it was an ambulance crew. They hadn't found it funny, or even ironic: they'd been concerned, swift, practical and serious. She didn't question the immediacy of their arrival at the time. It seemed only an aspect of their gravity. It was only much later that she realized, with a flush of ugly shame, that the Brigadier had somehow managed to telephone as he lay, that he hadn't, in fact, died in a moment. She hadn't attached any significance to the telephone lying in a tangle on the floor with everything else. She had, it turned out, just missed him.

Kitty was very good, when they'd returned from the hospital, even holding her hand in the taxi, and not expecting her to say anything at all. But what had been most helpful was what always had been helpful, Billa's opportunity, once alone, to sit herself down and give herself a good talking-to. She'd always excelled at that, whether it was the night before her wedding when, incredible as it now seemed, she'd almost decided that she was making a ghastly mistake in marrying the Brigadier as he then wasn't, or returning from the clinic five years later when the doctor had had to tell them that they would never be able to have children. (So, her wrongness before her wedding had been so quickly revealed that five years later it was a matter of 'them' in so personal an issue.) She'd given herself a good talking-to on their first night in their Ugandan quarters, with mould halfway up the walls and stinking like a wardrobe in which an animal had died, no food

331

in the house, no servants in sight, and the single thing that might have made her burst into tears, a long-unflushed lavatory. And she gave herself a good talking-to now.

The public aspect of the Brigadier's death simply hadn't occurred to her, though perhaps she might have seen something of it in the quivering, bright-eyed way so many of the village people had conveyed their regrets, as if they were trembling on the verge of quite a different sentiment altogether. It was only when the hateful obituary in the *Daily Telegraph* came out, only five days ago, which actually mentioned the circumstances of the Brigadier's death in its first sentence before going on, true, to his military record, that any such possibility had occurred to her. And then it only seemed to her like a single blunder in taste and tact, like a snorting-out of soup at the dinner table, which nobody, naturally, would ever mention again. But late the next day, the local television news had got hold of it, and they did not mention the Brigadier's life at all, but only the way, which was horrible enough, he had died, and treated it with vast levity. She had not been able to stop watching, once she had seen the outside of their house on the screen, until the report had finished and the man on the sofa had turned lightly to the woman on the sofa and said, with open amusement 'It's always the ironing-boards that get you in the end,' and the woman had actually laughed. Billa, now, wondered what sort of country she was living in.

The funeral, as she walked into the church in advance of her husband, like a wedding in reverse, Kitty at her side like an ageing bridesmaid, was as crowded as she could ever have wished. But it had arranged itself in a series of rings, the genuine mourners at the centre and becoming steadily more carnival-like the further out it spread until, at its furthest reaches with people who could never have known the Brigadier in life, it started to resemble the last stages of a rather ragged party. Irrelevantly, as she sat down in the front pew, she wondered where exactly she would draw the line in this, at what point she should stop inviting the attenders to come back to the house afterwards to eat Kitty's shrink-wrapped food. Certainly the inmost mourners – kind Miranda and Kenyon from the reading group with their little daughter, her face lowered, the neighbours, Billa's elderly cousin and, if he arrived, her brother they hadn't seen for three years, the Brigadier always rather objecting to his manner and his readiness to mount an argument from a standing start. Dear Sam and Harry had put on suits and white shirts and black ties; they had never been great pals of the Brigadier, who had had to be ticked off enough times for the way he referred to her cheese-flogging bum-bandit chums. They were here for her. There were plenty of people of that sort – not Sam's sort in the Brigadier's sense, just friends from the village, old comrades of the Brigadier's. She turned round and nodded with a subdued smile at General Franklin and his wife; it was very good of them to come all the way from Yorkshire. And, as well, there was what must be, in that very smartly turned-out young officer, a representative from the regiment. It was good of them, too.

But further away, there were people unlikely to have felt much personal grief for the Brigadier, such as the sluttish landlady of one of the worst pubs in Hanmouth, one they never went into. And next to her, in one of the back pews, a girl who lived in one of the houses at the far end of the high street, said in the greengrocer's to be an artist, along with much more about her history and goings-on with men. She was wrapped up in dark velvet scarves, blue and purple and swirling in patterns, like a Bashi-Bazouk, and although she wore a black dress, it was exactly the same dress she always wore, in a stretchy T-shirt material. The Brigadier hadn't known her, wouldn't have wanted to, and it was only by the purest chance that Billa had hung around in greengrocer's shops and heard her name: Sylvie. She was looking around her with frank interest, as if she were the sort of artist who might dash home to sketch the scene. But of course – the greengrocer's gossip had it – she wasn't at all that sort of artist, rather the sort that stapled a brick to a dead frog and called it art, as the Brigadier used to say. And beyond that circle, containing people like Sylvie – Billa was surprised that she actually knew her name – there were, outside the church, a couple of representatives of the media, one with a small television camera, with the name of an unfamiliar television channel on the side. There was nothing, surely, to be got out of the funeral for them. There, gawping on the pavement opposite the church, strangers not from the village, who had heard the story, and their children running up and down. It was exactly like the time, four or five months ago, when that girl had gone missing, believed kidnapped, and hundreds of rubberneckers had descended on Hanmouth. They might even be the same rubberneckers. The comparison seemed distasteful in the extreme to Billa. To them it seemed unlikely that anyone had actually died, that anyone could be conceivably mourning a death so very entertaining.

Well, that was to be expected, and Billa's irritation stopped, in practice, with people like the woman artist, who had forced her way into the church itself, never having known or spoken to the Brigadier in life. That was pushing impertinent curiosity to its limits. At the end of the service, making her way out of the church, Billa made a point of pausing by the woman's pew. She looked up, a little puzzled; she might not actually know who Billa was, and she hadn't even lived in Hanmouth that long. 'Thank you for coming,' Billa said, in a forced, kindly tone. 'I do hope you'll come back to the house afterwards. Since you made the effort to come and see Tom off.' Sylvie, if that was her name, had at least the decency to blush, taking the point. As if by inoculation, this comment ensured that none of the outer circle of rubberneckers pushed their intrusion any further. Those coming into the kitchen were exactly those she would have invited to a normal sort of party, plus the honourable addition of the young officer from the Brigadier's regiment.

'It was very good of you to come,' she said. 'I do hope it wasn't too tiresome a journey for you. My husband always thought of the army as one of the most important things in his life.'

'I'm proud to have been asked,' the young soldier said. 'It's important to keep a sense of continuity.'

That was so much a sentence from a memo, a much-Roneoed sheet of instructions for junior officers attending funerals, that she shouldn't have gone on. But she had always been a good hostess, and said, distractedly, 'I do hope you'll drop in again if you're ever in the area.' That was the wrong thing to say: this was just a uniform, paying the required homage to another uniform. The supplied mourner, like the regiment, felt nothing, and in a moment he excused himself and left. He had parked his car outside the house – a most unexpected little red Fiat – and she watched him, in his uniform, zap the door open, get in, and drive off in an embarrassed, stately way. She tried to remember times when the Brigadier had carried out this exact duty, long ago. He must have done; but it could never have seemed important.

6.

'"Hanmouth is home to a wide and varied community. Many families and older people have chosen to make their home here, and they appreciate its family atmosphere and the feeling of safety in its streets. With the installation of CCTV cameras without a gap from the end of the Fore street to the end of the Strand, and the Devon Police Authority's agreement to dedicate a single desk officer, PC Browning, to Hanmouth and its concerns, we can all feel much safer in a sometimes threatening and fast-changing world.

'"However, with the privilege of living in Hanmouth come responsibilities, and Neighbourhood Watch have long emphasized the importance of good, neighbourly behaviour, and the maintenance of a certain standard of acceptable behaviour. It was drawn to the attention of Neighbourhood Watch at its most recent meeting that two men, in the early evening of Saturday, the twelfth of July, were seen in a residential Hanmouth street dressed in an unacceptable manner. Though Neighbourhood Watch was clear that it has no intentions of imposing dress standards, and has no objection to fancy dress, it does believe that the 'fetish' costumes worn by these two were only designed to advertise their sexual preferences and should not have been worn in public in a town where many families with children of different ages live.

'"We understand that these men were guests of yours on this particular occasion. We would like to emphasize to you that a certain standard of behaviour is required not only of those visiting Hanmouth, but those who live here, too. We are sorry to have to bring this to your attention, but we feel that you should be aware of how your neighbours feel, as evidenced by a number of representations to Neighbourhood Watch. We are sure that you will want to tell your guests in future that, once in Hanmouth, they should behave and dress in the style which the families who live here have come to expect and enjoy." Fuck off,' Sam said, finishing reading.

'Who's signed it?' Harry said. They were in the sitting room of their house. Sam had screwed up the letter, before throwing it in the direction of the bin. Stanley, capering with a sort of dim joy about Sam's feet, had been misled by Sam pacing up and down into thinking that a walk was imminent. So often, before a walk, one thing after another – a woolly hat, gloves, keys, poo-bags, wallet, man-bag – had been misplaced or lost by Sam, and so often he had walked up and down in exactly this pacing way before he had found enough to go out.

'It's just signed Neighbourhood Watch,' Sam said. 'There's no name. Who's in Neighbourhood Watch?'

'I don't think we know anyone, apart from that John Calvin,' Harry said. 'Didn't Helena Grosjean used to be in it?'

'No, you're thinking of the people who lived there before Mrs Grosjean,' Sam said. 'The ones who had that really hideous water feature in their pocket garden. This is really outrageous.'

'Just throw it away,' Harry said. 'And stop stomping up and

down – I can't read the paper with that going on. It's just the usual crap. You know they hate us.'

'No,' Sam said. 'I don't think I did know they hated you and me.'

'Not you and me,' Harry said. 'They hate us, the gays. Well, they don't mind us if they don't have to think about it too much. But once they think about us, they realize that they do hate us, actually. Was it that night the mechanic came?'

'And that Italian.'

'Oh, yeah. That Italian.' Harry went off into a short but, clearly, agreeable reverie. 'Who brought him?'

'I was trying to think. Was it Juan Carlos? Another waiter from Paddington Park, was it?'

'They've discovered a ten-year-old, been under the rubble in Haiti for nineteen days – would you have believed that possible?' Harry waved the paper in Sam's general direction. 'He'd have had to have water, some access to water, wouldn't he?'

'Who do you think it was?' Sam said.

'I don't know, it doesn't give—'

'Not your earthquake victim, you fool. Who do you think it was that so upset Neighbourhood Frigging Watch?'

'Could have been anyone. I'll have a word with the lads. Someone did come in a strap and a kilt with their tits out, I seem to remember. I'll mention it, next time we have a gathering.'

Sam stopped pacing; Stanley promptly sat down, his eyes on his master, just as patient and fascinated as if Sam were a washing-machine or a hen-house. Sam looked, amazed, at Harry. 'No, Harry,' he said. 'No. That's not the point. Neighbourhood Watch have sent us a letter, saying that they don't like the way our friends dress, and can we have a word with them. Why the hell should we? Who the hell are Neighbourhood Watch to tell us what our friends can wear? If we don't tell them to fuck off now, they'll be asking if they can go through our cupboards, see if there's anything they *deem*' – Sam got a lot of mileage out of this word – 'unsuitable next.'

'Oh, yeah,' Harry said. 'I love it when you get all principled.'

'Fuck off, Harry,' Sam said. 'You don't like it any more than I do.'

'I don't really care,' Harry said. 'They didn't have their dicks out, did they, do you think?'

'Of course they didn't,' Sam said. 'It's not stamped, is it?' He went to the table and turned the envelope over. 'Did you see who put it through the letterbox – was it this morning?'

'No idea,' Harry said. 'A representative of Neighbourhood Watch. I don't know them, apart from John Calvin. Anyway, I didn't see.'

'I'm going round to see John Calvin with this,' Sam said.

In his lumbering way, Stanley capered about Sam as he picked up the lead from the coat-rack by the door. Walk time was before breakfast, late afternoon when Sam got back from the shop – Stanley was just too smelly to have hanging around the shop during the day, and he seemed happy enough retiring to his basket for a few hours if Sam popped back at lunchtime – and a quick walk down the street and a poo while gazing at the night sky. Stanley was confused but giddily delighted at this one, with both Sam and Harry at home – it was a Saturday – and a walk being offered at half past eleven. He took the opportunity.

There was that crisp blue day, with the suggestion of woodsmoke brought on by the colouring of the leaves, which in late September always brought happy thoughts of change and improvement to Sam. He supposed it was the memory of going back to school, which never left you, apparently. No one lit bonfires any more; and yet his childhood, at this time of year, on a September clear day, had been so full of bonfires that the suggestions and associations of autumn constructed an illusion. He could have sworn he could smell, was just about to smell, had just stopped smelling the smoke of a domestic bonfire. It was the best smell he ever smelt, and he strained after it. What did people used to burn in their bonfires? His father had had one every fortnight. Probably what people now were enjoined to recycle – garden waste, newspaper, paper packaging. He couldn't think that a square green recycling bin, full to the brim with old *Guardians*, increased the sum of human happiness in the way that a single bonfire could, casting its lapsang-souchong odours over a neat suburb of London, its gardens packaged and fenced and tidy. When he got back, he would phone his father, if he could work out the time difference. One of these days, he, and Harry too, they'd take the long journey to Auckland. Probably quite soon.

In the little communal garden where the war memorial stood, there were two hunched figures on the bench, looking outwards. They were not talking for the moment; they gave the impression of not having exchanged a word for some time. It was Catherine and Alec. Then Sam remembered who it had been who had brought the Italian, and that it had been on the same night, two months before, that they had gone first to Catherine and Alec's party. He considered greeting them; he knew he had said, more than once, how sorry he was. Could you go on saying how sorry you were when there was nothing else, really, to say? Instead, he began to walk past them without a comment; but Stanley's whuffling and wheezing did the trick, and Catherine turned round. Her face was tired and worn and slow. How did she fill her days when her son had been taken away from her?

'Why, Sam,' she said, and Sam said hello. Then her husband turned round, looked at Sam, and turned back again, to go on looking at the view. After a moment, Catherine gave a weak, watery smile at Sam, and turned back as well. They had not been seen at Tom's funeral, which anyone could have understood. Sam walked on with Stanley; he saw that Catherine had taken her husband's hand in her own, and they went on sitting there.

John Calvin lived in a house beyond Miranda's, on the Strand. It was a curious, unsatisfactory house, which had at some period been squeezed into a gap between two more substantial houses. If it had a good location, the house itself was evidently hard to live in. While Harry and Sam had lived in their house, four different people had lived in the Calvins'. But Calvin and his wife

339

had now lived there for some years. They apparently saw nothing wrong with its narrow, wedge-like arrangements, or with its lowering pebbledash front, practical against the salt water from the estuary, which made such havoc with other fronts, but inescapably ugly. No one had ever been inside Calvin's house. Sam rang the bell on the grey, unwindowed front door with a sense of boldness.

Calvin's wife stood there with an enquiring expression; she perhaps didn't remember or recognize Sam, and they had only met once.

'I was looking for John,' Sam said. Laura retreated into the gloom of the house without saying anything; her lank hair, parted at the top, the glasses through which she peered made her seem some underwater or underground being, some kobold called up from the depths and now allowed to retreat.

Calvin shuffled forward; his eyes flickered downwards to the piece of paper Sam held in his hand, and to Stanley, looking upwards in turn at Calvin. He said nothing; just an enquiring movement of the eyebrow.

'Hello, John,' Sam said, and waited.

'Hello there,' Calvin said uncertainly.

'I'd like to join Neighbourhood Watch,' Sam said.

Calvin stared. He scratched his head, first theatrically, in puzzlement, and then genuinely, as if by scratching he had brought on an itch. His scratching seemed to lift his Brylcreemed coiffure in one, like a trapdoor, and for a moment it stood up on the crest of his skull like a cock's comb. He raised his other hand to his head, and smoothed his white hair down into its usual cap-like structure. Behind him, his wife Laura could be seen approaching again. Sam felt he had said the one magical sentence that would summon this household like a box of djinns, and make it blink at his command.

'Well,' Calvin said. 'That wasn't what I thought you were going to say.'

'What did you think I was going to say?'

'Not that,' Laura Calvin said, in her low croak, from their sitting room. The front door of their house opened directly onto the sitting room rather than a hallway. It was a marker of social class on the Strand, whether your door opened onto a hall or a sitting room; a subdivision of a class that had already subdivided itself on geographical grounds. Sam knew, from occasional visits to these houses, that the wind from the estuary whipped under the door and chilled your ankles all year round, if you had no hallway. Calvin's brown and green sitting room, gloomily lit, seemed to be filled with ill-assorted and oddly shaped furniture, as if at the depot of an unsuccessful antiques dealer, and gathered in the direction of neither a television nor a fireplace, nor with regard to each other. The chairs and tables and lamps, even, sat and pointed, and ignored each other.

'No,' Calvin said. 'I didn't think you were going to say that.'

'Nevertheless,' Sam said, 'I would like to join Neighbourhood Watch.'

'It would be lovely,' Calvin said. 'But I'm not sure we really have room for any more.'

'I'm sure you could squeeze me in,' Sam said.

'I don't think we could,' Calvin said.

'Somebody sent us this letter,' Sam said, producing it. 'I wonder who it's from.'

Calvin peered, and flattened it out – Sam had been clutching it, and it had grown crumpled. 'It's from Neighbourhood Watch,' he said. 'It says so, there, at the bottom, doesn't it?'

'Yes, I read that,' Sam said. 'But I wondered who wrote it. I would rather like to speak to the person who wrote it.'

'Well, Neighbourhood Watch wrote it,' Calvin said, apparently genuinely at a loss.

'That's right,' Laura said from behind. 'Neighbourhood Watch did.'

'Well, I would like to come to talk to Neighbourhood Watch,' Sam said. 'When do you meet?'

'I don't think that's really appropriate,' Calvin said.

'Or possible,' Laura said, now coming up to the doorway. She was holding a mug with, unexpectedly, World's Greatest Mum written on it. The Calvins had no children, did they? Or were they grown-up and gone away? For the first time, it occurred to Sam that, with his unlined pink face and smooth white hair, Calvin could be almost any age. But then, gathering himself, Calvin shot into one of his performances.

'Oooh! No! Oooh! I tell you what – I tell you what, missus – no, go on, I'm telling you – there's ever such a lot, I mean-to-say, there's ever such a lot of them as would LOVE to come to Watch, as we call it. Ooh, we 'ave a laugh, ooh, we do. So you see,' Calvin said, coming back into his normal, or his most-used tones, 'we're always having to say to people who want to join that it's unfortunate, but due to pressures of space, this is your captain speaking with a health-and-safety announcement, the fire exits are at the rear, middle and front of the plane, we can't let everyone come who wants to join Neighbourhood Watch. I'm sorry, and it's unfortunate, but there it is.'

'So who's in Neighbourhood Watch? I thought Helena Grosjean was, but apparently she isn't. And I know Miranda Kenyon isn't, though she'd like to be, I dare say.'

Calvin looked at him blankly, kindly.

'I just wanted to know,' Sam said, 'who is actually in your Neighbourhood Watch group.'

'Well, I am,' Calvin said, with a laugh. 'Obviously I'm in it. Look, I don't think I can stand out here in the cold any more with the door open. The cost of central heating nowadays, it's summink chronic.'

'I don't mind coming in to talk it over.'

'That would be charming,' Calvin said. 'But Laura – my wife, here – she's very allergic to dogs. Comes up in hives a quarter of an inch high. Purple. No, we can't have your dog in the house, I'm sorry to say.'

'Stanley can wait outside—' Sam was in the middle of saying, but found that he was talking to a shut door, Calvin having said,

'See you soon,' and shut it in his face. There was a little rustle at the curtains – Calvin must have been the only person in the Strand still to have net curtains to shield his privacy and his wife's from the passing trade. Sam wondered if he could be Scottish. On the window, on two of the small panes between the leading, there was the orange logo of Neighbourhood Watch, its shouty capitals, a logo of inspection and observation.

7.

The restaurant was too close to a tube station – in this case South Kensington. Another two hundred metres away, perhaps down a stuccoed avenue, and it would have found it easier to claim some kind of elegance, make a stake on a regular, satisfied and sophisticated clientele. London was full of restaurants of the same sort as Sumac, named after an abstruse foodstuff, set up with an elaborately creative menu and the funding of a dozen of the owner's friends from banks or the City. The old restaurant, which had managed to stay in business only a year and a half before succumbing to the lack of enthusiasm of Londoners for a Peruvian ranch-style restaurant, was gutted. A new interior in magnolia and grey, with slate surfaces and white lilies everywhere, glass urinals and translucent orange marble doors to the toilets, all this would be installed with the backing of the owner's friends. But in the end it was too close to a tube station. The people who wandered in were tourists on their way to or back from the museums, and tended to be shocked when they saw the prices, and settle only for one dish and some water. The rich locals in their stucco terraces or their mansion flats, they tried Sumac once, said it was nice, said they'd be back, and then presumably went to a restaurant not so close to a tube station. Six months after opening, the white lilies were appearing only at weekends, and were still hanging about, browning at the edges, a week later.

Mauro thought they would be better off trying the techniques of Paolo Crichetti, and just delivering food to the table that the tourists hadn't ordered, and charging them for it whether they ate it or not. He had no idea why restaurant owners in London didn't seem to do that.

Mauro had worked at the restaurant for two months now, or maybe a little bit more. He had just started working there when he had gone away for the weekend with David that had ended so badly. Before this, he had been working in a pizzeria, and was keen to get away from the hot, noisy, oregano-smelling atmosphere. It was a good pizzeria, a gourmet pizzeria, one with well-dressed customers and with newspaper reviews in the window. Still, it was a pizzeria. Mauro thought of working in a crisp white shirt and black trousers, welcoming his favourite customers with a smile and dismissing the walk-ups with a shrug; he dreamt of working in a restaurant with a handsome blond sommelier with a black apron down to his ankles. London must be full of such places.

A boy Mauro knew called Luis had told him about Sumac. It was being started up by someone he knew, an Englishman called Oswald Bond. 'You should want to be in on the ground of this one,' Luis had said, and Mauro had gone to see Oswald Bond. Talking to him, Oswald Bond explained that he wanted something stylish; he wanted something innovative; he wanted something exciting. Mauro signed up.

Now, at this exact moment, Mauro felt terrible. It was his own fault. At first, Oswald Bond had promised, or seemed to promise, that Mauro could work whenever he wanted to, choosing what service he wanted to work and did not want to work. For the first weeks, Mauro had not worked the Saturday or the Sunday lunchtime services. But then Oswald Bond had said one week that he needed Mauro to work exactly those times. He gave the impression that it would be just for that week; but then, at the end of the following week, Mauro was put down to work the same shifts without any comment. Now he had worked for three out of the four last Saturday lunchtimes.

He hated it, because the Saturday lunch service drew in, almost exclusively, a disgruntled and complaining crowd of tourists straight out of the museums, unable to find anything else, unwilling to pay Sumac's prices. He was fed up of serving tables of seven a main course only, with nothing but tap water to drink, and a bare scraping of a tip at the end. Most of all, he hated it because it deprived him of his Friday nights; either a Friday night working, which gave the best tips and the nearest thing to a nice crowd Sumac ever saw, or a Friday night in the bars and clubs of Vauxhall.

Now, he stood in Sumac, and felt terrible. The night before, not working, he had succumbed to a phone call from Susie. He had met her and her dyke friends at seven in a Vauxhall bar, and had gone on from there. At five, he had found himself shouting into Christian's ear on a dance floor somewhere underground, somewhere under a railway arch, that he had to be 'on' in six hours' time, as if that were the funniest thing in the world. 'Darling,' Christian had yelled back, 'just have a disco nap, a strong coffee, a cold shower, and leave a line of coke on your dressing-table, baby. That'll get you out of the door. The Gods of Gay, they'll do the rest, baby.' He had followed the advice, not leaving the club until the lights went on. Now he looked at himself in the horizontal mirror that ran at head height around the whole space of Sumac, and saw how terrible he looked.

He was sweating slightly; his skin was blotchy and somehow both yellow and red; his eyes were bloodshot, and his hair had taken on a mad quality. A party of five Norwegians were giving their order. Two giant parents, a giant, massive-jawed girl and a seven-foot boy and, maybe, Grandma with her Nazi gaze. It was one thirty. Mauro had recited the specials for the ninth time, and guided the party towards the scallop and black pudding cannelloni the kitchen wanted to get rid of. He was alone on the service. Bruno, the English boy, the son of a friend of Oswald Bond who had been ineptly waiting for the last two weeks, had phoned in sick. Mauro doubted he would ever come in again. Oswald Bond, too mean or too constrained by the restaurant's lack of success to call an agency for help, had said, 'I'll step in,' but, as before, had quickly retreated to the bar, where he sat with what might be sparkling water.

Mauro went to the kitchen hatch, handed over the miserly order, and felt he had to go to and do something about his appearance. 'Table seven ready to order,' Oswald Bond said reprovingly.

'I'll be there in a moment,' Mauro said, going into the customer toilet. He had to do something. He splashed his face with cold water – he could smell himself, oozing the corruptions of last night, the pleasures, the old odours preserved and leaking in his flesh. He dried his face with one of the white towels kept in a pile by the sink. The single line of coke he had left to get himself going at ten that morning had worked, up to a point: he hadn't been late; he had presented himself in a clean white shirt and a clean pair of black trousers. He couldn't see himself getting through until one o'clock in the morning without a little more help. He felt for his mobile phone. But, as usual, he had left it behind the bar for safekeeping. Glen would come out to South Kensington with his bag of goodies, some time in the early evening, when Mauro would need it most.

It was then, Mauro standing at the urinal, that the catastrophe happened. Pissing, he felt a fart building up, and he let it out. Instantly he knew his mistake, as a hot wet weight filled his underpants. He was drunk, hung-over, under the loosening effects of the drugs from the night before, and for the first time ever, he had shit himself. With an awkward shuffle, the piss still dribbling across the floor as he rapidly went, he pushed the translucent marble door of the cubicle open, and, almost before it was shut, dropped his trousers and pants to the floor. He had no idea what to do. He kicked his slip-on shoes off, then his trousers, then made a bundle of his underpants. He emptied them of their disgusting load down the toilet, and cleaned himself, standing in his shirt and socks on the cold stone floor. He could not clean the underpants, not in the sink outside with a customer liable to

346

come in at any moment. He flushed the toilet again, and cautiously, retching slightly, he held the soiled underpants under the waterfall out of the rim. It did no good. There was no bin in the toilet; the underpants could not be worn again, could not be flushed away – these toilets were temperamental in their modern design and prone to blocking, and he would be the one who would have to unblock them, in any case. He could not leave the toilet with the soiled underpants in his hand, and the toilet offered no means of disposal. He was a man who had shit himself at his place of work. The bathroom door outside opened with its usual clang.

'What are you doing in there?' Oswald Bond said. 'I can't have this, Mauro.'

'I'm not well,' Mauro said. 'I'll be all right in a minute.'

'I can't have this,' Oswald Bond said again. 'You need to be out here, in a proper state, in exactly thirty seconds. You're disappointing me, now, Mauro.'

With a shuddering gesture, Mauro took the underpants and threw them up above the cupboard concealing the cistern. He pulled his trousers up, flushed and left the cubicle. Oswald Bond was still there, his hands in his pockets, wearing a sarcastic expression.

'Some restaurants measure the time their staff spend in the toilets,' Oswald Bond said. He had made one of his effortless passes between mate-of-yours to hyper-efficient boss; it was never quite predictable when one of these would happen, but it was usually at some vulnerable moment. 'I might start to think about that. I don't know what you were doing in there. I don't want to know how you spend your time when you go off for ten minutes alone in the toilet, because I think if I did know, I'd feel obliged to send for the police. Do you understand, Mauro?'

'I was ill,' Mauro said.

'You were ill,' Oswald Bond said. 'Like all the other times. Well, consider yourself told. I don't want to have to tell you again. And we can't have you absenting yourself from the lunchtime service for ten minutes in the middle of the rush. It just can't happen again. OK? Lecture over,' he went on, disconcertingly switching back to his previous, indiscriminately friendly mode. 'By the way, your phone was going a minute ago. I didn't answer it.'

In the end, he didn't have a chance to look at his phone until the end of the lunch service and the departure of the last complaining Scandinavian. It wasn't a number he recognized. It was a landline of some sort, but one from outside London. They hadn't left a message. Mauro resolved to start looking for another job as soon as he had got himself back in Oswald Bond's good books.

8.

The view composed itself slowly into six horizontals: sky, hills, mud, water, mud again, and the shoreline. It was a simple visual construction, and it coagulated out of a complicated blur. Catherine cried so often, these days. She had a full range of ways of crying; a set of categories she had explored from top to bottom. At one end there was the helpless tantrum, like being shaken by an outside force, where your joints and limbs ached and juddered; at the other there was the more or less constant access of moisture to your eyes. She felt, at best, as if she existed at the tender edge of a touching movie. The feeling of a tremulous beat somewhere in the chest, the gingery itch of water at the corner of the eye: she knew all about that. They sat, the two of them, on a bench in a small public garden on the Strand in Hanmouth. Catherine was returning from an intermediate state of weeping; neither the noisy nor the pathetic, but just a steady silent flow of water down her face. It came whether she thought of David or not. She had had no idea that she had loved her son as much as she had.

She held Alec's hand. It lay there, morosely. In some time her tears came to a sort of end; the landscape composed itself. She fished in her old brown handbag by her side, creased and folded like a boxer's glove, and tidied herself with a Kleenex. There were plenty more in there.

'I'll phone him again later,' she said. 'It was probably foolish phoning him at lunchtime. He'd be busy. It's a small restaurant – they couldn't afford to give him time off.'

'He'll have seen the number,' Alec said. 'He can call us back.'

'I'd like to phone again,' Catherine said.

'I don't like to see you getting into so much of a state,' Alec said. 'Best let sleeping dogs lie. He can get in touch with us. Maybe he just doesn't want to – you know.'

'People deal with these things in different ways,' Catherine said, for the hundredth time; she had applied this maxim to the difference between her grieving and Alec's, about the ways in which people greeted or avoided them – David's death had brought an end to anything resembling a social life in Hanmouth. She knew about the Brigadier's death, like a satisfied, hurtful carnival. Her grief was the object of communal shame, ignored, a kind of low-level and unsuccessful attempt to imitate what Hanmouth did best, apparently. Nobody wanted to do anything but cross the road or closely examine the house prices in estate agents' windows when they saw Catherine and Alec approaching, two people who had been bereaved whom they did not know well. Bereaved in a rubbish way. Now Catherine applied her maxim to the unknown ways in which Mauro, someone they had met only once, for twenty-four hours, might be dealing between shifts with the death of his partner. They really had no idea; they only knew that his way was different from theirs.

After that unexpected arrival of the police officers at their door, they had gone immediately to the hospital. How had they got there? She couldn't remember. 'His friend is there, too,' the policeman had said gently. They had nodded. She and Alec had sat in the back of the car, not quite understanding. She remembered them riding slowly along the Fore street in Hanmouth, a stranger bowing his head to look inside at them. It was the foolish-looking old man who had once snubbed her, the one who knew everything that happened in Hanmouth, everybody that mattered here, and who had made it clear that they did not count. He lowered his head as men used to when a hearse drove past; but then he must have seen the two of them, white-faced, as if they were arrested criminals. A brief raising, self-satisfied, of the head, and he was gone again, perhaps to spread the word. When they got to the roundabout outside Hanmouth and the enormous roadhouse pub neither of them had ever been to, the car speeded up. She did not know whether she wanted it to drive fast or slowly; in stately grief, or to rush to her boy. And then they had got to that unfamiliar town and its unfamiliar hospital, a name on a map only, and had been taken straight past Reception, with its load of waiting patients, into a treatment room, and there was David. She had never thought to see him like this. 'Where is he?' she had said after a time. They had not understood at first. It was made clear to her that Mauro had gone. He had left the hospital. In the days to come, she constructed his journey: he must have phoned for a taxi, gone to the station, got the train back to London. She could not understand it. They had gone through David's telephone, had called every name on it, and they had mostly come down to the funeral. They had not known where to hold it, and in the end had held it in Bideford. It was nearest to them, and to the hospital where David's body had been held, and his friends – Richard, Dymphna, some others – had come down to it. It made a small crowd, a sad afternoon. She had spoken to Mauro, and he had said he didn't know. Grief took people in different ways. In the end he had not come. What to do with the mobile phone afterwards? They let the battery run down, not wanting to switch it off for ever, and kept it in a cupboard, with all the other stuff.

'Do you remember,' she said eventually, 'do you remember when we went to the Proms that time.'

'Why are you thinking of that?' Alec said.

'It just came to mind,' Catherine said. It was before they were married – the summer before. They weren't even engaged. They had agreed to get married in the autumn, one Sunday afternoon in the park, and had married in April, on the second of April. 'Can't get married on April Fools' Day,' Alec had said. People seemed to take longer, these days. But before all of that, there was the Proms. Their 1960s were not the 1960s of pop festivals and free love and everything else, all that you saw on documentaries. It was a 1960s of living with their parents still, seven streets away from each other, of a good job and suits from Burton's, of library books returned on time and her resentful sister acting as a chaperone; of an outing, in the summer, to the Proms. They liked it; Alec had been keen on jazz, but just as keen on classical music. People were then. It was an August night, one of the hottest she could remember or imagine, and they had driven up to London in his little Morris Minor, black and shiny. He had curtains in the back window, neatly tied back, a favourite joke of the time among the sort of people they knew, and she was wearing – she was amazed she could remember this – a red-on-white polka-dot dress, not quite miniskirt – an inch or two above the knee with a white plastic belt. White tights, too – she'd regretted those tights later, what with the heat. What would Alec have been wearing? A charcoal suit, probably, and – yes – a thin tie. She could remember taking it between her hands, later in the evening. In the hall it was as if steam were rising from the auditorium, from the students standing, pressing forward, marking their spaces. They had got seats. 'I couldn't stand,' she said. 'Not through all of that. I would faint.' But she was saying that as they were taking their seats. Alec would never ask her to stand. He was always considerate like that.

They loved Tchaikovsky, they had agreed on that, and there was his violin concerto, played by Ida Haendel. They'd heard her before; they loved her grand, enormous, serious face, and the huge noise she threw into the auditorium. And after the interval there was something they didn't know, a symphony by Mahler. They'd loved that above almost anything. It was like storytelling; it was like the fairytale wanderings of a German shepherdess, going through travails and suffering, and coming out all right at the end. A week later, Alec had presented her with an LP of this very symphony; fifteen years later, he had come home with a huge object under his arm, all of Mahler's symphonies, and for weeks they had listened to them, one after the other, vainly attempting to find again the magic of that hot August night in 1968, and Alec coming out with her, his face red and hot, his shirt even sticking to his body, and saying, 'Wonderful,' and she saying, 'Truly wonderful,' back. By the time he had bought that enormous box set, he had needed to apologize for spending his money on such a thing. They had loved music. And afterwards, on the way back to the car – how *easy* it had been to park in central London then, forty years ago! – the tune in her head, surging on after the lovely song finale, the ovations, the exiting, had made her seize him and, not caring, she had pulled him onto the bonnet of a perfect stranger's car, and they had kissed for so long. The memory was sweet; it was combined with the thought that, of course, they'd had no car alarms then to set off. Now she thought of it, she did not think the tie had been narrow at all. He must have been wearing a kipper tie, one of the first. It had been fat in her hand as she pulled him towards her. She was sure of it.

'What on earth made you think of that?' Alec said.

'I don't know,' Catherine said. 'It came to mind. All of it, all at once.'

9.

'The important thing,' Kitty was saying, much later, 'is to keep busy. Find yourself an occupation.'

Everyone had gone, an hour or two before. Kitty had stayed on, at first bustling around tidying things up. But it hadn't taken all that long, and finally she'd sat down and started talking. Of course, it wouldn't do just to leave Billa on her own with the whole evening in front of her. They'd done the congregation and the guests, and in a while Kitty had got on to the subject of Billa's future.

'What I found,' she went on, 'was that all of a sudden, I had enormous amounts of time on my hands. I honestly hadn't realized how much time was taken up by just having a husband. Extraordinary. Really, when things are settled down, you must think about finding yourself an occupation of some sort.'

'A job, do you mean?' Billa said, trying to envisage herself behind a counter in a shop. 'No one would give me a job.'

'Oh, you'd be surprised,' Kitty said expansively. 'Not necessarily a job, though. All I meant was something to keep your hand in, a new skill, something to keep the grey cells ticking over. Learn a language. Take up painting.'

'Oh, I couldn't do that,' Billa said, aghast. The village was full of amateur painters, foisting their views of the estuary on each other, filling up their own walls in a manner Billa had always found depressing. Filling up each other's walls with paintings best understood as threats, or hostages: still more depressing.

'I'm sure you could, perfectly well,' Kitty said, not having understood. 'I was thinking,' she went on, finishing what was in her glass. 'More than anything, I would love to go to Italy some time. I was thinking perhaps of going, hmm, in the early spring?'

'Good idea,' Billa said. 'Won't be too hot.'

'Awful to go on your own, though,' Kitty said.

'I'm sure you'll cope,' Billa said. She heard herself – and, after all, Kitty only meant to be kind, had only heard somewhere that you ought to give the bereaved something to look forward to. 'Sorry. I just don't see it happening. Don't worry about me. I'll be quite all right.'

'Any more of this?' Kitty said, waving her empty glass.

Kitty's interest was one thing, but Billa's situation seemed to have turned her into a sort of public property, the concern of a considerable swathe of acquaintanceship.

'You really ought to take something up,' Kitty said one

morning. 'I can't imagine what you do, all day long.' They were in the little high street; Kitty had persuaded her to come out for a few small things.

'Oh, I'm quite busy,' Billa said. 'Sam!'

'Hello, Billa, love,' Sam said, just coming out of the greengrocer. 'I can't stop. We've got friends coming round tonight and I haven't done a thing. Are you two coming to the book club tomorrow?'

'Gosh, I hadn't thought,' Billa said. 'I haven't got on at all with the book, I'm afraid. Off you go, then – you see, Kitty, I am busy. If I'd only remembered to read the book for the club, of course.'

'I don't mean that sort of busy,' Kitty said. 'Always good to take something new up. I just want to pop in here.'

'Here' was the little greengrocer that Sam had just popped out of. Kitty used it, saying as she so often did that one had to support local businesses if the supermarkets weren't going to take over the world. Billa rarely bothered; she thought supermarkets were perfectly convenient.

'Good morning,' Kitty said, to the sour old pair who ran the shop, who said nothing in return. 'Just a few things . . .'

Billa stood there, making no attempt to look like someone who wasn't waiting.

'You might take a class in something interesting,' Kitty said. 'Learn to type. Or paint. Or there's the amateur dramatics. Garlic.'

'You might be right,' Billa said. Kitty, as she spoke, was waving her arms around as if she had suddenly been struck with this inspiration. She had quite forgotten that she had said exactly the same things to Billa immediately after the funeral. An unfamiliar young woman with a small boy, ginger-haired and frail-looking, came into the shop behind them.

'We'll just have some apples,' the woman said. 'Golden Delicious all right?'

'I only like Granny Smith's,' the boy said. They both had a flatly querulous London accent; holidaymakers.

'Well, they've only got Golden Delicious,' the woman said. 'They're quite nice.'

'I can't remember,' Kitty said, as if she expected Billa to help her out, 'whether I've got any eggs.'

Billa made a noncommittal noise. The London pair paid for their apples.

'On holiday?' the greengrocer's wife said, as she took their money.

'That's right,' the woman said. 'It's nice down here.'

'We like it,' the greengrocer interjected.

They watched the pair go; they were hardly out of the door when the greengrocer said, 'Grockles. Nothing ever good enough for them.' His wife laughed coarsely.

Kitty didn't seem to hear at all, but Billa flushed, as so often when someone let themselves down in her hearing. She'd only started hearing the word recently, and it had seemed the most repulsively provincial insult, a description of a Londoner only a real yokel could ever use.

She had always bought food more or less indifferently in local shops, or in supermarkets you had to drive to. Kitty maintained that you ought to keep the local shops going, that the huge supermarkets springing up everywhere were destroying small towns and the tomatoes had no taste whatsoever. Billa went along with this, weak-mindedly, in general. 'Do you know what?' Kitty said now. 'I've come out without any money at all. I'm just going to pop to the cashpoint.'

'I'll lend you the money,' Billa said, and it was only a bag or two of stuff, but Kitty was out of the door, leaving her basket at the till.

'That's the second time that's happened today,' the greengrocer's wife said.

'Oh, yes,' Billa said, but then, clearly, she was not being spoken to. She might as well not be there at all.

'What's that, then?' the greengrocer said.

'Someone walking out, saying they'll be back. Who was it earlier?'

'That fat chap,' the greengrocer said. 'Lives with his friend, the lawyer. He's a lord, too, they say. Like that, they are.'

'They're friends, are they?' the greengrocer's wife said. 'And the boyfriend a lord and a lawyer, too. What a waste, I'd say.'

Billa, standing there gazing at the bins of potatoes, felt all the invisibility that solitude, apparently, had conferred on her. She had heard Sam repeat exactly this story; the way that people referred to him and to Harry when there was no one around. It was as if the greengrocer were repeating a well-loved performance for the sake of an audience. But that was misleading, because there was no audience, not even her. This was the way that people always talked when there was nobody who mattered around them.

10.

She was almost outside her own house when she was accosted from the other side of the street. 'Mrs Townsend,' a voice said. Billa turned, and it was, unexpectedly, the woman artist who had come to the funeral. She'd thought she had seen her off. The woman was draped in blacks and purples; somewhere underneath there was a shape-fitting dress, but the surface was all shawls and drapes. She came across the road in an uneven, seesawing way, as if in something of a hurry; Billa waited, conscious of the need to be civil, briefly, avoiding the word 'waddling', even in her head.

'How are you?' the woman said.

'I'm very well, considering,' Billa said, in her unvarying formula. 'Of course, it's all been a very great strain, but I think I see my way clear now, thank you so much.'

'That's good to hear,' the woman said. 'I just wanted to say – I do hope you didn't think I was intruding. Coming to the funeral like that.'

This was so impossible a comment that Billa made no answer, other than moving her head to one side. Over the road, Kitty waved, returning from the cashpoint machine – Billa had quite forgotten about her, and had left Kitty's basket unattended in the greengrocer.

'I'm Sylvie,' the woman said. 'I thought you might not remember my name from before.'

'No,' Billa said. 'That's right, I'm afraid. I don't remember meeting you.'

Sylvie blew out her cheeks, emptied them, inhaled noisily and fanned herself with the flippers of her hands, although it was not at all hot. 'Well, no wonder,' she began. 'Of course, you wouldn't remember. It must have been a great shock. It was me, when those yobbos bowled you over in the street a couple of months back – I picked you up and got you into the little cheese shop your friend runs – Sam, is it?'

'Oh,' Billa said. Of all things, she hated snubbing the most; the act of pretending you were too good to say hello to someone, to be ungrateful for that small deed of reaching across to another human being. Always had. In the humiliations and sore moments of the funeral, she had been led, against all her principles, to snub someone she'd thought she did not know. To dismiss someone's kindness in such a way, that was not like Billa, she liked to think. She considered for a moment whether she could pass off her greeting at the funeral as an ordinary moment of gratitude; she did not remember her exact words, but knew from the way it hung in the air that she could not. 'Oh, my dear, what must you think of me? I am so sorry. It was so kind of you to come to Tom's funeral. And I never said thank you for what you did. I don't know what I should have done – probably still be lying in the road.'

'It's really quite all right,' Sylvie said. 'I didn't mean to tick you off, or anything. I could see you weren't yourself.'

'No, indeed,' Billa said. 'I certainly wasn't. I am really so sorry. It really isn't like me.'

'Anyway,' Sylvie said, 'I'm sure anyone else would have picked you up. I just happened to be nearest.'

'Even if that's true,' Billa said, 'it was you who *did* do it. I never said thank you. I'm so sorry.'

'You've said thank you now,' Sylvie said, smiling.

'And so we must be friends,' Billa said.

In a moment, they had established that they had nothing else to do for the moment. Billa asked Sylvie to come back for a cup of coffee – there was still some funeral fruitcake left, and would be for some months. But when Sylvie suggested that Billa come back to her house, to have coffee with her, not promising much in the way of anything else – 'though I could do you some toast' – Billa was tempted, and agreed. As Sylvie said, as they went companionably through the back lanes between wisteria and magnolia trees, past terraces and almshouses and the stately white houses of the eighteenth-century gentry, Billa had done enough entertaining for the moment. Sometimes it was nice to be someone else's guest, however inadequately entertained. And that was true. Billa thought of Kitty returning, flushed, from the greengrocer with her bag-for-life full of her week's greenery; she would knock on Billa's door, probably pushing at the same time, and be surprised Billa was out still, not available as the recipient of concern and sympathy. That – offering to be the recipient of concern and sympathy – was the most tiring form of entertaining, Billa had found, as tiring as making sure a small child had every-thing he needed. She was rather glad to be going to a strange house, even for an hour or so.

'I have heard of you,' Billa said, when they were in Sylvie's kitchen. 'Not by name, I mean. I've heard what people say about you.'

'I had no idea,' Sylvie said.

'No, I mean . . .' Billa said. 'Well, they say that you're an artist, that was what I heard.'

'If that's the worst . . .'

'Oh, yes,' Billa said. 'That's the worst of it, I'm afraid.'

'Well, I teach art to the kids in Barnstaple,' Sylvie said. 'Nothing so very elevated.'

'Do you not do art yourself?' Billa said. '"Do art" – that sounded strange. Do I mean "do art"?'

'"Do art" is just fine,' Sylvie said, smiling. 'Yes, I do art, even when no one's looking or when they're seizing my attention by trying to eat the pastel chalks or sniff the Copydex, which is how I spend my days, mostly, putting a stop to that sort of thing.'

'May I see some time?' Billa said. 'Your art?'

Sylvie put her coffee mug down, and appeared to assess Billa. The kitchen they were in was not as atrociously untidy as Billa had anticipated. There were two bowls for a cat by the sink on a sheet of newspaper, and the animal had scattered the dry food, which constituted its dinner, about a large area. There were two dinner plates, a saucepan and two wine glasses in the sink along with the breakfast things, and a finished bottle stood on the draining-board. The pine table they sat at could have done with a wipe – the crumbs from breakfast and spilt gobbets of muesli had been ignored. Billa had seen worse.

'May you see some time?' Sylvie said. 'Well, I don't see why not. I'm not a lady watercolourist, though.'

'Too many of those around,' Billa said. 'My friend Kitty, she's long ago run out of interesting subjects round here, so she's taken to painting the same things over and over. She's still getting through her photographs of her holiday in Tunisia two years ago – she props one up on the easel, and she just copies it, with her tongue out, you know.'

'I know exactly,' Sylvie said. 'What happens when she gets to the end of her photographs, or the usable ones, anyway? I suppose even Kitty takes some photographs you wouldn't want to turn into a watercolour.'

'She's nearly finished, I believe,' Billa said. 'Nearly got to the bottom of the pile. Not that there is a pile, it's all digital nowadays. I presume she'll go back to painting the view from the Wolf Walk. Or she could just go on holiday somewhere else and take some more photographs. But you're not an artist like that.'

'No,' Sylvie said. 'I'm not much like Kitty. I used to be – I used to put marks on paper and canvas and turn solid stuff into shapes on pedestals. I even carved a piece of elm, once.'

359

'Lovely grain,' Billa said. 'I know that much – it has a lovely grain, elm.'

'Yes, indeed it does,' Sylvie said. 'But I teach kids to do that sort of stuff all day long, and I don't really feel like starting up again when I get home. I do different sorts of things nowadays.'

'And can I see?'

Sylvie gave her, again, that assessing look; then she apparently decided that Billa would do. She got up, and together they went into the garden – the lawn needed a trim and the beds a once-over to get rid of the weeds but, like the kitchen, no worse than that. The outhouse, or perhaps studio, was not connected to the house: you had to go out of the kitchen door and across the patio, Sylvie explained. It was good on a winter morning to feel that you had to go to work – to leave your cosy home and travel, however short a distance, to your place of work. Commuting was good, Sylvie explained; a commute that lasted twenty seconds was good enough for her.

'Here we are,' Sylvie said, throwing a switch; a brilliant fluorescent light flooded the studio.

'If you cleaned all those leaves off,' Billa said, nodding upwards at the glass roof, 'you wouldn't need artificial light at all.'

'You're probably right,' Sylvie said. 'I ought to do it. I have a terror of crashing through, though – getting up there on a ladder, leaning too far over, losing my balance, and—' She shuddered. 'I couldn't.'

'Get someone in,' Billa said. She had never been in an artist's studio before, if you didn't count Kitty's box room where her easel and paints and unsold works were stored. It was unexpectedly orderly. In pigeonholes to one side were pages of magazines, torn out roughly and labelled with the signs of male and female, and boxes of artists' materials – pastels and oils, pencils and charcoal – were shelved above stores of paper, sketchbooks and two large blank canvases. The work surface was two or three metres across, in white Formica, and an efficient-looking array of glue, scissors, rulers, pencils, rubbers, sharpeners sat in an office-tidy by the side of a small guillotine and a photographer's spyglass. Propped up was what looked like a finished work. Billa's eyesight was not quite what it had been, and she murmured, 'Impressionist, I suppose you could call it,' at this pink, dappled, throbbing image. It didn't seem to depict anything in particular, but the rippling effect of small strokes of paint in shades of pink and white and brown did remind her of impressionist paintings she had sometimes seen on an occasional trip to London and the Royal Academy. She put her spectacles on, and immediately saw that brushstrokes had not created this effect, but a thousand miniature, collaged pieces of magazine print. 'Ingenious,' she said politely, moving closer, and then, all at once, it was apparent what everything, every component of the image was: a man's parts, cut out and glued on.

'My word,' she said. 'That startled me.'

'It tends to do that,' Sylvie said. Her expression was unreadable; had she meant to shock an old woman who had insulted her? Billa thought not. Sylvie was direct, and was showing Billa her work, no more than that.

'So,' Billa said. 'You cut these out of, what, magazines? And then what? Forgive me – I would just rather like to know what the process is.'

'I put them in jars first,' Sylvie said. 'These jars.' There were nine, darkening by degrees from left to right. 'I arrange them by colour, really. The very pale ones here – the darkest ones here. I'm only really interested in colour. The other things . . .'

Sylvie went on explaining, about the glue, the canvas, the glaze, the difficulties of sourcing the material, and Billa went on saying, 'I see, I see,' at first politely, but then with real interest and engagement. It seemed to her to be an interesting undertaking. She herself had never seen a man's genitals in life, apart from Tom's – she searched her memory, but apart from a visit to *Equus* twenty years ago, one or two things like that, that seemed to be the case. 'I see,' Billa went on saying, enjoying Sylvie's seriousness, and placing her in context among the ceramicists and the tapestry-makers, the perpetrators of macramé and the proponents of batik. She did seem to have her careful, devoted place in the town; the maker of *découpages*, as Sylvie called it; the community cutter-out of willies. By the end of the morning Sylvie had handed Billa a pair of curved-blade scissors, and Billa was cutting out the crucial parts of nude men, perfectly handily.

11.

Miranda had been talking for only five minutes when the door to the lecture room opened behind her. She paid no attention. Students were never good at turning up on time, and she let them come and go more or less as they chose. She continued talking from her notes on *Robinson Crusoe*. It was a windowless room, ill-lit by theoretically adjustable lights, and this lecture was time-tabled for three o'clock in the afternoon on Thursday, a graveyard slot. Miranda herself liked to take a brief nap around this time. She was used to facing a slumped and dull-eyed audience with conspicuous gaps in it. She was surprised, now, that the students grew suddenly alert, that they had started to talk among themselves, their pens and pencils abandoned above their note-taking paper.

'As I was saying,' Miranda said, to get their attention back, turning to one side to see what, if anything, had created this disturbance. To her alarm, standing inside the lecture room were two policemen, each holding his cap in his hand.

'Could I have your attention, please?' one policeman said, and the walkie-talkie at his belt crackled into electric life. 'I'm going to have to interrupt this lecture. Is there a Faisal Ahmed in the room?'

'Faisal,' Miranda said, correcting the policeman's pronunciation. 'No, there isn't. There's no one of that name in this lecture hall.'

Faisal Khalil had been sitting in the third row. Was it an illusion, or had the girls to either side of him drawn away somewhat? He now raised his hand, perhaps conceding that, since he was the only person in the room who was not white, it was only a matter of time before the policemen asked him directly who he was. 'I think you might mean me,' he said. 'Ahmed's my middle name.'

The larger of the two policemen looked at him, and went outside. He could be heard talking indistinctly into his walkie-talkie. An excited murmuring broke out in the hall.

'Quiet, please,' Miranda said, and then, to the policeman, 'Who gave you permission to come into my lecture?'

The policeman ignored this, and in a moment his colleague came back in. 'That's right,' he said to Faisal. 'Are you Faisal Ahmed Khalil?'

Faisal agreed that he was.

'Confused your surname and your Christian name,' the policeman said.

'I don't have a Christian name,' Faisal said, reasonably enough.

'We need you to come with us, please,' the policeman said, brushing this irrelevant objection aside. Faisal, with resignation, as if he had been expecting something rather like this all his life, got up, taking his book, his notepaper, his pens and pencils, and followed the policemen out.

'I'm going to leave it there for the day,' Miranda said to her audience, though she had only reached halfway down the first page of her notes on the nature of capitalism and *Robinson Crusoe*. In any case, she had lost their attention now, and would not be able to regain it. They could just jolly well go and read a book on the subject. She left the lecture hall in time to see, through the glass double doors, Faisal Khalil being helped – not pushed, but definitely helped – into a squad car. With her documents, she hurried upstairs to Benjy's office. She knocked, briefly, and then entered without waiting for a reply.

Benjamin was sitting at a table with someone she vaguely

363

recognized as some administrator or other from the university headquarters. They seemed to be going over some figures.

'Did you know this was going to happen?' she said immediately.

'I'm sorry, Miranda,' Benjamin said. 'I'm in the middle of something here.'

'This is most important,' Miranda said. 'Did you give the police permission to come into my lecture?'

'I'm sorry,' Benjamin said. 'I don't know what you're talking about. Miranda Kenyon, one of our senior lecturers,' he added, as an aside, to the administrative bod.

'Two policemen just came into my lecture in Theatre Three,' Miranda said. 'They told me to stop what I was doing, and demanded to know if Faisal Khalil was there. Then they took him away. Did you give them permission?'

'I'm sure they wouldn't have come in without permission,' the administrative person said. Miranda recognized him now – he was one of several deputy vice-chancellors. 'I'm sure they had a very good reason for coming in.'

'And I'm sure they didn't,' Miranda said. 'Benjamin. Did you give the police permission to come into my lecture and arrest a student in front of a hundred other students?'

'I don't think I need to answer that question,' Benjamin said.

'I really don't think we can resist the police in the legitimate conduct of their duties,' the deputy VC said. 'I really don't think this is something for you to get worked up about.'

'I think I should also say that the student was the only student in his year from a non-white background,' Miranda said. 'I have no idea what he is supposed to have done, but it doesn't look very reasonable to me.'

'I'm sure the police know exactly what they are doing,' Benjamin said, taking his cue. 'I very much doubt that there is anything for you to worry about here.'

'So you're happy, are you, that the police come in and arrest our students in the most public way imaginable, without bothering to inform us? Is that how we are going to start running our disciplinary procedures now?'

'I'm sorry, Miranda,' the deputy VC said urbanely. 'Miranda? Is that right? I'm sorry, but we really are in the middle of something very important here. We've heard what you have to say, but I think we have to ask you to let us get back to all this.' He gestured at the table top before him, covered with papers – accounts, discussion papers, institutional proposals, every one of them written by people who believed that you said, 'This proposal was considered by the VC and I in March 2007.' Miranda turned and left the pair of them to pursue the work of the enemies of literature.

'A little bit less concern on that one's part for the welfare of students, a little bit less intrusion,' Benjamin said. 'That would be very welcome, to tell you the truth.'

'I recognize the type,' the deputy VC said, perfectly calmly.

12.

'Amy was, like, can you tell the lead singer that I, like, want to marry him, and she was, like, well, you can go on MySpace and tell him, or I'll take your number and I'll tell him. Anyway, how was your weekend? Oh, cool. Because one really dodgy one called that William something. You know Amy's friend Joe who's like blond, it's his birthday, so they managed to get him a ticket to go, and the trombonist was incredible, he like did not stop dancing, it was incredible. We were like in the top seats, in the circle, he wouldn't stop shaking his hips the whole time and the lead singer wouldn't stop shaking his hips the whole time, and the trumpeter, he was all dressed in white. But the whole place smelt of wee!'

Ahead of Mauro, a girl sat, talking into her telephone. She had been talking like this since the train had left Paddington station; talking into her headset intently, hardly making sense at all. They had stopped at the first station on the line, Reading, and the girl had gone on talking; they were pulling out now and the conversation was going on. 'That's crazy,' Mauro said, actually out loud, at the volume and nonsense and unstoppability of it. Around her people were staring and raising newspapers, and talking about her in loud voices. 'There were some really weird types there,' she went on at top volume. 'Yes, just at Reading.'

Mauro had only once taken the train in England before, and he had not very often taken one even at home, in Italy. He knew how it was done, but there had always been people around to give him a lift and, anyway, he hadn't gone to so many places, or needed to. He had done it all wrong. He had turned up at Paddington, queued, and asked for a ticket to Hanmouth. The man behind the counter hadn't understood, or hadn't known where he was asking for; Mauro had spelt it out, as best he could, and the clerk had looked it up. Finally, he asked for a sum of money so outlandishly large that Mauro had said he didn't want a first-class ticket. He was corrected; thought of walking away; thought of David's parents, waiting for him; and resentfully, crossly, with a sense that he was doing the right thing here and it was costing him nearly a hundred pounds, he handed over his bank card, almost hoping that it would be refused. When he had caught the train before, that one time, he had not paid. It had been a Sunday, escaping from the hospital to which David had been taken, and Mauro had correctly calculated that there would be no ticket checkers at work. Then, he had not paid for his ticket; now, on a more serious obligation, he felt he ought to.

His overdraft, in the event, bore the brunt, and he got onto the first train to Bristol, after which he would have to change. He sat down in a seat at a table, but in a moment a family of four came up – overweight, overladen, puffing and morose – and stood, examining their little orange tickets, talking to each other with theatrical bafflement. Eventually, Mauro understood that they wanted him to move; that they for some reason considered the seat he was sitting in to be their seat. The English were strange;

they forced him to move and to recognize his mistake without addressing one word to him, or even looking directly at him. Mauro went on through the train. His instinct had been to sit down in the next empty seat, but now he understood what the small tickets at the back of each seat signified. He went on, from carriage to carriage, as every seat seemed to be taken; reserved, but not taken. Eventually he had come to a carriage, an inhuman, overstuffed, overheated, sweet-smelling carriage, in which no seat was reserved, where people like him who had not planned or reserved were placed. These incompetent planners jostled and shoved, and squashed up next to each other. Mauro wanted to go on; but when he eventually reached the far door, he saw another thicket of white reservations in the carriage to follow. He turned back, and sat down in a seat going backwards, thinking himself lucky. And then the girl in the seat ahead of him answered her phone, and began to talk.

It had been a surprise to get a phone call from David's mother. That day had unravelled in a dreamlike sequence. An ambulance had arrived, and Mauro had been taken downstairs by the policeman to ride after the ambulance in a police car. He had sat in a 'Relatives' Room' for some time – of all that day, he remembered best the apricot and peach shades of that dull room, and the boredom he experienced while sitting there. He had paced around, had counted the flowers on the picture on the wall, had conducted minor experiments with his body – could you place your feet toe-to-toe, so that they formed a straight line? He had emptied and repacked his bag; with some shame, he realized that somebody had found that pretty little enamel bird in his belongings and had removed it. He honestly didn't know why he did these things. That was the sort of behaviour he was supposed to have put a stop to. A nurse had come in, asking if Mauro wanted to phone David's family, but Mauro thought it was best if the hospital did it. Did he have a number? No, he did not; but David would have one, on his mobile phone, in his pocket, no doubt. 'It's really probably best if you call them, if you know them at all,' the nurse

said. 'I know it's difficult, and we will call if you still want us to
. . .' Mauro still wanted them to. At that point, it occurred to
Mauro that, along with his mobile phone, David might still have,
in his pocket, the half-gram of cocaine he had boasted about. When
the nurse had gone to get David's mobile out of his pocket, or
out of the tray bearing the innumerable minor possessions with
which David pouched out his hips like a cud-chewing ruminant,
Mauro yielded to temptation. He left the room, walking swiftly,
and soon came to the front entrance of the hospital. A taxi was
there, into which Mauro stepped sharply, believing in the gifts of
the gods. 'For Roberts?' the driver said unbelievingly, and Mauro
agreed that he was Roberts. 'To the train station?' the driver said,
and Mauro, hefting his weekend bag onto the seat beside him, said
that that was what he had asked for over the phone, wasn't it? He
had got on the first train to Bristol, which he knew was a big city;
he had changed, walking over the platform; he had got on a train
to London, and at London the gates had been left open, and he
had walked out of the station, his bag banging against his knee as
he walked. He hardly thought about David at all, and before he
got on the Underground, he telephoned Christian and asked him
if he was around, and what he was up to, now, this second.

   Now, his train reached Bristol, and he changed, walking
between platforms; he thought of getting a coffee at the little stall
underground, but he was late, there was a queue, and he remembered how much his ticket had cost him. The next train was
smaller, only three carriages, and stopped at ten towns on the
way to Barnstaple. Four or five passengers greeted each other as
old friends; there was none of that resentful silence underneath
a single mobile-phone monologue, and conversations started up.
At Barnstaple he changed again; a small-city urban pride seemed
to mark the station, with its flower tubs and its decorative frescos
of travellers in a Renaissance style. The train to Hanmouth was
waiting at platform one. 'Have you got a ticket for this train, sir?'
a guard said, and he showed him his authorization. In the train,
the passengers all seemed to know each other now, chattering and

waving like a school outing, like a party, like crows on a line, and Mauro felt almost left out. He wondered if he would see those two men again. Not very likely: he wasn't going to stay even one night. As the train went from station to station, leaving the outskirts of Barnstaple behind and reaching stations with a claim to independence, Mauro looked outside, and recognized nothing. He had told David's parents when his series of trains would bring him to Hanmouth. It reached the small station, going over a level crossing with cars and foot passengers waiting on either side, some with dogs looking up excitedly at the great roar of a small suburban train. On the platform was an elaborate piece of topiary: 'Hanmouth' it spelt out, in some sort of hedge material, and waiting there were David's parents. They peered into the carriage as the train came in, but it was easier for Mauro to see them, looking sober, strained, heavy with worry. They were holding each other's hands like children.

'Hello, Mauro,' Catherine said, shaking his hand with a sort of smile.

'Did you have a good journey?' Alec said, and Mauro agreed that he had.

13.

'We can talk tomorrow,' Ahmed Khalil said to Tony, ushering him out of his office and turning the lights out. 'It's a lot to digest, I know, and you'll want to think about your options.'

'I've thought about my options,' Tony said, walking almost backwards before Ahmed. 'I've done little else but think about the prospective future of teaching German in this town, little else for months on end.'

'And now, you'll have the opportunity of teaching Film and Media, too,' Ahmed said. 'Or not. As you prefer. Have a think about it overnight, over the weekend.'

'I'd rather talk about it now,' Tony said.

'That's not possible,' Ahmed said. 'I'm sorry, Tony. That's not possible.'

It was a Thursday night. A few weeks ago, Ahmed had given Kenyon a key to his house – it seemed the sensible thing to do, so that Kenyon could come and go with the minimum of disturbance. Since then, Kenyon had found a way to leave work in London soon after lunch on Thursday. He would say, he told Ahmed, that he had to work at home, and it was true that he arrived with a briefcase with his underwear in it. Ahmed had no idea what Kenyon told his wife; she had never telephoned him, as far as Ahmed knew, when Kenyon was at Ahmed's. Today Ahmed had been kept at work somewhat by this meeting with Tony, after the end of the school day, about the future of German teaching and the need for Tony to find some more specialities to justify his existence. He thought of Kenyon, quite probably already at home in Missouri Avenue, waiting for him, and his pleasure seemed to start from nothing. He unlocked the car door and slid nimbly in.

'Wotcher,' Kenyon said, as Ahmed came through the front door. He wasn't, as once before, lying upstairs in bed – Kenyon was not the sort of person you would expect to do that, and in the end he had had to call downstairs to attract Ahmed's attention, half an hour after Ahmed had come home. He came towards Ahmed, and they kissed; a big, deep, smiling kiss. Kenyon was wearing Ahmed's old leather slippers, Ahmed noticed; it was a great pleasure to Ahmed that he and Kenyon were exactly the same size in almost everything; the same five foot seven, the same size eights, the same thirty-four around the waist and sixteen round the neck, and a pleasure that Kenyon could come into Ahmed's house and comfortably put on his cracked and soft butter-yellow slippers. Once, they had experimentally dressed in each other's clothes; they had expected to be amused, as if at fancy dress, as if at disguise, but in the event they had looked perfectly unremarkable. They just seemed to fit into each other, and had done ever since they had met at adjoining tables in Caffè Nero that time, Kenyon passing the time while Miranda took an extra-mural class. They had started talking, had gone on, had walked in the same direction, and surprisingly had been in bed together only two hours after Ahmed had knocked a glass of water all over Kenyon's shoes. 'It's only you,' Kenyon had said, more than once, explaining his general tendency. 'It only seems to be you, I think.'

'Well, I don't mind that,' Ahmed said. For him it was not just Arthur, as he called Kenyon, almost the only person alive to do so. Or, rather, it had not just been Arthur, in the past. But now it was. He liked his broad face, his puzzled eyes behind the enlarging lenses of the long-sighted, his perpetual schoolboy untidiness, his hair sticking out at the end of the day in all directions, his nice neat little mouth, the dusting of freckles across his wide, white, milky shoulders. He liked him all, in fact. Sometimes Ahmed even looked at Kenyon and thought about the future.

Kenyon looked at Ahmed too; he liked his bemused, open, problem-solving, capable face, the brilliant whites of his eyes and of his teeth, when he smiled, the smooth colour of his cheeks. He wondered what Ahmed was thinking; he seemed pleased to see Kenyon.

'I've only got chicken breasts from M and S,' Ahmed said. 'And a salad. Is that OK?'

'That's fine,' Kenyon said. 'I don't come here for the food. What's up?'

'Oh, the usual,' Ahmed said. 'People being difficult for the sake of it at work. A fourteen-year-old pregnant.'

'Wasn't there a fourteen-year-old pregnant a month back? Is it the same one?'

'No, a different one. It must be catching. And,' Ahmed hurried over this one, 'Faisal's in trouble. My son Faisal.'

'Oh, yes?' Kenyon said. 'Sorry to hear that.' He loosened his tight grip around Ahmed's waist, leant back, inspected Ahmed's face. He didn't give the impression of being particularly concerned.

371

It came to mind that Faisal studied in the faculty where Miranda taught. Kenyon did not want to mention that, or bring it up.

'He calls himself Phil,' Ahmed said. 'Or he used to. I think he might have started saying Faisal again.'

'Nothing serious?' Kenyon said.

'Serious enough,' Ahmed said. 'Let's not talk about him.'

'I've never met him,' Kenyon said. 'Where does he live?'

'A hall of residence, just five minutes' walk from here,' Ahmed said. 'I don't know why. They know their own minds; he didn't want to go on living with his father, though he still brings his washing home. His bedroom's there for him.'

'I'm counting the days,' Kenyon said.

Ahmed looking enquiringly.

'Till Hettie moves out. She's going through a difficult phase.'

He really didn't want to spend time talking about their children, about Faisal and about Hettie. For a moment an absurd fantasy crossed his mind in which the pair of them met, got on, fell in love. A curious-looking double wedding took place in Kenyon's mind.

Ahmed's house was a Victorian terrace, on three floors, the downstairs window bellying out over a pocket-handkerchief of earth and the bald remains of neglected shrubs. The house, on the other hand, was neat, new-furnished and a touch anonymous; Kenyon had sometimes wondered that there was hardly anything identifiable as coming from Pakistan in the house, but of course Ahmed had never been there, was born in London in the late 1960s, and since what sounded like a painful and humiliating divorce, he and his son had lived a completely English life, eating Marks & Spencer ready meals on Habitat furniture. There might be an aspect of deliberate separation in this, Kenyon believed, but he knew many professional people like this, even in India and Africa, who had, apparently, an enthusiasm for stripping their circumstances of anything that could locate them within a thousand miles of any particular place. Ahmed's surroundings, his house, his décor, the food he ate, the way he talked and dressed, were studiedly anonymous and unspecific. Really, though, it was not the smooth, unspecific, interchangeable professional in Ahmed that Kenyon was drawn to and liked so much. He put it no more strongly than that.

Now, after these months, he knew Ahmed's house from top to bottom, even the preserved bedroom of Faisal. Ahmed must have forgotten that he had shown him that, too, the first time he came here. Kenyon now took the plastic bag from Ahmed's hands, placing it on the floor in the hallway. Ahmed, in his kindness, had bought a bottle of wine – Ahmed did not drink, and had no real insight into it beyond spending more than seven, less than ten pounds on a bottle, often bringing a heavy sparkling Australian red to drink with fish, or cava to accompany a beef pie. He would sit and watch Kenyon drink it, steadily, politely, appreciatively, and Kenyon had never made a suggestion about the wine next time, or wanted to. Now he took Ahmed's hands in his own, right in left and left in right. He kissed Ahmed, and Ahmed's lips stayed fastened on his own as he walked backwards up the stairs; whether Kenyon was leading him backwards, whether Ahmed was following him, neither could have said, and they were both thinking, oddly, the same thing: what it would be like to be there, walking forwards or backwards on the stairs, kissing the person who was now kissing them. Kenyon thought what it would be like to be Ahmed, kissing Kenyon, and Ahmed thought what it would be like to be Kenyon, kissing Ahmed. They happily envied each other; and quite soon, bumping into tables and chairs and even picture frames on the way, their eyes closed, they came to Ahmed's neat bedroom, and fell like one body onto Ahmed's bed.

14.

The Wolf Walk, on maps, extended upwards out of Hanmouth like a finger pointing to the heavens. The Strand petered out in a last flourish of Dutch houses, a Queen Anne customs house and a 1930s villa, now expensively restored by the hedge-fund abstractionist with steel, frosted glass and a double ash door on a central pivot. Then the road turned left, and a small cobbled jetty led the walker onwards: to the Wolf Walk.

It ran alongside a sloping harbour wall of cemented stone, almost five feet high; over the wall, there was a neglected pear orchard, which could not be expected to do well in the prevailing atmosphere of salt and mud. No one knew who that belonged to. The Wolf Walk itself was an almost straight path five feet wide, edging the estuary. Wading birds, coots, gulls, ducks picked their way along the velvety mud, ignoring people on the Wolf Walk, digging with their bills for estuary worms and grubs, taking short runs at each other to bully enemies off a fat patch. People said on a fine day they could come down here and watch them birds for hours. They were comical, weren't they, people said. It was a good place to sit and watch.

Along the half-mile stretch of the Wolf Walk five solid benches had been placed, dedicated and screwed down after an unfortunate incident with a large group of drunk students who had thrown one bench into the estuary. The jetty by the quay was a more popular place for the dedication of benches, and they fairly lined up, arm to arm, there. The Wolf Walk was more of a stride, as they said. Perhaps it would be beyond the reach of frail old people in their last days, when they might be asking sons and daughters if, when they were gone, they would put up a bench with their names on it. There were five such benches, dedicated to Marjorie, to Alan and Queeny, 'who loved this place', and two other old people.

The one everyone remembered was to Tracy Wood, at the very far end of the Wolf Walk, where the long finger on the map curved slightly and the path came to an end, pointing northwards out to the mouth of the estuary, the Bristol Channel and the open sea. The only options here were to turn back, or to turn left to the dull bird sanctuary where no one ever went. Here, at the turn, the setting sun could be heavenly, with the clouds at sunset gathering about a salmon-coloured light, a great draw to photographers and watercolourists. Here was Tracy Wood's bench, which people remembered because it was to a girl who had died at thirteen, in 1978, with no other information. It was said that her family must have moved out of the area many years ago. Information differed as to who she was, how she had died, what her story was. The population of Hanmouth, despite what it believed about itself, was too transient to remember a dead girl like that for thirty years. Not a single house on the Strand was still lived in by the person who had lived there in 1978. But still, sooner or later, every inhabitant of Hanmouth would walk right to the end of the Wolf Walk, taking note of the good long lives the other people had lived who were commemorated by benches, and then see Tracy Wood's: she had died at thirteen or perhaps even twelve. The dates did not specify anything beyond years. They would turn to their companions and say the same thing: 'How awfully sad.' But she had the most beautiful view, the one right at the end of the Wolf Walk.

No one knew why it was called the Wolf Walk. There was a romantic tale, and a blunt, boring explanation. The blunt, boring explanation was that it had not, originally, been 'Wolf' at all, but had been corrupted from its original, which was Wharf Walk. The Dutch merchants who had settled here and developed it as a small port and prosperous little town had spoken much as Dutch people speak today, with a pronounced *r*, even in the middle of words – 'an intermediate *r*', the amateur historian who worked in the bookshop would explain, as he had looked into it. A Dutchman saying 'Wharrrf', deep in the back of his throat, would to an Englishman sound very like someone saying 'Wolf', and the name was corrupted. Nothing so very remarkable: it was the walk to the wharf.

But others objected that the wharf was not there, and never had been, and that if the Dutch rolled and made a meal of their intermediate *r*s, then so did the men of Devon – rather famously so, in fact. And it was rather odd that they would not understand a word like 'wharf', which they heard every day of their lives, and would mistake it for the name of an animal none of them would ever have seen. 'Those romantic explanations,' the amateur historian who worked in the bookshop would say, 'are always wrong. Always. Take it from me. If there's a story attached to a name, a place name, then without the slightest doubt, the story was made up some time in the nineteenth century. Do you know,' he went on, in a practised way, 'the story of how the word "posh" came to be? An interesting example, and also quite wrong.'

His listeners would do their job and listen, impressed. But they liked the story, which, too, was told in the amateur historian's self-published little account of Hanmouth, sold in the bookshop – he knew and half respected his audience, after all. They read it, or heard it, and told it again.

Some time ago – well, there must have been kings and queens and therefore a date, but was it bad King John, or Richard the Lionheart, or Alfred the Great? – but a very long time ago, England was a great deal more wooded than it is now. If you look over the estuary, towards the castle, you'll see a patch of forest. That's not a planted forest, not one grown in the last fifty years for paper, but the last scrap of an ancient forest. Round here, round where Hanmouth is, it was once all forest. If you went into the forest and lost your way, you'd maybe never come out again. Nowadays, of course, there's nothing in the forest bigger than foxes and the odd grumpy badger, but years ago – at this time – there were other things. There were bears living in there – they got fat, the bears, on honey from the bees. And there was one old grey wolf.

Hanmouth was here, then. It was smaller and there wasn't a ring-road or any Dutch houses or any little jewellers' shops on the Fore street. But there was a church – not the church on the spit we've got now, that's only Victorian, but on the same place, there was a church. And there was a quay, because there's been a quay and there's been trade in Hanmouth as long as there's been

Hanmouth. The quay came before anything else. There was a castle – the lords over there, we know they were there before the Conqueror, because one of them married one of the Conqueror's knight's daughters. He was clever, the lord, like that, the only one who ever did that. And he hung on to his lands and built the first castle that ever stood there on the ridge. And there were houses – dwellings, huts, whatever they might have been. Nobody knows what they would have looked like.

The old grey wolf lived in the forest. He always had. He went back beyond the memory of even the oldest people who lived in what would one day be named Hanmouth. He hunted around half of the county, never coming far out of the forest in his hunt. He lived on small animals and the infants of larger animals; he lived on chickens and rabbits and red squirrels. 'Were there rabbits as long ago as that?' a well-informed listener might say, going on to suggest that he supposed there were potatoes and tobacco in the villagers' gardens, too. 'Of course there were rabbits,' the teller would say. 'There's always been rabbits in England.'

Only very occasionally, in the middle of a winter that froze the ground and the estuary to the same white hardness, did the wolf venture out into the little huddled settlements, and seize, if he could, a baby. The villagers accepted this, more or less. It was foolish not to guard a baby against the wolf, but the wolf had to eat too. But one year, the spring came, and a mother set her baby out in its swaddling in the sun, and the wolf came for it. A high thin scream, quickly silenced; the great haunches of the wolf sidling off into the forests where it never grew light.

The lord said that the wolf had got a taste for human flesh above the usual diet the abundance of the forest provided, and it must be hunted down. They set out, with torches and improvised weapons. They blocked off the wolf's known runs; the lord and his cronies, they mounted on their horses, three hands smaller than any hunter today, and at the end of the day, the wolf, tired, hungry, and bewildered with rage, found himself just there, where the Strand now runs out, and the path goes on, up towards the mouth of the estuary and the open sea. That path, it had always been there, and it never had a name, until the wolf ran from the hunters, ran along the Wolf Walk. It came to an end, and there was nowhere for the wolf to go; the orchard wall to one side, the estuary on the other, and it was at its fullest. There were rushes then, wild rushes, and the wolf plunged into them to escape the fall of arrows hailing down on him. 'After him,' the lord would have said, but before the serfs and the villeins could jump into the mud and the rushes, they all saw an astounding thing: the wolf running, his head held low and pointed, across the mud flats towards the other side of the estuary, and then, skimming across like a flat stone that's thrown on a lake, across the surface of the estuary itself, across the water. They didn't follow him then; their bows, they let drop, and watched the wolf go. He disappeared into the rushes on the far bank, and they watched them ruffle and move as if with a wind, and then he was into the forest, and lost to them. They watched the wolf go, with their bows lowered. A sort of respect. That is the story of the Wolf Walk, the walk the wolf took. And what happened to the wolf? people would ask. Well, it went back into the forest, and occasionally stole a baby, just as before, but the people of Hanmouth never went after it again, and it died at a good old age. One of the last wolves in the west of England, and after that, the path that goes down to the very end, it has always been called the Wolf Walk. And why shouldn't it be true?

15.

At the end of the Wolf Walk, on Tracy Wood's bench, three people sat. It must be one of the last fine days of summer – an Indian summer, everyone said. Mauro had thought of making a comment on Tracy Wood's bench, the same one that everyone always made, but he saw just in time that it would not be a good idea. Catherine had cried when he had embraced her, on the railway platform; she had cried again in the flat, as they were sitting having a cup of coffee. A walk had been suggested, and Mauro had taken them up on it. He felt that in the open air, he could escape any suggestion that he should stay the night. The thought came to him that he could, perhaps, make an excuse once they had had their conversation out here. He need not, perhaps, even go back to their flat, but just say goodbye here, and go back to the train. It seemed bizarre to travel for two and a half hours, spend half an hour with David's parents, and then go back again, but – Mauro's thoughts shuffled rather – nothing, no effort was too much for Catherine and Alec. He didn't mind coming down one bit. But all that would be wasted if he mentioned Tracy Wood, dead at thirteen in 1978 and a bench put up to her. Catherine would cry for a third time, and his departure would be put off for an hour at least.

'It's really lovely here,' Mauro said, referring to the elaborate view, out to sea and over a wooded slope on the other side of the estuary.

'It is nice,' Catherine said. 'Sometimes I come down here at twilight – you can see the lights of the towns on the other side. Look . . .'

She gestured at the birds, gathering now at their feet. They seemed to be expecting something, all looking upwards in their callous way.

'We should have brought some bread,' Alec said quietly. 'They like it better when it's wet, the ducks. After a dry spell, there's not much for them to eat, I suppose.'

Mauro felt in his pockets, as if he might have some food there to offer the ducks. But he had nothing to offer anyone; just chewing gum.

'I'm sorry I haven't been down before,' he said impulsively. 'I'm sorry I couldn't come to the funeral.'

'Well,' Catherine said. 'Well, we understand. It was really very hard for everyone, that day. I don't think it's for us to say what you should do.'

'I should have come,' Mauro said.

'It doesn't matter,' Alec said. 'We're glad you've come down.'

Mauro looked at him out of the corner of his eye. He never felt that Alec liked him in the slightest – actually, he had felt from something or other David had said during that argument in the car that Alec was on to him, didn't think him at all authentic. In his dry way, Alec had now said something authentic. He wondered why he had. Mauro saw, too, that Alec's face was thinner, that whatever he had been through in the last few months had stripped the flesh from his face and handed him his grey old age.

'You see,' Catherine said, 'we don't know so many people down here. We only moved a year ago, after all. We have friends.'

'We have friends,' Alec said.

'But, of course, none of them knew David,' Catherine said. 'It's hard to talk to them about David.'

'So we're glad you've come down,' Alec said again.

'That's all right,' Mauro said. He was, after all, a good person. He had come down here for no reason of gain; he was a link for them with their dead son, and he could provide that, he thought.

'Do you think –' Catherine said, and now she was surely going to cry again '– do you think David was happy? I mean in general.'

'You don't think he was?' Mauro said. 'I mean – what do you think?'

'It was the way he was found,' Alec said. 'That was a shock. That didn't seem like a happy person, happy in general. It's been hard for us.'

'Maybe I think you don't have to think about that, not too much,' Mauro said, aghast. He saw how implicated he was in these details.

'We try not to,' Catherine said. 'But I can't help wondering whether David was happy or not, and if we did enough for him.'

'Perhaps some people don't have the gift, the talent, for being happy,' Mauro said. 'I'm sure you did enough for him, you did everything you could for him. Maybe it was just in him, he couldn't be happy, whatever you two did.'

'No,' Catherine said. 'When I said "we", I didn't mean just me and Alec – I meant you as well. Don't you ever wonder that?'

Mauro hesitated. He felt so little involved in this. And that was unfair – if she knew that he was not drawn to David by desire or, much, by liking, she would surely see how enormously unselfish he, Mauro, had been from beginning to end. David's search for happiness had dragged him in, and somehow turned him into David, with all the demands and exhaustion that misery made of you. For no very good reason, Sumac came to mind, and the fact that he had phoned in sick this morning, from Paddington station, ignoring the telephone ringing back all the way to Hanmouth. He just couldn't have stood to go in there today, not after what Oswald Bond had said to him yesterday. He knew he was going to get the sack when he went back there tomorrow. That was David's fault; by involving himself in David's concerns and by trying to make an effort, he had somehow dragged himself down into the circumstances of David's life, as if to take his place. Mauro thought about it: he was overwhelmed with a sense of his own selflessness.

'I tried, I think,' Mauro said. 'I think he was happy for a time, with me. I don't know. I would have tried to make him happy, I would.'

'That's nice to hear,' Catherine said, but Mauro did not know what else he could have said. 'Maybe he didn't have a gift for happiness, like you say. He was quite an unhappy little boy, even. I don't know what else we could have done.'

'Me, I don't know, too,' Mauro said.

'We've been dealing with all the business,' Alec said, quite briskly. 'There's a surprising amount to get through, what with the inquest and winding up David's affairs – of course, he hadn't set his affairs in order. He had no reason to at his time of life, but that made a little more work for us, as you can imagine. We've sold his flat in St Albans – we thought about it, but it seemed the right thing to do, when the property market seems to have peaked and just started a downward slide. We've put all his stuff into storage for the moment.'

'We paid some removers to do it,' Catherine said. 'I honestly didn't feel I wanted to deal with it. But it's all in storage, all in boxes.'

'If there was anything that you wanted – something to remind you of David – anything at all . . .' Alec said.

Mauro thought: he had no idea. He had never been to David's flat in St Albans. He had no idea what was there, what his furniture was like, whether there were ornaments or pictures. All he knew was what he saw David in. For a moment he thought about asking them if he could have David's car, but something suggested to him that that would not do as a keepsake. Surely David had had a CD player, a television, a sofa. But then he saw that he had better play safe. 'There was a belt he used to wear,' Mauro said. 'It was a black belt – he always wore it. And there was a silver bangle, too. I often think of him wearing that.'

Catherine and Alec visibly relaxed. They shared a look. 'That's easily done,' Alec said. 'If that's all you want, of course.'

'I can see you only want something to remember him by,' Catherine said.

'Yes, just that,' Mauro said, lit up by his own selfless nobility. Just a black belt and a silver bangle; that would do, that would be the request of someone of great style and dignity. And he remembered that nobody seemed to know about the £2,400 David had lent him.

'We've just sold the flat in St Albans, as I say,' Alec said. 'It's not quite come through yet, but once the authorities have done their worst with it, there will be something. David didn't leave a will, you know, so I'm afraid it all comes back to us as his next of kin.'

'That's all right,' Mauro said, and again that look was exchanged between Catherine and Alec.

'We don't think it's quite fair,' Catherine said. 'We've been talking about it, and we think that we'd like to give you a present. After all, you were David's friend at the end of his life, and you might expect . . .' She trailed off.

'We thought ten thousand pounds,' Alec said bluntly.

Mauro was a Roman, and at this, a Roman response came: 'That's all right,' Mauro said. 'I don't want any money. To remember David – just his belt, and his silver bangle.'

Catherine and Alec both breathed out; a heavy, relieved breath, and Mauro immediately thought of withdrawing his noble statement. I don't want any money, he had said, I don't want any – that nobility had risen up from somewhere, he had no idea where, and turned down ten thousand pounds. He could have done anything with that. Just at that exact moment, surprised by a statement of money, the temptations of nobility, of selfishness, had struck him, and there had been no resisting them. Now it was Mauro who wanted to cry, to say, 'No, I was only joking,' or even 'You insult me with your ten thousand – I want fifty thousand.' But it was all impossible, and he would have to live with his terrible unaccountable whim.

'We've got the belt and the bangle, I know,' Catherine said. 'If it's the ones you meant. He was wearing them at the end. If you come back, we can wrap them up and give them to you now.'

'No,' Mauro said. 'I think I'd like to go home now.'

'I know,' Alec said. He actually reached around Mauro, sitting hunched on the bench, as if to embrace him, but instead clapped him awkwardly between his shoulder-blades. 'It takes it out of you, all this.'

'We'd like you to have this, too,' Catherine said, and from her bag she produced a paperback book. She gave it to Mauro who, puzzled, took it from her. 'It was the first thing – the very first thing – David wrote. In his job, you know. I thought you would like to have it.'

'Yes,' Mauro said, turning it over, not understanding in the least. What had Mr Poppers written? When had he written a book? But it did not have David's name on the cover, and Mauro didn't feel he could enquire any further. 'I'm very happy to have this,' he said in the end, though the book was an ugly thing, bright pink and with an amateurish drawing of a sort of landscape. 'Thank you.'

'Do stay in touch,' Alec said, and now the pair of them got to their feet. 'Shall we walk you to the station? You did say you wanted to go home, didn't you?'

'This is called the Wolf Walk,' Catherine said. 'There's an interesting story behind the name, I believe.'

They were just in time for the half-hourly train into Barnstaple, and they waved him off. His face at the train window had a puzzled aspect. Theirs, they suspected, a relieved and unburdened one. They stood and watched until the train was quite round the wooded bend.

'That's one thing,' Alec said. 'They didn't marry, or anything like that.'

'No,' Catherine said. 'I don't know why you thought they might have, but they hadn't. And he doesn't want anything from us.'

'That's a relief,' Alec said. 'I couldn't have borne any more engagement with the legal profession.'

'I know,' Catherine said, and as the level crossing raised, she took his hand in hers, and they walked down the hill homewards, two small figures in a posture of shyness.

16.

In the train to Bristol, Mauro looked at the book. He had not read a book from beginning to end since he was at school. He had no idea Mr Poppers had written one at all. He turned the ugly object over, and read what was written on the back cover.

'One day,' he read, 'hope and love enter your life, with a special smiling face which seems meant just for you. And you know that happiness is your destiny, embodied in the sweet loving expression of someone who adores you. Maybe they were waiting for love and saw it in your face too. Like two beautiful people looking through a window at each other, sometimes they think it is a mirror. Love is the only thing which matters in this world, and we make it for ourselves by not thinking of ourselves, but of that special smiling face which maybe hasn't come along yet. And love is what survives of us, somewhere, in the special magical garden after rain we call our heart.'

Mauro read it from beginning to end twice. It seemed to make no sense at all. Then he felt in his pocket, got out his wallet, and saw that he had a ten-pound note. Shortly, there was an announcement that the buffet car was open for the sale of snacks, sandwiches, hot and cold drinks and light refreshments. Mauro thought he would risk an English cup of coffee.

17.

All summer, since the disappearance, it had been hot and dry – a proper picnic summer, people said, and once or twice they did take a picnic out, with a sense of occasion. A barbecue summer, the Met Office said, and that was more like it; the blue smoke of burning pigs' meat, the crack and ear-fizz of bottles and glasses being dropped and smashed hung over the patched-up gardens of Barnstaple all summer long. The flesh of Hanmouth was given an outing; and whether in gentlemanly knee-lengths with sandals and a short-sleeved shirt, or – their sons – cut-offs and flip-flops, or spaghetti-string tops, cystitis-tight shorts and high-heeled shoes, the flesh of Hanmouth and Barnstaple flushed angry red before subsiding into a country brown, a ploughman's tan.

The flesh of the country grew brown, too; the moors a feeble beige, a dried-out dead colour. On his way to London at the bookends of the week, Kenyon noticed that the chalk horse at the midpoint of the journey had almost disappeared, so drab and pale had the turf it was cut in become.

The crops wilted and browned; those who fancied themselves country folk talked gravely of the consequences of this dry spell.

People had known hotter summers, and at the end of August, around the Brigadier's funeral, there was a sudden drop in temperature, which seemed like the beginning of autumn. But it had not rained, and the temperature had crept up again for a last burst, an Indian summer, mid-September. Only now it rained.

The clouds swept up in a great mass from the Atlantic, black-bellied and angry, and they hit something in the air – the Met Office could have explained what. First some fat drops, hitting the dust on the street, and then the collapse of the skies; girls ran through it, nothing to shelter under but their handbags. A single flash, somewhere over the castle, and simultaneously a great explosion of thunder, like a bomb going off, people said.

What a treat for the farmers, the husbands of Hanmouth observed, hurrying inside, carrying the Sunday papers from the garden. There was a wash of beautiful fragrance from field, park and garden that had been locked up for months; a wash of fragrance, too, from the estuary, trickling along at the bottom of its course. In less than half an hour, the sloping streets of Hanmouth were bordered by rivulets, fast becoming brooks, a twist of bright water running down to the drains and the earth.

What a treat for the farmers, the husbands of Hanmouth said again, and nobody rushed to get the washing in; that was all done in tumble-driers these days, even in an Indian summer.

18.

'I suppose the farmers will be glad of it,' John Calvin said, in their sitting room, reading the paper. Laura agreed that they would. He was sitting reading the *Observer* with one sock off, occasionally giving the sole of his foot a small poke with the end of his crossword pencil – he suffered, always had, from athlete's foot, a positive martyr to it. Laura was at her Sunday-morning task of ironing Calvin's shirts. He liked to have them ironed and

ready, twelve of them, on Monday morning, for the week ahead
– a daytime shirt and an evening shirt. After the shirts, there were
the trousers to put a crease in, his underpants to iron, his handkerchiefs, and then his socks.

'Ooh, arr,' Calvin said, in an uncommitted way. 'It's terrible,
this collapse in house prices, Laura.'

'Really?' Laura said.

'It says here, house prices have come down twenty per cent in
a year. Twenty per cent!'

'Have we lost money on our house, John?' Laura said.

'No, not yet,' John said. 'It's got a long way to fall before that
happens, Laura.'

'Oh, good,' Laura said. 'Because I would really worry about
that.'

The two of them remained absorbed in their different tasks for
a minute; John Calvin reading about house prices, and Laura
Calvin finishing the last of her husband's shirts.

'I think it may be time for Neighbourhood Watch, Laura,' John
said.

Laura set down her iron with a bang, point upwards. 'I thought
Neighbourhood Watch was on Tuesday nights, John.'

'It usually is, Laura,' John Calvin said. 'But it isn't always.
Today Neighbourhood Watch is on a Sunday.'

'People will be confused,' Laura said. 'The members of Neighbourhood Watch. They won't know to come, will they?'

'Oh, yes,' Calvin said. He bent down, picked up his sock,
turned it inside out and put it on again. 'They're all coming.
They're all very excited and interested.'

'Well, I can only do biscuits,' Laura said. 'I haven't made
anything else. There are those walnut biscuits I made yesterday,
and there's a packet of chocolate Hobnobs.'

'I thought you made a lemon drizzle cake on Friday, Laura,'
John Calvin said. 'I distinctly remember you saying so, and we
had a piece each, yesterday, at our morning coffee. I told you I
thought it was delicious and moist. Did we finish that?'

'No, John,' Laura said. 'You're right. There is some lemon drizzle cake. They can have that.'

'Mrs McGillicuddy from the dairy I happen to know especially likes lemon drizzle cake,' John Calvin said. 'And Signor Abbagataglia, the pizza chef, often brings a cake typical of his native Sicily to pass round. Poor Dr "Taff" Williams has been put on a strict diet by his new young wife, Blodwen, to get his blood pressure down.'

'Fancy him not worrying about that sooner!' Laura Calvin said. She bent down and unplugged the iron, set it down on a granite square. She carried the washing through to the kitchen, returned and started to fold up the ironing-board. 'And him a GP, too.'

'So he won't be eating anything at all, Laura,' John Calvin said. 'Though I have known him to sneak a bite when Blodwen was not in the room. "Nary a word, boyo," he said to me on one occasion, and winked. And then I know Mrs Patel will definitely be here, late as usual in her comical way. I am sure she will bustle into the room, fifteen minutes late, demand that we start again from the beginning of the agenda, and misunderstand almost everything while eating the rest of the lemon drizzle cake. She is really too fat, Mrs Patel is, with the sedentary life she leads.'

'Would you call Mrs Patel fat, John?' Laura asked. 'I would not have thought she was as fat even as Dr "Taff" Williams.'

'Yes,' John Calvin said. 'Yes, she is really quite definitely fat. Most people would describe that as her defining characteristic.'

He picked up the newspaper again, flapping it open in a decisive way.

'It's simply pouring it down,' Laura said. 'Are you sure that they are going to want to come out in this weather?'

'We airrn't made oot of sugar, hinny,' John Calvin said, from behind the newspaper, imitating Mrs McGillicuddy from the dairy's voice.

'I wondered whether it might not be more convenient for everyone to hold it on Tuesday night,' Laura said. 'Then I could make some really nice canapés, and I don't believe there's any sherry in the house to offer them.'

John Calvin threw down his newspaper. 'No, Laura,' he said. 'Neighbourhood Watch is happening this morning. In fact, it's happening now. Look, there's Signor Abbagataglia. I'm so glad he managed to get time off from the pizza parlour.'

Outside, through the window, it was Sam and his dog Stanley; they were rushing home through the rain, as fast as either of them could manage. But Laura, her ironing done and out of sight, quickly laid out six plates around the pale oak dining-table, where John liked to hold his Neighbourhood Watch meetings.

'Here is Signor Abbagataglia,' Laura said, without opening the front door – they didn't go that far, but making a gesture.

'Beh – iz-a luvverly to see-a you,' John Calvin said. 'Beh, cannot-a believe-a the rain. Rain-a, rain-a, go away, we say inna my country. And-a the beautiful Laura—'

A certain amount of frank kissing then happened. Signor Abbagataglia was a terrible flirt, unable to restrain his libido or his desire when he saw Laura. But everyone accepted that. 'And Mrs McGillicuddy – how lovely to see you, Morag – and Dr "Taff" Williams. Now, Dr "Taff", I know dear Blodwen is keeping you on a strict diet, so we won't tempt you with any of those delicious little sweet things you like so much.

'Or maybe just the one it is, boyo, if my drift you are getting it is, Mrs C,' John Calvin said, pulling out Dr "Taff" Williams's chair. Laura went into the kitchen, fetched the two-thirds remainder of the lemon drizzle cake, and the walnut biscuits she had made yesterday. She wished she had got round to the choc-olate and star-anise brownies she'd read about in yesterday's *Guardian*.

'And, och, who else are we expecting the day, laddie? See's yon cookie, Laura,' John Calvin said, from behind Morag McGilli-cuddy's chair.

'And who else would it be but Mrs Patel?' he went on in his own voice. 'Mrs Patel, has she ever arrived on time for anything, in her entire life? Dear old Mrs Patel – where would we be without her?'

The company all laughed, except for Laura, who was wondering whether she had forgotten anything. 'I'll bring the tea in a moment, John,' she said. He gave her a warning glance. 'Everyone,' she said.

'I think we *won't* wait for Mrs Patel,' John Calvin said, as he did at every Neighbourhood Watch meeting. 'Mrs McGillicuddy – Dr "Taff" Williams – Signor Aggabatablia, I mean Abbagataglia – I *will* get your name right one of these days, I really will! – do sit down, one and all. There's a lot for us to get through today. Neighbourhood Watch. Neighbourhood Watch . . .' and he went on rearranging the papers that were always kept at the end of the pale oak dining-table in a pile. 'Yes. Well. As I promised,' John Calvin said to the empty table, 'I did meet with the local constabulary, on everyone's behalf.'

20.

Kenyon stood by the cashpoint machine on Hanmouth Fore street, and fed his card in. He was sheltering under an umbrella: it had been raining steadily, sweetly, all day. He entered his four-digit security code, and pressed the button for cash withdrawal. He indicated that he would like a hundred pounds – it was Sunday night, and he would need some cash in the morning, when he went to London.

The machine made an electronic murmur, and then produced a message: 'INSUFFICIENT FUNDS', it said. Kenyon looked at it, with a flush of heat all over his head. It was the ninth day of the month. This was impossible. But then he saw how very possible it was. The card was returned to him, and he performed the same cycle, this time asking for a mere fifty pounds. There was the same noise, and it again produced the message: 'INSUF-

FICIENT FUNDS'. There was really no point in trying the credit card – he knew that was at its absolute limit, or somewhat beyond. The letters from Barclaycard he had taken to placing unopened in his briefcase, and disposing of in his office shredder without even reading them. He told himself that they were probably circulars, anyway, of no interest. But he did not believe that.

What was it all spent on? Nothing. Just a place to live, eating out when Miranda didn't want to cook, the occasional trip to the theatre or to the cinema, the occasional painting, three times a year a holiday, and then there were clothes, bills, things like that. You couldn't live without any of that, you just couldn't. Miranda earned £47,000 a year: he earned £62,000 a year, and the pair of them had no money at all. It all went on the gigantic mortgage. The card was returned to him, and once more he typed in his security code, indicated he wanted to withdraw some money, and typed in ten pounds. The message came back, but a different one: 'SORRY THIS MACHINE ONLY HOLDS £20 NOTES. DO YOU WISH TO REQUEST A SUM AVAILABLE IN £20 NOTES?' Kenyon agreed that he did, and asked for twenty pounds. There was a small solitary noise of consideration from within the machine, and then, amazingly, it produced a twenty-pound note, and thanked him for his custom. That was it, then: Kenyon, at this moment, had somewhere between twenty and forty-nine pounds in his bank account, or rather, his bank was prepared to lend him a further sum, between twenty and forty-nine pounds. Some years ago, a person would be allowed to remove twenty pounds if he had twenty pounds; now, a person would be allowed to remove twenty pounds if that was the sum remaining in his many-thousands overdraft facility, which in any case Kenyon had no recollection of ever requesting. 'Retrench, retrench, retrench,' Kenyon said to himself as he turned back towards his house, his impossible million-pound house with the £600,000 mortgage on it. He greeted a couple he knew, also out walking under umbrellas: it was the new couple. Their names – she was Catherine, he remembered. But they did not stop to speak to him beyond a brief greeting. Miranda would lend him some money. She would have to. After all, he'd lent her three hundred pounds at the end of September, to tide her over.

21.

Each polished surface in the sitting room on the first floor was a still life; each painting on the wall was also a still life. On the good antique walnut surfaces of the side tables, the low glass coffee-table, a modern 1960s console under a Mary Fedden, an arrangement had been placed. They were unchanging. On the walnut table by the side of the sofa, there was an enamel snuffbox, a 'netsuke toggle', as Billa referred to it, of an octopus embroiled in a struggle with a crab, and a brownish sort of ashtray, as well as an occasional light; on the console table there was a huge Swedish vase and what Billa recognized her guests would mostly consider a macabre object, a horse's hoof half-encased in silver filigree, said to be the relic of the last cavalry charge Tom's regiment ever made. Even on the coffee-table, the picture-books changed from time to time, but their general arrangement never; Billa went up to London from time to time, saw an exhibition every so often, came back and put the catalogue in the place that the catalogues had always been, next to another ashtray, a half conch shell rimmed, again, with silver. Neither Billa nor Tom had ever smoked, and their guests did not – had not – either; it would not, however, have suited them to be considered a non-smoking house.

'I went to this,' Sylvie said, picking up an exhibition catalogue. It was of Matisse and Picasso. She opened it. 'I loved this show. God, was it as long ago as that – four years?'

'That must have been the last thing we went to,' Billa said. 'Kitty and I, we used to be rather good at getting up to town, going round the shops, taking in things like that.'

In fact, she had very little memory of the exhibition. It had for four years been sitting, in book form, on her coffee-table, a trophy brought back and then ignored. She had retained almost nothing of the exhibition itself, only enough to tell Tom a few things, pass on some impressions to Miranda and Sam and anyone else who might be polite enough to show an interest, and then she had forgotten about it.

'Don't you go?' Billa said. 'You must head up to London, surely. To see art, I mean.'

Sylvie paused with her coffee cup halfway to her lips; blew judiciously on it; lifted it slightly, scraping it on the edge of the saucer, then poured the residue that had slopped into the saucer back into the cup.

'No,' she said eventually. 'No, I don't. Not if I can really help it. I know I should. I'm terribly lazy. Do you mind if I have a cigarette? I'm simply dying for one.'

'Not at all. Don't you need to keep up with stuff?' Billa said.

'Keep up? You mean what everyone else is doing? No, I don't feel that need. You can get ideas anywhere.'

Billa, who believed that Sylvie's art extended only to cutting men's parts out of dirty magazines and pasting them on canvas, said nothing to this. Her friendship with Sylvie had developed into cups of coffee on the mornings when Sylvie wasn't teaching in Barnstaple, and, once or twice, a glass of wine in the early evening. Tom had formerly looked after the wine, and he'd done it well; there was an enormous amount down there under the stairs, it seemed to Billa, and some of it, she believed complacently, was really rather good. She knew nothing about wine, except that if one of Tom's bottles were covered in dust, it was probably a valuable one. He had never encouraged her to fetch a bottle; that had always been his job, and he could take a surprisingly long time about it, weighing the claims of this and that. Now that he was dead – Billa's unaccommodating formula to herself – Billa would just go down, fetch up a bottle of red or of white, open it, and drink some of it with Sylvie. 'This is really delicious,'

Sylvie said once or twice, startling Billa, to whom 'delicious' was more likely to refer to food, even to the bowl of peanuts than to a glass of wine. One day soon, she would get in someone who knew about this stuff, and probably offload some of the best bottles. She had to admit, she didn't really appreciate Tom's collection.

She appreciated Sylvie, though. She was the only visitor she had, these days, who arrived without bearing some kind of food-stuff, usually handmade, for Billa to heat up. At the first, there had been so much more than Billa could reasonably get through that she found herself eating heavy lasagnes, shepherd's pies, moussakas, fish pies and pots of stews at lunchtime and supper-time; the donators would always want their dishes back, so one couldn't simply bung them in the freezer. The cakes and biscuits could be put on one side, but fewer people thought that would be what Billa would want or need. They thought, evidently, that she would not be up to the challenge of making a pie, and yet would welcome a made dish like that. Like W.B. Yeats and his nine bean-rows, Billa suffered under a terrible and exhausting glut of layered savoury dishes. Her fridge and pantry looked like a horizontal, clingfilmed archive.

Sylvie had arrived, once, with a packet of tea – evidently quite nice tea – and that had been that. They had drunk the tea, commented on its deliciousness, and got stuck into one of Kitty's coffee cakes. Not so delicious: made with coffee essence, evidently, and not with coffee. Kitty's cooking had never quite moved on from the style she had learnt as a girl, in the 1960s. Billa and Sylvie had thoroughly dissected it at the time: on the other hand, they had also eaten the cake.

Sylvie was relaxing company, flopping down on the sofa and talking over this and that. She hadn't known Tom, and that was all to the good.

'What news of Tony?' Billa said jauntily. Outside, there was the clatter of a ladder against the wall – the window cleaner, she expected.

'Ah, Tony,' Sylvie said. 'Counting the days. I told him for the fifth time at least that he ought to be finding somewhere else to live. He seemed surprised. I don't know why. I want my house to myself again. On top of that, I hear he's being made to retrain and teach media and film. No call for German, these days. He's not very happy about that.'

'Can you teach media and film? Oh, making it, you mean.'

'No, just watching it. And then talking about it afterwards. Analysing it, you know.'

'I see,' Billa said. She was determined not to be an old stick about these things. 'I think I recognized him in someone on the Wolf Walk the other morning. Does he have a—'

There was a sharp high noise very close at hand, outside the house, exactly like a dentist's drill, amplified. Someone was drilling into the brick of the house.

'Having work done?' Sylvie said.

'No, not at all,' Billa said. 'I wonder – what in the world –'

They went to the window at the front of the house, and there, at the top of a grey steel ladder and effectively just by them, was a man in overalls and goggles, applying a drill to Billa's brickwork. She rapped on the window; he stopped, and amiably smiled at her, raising the drill like a pistol, in some sort of greeting.

'What on earth's he doing?' Sylvie said, but Billa had put down her coffee and was already hastening out. She followed her, down the stairs, along the flagstoned hallway and through the heavy front door. Outside, there was a van reading 'Homeland Security' in urgent, diagonal lettering, a lightning bolt to either side.

'You've made a mistake,' Billa shouted up at the man. 'Stop immediately. There's no work due to be done on this house.'

'Can't do that, I'm afraid,' the workman said. 'I'll check again, if you like, but it's definitely here we're scheduled to put it up.'

'Put what up?' Sylvie shouted, but the workman had started up his drill again. 'I said, put what up?' He could not hear her above the whine and grunt of the drill. A small group of pensioners was gathering opposite, just by the Conservative Club; the same sort of people who always gather when some sort of disagreement seems likely to enliven a street. Sylvie took hold of the bottom of the ladder and gave it a gentle shake. It was enough to bring his attention back to them, and he switched his drill off.

'Are you mental?' he shouted. 'You could have killed me, then.'

'Like that?' Sylvie said. 'You must be joking. That wasn't dangerous. This' – she shook the bottom of the ladder somewhat harder – 'is dangerous.'

The man slid down the ladder very sharply. His mate – a fat spotty boy of eighteen or so, his arms folded and his jaws engaged about a piece of gum – emerged from the little van. 'Are you mental?' the workman said. 'What the hell do you think you're doing?'

'That was exactly what I was going to ask you,' Billa said crisply. 'This is my house. What are you drilling into it for?'

'You just tried to kill me,' the man shouted.

'No, I didn't,' Sylvie said. 'I shook your ladder. Now, what are you drilling into my friend's house for?'

'I don't have to talk to people who just tried to kill me,' the workman said.

'Ass right,' the fat boy said.

'Shut up, Brandon,' the workman said. 'I'm just here to do a job.'

'Ass right,' the fat boy said.

'That's right,' Sylvie said. 'As your friend says. We just want to know what the job is. You must have the wrong house. My friend doesn't know anything about it.'

'No mistake,' the workman said, and from his overall pocket, he pulled out a letter with the heading of the Devon and Cornwall police service. He handed it over to Billa and Sylvie – his breath sweet-smelling with rot and uncleanness – and together, the three of them read it.

'That's ridiculous,' Billa said. 'I never asked for a camera to be fixed onto my house.'

'You don't have to ask,' the workman said. 'The police decide where it needs to go, to keep watch over a town, and then they ask me to pop one up. They prob'ly should have notified you,' he went on, in conciliating tones. 'That's bad, that is.'

'Well, it's not going up,' Billa said. 'I don't want one.'

'But it's not your say, my love,' the workman said. 'It's the police and the local community who decide together, and they've decided, they have, that they want a camera just here, because otherwise they wouldn't get to see – well, I don't know what they wouldn't get to see, but we got our instructions.'

'There's a bloody camera just over there, there, on the Conservative Club,' Sylvie said. 'And there's another one, look, twenty yards away, over Sam's shop. There's hundreds of the bloody things.'

And then, quite suddenly, like someone dropping water into a supersaturated solution, and it turning quite at once from a damp solid into a liquid, or, as she put it to herself, like a person placing that final straw on the back of the camel, Billa saw what she had not noticed, had not thought of any significance: the fact that from one end of her town to the other, every fifteen metres, just out of reach of a leaping person, there was a camera.

'I don't want it,' Billa said.

'Well, it's not up to you,' the workman said.

'I don't want it,' Billa said.

'The local community has asked for it,' the workman said. 'And the police agreed with them. They should have notified you, though, as the owner of the property to which the aforesaid camera is proposed to be affixed. That's bad, that is.'

'I'm in the bloody local community,' Sylvie said. 'And nobody asked me whether I want any more cameras filming my arse as I go from one end of the Fore street to the other, and the answer would have been no, by the way.'

'Ass right,' the fat boy said, shifting his allegiance.

'Yes,' Billa said. She was uncomfortably aware of more people on the other side of the road, gawping in fascination; she would not turn to look at them, in case she recognized some of them, letting themselves down. 'Yes, who exactly has asked for this?'

'It's the local community,' the workman said. 'I said, it's the local community. Now, if you don't mind, I've got to get on with this job. There's another two today I've got to affix, in Cullompton, and Iddesleigh village square. And if,' he said with dignity to Sylvie, 'you would be so good as to restrain yourself from shaking the ladder and attempting to kill me in the course of my duties, I would be most grateful.'

'Not on your life,' Sylvie said. 'We want to know who's asked for this.'

'Is there a problem, Billa?' Sam said, leaving his shop over the road with the door open. He was wearing his blue and white cheesemonger's apron.

'Yes, is there some kind of problem?' a man said, speaking to the workman rather than to Billa or Sylvie. He had a white, smoothed-down cap of hair, and a dark blue overcoat, an elegant pencil with a quizzical expression. It was John Calvin. 'This is all in order, isn't it?'

'Sam, they're putting up a CCTV camera on my front wall,' Billa said. 'No one told me. This gentleman just arrived and started drilling into my wall.'

'And this *lady*,' the workman said, pointing at Sylvie, 'comes out, and she starts—'

'That can't be right,' Sam said. 'Surely. There must be some mistake.'

'I don't believe so,' Calvin said, smiling faintly. 'Neighbourhood Watch has been discussing these things, and we requested an extra camera or two. For security. There really has been a lot of trouble in Hanmouth. Well, Neighbourhood Watch discussed it, and then—'

'I tried to join Neighbourhood Watch,' Sam cried. 'I got turned down. Come on, Calvin, who's in your fucking awful Neighbourhood Watch group?'

Calvin gave a smile – a general smile, aimed at no one in particular. 'It's all been discussed,' he said. 'I don't think anyone will find anything to complain about. Apart from people who think they have a right to walk the street indecently dressed, of course.'

'Oh, fuck off,' Sam said. He walked over to the ladder, still leaning against the wall, and took it; he was a strong, compact man, and with a single gesture he threw it down into the road. It narrowly missed the front window of the Conservative Club, now filled with curious hangers-and-floggers.

'Hey!' the workman shouted.

'It's for all of our safety,' Calvin said, quite unperturbed. 'And if you have nothing to hide, you have absolutely nothing to fear. After all, Mrs Townsend,' he gave an unspecific gesture in her direction, not quite a bow, more of a simper, 'I know that your husband met a very sad end recently. Quite unnecessary. If some-body – some friendly person, watching out for all of our interests had been able to take a look, now and then, at what was happening just here, at your front door, we probably could have got help to your husband, couldn't we? It's too late for him, of course, but, as Neighbourhood Watch were remarking—'

'My husband died inside the house,' Billa said, her tone low, but her voice carrying and decisive. 'Are you proposing to place cameras inside our houses?'

'No, no, of course not,' Calvin said, laughing gently. 'That would really be absurd. My meaning was only that, had Tom – Mr Townsend,' he corrected himself, seeing something in Billa's eyes, 'known there was a camera outside, he could possibly have hauled himself out, attracted attention—'

'What complete rubbish,' Billa said. 'Really, you can leave my husband out of all of this.'

'And you – you can pick my ladder up,' the workman said to Sam, who told him to fuck off. 'That's nice,' he said to the fat boy. 'Lovely manners people have round here in Hanmouth. Did you hear that? Fuck off, he told me to. That's charming.'

'This gentleman's just going to finish the job he's here to do,' Calvin said, as if a compromise had now been reached, 'and afterwards we can all sit down with a nice cup of tea, and talk about everything. How does that sound?'

'I'm calling the police,' Billa said. 'I don't believe you can just do this without asking first. And in the meantime, as my friend Sam says, you absolutely can fuck off.' There was a small outbreak of excitement among the gawpers on the other side of the street: they hadn't expected someone of Billa's appearance, one of the gentry, to know or use the expression.

'By all means call the police,' Calvin said, with a smile and a streak of ice in his tone. Billa stopped; she looked at Calvin; he seemed genuinely relaxed about the attendance of the police, and in a second, she understood why. All her life she had believed that she could call the police: that, in the last resort, they would come and protect her and Tom against threats of violence and anarchy. Now she understood what the police were. She and Sylvie went inside and upstairs, and after a few minutes, they heard from the first-floor drawing room the clatter of a ladder being placed against the Queen Anne brick, and shortly after that the whine of a drill going into the soft red composite of the Queen Anne brick. In an hour, a white downward pointing camera was affixed to the wall. You could see its shape from Billa's armchair.

22.

Greg Lucas hadn't bothered to change the satnav, or switch it off, and all morning it had continued trying to direct him towards yesterday's job. 'Turn left at next junction,' it said, and Greg drove the lorry straight on. 'Continue in a straight line for five hundred metres,' it said, and Greg turned directly right. It would fall silent for a few moments, recalibrating, and then, in its bright, womanly way, would just say, 'Turn left in two hundred metres, then left again.' Greg reached the little crossroads, and turned right, towards Hartswell village. He knew roughly where he was going.

He liked some kind of noise in the cabin of the lorry; that was why he kept the satnav on without troubling to inform it of his real destination. Usually, too, he kept the radio on. Later, he was able to say that he had arrived exactly at twelve noon, not just because that was when he had arranged to come, but because as he was driving up the lane, *The Ken Bruce Show* was coming to an end, and Ken Bruce was handing over to Jeremy Vine. That was on Radio 2. Sometimes Greg liked Classic FM. There was no sloshing in the vessel at the back and, despite what people thought, no smell either – not that Classic FM or Ken Bruce would hide a smell. He liked to have the radio on, and today, the satnav woman patiently trying to correct him.

He enjoyed his job. He never tried to disguise what it was he did for a living with an elaborate phrase. He did the rounds of most of Devon and parts of Somerset and Dorset, too, emptying domestic cesspits and septic tanks. It had never been worth anyone's while running sewage outlets beyond the villages and towns, and hundreds of houses in this part of the world flushed their waste into a septic tank or cesspit, buried under the garden with just a discreet little drainage cover. It was a legal obligation to run water to these houses, Greg believed, but you couldn't force a local authority to install a sewage pipe. The cesspit, or septic tank, was the most cost-effective solution. Most people in the country recognized this, and did not think of Greg as doing anything but offering a good professional service. Apart from the occasional joke directed at his children, he thought he was respected in the community. The white boiler-suit helped, tucked into his heavy socks and white rubber boots, and the white lorry, which the boys at the depot cleaned every other day to keep it sanitary-looking.

Septic tanks needed to be emptied regularly, but not as often as a cesspit, which took everything. Septic tanks cleaned the water, and let it drain away into the surrounding land inoffensively. Many of Greg's customers opted for an annual service, perhaps twice a year at most. For a small family or a couple, living alone, that would probably be sufficient. Though everything went into the cesspit – bathwater, water from the washing-machine and dishwasher, grey water as well as bodily waste and water from the lavatory – what remained to be taken away was nothing more than what Greg's industry referred to as 'sludge'. They were big tanks, designed to be forgotten about from one equinox to the next. Greg's visits could be festive occasions, and he was often popular with the children of Devon, craning out of their kitchen windows, standing restrained in their back doors, or even being allowed to watch in the garden as he hoicked up the manhole cover and fastened the vacuuming pipe to the securely fastened airlock. They were fascinated by the thought that the poo and wee of their family had been stored up like a valuable commodity for months on end, just under the lawn where their chickens, perhaps, pecked heedlessly. Now the poo-man, as they often called him, had turned up with his lorry to suck it all up and drive off with a cheery mobile reservoir of shit. 'And then what do you do with it?' a little girl or boy could be relied upon to ask, but Greg always refused to answer that, asking them instead what they thought he did with it. Their eyes grew big; Greg sometimes thought what they would grow up thinking.

Today's visit was to a man whose family had lived there for years. He lived there alone now. His mother had died five years ago. Not many people knew him; he kept himself to himself, not an unusual habit in this part of the country, bordering on the great moor. Living on his own, he did not need to call Greg as often as others. Probably he had bachelor standards of cleanliness, too, which meant that the septic tank would fill up with the residues of bathwater and other grey water that much more slowly. Greg tended to come up once every year and a half, no more than that. It was dangerous to leave a septic tank unemptied, but sometimes on his eighteen-monthly visit to the little thatched-roof cottage, buried like a mushroom beneath the level of the lane that led nowhere, Greg had found that the tank was not yet full.

Greg reversed from the lane into the semi-abandoned domestic garden beside and behind the house. 'Turn left,' the satnav woman said, without abandoning her calm composure in the face of Greg's perversity, 'and continue for three hundred yards.' It was the way Greg had come; she seemed not to want him to come here at all. The customer was already out of the house, shutting the door behind him to keep the heat in. It had been a lovely summer, but now, in October, there was a definite nip of autumn in the air.

'It's been a bit longer than usual,' the customer said. Greg looked at the invoice: Terry Strutte. He didn't know why he hadn't remembered a customer's name when Lucas's Septic Management had been dealing with him for so long, and his mother before him.

'No,' Greg said, hopping down from the cab of the lorry and putting his heavy-duty gloves on. 'It's the same as it usually is. Just eighteen months since the last time, or a week short. We must have sent you a card reminding you.'

'Well, there's a problem,' the customer said. 'I don't know why.'

'Let's have a look,' Greg said, following the customer out to the back of the property. There were two main problems he had to deal with: one was the tank backing up and sending waste water back up the toilets in a house. That often happened in winter, and was pretty unpleasant. The other was seepage out of the service area, the manhole, leading to foul odours and worse. That could be dangerous. Fortunately, a customer tended to notice one of these things quickly, and wouldn't let it run on for long. In this customer's case, there was some seepage; Greg could smell it as soon as he had got out of the lorry.

'What's the problem?' the customer said.

'It's full, it's leaking,' Greg said. 'We'll sort that out for you, no problem. The smell'll go in time, once we've emptied the tank. I'd stay well clear of the garden for a couple of weeks, more if there's no rain.'

'I don't come out here that much,' the customer said. Greg could see that. There was the remains of a vegetable patch, the

403

troughs still there, some things that might once have been vegetables – carrots, cabbages, the ruin of a single bean-row, a mass
of potatoes – now running to seed and colonizing the lawn around.
'It was my mum who liked gardening,' he went on. 'Grew half
our food on the table, she did. I'm too busy, I am.'

'It's nice to sit out in the summer, though,' Greg said. 'You've
got a good situation here, right on the moor. Nobody disturbs
you, I reckon.'

'Are you going to start now?' the customer said.

'I'll do that,' Greg said.

The customer went inside, shutting the door carefully behind
him. Greg unhooked the large pipe from the back of the lorry,
and, whistling, took it to the service area. The ground about was
really sodden, and the odour quite marked. He lifted up the
manhole cover, and fastened the pipe to the outlet. There was
definitely some overflow, and it must have been apparent for at
least a week. He wondered why the tank had filled up so much
more quickly than before, and why the customer hadn't called
immediately. He must have changed his habits in some way. With
a bit of luck, though, the tank would be at fault and need replacing,
a job that couldn't be delayed. Lucas's Septic Management would
do all right through this recession they were talking about; it
wasn't a service that was delayed when money was short.

The machine began its familiar, grinding, sucking roar. Greg
went back to the front end of the lorry, took his heavy gloves
off, placing them between his knees. He took a cigarette from a
packet on the dashboard, and smoked one, half listening to the
industrial noise. You could see the moor from here, and what
must be skylarks, dipping and soaring. Probably if you turned
the machine off, you would be able to hear them at their song.
It wasn't because of that but because the drainage system was
making a peculiar noise that Greg went to the back of the lorry
and turned the machine off. It often did this, signifying some sort
of blockage; in ninety-nine cases out of a hundred, you just needed
to turn it off, leave it for thirty seconds, and then switch it on

again. Even Greg dreaded that hundredth case. It was incredible what people would put down their toilet outlet.

After the cheerful, grinding noise of the engine was switched off, the air of the moor sang in his ears. It was so quiet out here. Greg spent his life going between remote and cut-off houses, but this was still more remote than most. In Devon, there was often a distant hum of a motorway, even in quiet retreats, but there was nothing here that was not just as it had been a hundred years ago. On the air, a high long note hovered, floated, urgent and remote. It was surprising how much the song of a bird could sound like someone screaming, thinly. Greg listened again, and then he understood that it was not a bird at all. That was not a bird, singing, and it was not that far off.

Half turning towards the house, he saw the customer standing at the kitchen window. Whatever happened, he must not turn with suspicion in his face to this man. Greg Lucas was not a heroic person. He had followed his father into his small business; he had never thought of moving away, to go into the world, to test himself against the demands of a new existence. He understood now what bravery was, and what was asked of him. What he had to do was quite clear, and he had to do it now, not go away to ask for help.

As a rule, those in Greg's business would never even ask permission to enter a house, but Terry Strutte – that was his name, Terry Strutte – he would not know that. Greg went, a cheerful expression maintained on his face, to the back door. The customer half opened it, warding Greg off; but from here, the intermittent sounds of the child screaming were unmistakable, a thin, muted, but discernible sound. Greg must continue as if there was nothing wrong, nothing at all.

'There's some sort of blockage there,' he said. 'It's a bit more complicated than I thought. I'm going to need to call my colleague. He's got the –' Inspiration failed Greg. There was nothing at all he could think of which his brother Ed might have to hand that he did not. 'He's got the oojamaflip.'

'OK,' the customer said. 'I'm not going anywhere. It's my day off from the stables. You call, and we'll wait.'

'There's no reception out here,' Greg said. 'I need to use your landline, if I may.' He could see the telephone from where he stood, on a small table by the front door. It was a cottage where nothing much intervened between the back entrance and the front entrance. 'I'll take my boots off,' he offered.

'OK,' the customer said unwillingly. Greg, sitting on the step, unhooked his sanitary white wellingtons, smeared with mud and worse, and swung himself round into the kitchen. In here, the sound was really unmistakable; a girl, screaming as hard as she was able. It was impossible to ignore. For the first time, Greg looked directly into the customer's eyes: it was a face of fat weakness, marked with thin, colourless eyebrows and white stubby eyelashes, like a pig's; his untidy mouse-blond hair, thinning on top, and eyes of pale, mad blue, one careering off to one side evasively. People who lived in the remote fastnesses of Devon sometimes looked like this, the product of cousins marrying each other over generations. But into this weak face, something like a decision came.

'Excuse me,' the customer said. 'I'll just be a minute. Hang on.' He walked past Greg, into his back garden, and then very quickly across the sodden earth, stepping carefully over the silent waste pipe, and then, more swiftly, through the gate in the garden wall, and on. He was almost running now, without direction or aim, just running away from Greg and the noise, which, Greg could hear, was coming from under the kitchen flags. From under the house. There was nowhere the customer could go. That way was the moor, nothing else. Greg let him go without shouting, without caring. There was a reason why the prison was set in the middle of the moor: because you could not get anywhere on your own, and after a while, you were glad to give yourself up again. That was what his old man had always said.

The sound had continued unabated, and now there was a hammering, too, as if something was being beaten against the walls, or rather, against some pipes. Greg listened, and in a moment worked out the quarter of the kitchen the sound was coming from, and then the particular flag. It made a hollow sound. He looked about him, and there was an iron pipe with a flattened end, a home-made tool, propped up beside the dresser. Greg had always been handy, and he saw immediately how this would work; he saw the groove in the side of the stone. He pushed it down, and levered, and it came up easily. The screaming filled the air. There was a flight of stone steps leading down into a cellar, into the dark. The screaming stopped as if a stop had been put on it.

'It's all right,' he said. 'I'm here to help you.'

There was silence from the cellar.

'Is there any light?' he said. 'He's gone. I need to put some light on.'

A small voice, a girl's voice said, 'Just underneath the trapdoor. There's a switch.' It was surprisingly close. He felt underneath the trapdoor, all round, and there was the switch. He put on the light, and walked down a couple of steps.

'He's gone,' he said. The girl, in a dirty pink sweatshirt, her hair lank and her face greasy, looked at him with such a look; afterwards, he said to the camera crews, to journalists, and in years to come, those who knew him who would ask him about this moment, he could never tell anyone what that look had meant. You would never want any harm to come to this little girl again, he would say. There was a look in her eyes; it was the wide, focused look of an animal in a corner. Of course he knew exactly who she was. She could not be anyone else.

'You're China,' he said.

'How do you know my name?' she said.

He was baffled by that. 'It doesn't matter,' he said. 'You're all right now.'

'That's what he said,' she said. 'If you come near me, I swear, I'll kill you, I swear I will.'

'I'm here to get you out of here,' he said. 'I'm not going to—' He couldn't say it.

'You stand there, at the top of the steps,' she said. 'Don't you come near me. Has he gone?'

'Yes, he's gone,' he said. 'I'm going to phone the police, and they'll come to get you. It's all going to be all right.'

'I don't want the police,' she said, and then, quite abruptly, she started crying. 'If you come near me, I'll kill you.'

'I'm not going to come near you,' he said. 'It's best if I call the police.'

'Who are you?' she said. 'You're not a friend of Marcus's?'

'No,' he said. 'I'm the poo-man. You're all right now, China.'

'But how do you know my name?' she said.

23.

Up the hill came a steady flow of families in their best clothes: fathers in suits, or at least a jacket and tie, limping mothers in practical but newish combinations and evidently uncomfortable shoes. The prospective students were, to Miranda's eyes, disappointingly clean and cheerful-looking. She remembered her own student days, nearly thirty years back at Oxford, how they had scowled and refused to work, and worn the same clothes from one end of term to the next. The idea of pleasing the elders had never, she believed, occurred to any of them. Then, people had been much more independent, too, surely. She vaguely remembered going to open days at universities, but no one would have thought of inviting parents, or involving them in where their children were going to go. Didn't think of them as children, either.

At some point, the parents had started turning up. They were greeted not with ridicule or amusement by the cooler, less dependent kids, but as a matter of course. Now it was a rare prospective who showed up without one or other of their parents. Miranda, in her tidy office with its ranks of the English poets in alphabetical order, looked out of the window with its pair of spider plants at the cautious, sullen groups failing to mix with each other. She thought like an old fart of how everything had changed. They walked, the lot of them, with the apparent knowledge that someone was watching them closely. From her third-floor window, Miranda watched them closely. She regretted how much things had changed under surveillance and expectation.

Seven times in the winter and spring, the university at Barnstaple mounted open days for prospective students and their parents, always on a Friday. The students had had their offers, and now merely had to achieve them. Barnstaple was somewhere between the seventy-fourth and eighty-seventh best, or perhaps worst, university in the country. A student with only quite moderate grades could expect to be welcomed here with open arms. But still they came with their nerves visible on their faces, embodying the disappointment or the hopes of their families, and still the faculties of Barnstaple struggled to make them welcome, to put on a little bit of a display.

The head of the faculty, Little Benjy, had always been less than friendly towards Miranda, but now his coldness had been reinforced by an illusion of being in the right. His muttered greeting had sunk into a curt nod, and now an assessing gaze. Miranda knew about the historically established degrees of snubbing – the Cut Sublime, when you pretended to be very interested in a nearby object, the Cut Indirect, when you pretended not to see the person, and the Cut Direct, when you gazed into someone's face and ignored their greeting, if any. These days, Little Benjy was performing the Cut Direct, and there was something self-righteous about his interrogating, ignoring gaze. To a direct enquiry, Benjy had replied that the matter of Faisal Khalil being arrested in a lecture hall was now beyond both of them, meaning that it was more important than Miranda, at least. Pressed further, he said curtly that the university was convinced the police had had good reasons for arresting Faisal, whatever they might be. Asked still further whether the police were going to make a habit of entering classrooms without notice to arrest students, Little

Benjy said that he was very busy and had no intention of pursuing this matter any further. Miranda replied that that might be his intention, but it was not hers. She was sure he would understand. The era of the Cut Direct, enacted four times daily on staircases and corridors and in the pathways between buildings, now began in earnest.

The tasks for post-offer open days for prospective students passed between faculty members. Today was Miranda's turn. The faculty held a talk in a lecture theatre about the work of the university, highlighting what institutional successes could be scraped together and emphasized. Then there was a brief pseudo-lecture, mounted by a junior member of the faculty on some popular work of recent English literature – this year it was going to be on Mark Haddon's *The Curious Incident of the Dog in the Night-time*, which experience had shown was one of very few books that the parents of any students, prospective or otherwise, might have read. The students themselves, prospective or otherwise, had of course read nothing at all. Then the students were taken off to pseudo-classes and their parents wined and dined, or at any rate given a cup of weak coffee and a glazed yellow Danish pastry and chatted up by members of the staff.

There were better things for Miranda to be doing on a Friday afternoon, and these talks were generally delegated to members of the faculty who had not yet lost the will to live. In the email that had arrived the week before, telling Miranda it was her turn to give a talk to the parents, Miranda detected the hand of Little Benjy and his tittering cadences. She had not protested; she gathered herself; she prepared some brief notes, which were now on the desk before her in a yellow folder.

There was a knock at her door. Through the reinforced glass, the White-Queen-like silhouette of Sukie made itself clear. Miranda made no response, and in a moment, another knock came. If she could see Sukie's outline, then Sukie could see hers. But she made no response.

'Are you there?' Sukie said, half opening the door. 'Oh – you are. Are you disturbable?'

'I *was* making some notes on something,' Miranda said. 'But now I'm quite finished, I believe.'

'Well, it was nothing so very important,' Sukie said. 'It occurred to me that it's been an absolute age since we had you and Kenyon over to dinner, and, hey, I thought, let's go crazy and fix a date.'

This was untrue: Sukie had now had Miranda and Kenyon over to dinner three times in succession, without Miranda and Kenyon making the slightest effort to invite them back. Miranda believed that the invitations came originally from Sukie's son – it was Michael, wasn't it? – who was hanging round a lot with Hettie. There had been three awkward evenings there with the six of them, Michael and Hettie sitting at the far end of the table, contributing nothing. Miranda guessed that this invitation was as near as Sukie could reasonably get to asking Miranda if she and Kenyon were proposing to ask her and her husband Lloyd over any time soon. But Miranda had calculated the cost of having Sukie, Lloyd and silent Michael over to dinner, and found that it could not be done for under two hundred pounds with decency, three courses and some restocking of the drinks cabinet. You could not respectably refuse if someone said 'I'll have a gin- [or vodka] -and-tonic,' before dinner, though you could laugh off a lack of Campari or sherry; you could not admit there was no whisky or brandy in the house after dinner. And there had been no gin, or vodka, or whisky, or brandy in the house for six weeks now. Sam had come round and polished off the last of the Campari ten days before. Miranda had calculated the cost of entertaining the three of them, or anyone else. She had considered that Sukie was actually here only from January to January before she returned to Quincunx College for good. She also remembered that all Americans regarded all English people as sponging, mean and unfriendly, and she didn't see why she shouldn't contribute to the stereotype, just a touch. So she now said, 'Well, that's very nice of you, Sukie. Whenever suits you, truly.'

411

'I'll have a look at my diary, and at Lloyd's,' Sukie said, defeated. 'Are you busy?'

'I *am*,' Miranda said. 'I'm just about to give my standard jollying-along speech to the prospectives and their mums and dads. I'm on in five minutes, actually. Were you going to have a cup of tea?'

'You read my mind,' Sukie said. 'Well, another time, then.'

'I might pop along later,' Miranda lied. 'After I've done my bit. It won't take all that long.'

'I dare say I'll still be there in half an hour,' Sukie said. 'I'll walk down with you. How's Hettie?'

They left Miranda's office, and she locked it up carefully. The night before, she had emptied her desk of anything she considered important; she had run along the office shelves for anything she had any emotional attachment to. There had been half a dozen favourite copies of favourite books; she had found a copy of Natalia Ginzburg's *Family Sayings*, the book Kenyon had handed over when they had first met. It had been his first gift to her; he had said, at that table at the back of the old Café Pelican on St Martin's Lane, long and thin as the car showroom it had once been, green and gold as Hammersmith Bridge or Harrods, that it was a book he loved and he hoped she would love it too. It had been after *Götterdämmerung* at the Coliseum. It must have been 1978, and Miranda was halfway through her PhD. And she had loved the book, and, though it had nothing to do with her work, it had ended up in her office. The night before, she had taken it home, with a few other favourite books, and some vital papers, and this morning, she had tidied her desk like a woman facing execution. She was, she believed, an orderly person.

She agreed with Sukie, as they walked down the stairs, that Michael and Hettie were good kids; that they were good together; that it was kind of touching to see them together. And all of that was true. Her mind was on the yellow folder under her arm. It contained not only her file copy of the speech she gave on these occasions almost every year, the text much amended by hand, but a series of notes on more recent events. There was an account of what had happened when Faisal Khalil had been hauled out, an honest first-person account including the officers' names and numbers; it contained all the emails and summaries of the phone calls and meetings she had held since with the university, the police force, with human rights groups, and with the trade unions, both of university teachers and of students. To Miranda's slight disappointment, the police had charged Faisal Khalil not with terror-related offences – she had been absolutely sure they were going to drag him off to Guantánamo Bay in an unmarked aeroplane. They claimed, instead, that he had been selling horse tranquillizer to his fellow students to help them to obliterate a segment of their Saturday nights. But that hardly mattered. She did not believe it, and if she had believed it, she thought that they could not simply turn up and interrupt the process of education in that way. She took her yellow folder with her, not because she was going to refer to it in the next hour, but because she thought she would need it, quite soon.

The prospective students and their parents were milling about in the foyer in front of the lecture hall. Miranda was struck by how much the children looked like students already, clean-haired and clean-faced, their only distinction from the enlisted many their expressions of nervousness, of a wish to please or impress, of a concern for what she might think of them. She felt like reassuring them. She would be gone by the time they arrived here.

Miranda, smiling, made her way through the crowd. There were a few current students she recognized at the front, pink with self-importance and confidence. It was usually the plainer, less socially successful students who volunteered for this sort of thing. 'Well,' she said to one of them. 'Shall we make a start?' The student pushed open the door, and Miranda led the way in. The student volunteers, then the parents with their prospectives followed, finding their places; then at the back, Karen Chu, one of the newest of the faculty. She had come to see how it was done, no doubt. Miranda had known there would be someone

413

here, someone to report back. She was pleased it was Karen Chu, who would not exaggerate or invent material or misunderstand. Karen Chu was a bright girl: she had published two books before she was given employment at Barnstaple; she could be relied upon to play her part.

Karen Chu stood up, a glamorous, tousled figure with a parrot's quiff, a semi-Mohican, a polo-neck in electric blue and black leather trousers. 'Welcome,' she began, and introduced Miranda in generous terms.

'Well, that's very kind of you, Karen,' Miranda said. 'And at least I hope you can see that we are a friendly faculty – we like to see the best in each other. Thanks very much – are you staying? Oh, good. I'm going to talk for about twenty minutes, no more than that, maybe a little bit less. I want to leave lots of time for questions. You must be bursting with questions. I know how daunting it all seems! Or if you don't want to ask a question in front of everyone, for whatever reason, then we'll be around afterwards for tea or coffee and Danish pastries, along with lots of other folk from the faculty, and do come and ask us whatever you had in mind then. Now then – where was I? Let me tell you a little bit about the faculty here. We're quite well established – we were part of the original Barnstaple Training College, a sort of extramural part, before we became first Barnstaple and North Devon Polytechnic, and then the University of the English Occident, as we are now, though of course everyone calls us Barnstaple Uni – it's easier to pronounce, we find.

'If you believe these things called government statistics, which I'm not sure I do, however flattering they might be, we at Barnstaple University are somewhere between the seventy-fourth and eighty-seventh best university in the country. Now that might not immediately sound very impressive, I know . . .' a pause here for polite laughter '. . . but I'd like you to remember two or three things. First, the English faculty here is rated a little bit higher than the university as a whole, somewhere between the forty-seventh and the fifty-fifth best in the country. No one else in the university does as well as we do. So your son or daughter would have the confidence of studying at a faculty which is better than any of the other faculties. The second point I would like to make is that the university, a mere five years ago, was only the hundred and fourth or hundred and fifth best university in the country, so we have improved a good deal. And third, I should point out that in this country, there are one hundred and seventeen universities, and ninety-seven English faculties. What that means is that there are – excuse me, my maths is really a little rusty, though I find I use it more and more these days – there are up to forty-three universities in this country which are worse than this one. And as many as fifty English faculties which are not as good. Hardly any of our graduates leave us with anything but a first or a two:one – we only awarded one two:two last year, out of a cohort of sixty-four. These are impressive statistics, ladies and gentlemen.'

(Those in the audience more eager to make a mark on this open day, who were showing off by taking notes, now wrote down 'impressive statistics' in their new notebooks.)

'And believe me,' Miranda continued, 'with the employment statistics as they are, we are providing a vital service. We are offering young people who, even thirty years ago, would not have had the chance of higher education, and would have had to become plumbers, builders, cooks or carpenters, we are offering them the chance to come to university. We are a vocationally focused faculty, and many of our graduates find employment within a year of leaving the university. But more than that, we find ways to enrich our students' lives. Many of our students are imbued with a love of literature, which lasts almost until the day they graduate.'

(Karen Chu gave Miranda a sideways look from under her Mohican, or was it a Mohawk, or was it neither? The audience, though, seemed to hear nothing so very odd, and it was clearly a new experience for many of them, to listen to a woman being allowed to speak without interruption. Some of them were writing down the words 'love of literature'.)

415

'We're a very young faculty – I sometimes don't know whether I'm talking to a student, straight from school, or a brilliant new colleague who's just finished work on some manuscripts of Geoffrey Hill, or Milton, or whatever they happen to be working on. We're very friendly and approachable, as you just saw – we pride ourselves on our approachability, in fact. Approachable not just by your sons and daughters, but by you, too. If you have any concerns about your sons or daughters, then please don't hesitate to get in touch. And we in turn will get in touch with you if anything seems to be going wrong with your children's studies, if it seems appropriate to do so.

'And you will be wondering, either now, or when you come to see us, whether we are going to take care of your children. Do we exercise our duty of care? Do we make sure that they're not going to get into trouble? Well, I can assure you that we keep a close eye on them – we tick them off on registers at every class as if they were six-year-olds, for instance. We insist that they come to see us with their work twice a term, so that we can make sure they're doing everything they should be doing. That's because, ladies and gentlemen, we don't really trust them. But you might approve of that. So you will be asking, what about that duty of care – what happens when my son or daughter needs help?

'Well, I can tell you straight away. The university will wash its hands of them. The university doesn't give a toss if the police service comes into a lecture hall to arrest one of our students, your children. The university doesn't even ask the police if they have an arrest warrant. The forces of law and order can trample all over your children, and the university won't do a single bally thing. So I'm saying this to you. If you want your children to get as reasonable an education as their limited achievements entitle them to, then send them here. Why not? If you want them just to be in a place not too far from home, where there might be a few hundred books, then this is as good as anywhere, I suppose. But if you want to be sure that they're going to be looked after

416

properly, then I've got this to say to you. Send them somewhere else. Send them to one of the – what was it? – forty-three universities in this country which are worse than this one, one of the fifty English faculties where, bloody hell – *fifty* English faculties worse than this one, some of them, they wouldn't be able to read a bloody book – yes, send them there. I don't suppose it matters a great deal in the long run. And now I want to say a few words about research income.'

At some point in the previous five minutes, Karen Chu had got up from the chair she had been occupying, facing the audience. Now the door to the lecture hall opened, and, with red face, in came Little Benjy. He had come so fast that he hadn't had time to put his shoes on, and he appeared in his black socks. 'I'm sure there'll be time to answer all your questions very shortly,' he said, laughing lightly in the face of twenty raised and cross arms. Some of the parents were even beginning to call out their observations, remarks, questions without waiting to be invited. 'Now I'm going to hand you over to Dr Karen Chu, who will be talking to you about what it's like to live and work at the University of Barnstaple. Dr Kenyon will be leaving you now, but I'm sure we can answer any of the questions raised by her talk later in the afternoon.'

Miranda gathered up her yellow folder, and followed Little Benjy out of the lecture room.

24.

'The thing is,' Kenyon said rather later, at home, 'they went down the list, one after the other, and there was nobody. Nobody at all.'

'This is the Treasury, is it?' Miranda said. They were both quite calm; Hettie was upstairs; from somewhere a bottle of gin and a bottle of tonic had been procured, and even a couple of slices of lemon. They were jolly well having their Friday-night drink. 'Where you used to work?'

'That's right,' Kenyon said. 'It was the Treasury I was talking about.'

'I see,' Miranda said. 'And what was this for – I'm sorry, I'm being awfully stupid, I know.'

'It's the head of their new Deficit Unit,' Kenyon said. 'I don't know whether you know, but the country's really in a bit of a sticky situation. It honestly is. We gave such a lot of money to those awful bankers.'

'Awful, awful bankers, I quite agree,' Miranda said, thinking of the occasion at the end of last month when the cashpoint had rudely refused to give her any money. She had had to borrow three hundred pounds off her own husband, like a student. So rude.

'And now we don't seem to have any at all ourselves. Less than none, really,' Kenyon said.

'Well, that is bad luck,' Miranda said. 'You mean the nation when you say "we", I presume.'

'Yes, indeed, I meant us the nation. And so the Chancellor – you know, the Chancellor of the Exchequer, the big cheese with the eyebrows – he's decided that he needs a Deficit Unit to run around thinking of good ideas about how to raise money.'

'Well, you could just ask those awful bankers for all that money back, couldn't you?' Miranda said. 'Golly, how I loathe capitalists. I could toss a brick through their windows sometimes.'

'I suppose we could,' Kenyon said, his voice going into falsetto. 'Ask them for the money back. I don't suppose they'd take much notice if we asked them. In any case, they had a chap lined up to be the head of this new Deficit Unit, though I don't suppose even he was doing it very willingly. His name was Barraclough. I don't know if you remember him from a Christmas party, or something like that.'

'No,' Miranda said. 'I can't say that I do, I'm afraid, darling.'

'Well, he had just agreed to do it, when – do you remember

418

that extraordinary day, when I came back from Paddington, and there had been that shooting on the concourse? About six months ago? Do you remember?'

'Oh, yes,' Miranda said. 'Awful. Frightful.'

Kenyon eyed her: he was not sure that he had ever managed to tell her about the event in a way that she would remember. 'Well, it turned out that one of the people that chap shot was my former colleague Barraclough, who was just on his way home to Oxford, poor fellow. Shot through the head. Dead as a doornail. So ever since then, the Treasury, they've been running down the list of people who might, just might, be prepared to head up this new Deficit Unit.'

'And they still haven't found anyone?' Miranda said. 'That seems rather a long time.'

'Oh, you know the Treasury,' Kenyon said. 'Like God in the hymn, a thousand ages in their sight are like a moment gone. And, anyway, everyone they offered it to said they wanted to think it over for a week and then said no.'

'But why?'

'Why do you think? Awful job, can't achieve anything, public obloquy and shame. But all the time their desperation was rising and so were the sums they were offering the candidates, interestingly enough – I heard they had to go back to the Cabinet Office three times, strictly between you and me. And a couple of weeks ago, they remembered that they'd donated me to the AIDS in Africa people.'

'Not donated, darling, seconded,' Miranda said.

'Quite right, seconded,' Kenyon said. 'They'd rather forgotten about me, I dare say. But two weeks ago, I had a telephone call about this, and the long and the short of it is that – well, you're looking at the new head of the new Deficit Unit. I suppose if I'd said no, they would have had to offer the job to Robert Peston off the *News*.'

Miranda's eyes were gleaming with love, or moisture, or contemplation of the mere future in which she and Kenyon and

Hettie could go on living in their million-pound house, currently bankrupting them by the day.

'How much?' she said, her voice low and thrilling.

'Well, that's the rather good thing,' Kenyon said. 'It's going to be about twice what I earn now, or a little bit more. The negotiations had reached such a pitch before they even got to me, you have no idea! And the other nice thing is that they've agreed to regard me as a candidate recruited from the outside world, not from within the public service at all.'

'So?'

'So I get a lovely big sum of lovely money for just coming back to the bosom of the Treasury. They thought I would say no unless they gave me—'

'But I thought we had no money, I mean, not us, I mean the country, didn't you just say?'

'Well, yes, but this is sort of different money. They can justify that.'

'How much?' Miranda said again.

'Oh, somewhere around three hundred thousand,' Kenyon said. 'Something like that.'

Miranda drank her gin-and-tonic in one; her manner quite changed. 'Well, that is a nice lot of different money to welcome you home with,' she said. 'I am pleased for you. Of course, it's not really about the money, is it? I am glad they're recognizing you, at last – I rather thought they had forgotten all about you, tucked away in Islington like that. And I've got some news too, rather along the same lines. Really very much along the same lines.'

'I don't suppose you're going to tell me the university's going to give you three hundred thousand, too?' Kenyon said, laughing.

'Well, I don't know how much it will be in the end,' Miranda said. 'But there was a bit of a hoo-hah today, and after a little bit of a conversation with Little Benjy and his Big Boss – golly, it sounds like a play by Brecht, doesn't it, darling? – after that little bit of a conversation, I reckon that they see the future of the faculty as being a little bit Miranda-less. Boo-hoo. But they did say that they would be sure to give me a lump sum if they had to ask me to go, a nice big lump sum. So we've both had some very good news. I think, between the two of us, we could probably pay off the mortgage in one go, when the money comes through, and then we won't have any difficulty living on your salary, I suppose. Probably have a hundred thousand or two left over, as well. For a rainy day.'

'As much as that?' Kenyon said, whose thoughts were all on Ahmed, on how he could juggle a five-day-week job with his lover; and he was thinking about a flat in London, and a job in London for Ahmed. 'As much as that? Miranda – what is it that you've done?'

'Oh,' Miranda said. 'Well, the awful thing is that Benjy's big boss made me promise, as a condition of all of this – I mean, we're only just beginning on discussions, but this was his absolutely first insistence – that I would never, ever repeat to anyone the ghastly things I said today. So I don't think I will. I know it sounds awful. Maybe one day I'll tell you what it was. But anyway. That all sounds like very good news, I must say. Gracious heavens, what's that noise?'

At the window there was a distorted and inhuman face; it was Stanley, Sam and Harry's basset hound, emerging from the winter darkness, and for some reason best known to himself, gazing into Miranda and Kenyon's sitting room at the two handsome figures. He gave the paintwork an appraising lick, making the window frame rattle again.

'He shouldn't be out this late,' Miranda said. 'He knows he shouldn't. Stanley. Go home, Stanley, go home.'

'No, Stanley, we're not letting you in,' Kenyon said. 'God knows what you've been rolling in. Go home.' Stanley went on gazing, occasionally shaking his rump loose, as if he had never seen anything so fascinating as two people sitting opposite each other, their faces lit by table lamps, one with a tie loose about his neck, the other sitting upright in a black geometric dress, a black geometric haircut, slightly grown out, looking at him with concern and, perhaps, something like love. And, in a moment, Miranda picked up the telephone sitting on the side table, and called Sam to come and fetch him.

25.

Whenever Hettie left the house, she liked to count the steps between one landmark and the next. Between the front door and the fish shop: 247. In the other direction, to the very end of their street and the beginning of the Wolf Walk: 485. From one end of the Wolf Walk to the other and Tracy Wood; 170. (Hettie could cry when she thought of Tracy Wood, and the strange thought that she, Hettie, was now older than Tracy Wood would ever be. Somewhere, they were friends, she and Tracy Wood.) From the station to the Crapping Juvenile: 463. From the town hall to the swings at the Rec: 733.

She had always done that, and did it now when she was alone. If she was with Michael, her thoughts ran in different directions. She had sometimes thought of telling him that she counted her steps when she walked in Hanmouth, but not yet. He might think she was mental, so she did not. Perhaps before he went back to America, she would tell him. Whenever she left the house, she took a deep breath, as if about to place her head under water, and said a giant ONE in her head, whichever way she was going. She could count Hanmouth from one end to another. As she walked, it would unroll under her stamp and pace and jog.

In the last days and weeks, she had had a new task to add to the counting. She had had Billa Townsend, the old General's wife, to look out for. She had thought a lot about the way the General died, and every way she looked at it, she was to blame. Hettie saw the old General, going to one cupboard after another, looking for the ironing-board. All his life, his wife had done the ironing, but she couldn't now, because she'd fallen over and hurt herself somehow. So he would have to do it. His wife, Billa, she was out and she couldn't tell him where the ironing-board was kept, even. And then he went upstairs, and found the ironing-board in an upstairs cupboard. He didn't know how to do it, so instead of getting it downstairs while it was still folded, he thought it would save time to unfold it on the top landing and carry it down like that. But unfolding an ironing-board is a complicated thing. Hettie knew that. And somehow, there, standing on the top step of twenty, trying to get the ironing-board out, he caught his foot in it, and then it all came down like a pack of cards, whoosh, bang, thud.

Billa would not know that it was Hettie who had knocked her over, but she would forgive her when she saw how difficult it had been for Hettie to make this confession. She would clutch her to her chest and perhaps they would both cry a little bit. So as Hettie walked around, she lifted her head up and scanned the people, looking for Billa.

It was dark outside, and Kenyon and Miranda were talking about money downstairs – they were talking about how rich they were, from what Hettie could overhear. She quietly walked downstairs, looked into the kitchen, and there was nothing but bags from Sainsbury's sitting on the work surface. Dinner would still be some time away. She had come downstairs intending to get her *apéritif* and sit with her parents, making sophisticated conversation, but Kenyon and Miranda talking about how rich they were made her feel a little bit sick. She decided to go out. As silently as she could, she went through the hallway, picking up her Puffa jacket, lifting up the latch and stepping out. She closed the door behind her, and then, all at once, there was a dog at her knees. She recognized it: it was Stanley, the dog of those two old gays. Hettie knew where they lived; she decided to take him back.

That was more of a task than she had anticipated. Stanley, she knew, liked to sit and watch anything. He had probably been there staring in at the window, or looking at their chickens over the road. If someone came to investigate him, he would leave his post to sniff at them, but would usually return afterwards to his post of observation. He showed every sign of doing that now. Hettie seized his collar – he was a surprisingly big dog – and started to haul him behind her. The weight of him, the solidity and bone of his head and jaw, resisted her efforts. In a moment he would sit down, and then she would have to give up and leave him there. She supposed he would find his way home eventually.

But all of a sudden, Stanley's attention was taken by something in the middle distance, and he stopped trying to turn himself into an obstinate dead weight on the pavement. It was a somebody, rather than a something; and, as it came under the street lamp, Hettie saw that the person Stanley was trotting towards was Billa Townsend, the General's wife. Hettie followed Stanley. This, she thought, was her moment.

'I know this wretched dog,' Billa said, jabbing at him with her parrot-headed umbrella. 'Hello, Hettie. It's Stanley, isn't it?'

'Yes, I think it must be,' Hettie said. 'Anyway, he knows who you are.'

'And I should hope so, too,' Billa said. 'He shouldn't be out like this. I dare say Sam will be getting worried. Are you in a hurry?'

'No,' Hettie said. One of her rules was that she never admitted to a grown-up when she was on an expedition of discovery and thought; never said when she had just left the house with no particular end in mind. Inspiration struck. 'I was just going out to the Co-op to get some butter and milk. My mum's run out.'

'Oh, well,' Billa said. 'I've got nothing so purposeful to do. I was just going to go for a small walk before my dinner. I tell you what – I don't suppose it will take five minutes – why don't we take Stanley back to Sam and Harry's? It's just up the road here.'

'OK,' Hettie said. Stanley seemed much more willing to follow Billa than her. That seemed unfair.

'What a bad, bad, bad dog,' Billa said encouragingly. 'Aren't you just?'

Hettie's courage was high now, and before Billa could say anything else, she said, 'I'm really sorry about your husband.'

'Oh,' Billa said.

'Dying like that,' Hettie said to explain. 'It must have been a terrible shock to you and I hope you're feeling much better now.'

'Well . . .' Billa said. 'Thank you. I think. It was . . . it was a great shock.'

'But the thing is, I've got to tell you, I've got something I need to get off my chest, and I hope you'll understand,' Hettie said. 'I feel terrible about it, I really do. You see, I think it was really my fault, mine and that Michael's.'

'Hettie, I really don't think—'

'I've got to explain,' Hettie said, and did so; how she and Michael had, without meaning to, knocked Billa over and not stopped to pick her up; how it must have meant that she couldn't do stuff around the house, and the General – 'Brigadier,' Billa corrected mildly – had had to make an attempt with the ironing-board, and—

Hettie came to a stop. They were half lit by the orange glow of a streetlamp; Billa's hairy capable old face looked no more cross than usual. The orange light had made a strange colour out of her usual green gilet and fisherman's jumper underneath.

'Well, you have been worrying, I can see,' Billa said. 'But it wasn't like that, it really wasn't. My husband always did the ironing, whether I was fit or not. It was his task around the house. So he wouldn't have been struggling with anything he hadn't struggled with a hundred times before. Mind you, it was very bad of you to knock me over and run away like that.'

'I know,' Hettie said humbly. 'I'm sorry.' She couldn't wait to tell Michael it was all all right and it was the General's – the Brigadier's – fault and no one else's.

'And here comes Sam,' Billa said. 'Were you looking for this reprobate?'

Sam came down the lane. When he came into the light, he was in a leather jacket, an elaborately decorative lead in his hand. He

425

shook his head reprovingly. 'He just took himself off for a walk,' he said. 'Your mother phoned, Hettie, to get me to come and fetch him. I suppose he would have come back sooner or later.'

Sam bent down, and fastened the lead to Stanley's collar. He turned homewards, but decisively, unarguably, Stanley sat down where he was and began to make a high-pitched noise of complaint.

'Oh, God,' Sam said.

'I don't think he wants to go home,' Billa said. 'I think you're interrupting his walk.'

'Well, that's just too bad,' Sam said. He tugged again, and Stanley, an immovable object, remained just where he was. 'There's nothing for it,' Sam said. 'I'm just going to have to take him on his walk.'

'Where does he go?' Hettie said.

'He likes to go down to the end of the Wolf Walk and back again,' Sam said. 'He's not completely stupid – he wants to go to the very end and then turn back again. I know – he's just been in that direction.'

'Where they were putting up a camera today,' Hettie said.

'No,' Billa said. 'That was a week or two ago – it was on my house.'

'No, it was at the end of the Wolf Walk,' Hettie said. 'Me and Michael –' she shrugged, as if in response to a comment '– we were down there today, this afternoon. And it WAS cold! But we didn't mind. We were on the bench of the dead girl—'

'Tracy Wood,' Billa said, and the three of them smiled.

'That's right – and a van came and parked at the other end of the Wolf Walk. And I could see, they WERE cross, because first they had to get all the stuff out of the van, then they had to huff and puff, carrying it all that way – it's a hundred and seventy steps – they couldn't get any nearer. And then when they'd got their stuff down by Tracy Wood's bench, one of them stayed by it, and the other one had to go back three times to fetch his ladder and his tools and something else they forgot.'

'There's nothing down there worth filming,' Sam said. 'Or only sticklebacks or something. How ridiculous. What on earth are they doing, putting up a camera there?'

'They've gone stark staring mad,' Billa said.

'Who's gone mad?' Hettie said. 'No, but they said, because we asked them, they said they wouldn't leave their stuff unattended, they said, in this town. They said there was people who were mad around, who would probably throw it all in the estuary if they weren't there to watch over it. They meant us, but they couldn't say so because it would be rude. And we wouldn't have thrown it in the estuary, because Michael said he wanted to see them putting up a camera on the wall and, anyway, we'd have had to go past them on the way back. After we'd thrown everything in. So we didn't.'

'That's you they're talking about,' Sam said to Billa.

'What nonsense,' Billa said. 'What on earth says that they can put up a camera on top of my house, and a camera at the end of the Wolf Walk where nobody goes? I want to see this with my own eyes.'

'It's that John Calvin, I bet,' Sam said. 'Let's go and give him a piece of – no, let's not. I know what he'd say.'

'I can imagine,' Billa said.

Together, the three of them set off, Stanley sniffing at everything in his path. As they went down the Strand, they could hear voices calling within the houses for each other: Jack, they shouted, or Come here, or Have you seen this. As they walked, they looked through the windows of the Lovells' house, John Gordon's as he laid down his cello and called for his wife, the Kenyons', with Hettie's parents sitting, each in their own armchair with a drink in hand, past Helena Grosjean's white-slatted beehive and her orderly house, past the abstract-expressionist hedge-fund trader, past the off-duty newsreader's; and he, like all the others, was watching the news. Hettie and Sam and Billa walked past all these houses, either glimpsing a sequential fragment of the news or seeing an interior blue television glow, and heard the inhabitants of the Strand calling out to each other in their houses to grab their attention. On each television screen, glimpsed through each window, was the same thing: a girl's face, the photograph of the kidnapped girl which had been everywhere earlier this year, and then the mother in handcuffs, a field, a police van besieged by photographers, hammering vigilantes, the mother and her man, white-faced, on a stage with policemen; and then a house in the country, a ramshackle falling-down house, thatched and squat. As they walked down the street, Hettie and Sam and Billa looked with interest at each glimpse of the story, unfolding on twenty television screens through the window. They would not stop to gawp through a window, and it came to them in flashes. And then, through one window, a girl, stepping out cautiously into a crowd, or so it seemed, a girl pale, thin and luminous, only about eight, her hair scraped back into a bun, her eyes transmitted on the forty-two-inch screens of the Strand, huge, glowing, full, as she came out of her captivity, of a pained understanding of what light was like.

'They've found that little girl,' Sam said.

'The mother must be in prison,' Billa said. 'I don't know how—'

'Awaiting trial,' Sam said, and they discussed the finding of China, her likely future, her permanent separation from her parents and siblings all the way down the Strand, and onto the Wolf Walk.

At night, though the Wolf Walk was lovely, nobody came here. There was a single, warm, romantic light halfway down it, casting into the night and the shadows. The curve of the Walk was perceptible, and underneath, on the apron of mud, a colony of fat stones revealed themselves, as the three of them walked by, as sleeping ducks, each raising its head with a bewildered muted bark, before ruffling its feathers and settling its head again under its wing. There was no one else on the Walk. From the mid-point, under the lamp, the new camera was visible: a white box, pointing downwards.

'There it is,' said Sam. 'What on earth are they doing putting one up here?'

'Well, the workmen said that someone had once thrown a bench into the mud from here,' Hettie said. 'And they'd never found out who had done it, but now they wouldn't do it. And Michael and me, we'd been—'

'Kissing,' Billa supplied. 'Don't be so shocked. We've seen most things and even heard of kissing.'

'Yes, we'd been kissing, but of course we didn't want to go on, there on Tracy Wood's bench with a camera on top of us. You don't know who's going to be looking at you! And we'd only come here because our usual place – you know, we've got a usual place we go, I can't tell you where, it's secret – but the usual place, it had been taken over by a lot of people with binoculars, that's the only reason we'd come here to the Wolf Walk. Look, there it is.'

They were underneath the camera. The wall there was only six feet high, and the camera had been awkwardly affixed, and surely ineffectively. From there, nothing much could be seen, unless the criminals actually sat down on Tracy Wood's bench to carry out their wickedness.

'So Michael said to the man it was an intrusion, that we come out here to get a bit of peace and quiet, and he said, the man, after he'd put up the camera, he said, "I know the sort of a bit of peace and quiet you've come here for," and they laughed, they laughed at us, and his mate, he was a fat man, he said, "That's right," and then one of them, I don't know which one of them it was, they said, "If you've nothing to hide you've nothing to be frightened of." But when they'd gone, and the little red light came on to show it was filming, me and Michael didn't want to go on doing what we were doing. Michael said the moment had gone, really.'

'Well, of course it had,' Billa said. 'This is down to John Calvin and his Neighbourhood Watch.'

'I don't believe in Neighbourhood Watch,' Sam said, and he reached up and poked the camera. 'I don't believe there's anyone there at all. Look, you can move it.'

He gave it a firm shove, and the camera did move two or three inches, pointing now towards the castle. It must have been designed to be placed out of reach of the observed populace, and the workmen had been doing their best with an unsatisfactory place for the CCTV. 'That's better,' Sam said.

'They're awfully tinny little things, really, aren't they?' Billa said calmly. 'Not made to last at all.' With her parrot-headed umbrella, she gave it a firm knock on its side; it rattled like cheap tin. She gave another knock, and now you could see the dent in the side.

'You'll get into trouble,' Hettie said. 'It can't see you, but they'll be able to tell from your voice who's done that. You don't want to do that, Mrs Townsend.'

'These things don't have any kind of sound equipment,' Billa said. 'It's just a digital camera.'

She moved round to the front, and peered into the dark lens; it was a dark view into emptiness, into the dead recording eye. She took a step back and, with a sharp rap with the beak of her parrot-headed umbrella, shivered the glass. 'There you are,' she said.

'Oh, my God,' Hettie said. 'I can't believe you just did that.'

'Want a go?' Billa said, and handed her umbrella to Hettie. Hettie took it disbelievingly and, from one side – not wanting, perhaps, her face to be filmed in the last moments of the camera's life – she rapped on the lens. At first she rapped timidly, then more strongly, then gave the lens a good whack or two. It was shattered; fragments of glass on the pavement. 'It's quite easy,' Billa observed. 'I think I'm going to have a go at the wretched one on my house. I don't see why I should put up with that one, either.'

'There's one on my shop,' Sam said. 'I'll be doing something about that, first thing tomorrow morning. And look – look how bad the workmanship is. It's hardly fixed on the wall at all.'

He pulled at the base of the camera, which came away from the old wall, its cement and brick, quite easily. He tugged again, and the cables at its base yielded, tearing out of the camera's box.

Panting, he held the dead, dented and smashed camera in both hands.

'It's a bit heavier than it looks,' he said. 'And it's got my fingerprints all over it. It needs to go into the estuary, don't you think?'

Hettie and Billa agreed; and with two or three good heaves, Sam sent it on an arc over the mud. It landed in the central stream of the estuary with a great splash and a gloop. There it would lodge in the mud; the flow would quickly bury it, and wipe away any mark of who had disposed of it.

With a quiet, burglarish demeanour, hardly speaking, the three of them made their way home. Stanley, who had been waiting patiently while they smashed up the camera, seemed like a reluctant and disapproving governess. 'Goodnight,' Billa and Sam said to Hettie, and 'Goodnight' again to Miranda, as she opened the door, wondering where on earth Hettie had got to; 'Goodnight,' Billa said to Sam, as he turned up his little road, his shoulders glittering with ground glass; and she went on another three hundred yards to her house. There was nobody about at all; the curtains of the town were drawn, the streets quiet and undisturbed. Underneath an observing black eye and its red blink, she let herself into her house. She had no idea who would be watching her return. They had made no difference, she knew; indeed, they might have shown that this town needed to be watched, from one end to the other. In a few days, the camera on the Wolf Walk would be replaced. Billa thought she would heat up a gifted lasagne, and might even enjoy a glass out of one of Tom's best, or at any rate one of his dustiest bottles of wine.

26.

The clocks had changed a month ago. It was already dark when the doorbell went on a Saturday night. Stanley had occupied his absolutely central position on the sofa, his head and ears on its brink, watching *Doctor Who* with apparently total absorption and comprehension. In his right side, Sam's stockinged feet; Harry's stockinged feet pushed into Stanley's left. Stanley had had his patiently endured bath, as he did every other Saturday – he didn't seem to take much pleasure in it, but he put up with the process. Sam and Harry took enough enjoyment in it for three, splashing around the white double bath, switching on the Jacuzzi tap to startle Stanley, making izzi, oozi, duzzi noises and whisking up the dog shampoo into great wet meringues before rinsing him off and drying him with his special, marmalade-coloured, Stanley-coloured towel. And now Stanley smelt, if not exactly sweet, pleasantly doggy rather than frankly suppurating. From time to time, Sam passed Harry a bowl of olives, of cheesy puffs, of dry-roasted nuts. The snacks lived on the right arm of the sofa, with Sam's Negroni, and Sam was in charge of them; the remote controls for stereo, television and DVD sat on the left arm, with Harry's Whisky Sour. As the cheesy puffs in particular passed over Stanley's head, his expression raised itself upwards, rather as if deploring the snack than begging for one. If Harry was in the kitchen, Sam would sneak Stanley one: when Sam was refilling his Negroni, Harry would do exactly the same thing. Both believed that the other did not know. Stanley did not let on, as he snapped up the illicit cheesy treat.

'Which are those?' Harry said.

'Which what?'

'Those ones. Are those the Sontarans?'

'No. The Sontarans are the ones with the big heads. These are the—'

'Are they the ones who are made out of human fat?'

'No, those are the – I can't remember what those were called.'

'I liked those.'

'Can you just shut up and watch, darling?'

'I can't watch it if I can't follow it.'

'I don't know why you can't follow it. Children of six can follow it. It's made for children of six.'

'You knew where you were with the Daleks. Why can't they bring the Daleks back? I enjoyed those.'

'They were on only last week.'

'What were they doing?'

'Taking over the world.'

'Are they still at that old game?'

'You mean —'

'I mean, they must have tried dozens of times now, and they never succeed. Don't you think someone might advise them that they might be being too ambitious, aiming at taking over the world?'

'Sort of interplanetary Peter Principle, you mean?'

'Every alien is promoted to the level of its incompetence. Exactly. If they started with something a little bit smaller – say if they decided just to take over Kansas, or Malta – they might be a bit more successful. Work up from there.'

'What just happened?'

'I've no idea. Something blew up. Was it Queen Victoria?'

'No, she's not in it this week either.'

'Well, I can't understand a single thing that's happening, I must say. I only understand it when there's gays in it.' Harry took a deep judicious drink. 'I bumped into that John Calvin this afternoon,' he said.

'Oh, yes.'

'Did you know they're moving?'

'Really? Sudden decision?'

'No,' Harry said. 'He said they've been thinking about it for a while. But I don't know that they really have. And now *Doctor Who*'s finished, and I didn't understand a word of it. I'm sure it was all very exciting.'

'I've seen it before, actually,' Sam said. 'It was something to do with a parallel universe.' Just then the doorbell rang; a fierce possessive ring. 'I was just on the verge of remarking how nice it is to have a Saturday evening in for a change, without having to think about what to wear or what to talk about, just you, me

433

and that thing not stinking the place out for a change. And then off it goes.' Out in the street, a grunting roar, a car with inadequate silencing, sounded, and was off. The doorbell rang again, querulously, and Sam heaved himself up. 'God, I'm getting fat.'

'The two of us,' Harry said. 'It's probably the coppers, come to get you for throwing the camera into the estuary.'

'You're not supposed to say that,' Sam said, opening the door. The man from the other month – Spencer – the man from the garage, he was standing there with a grin on his face. He was in a tight white T-shirt and a pair of low-cut jeans, which, between them, opened in a gap, showing his belly button and a firm, directionally furred upper pubis. He had a bottle of wine in his hand.

'Hello, guys,' Spencer said.

'Hello there,' Sam said, raising an eyebrow. 'Spencer, isn't it?'

'Are you going to ask me in?' Spencer said. 'Are the other guys here yet?'

'What other guys?' Sam said. 'Did we know you were coming?'

Harry was not the world's best diary-keeper, and it was just possible that he had forgotten about an invitation.

'Come on,' Spencer said. 'It's the first Saturday of the month, isn't it? It's time to party. OK?'

Harry had been drawn out into the hallway by Spencer's noise; standing in the door to the sitting room, a glass in his hand, barefoot and in a cardigan and an unironed shirt, he was not at his most sexually irresistible. 'What's up?' he said eventually.

'Isn't it tonight?' Spencer said. 'I thought it was tonight. I thought it was going to be round here tonight. I thought I was going to be late, and all the other lads, here already, getting on with it.'

'Not as far as I know,' Sam said. 'I haven't heard from any of them for a month. Peter asked us all round, six weeks ago, but we couldn't go. No one's mentioned anything since then. God, I hope they aren't all on their way.'

'Yeah,' Spencer said, dropping into a low growl, and advancing

on Sam, giving his neck a good pinch between thumb and fore-
finger. 'Yeah, I hope they aren't, too – just the three of us, eh?
That'd be good, too – just you, and me, and—'

'It's a nice idea,' Harry interrupted. 'But I don't think so. Maybe
some other time.'

'Oh, come on, man,' Spencer said. 'I've come all the way from
Ottery. My – my lift's gone now. Don't waste my journey, mate.'

'Yeah, well,' Sam said. 'You should have phoned first. Sorry
about that. Some other time.'

'You never gave me your number. So fuck you,' Spencer said,
dropping his hand and opening the door behind him.

It was cold outside, and Spencer was only wearing a T-shirt,
so Harry called after him, 'You can wait inside while you call
your wife – oh, he's gone.'

'That must have been a disappointment,' Sam said, as they went
back into the sitting room. *Casualty* was just beginning.

'Yeah, poor old Spencer.'

'You don't mind, do you?'

'What – turning him out into the cold? No. Not at all.'

'Sexy bugger,' Sam said.

'But mental,' said Harry. 'More trouble than he's worth. Nice
evening in, just the two of us, that's the ticket. She won't have
got far, his wife.'

'That'll be an interesting conversation on the way home. You're
not saying we're giving up on all that, are you?'

'What – the lads, the gathering, the sexy mechanic someone's
once had? What do you reckon?'

'You're not saying that you and me, we're never going to have
sex with anyone else, the rest of our lives? You're saying that
from now on, it's just you and me and being faithful to each
other?'

'No, darling,' Harry said. 'No, I'm not saying that. I would
never say something like that to you. I couldn't hurt you like
that.'

'Love you,' Sam said, and almost crushed Stanley as the two

of them kissed on the sofa. When they were done, Sam got up, in his stockinged feet, and went into the kitchen with their empty glasses. In the fridge, there was a nice leg of lamb. It had been for Sunday lunch, but it might be rather nice to have it on a Saturday night with some roast potatoes and some green beans. The nights were really drawing in now: he pulled down the blinds over the sink, though they looked out on nothing but their garden, and nobody would be looking in from there. All around the house, the curtains were closed; the phone, the doorbell could be ignored; from now until tomorrow morning, they could be on their own, undisturbed and unobserved. Sam filled up Harry's glass, and then, with Campari, gin and red vermouth, his own. It was his third: but the important thing about a Saturday night in with Harry was that there was no one counting, or watching.

London-Geneva
March 2010